ELECTRIC EEL: BLOODBATH

A NOVEL BY MICHAEL COLE

SEVEREDPRESS

ELECTRIC EEL: BLOODBATH

ISBN: 978-1-922861-18-4

CHAPTER 1

The red ball of flame soared high into the night sky until it was so far away it resembled a dying star. Appropriately, the resulting explosion resembled a supernova, sending sparking clouds spreading below the clouds. Sparks crackled and fizzled out, and soon the smoke faded away to nothingness.

"Happy Fourth of July," Russell Bean muttered to himself. He stood on the fly deck of the seventy-foot motor yacht *Dream Wrecker*, listening to the moaning sounds from the aft deck directly below. Against his better judgement, he peered over the side at his two companions below. As he suspected, Wade Stevens was on top of the brunette Jessica Barter, burying his tongue in her mouth. One hand crept under the right shoulder strap of her bikini top. It pulled gradually down the length of her arm, which was wrapped around his bare back.

It continued coming down, peeling the cuff. Wade's mouth moved to her neck. She cocked her head to the side, giving him full access. Her eyes squeezed shut while she moaned with pleasure. She opened them, intending to fixate on the physical pleasures of Wade's body. Instead, she found herself staring up at Russell's smirking face.

"Hey! Creep! Get back at the helm where you belong!"

Wade sprang off her and looked up at the fly deck, only catching a glimpse of Russell's long black hair as he ducked away.

"I'm gonna kill you, man!"

"Sorry! Had to investigate a noise complaint!" Russell replied. Wade couldn't help but smile as he listened to the idiot cackle to himself. He felt Jessica's arms creeping over his shoulders, pulling him back down.

"Did you *have* to bring him?" she asked. Wade didn't reply. The answer was *yes*, unfortunately. This little sailing trip was supposed to be a celebration of all three of them completing their four year degrees at the University of Miami. All three had a couple elective leftover in order to get their degrees, so rather than waste time, they attended the accelerated spring semester, which concluded two days prior. Of course, now he wished it was just the two of them. Hell, he couldn't ignore how great she looked in that bikini, especially in the moonlight. With that thought in mind, he stroked her hair and resumed nuzzling her neck.

"He's gone now. We can resume."

"No!" She leaned away. Wade's lips followed like a homing missile. Jessica planted both hands on his chest, stopping him. "I'm serious."

"So am I," he said. He took one of her wrists and kissed it. Jessica smiled, her eyes faltering to his perfectly cut physique. It almost worked, until she heard Russell's wandering footsteps above them.

"He's still up there," she said.

"Eh." Wade shrugged his shoulders. "Let him watch. He needs to learn how it works sometime!" He leaned in. Somehow, Jessica's arms failed to resist. Instead, like they had minds of their own, they wrapped themselves around Wade's neck, allowing the fun to continue.

Right then, another rocket blasted from the fly deck. It exploded prematurely, sending hot red sparks raining down on the yacht. Wade and Jessica jumped to their feet, briefly dancing around the deck as hot specks struck down around them like meteorites.

Wade sneered at the culprit. "Jesus, Russell! You crazy nutjob!" Russell's puffy face peeked down at them. Wade proceeded to check himself for any burns, then started inspecting the deck. "Seriously though, dude, if you get any burn marks on my dad's boat, *I'M* gonna be the one who'll suffer for it."

"Hey, I didn't manufacture these stupid things," Russell retorted. He cleared his throat and gazed down at the two college athletes. "I'm sorry if my firework show is interrupting yours."

Jessica straightened her top and started heading for the cabin.

"Where are you going?" Wade asked.

"Getting a sweater. It's getting chilly out here," she answered. Wade's disappointment was plain on his face.

"It is not," he said. He shot up a fiery glare at his college roommate. Jessica wasn't cold, she just didn't want her body to be constantly peeped at by the increasingly annoying Russell Bean.

Wade hurried after Jessica, catching her at the door. His hands fondled her midsection, gradually working their way down. She offered no response. The magic had ended.

Not willing to give up, he leaned to her ear to whisper. "We can go to my quarters." Jessica closed her eyes and leaned her head back. There was no resistance to his touching. Wade felt a sliver of hope. His lips found their way to her neck. "We can shut the door. Have a nice comfy bed. Just you and I…"

Jessica exhaled agreeably. She opened her eyes, turned back, and nipped at Wade's lower lip. Her new desire was quickly eradicated as a bright flash reflected off the deck.

"Ugh!"

"Hence, the cabin," Wade said, knowing what bothered her.

"Not while *he's* awake," she said.

"Not while he's…?"

"I can't," she said. "I'm not doing it while he's up and about. I don't trust that creep."

Now, Wade was REALLY regretting the decision to let Russell tag along. He marched back to the aft deck and gazed up at his former roommate. Russell stood at the back railing, staring out into the water.

"Do you really have to keep shooting that stuff off?"

Russell looked down at him, his face flabbergasted. "That wasn't me!"

"Oh, yeah, sure," Wade said, pointing out into the empty ocean. The full moon offered a vast view of the world around them. There wasn't a single boat in sight. "I guess it was the fish shooting off fireworks?"

"Wade, it wasn't—"

"Please man, will you just cut it out? Jessica and I, we're…"

"There! Look behind you," Russell said, pointing into the water. As his friend spoke, Wade saw the white reflections of flickering light. He turned around and looked out over the transom.

"The hell?"

The lights continued flickering. Whatever they were, they were deep beneath the water. The way they glimmered reminded him of a busted transformer. In fact, some of the lights seemed to let off sparks that traveled for several feet before fizzling out.

"You have any idea what that is?" Russell asked.

"Not a clue," Wade replied. Jessica joined him at the deck, her eyes widening at the phenomenon.

"How deep is it here?" Russell asked.

"This far off Maxwell Island? Can't be more than a few hundred feet," Wade answered.

"Maybe it's a damaged power cable. There's a bunch of cables that go from the island to the mainland," Jessica said.

"I don't think so. We're over on the north side. The cables are on the west," Wade said. For a few moments, the lights ceased. The grads waited in silence, their hearts pounding with anticipation.

"Maybe it's gone," Jessica said. They waited another minute.

"Maybe we should radio it in," Wade said.

"And say what? Unexplained flashing lights a half mile off East Beach? Who'd come out here to inspect that? Besides, it's gone," Russell said. That last word had barely left his lips when a new series of flashes began. Each ball of light was larger than the last, lasting merely a second. They soon got so bright that the whole ocean seemed to light up.

"Maybe we should get out of here," Wade said.

"Sounds good to me," Russell said. "Because I think they're getting closer." Wade watched carefully. Russell was right. Before, they were over a thousand feet out. Now, they were only half that distance away. He didn't like it. He hurried inside and climbed the steps to the pilothouse, followed closely by Jessica.

"What could it be?" she asked, her voice bordering on frantic.

"I don't know, babe," he said. He cut the wheel to starboard and reached for the throttle. As he did, another flash streaked through the window behind him.

"Wade?" Jessica said. He saw her looking through the window, her hands cupped over her mouth. She tensed, on the verge of screaming. Wade looked out into the ocean. The flashes were only a few meters off the starboard quarter, each one blinding.

The next flash took definitive form. There was no mistaking its shape: it was a bolt of lightning under the water. Its jagged shape passed under the stern and hit the keel. Electric currents, hot as molten lava, traveled across the length of the vessel in the blink of an eye. As quickly as it appeared, the electric bolt vanished, only to be replaced by the orange flash of eighteen-hundred gallons of fuel simultaneously igniting. Wade and Jessica felt a rush of flame before the shockwave ended their lives.

The yacht burst into a ball of flames, sending chunks of the fly deck hurtling into the ocean. Among them was Russell Bean, his midsection partially coated with fire. Reeling head over heels, he hit the water and sank several feet, completely stunned.

After several seconds, he finally felt the sting of ocean water on his eyes and fresh burns. His scream dissolved into a series of air bubbles. He regained enough control of his senses to begin paddling to the surface. Even now, he wasn't really sure what happened. He had seen the electric bolt, then all of a sudden, he was thrown from the deck.

He broke the surface and sucked in a breath, followed by intense coughing. Bright orange flashes to his left caused him to turn, and he saw what remained of the smoldering *Dream Wrecker*. All decks were ablaze, the ship nearly broken in two. The entire portside had been blown outward, exposing the engine room and interior compartments.

Suddenly it hit him. *Wade...Jessica!* He remembered them going into the pilothouse, which was completely ablaze. Consumed by shock, it took several seconds for him to realize the white flashes were now directly below him. He looked down, seeing each spark larger than the last.

He hyperventilated, unable to take his eyes off the sight. With each flash, he noticed a shape. Something large, quickly rising toward him. As it got closer, he saw giant black eyes reflecting the light. Then teeth, clenched together. There was a moment of darkness. When the next flash came, those teeth had separated, lining an enormous mouth.

Crushing pressure and stabbing pain struck at once. An impossible force dragged him beneath the surface. Clouds of blood billowed around him like smoke. He felt sharp objects ripping deep into his belly like spikes, crushing his hip bones, legs, and pelvis.

The creature shook him like a ragdoll, its teeth continuing to mash. Muscle tissue tore, tendons snapped, and internal organs spilled out with the blood. It savored the taste of his flesh, taking its time mashing him up before swallowing.

Its body like one enormous fin, it slithered through the water like a snake in search of new prey.

Up above, the ocean calmed, its surface reflecting the orange glow of a burning ship.

CHAPTER 2

The summer months was usually the customary time for most people to break the mundane routines of employment for a week or two, in favor of the escapism brought by vacations. For the staff of the Maxwell Island Police Department, it was the opposite. Vacation time was denied, overtime was often mandated, and the casual patrol and donut munching was replaced with an endless hassle of vandalisms, complaints, and an endless enforcement of laws.

In her second year as chief, Silvia Remar had grown used to listening to the grievances of her staff. Each summer brought with it the tune of those complaining of missing out on family trips, birthdays, baseball games, and general home time. Silvia tolerated the verbal grievances from her staff. All it amounted to was them venting steam. What she didn't tolerate were lies and malicious behavior. In her first year as chief, she had received a time-off request in July by a five-year officer, claiming that a family member had passed away. Naturally, she had granted the request, only to find out a month later that the so-called funeral was actually a trip to the Grand Canyon. Unable to fire him for the offense, she decided to make an example of him, and had the officer moved from his much desired 7:00a.m. to 3:00p.m. day shift to midnights.

By June 1st, the first wave of vacationers began arriving on the beaches of Maxwell Island, doubling the population. That new number would also double by the 25th, when the *Gota ja' Titan* meteor made impact in the Atlantic. The resulting tsunami wreaked havoc along the Florida Keys, resulting in tremendous damage, which in itself resulted in many mainlanders cancelling their upcoming trips. Those who did not want to see their summer wasted turned to other avenues. Some chose

Maxwell Island. It was close enough to Florida to get that tropical feel, and far enough north that the tsunami did not cause much damage.

By the end of June, there was a vast spike in the population, which usually had the small island jampacked with fifteen-thousand vacationers. This summer, it was upwards of eighteen-thousand. As with many coastal and island communities that depended on tourist spending for their revenue, Maxwell Island welcomed these visitors with open arms. Lake house rentals, cabins, and hotels were usually booked months in advance. Fishermen looking for extra revenue charted out their boats for anyone hoping to bag the big one. For the island population, the tourists brought money.

For Chief Silvia Remar and her staff, they sometimes meant trouble.

It was 11:18p.m. on Tuesday, June 30th, and already the Chief was up to her neck in reports. She overheard the briefings for third shift during shift change, as well as the gripes from two afternoon officers that she mandated to stay over. She took no pleasure in it, but had little choice. They had over eighteen-thousand people on this island, and she only had twenty-two officers to contend with them, including one sergeant on first and second shift, who took turns to cover the vacancy on third, one lieutenant, and no deputy chief to help manage things.

Since her arrival at 6:48 that morning, she and her officers had to respond to twenty-five larceny reports—most of which were simply misplaced items that were recovered later, twenty-one vandalisms, six fights, seven medical calls–of which one was a heart attack after a four-hundred pound middle aged man thought he could down three foot-long chili dogs in the hundred-degree sun after eating an elephant ear. Combined with patrolling the beaches, petty theft and vehicle crimes, hotel complaints, and making sure the banks were well-protected, Silvia felt like she was at war each day.

Not one to demand something from her crew that she wouldn't do herself, she was practically living in the office. Unlike the officers below her, she didn't have the luxury of overtime. It was the price of good leadership, and Silvia didn't mind. Her only gripe was that the extra duty cut down on her gym time. At thirty-eight years old, she weighed exactly the same as the day she graduated basic training back in '01.

Oh, what could've been. With the thought came a pinch in her lower back, accompanied by a tingling of sciatica in her left leg. Silvia shifted in her seat, relieving pressure from the degenerated disc that cut her Army service short after only a year. With that pain came bitterness. Come October, had life not thrown her a curve ball, she'd be retiring after twenty years. Instead, she had to endure two years of intense physical therapy, followed by occasional visits to a chiropractor, in addition to two epidural shots every year. She had fooled herself into thinking she could re-enlist, until arthritis was added to her condition at age twenty-three.

Silvia could tell she had been trapped between her office chair and the driver seat of her patrol car for the past month, without any significant striding motion in-between. At her age, she needed sixty-minutes a day on the treadmill to keep that disc in place, but with the heavy workload, she was practically living at work. There was no getting used to disc pain. Thirteen years ago, she needed a strong dose of steroids to get her through the police academy. Despite barely getting through the physical aspects of the academy, she fooled herself into thinking she would adapt. But the weight from the duty belt, Kevlar, flashlight, taser, and various other equipment quickly wreaked havoc on her spine in her first year in the Miami PD. As a result, she found herself stuck on light duty, shuffling through an endless series of reports.

Her fingers punched an endless stream of words into the computer. **Classification of incident:** *Possession of controlled substance.* **Time:** *2233.* **Location:** *Harmon Hotel.*

Oh, how her police career had come full circle.

Realizing her typing had slowed, Silvia tried to retract the thought of her two years in Miami. The only thing worse than the pain was the humiliation. Ten years later, she cringed inwardly from the many eyes passing by her desk as her colleagues went in and out on patrol. Each glance displayed pity for the girl in her mid-twenties who was falling apart physically, lacked any other skillset, and couldn't even keep up with the tasks of her desired career.

That damn pity landed her in Maxwell Island Police Department. It was always said 'It's not how good you are, but who you know' that got you ahead. In Silvia's case, it couldn't have been any truer. Lieutenant Rick Stein, a good guy, well-meaning…didn't even realize he was taking her humiliation to a whole new level.

"I know the Chief on Maxwell Island. He's looking to fill a spot. It's a good, easy gig. Same fifteen-hundred residents for nine-months out of the year. Only busy time is during the summer. The officers there don't carry as much gear, so it won't be as physically demanding. Chief owes me a favor. Say the word and I'll get you in."

Every fiber in her being wanted to tell him to take that offer and shove it up his ass. "Easy gig, my ass." She didn't join the service and police force in pursuit of easy gigs. Her ego soared with the spirit of a woman in her twenties feeling that she had to prove something to herself. Unfortunately, the only thing stronger than her ego that day was the pain.

Instead of "Shove that job up your ass" it was "Please. Oh, God, thank you."

She checked her watch. 11:32p.m. Her alarm was set for 5:30. Ten minutes to get home, and with fifteen minutes she had to dedicate to some physical therapy exercises…at best she'd be getting five hours of sleep. She finished typing out the incident details then saved the files.

"Dispatch to Car Three."

"Go ahead, Dispatch."

"Can you take a look over at East Beach. Someone reported hearing a loud noise. Like a crack of thunder."

"The Fourth of July crowd has been rolling in, Dispatch. Probably just fireworks."

Silvia snatched her transmitter from her shirt collar. "Zero-One to Car Three, just do a drive-by and check it out." It was clear from the few moments of radio silence that they were surprised to hear her voice this late.

"Will do, Chief."

Silvia clipped her microphone to her shirt and began shutting down her computer. She heard footsteps in the hall, then a knock on her door.

"Come in," she said. The door, already open a crack, swung in the rest of the way, making way for the six-foot-two Sergeant Royce Boyer.

"Long day, eh, Chief?" he said.

"Too long," she replied. She forgot he was coming in tonight to cover the third shift Sergeant vacancy tonight. His ego was like an overloaded nuclear reactor, and everyone around him often felt like they were dying of radiation poisoning.

Silvia could tell by the narrow expression in those brown eyes that he was annoyed. Royce was one of those people who loathed having a younger person as his superior. Even more so, he hated micromanagement. She knew, as it was an argument he frequently used when applying for the position when Chief Engler retired three years ago. Silvia remembered the constant interviews with Mayor Joellen Marsh. It was like a political campaign, only the loser didn't fake the gracious demeanor of defeat. She pushed herself from her desk and stood up.

"I thought—" She froze and sucked in a deep breath, trying not to gasp. *Shit, I stood up too fast.* She waited a moment, then eased her back into a straight posture. She would be feeling this in the morning. "I thought you were dealing with that call at Free Willis Bar."

"Over and done with. Only took five minutes," Royce said. "Just had to talk the bad boys down. They went home. Case closed. I'm good like that."

"Dispatch stated there was an assault."

"Two bucks threw a few jabs over a hot babe. It happens everywhere, especially this time of year. I'm not in the habit of arresting everyone who isn't a boy scout."

And there it was again. For ten years, she had to listen to how the Sergeant worked in NYPD. Not a chill day for the eight years he was there. Always a drug bust, a fight, a domestic call, a shooting, and Silvia knew not to get him started on the terrorist threats. All that *real* police work didn't leave much time for the petty stuff. In actuality, it was disguised showboating—a reminder that he had more *real* police experience than she did. Silvia suspected that's what he was doing every time that USMC forearm tattoo was faced toward her. Two terms active duty, with one Purple Heard and a Bronze Star. All of this added to his resentment that Silvia was chosen over him by the hotshot progressive mayor, or as he called her—the bitch that slashed the department's budget by a third.

Silvia didn't have the temperament for his attitude tonight. She wanted to get out as soon as she could. Of course, that's what he wanted—for her to be intimidated. She didn't want to admit to herself that it was working.

"Before I forget, did you get my email?"

"Which one?"

"I tried looking up the files for the Vic Pally incident, but it wasn't there," Silvia said.

"Oh, that," Royce said. Silvia knew the tone; 'Why is that so important?' The Sergeant cleared his voice, obviously looking for a more diplomatic way of putting it. "Nothing came of it. We searched the parking lot. Didn't find anyone carrying drugs. No vehicles were broken into. I told Dispatch to log that we didn't find anything and called it a night."

"I see," Silvia said. "While you're here tonight, have it written by the time I get back. Mayor is asking about it."

"Rather some tourist bitched," Royce said.

Silvia's sciatica nerve pulsed. So much for diplomatic. She took a breath, keeping her temper down.

"Steven Pack. Not just some tourist."

"Ah, Steve. I should've known. Now it makes sense why Marsh wants him looked after. Gotta keep those sponsors happy, or else she'll have to find a new way to fund her next campaign."

"Regardless, get it done please. And have someone check the beaches," she said.

"I thought Island Counsel was extending the hours to midnight," Royce said.

Nice try. "No, they *want* to. Mayor hasn't agreed to it yet. They still close at twenty-two-hundred."

"Will do, then. Just know, the more our guys stray from the town areas at night, the more trouble the tourists get into. They watch for this stuff."

"I'll talk to the Mayor about getting some more help in the summer months," she said. Royce backed out to make room for her. Silvia shut the office door and pulled her truck keys from her pocket.

"By the way, you never got back to me. Is she asking for more police presence at the Belanger Festival?"

Silvia was halfway out the door. She looked away to hide that she was squeezing her eyes shut. *Shit! I forgot to ask.*

"She hasn't answered yet. She's been busy with meetings with the energy company, making her public appearances with the tourism industries, and her weekly battles with Chief Financial Officer for construction on the water treatment plant." She could tell he saw through her lies. Not like she was going to win his respect anyway. It was no secret that he thought she was just a glorified administrator who'd had the filing department overloaded with redundant reports. "I'll get with her first thing in the morning and get it straightened out."

"Okay. But I hope she doesn't expect much if she wants a police presence on the beaches at the same time."

"I'll make sure she's aware. See you in the morning," Silvia said. She embraced the cool night air as she walked out to her truck. It was the only good thing she had going right now. That pinching in her back was only getting worse. As much as she didn't want to sacrifice sleep, she would have to do at least a half-hour on the treadmill, followed by another half hour of her exercises. Hopefully, she'd get the disc worked back in enough so it wouldn't give her hell in the morning.

She eased herself into the seat and started the truck. She backed out of her space and went for the exit. As she started to make the left hand turn to go home, the radio blared.

"*Uh, Dispatch. This is Car Three over here on East Beach. Has anyone called the fire department?*"

"*No. Need me to get ahold of them?*"

"*Yeah, please. I'm standing on the beach right now, and I'm looking at a fire out on the water..*"

"*A fire—on the water?*"

"*It's definitely a fire. Not a little fire—it's HUGE! I think there's a boat out there that's gone ablaze.*"

Silvia cut the wheel to the right and put on the flashers, then sped her way to East Beach.

CHAPTER 3

From the backlot behind The Silver Pearl Tiki Bar, the burning yacht looked no larger than that of a small candle. Silvia parked her truck near two patrol cars already on scene and gazed at the flame through her windshield. Fifty feet past the guardrail were two patrol officers, standing just a few feet from the shore.

Silvia stepped out of the truck and found the open gate. She was grateful, as climbing over the guardrail would be a nightmare on her back. The two officers turned to look at her as she jogged across the sand to meet them. On the left was Officer Graft, a regular third-shifter. He resembled the kind of cop you'd expect to see on TV; moderate build, black mustache, easygoing demeanor. It was the opposite of the other officer: Zirke. He was at the start of a double shift, which would lead to his normal time on days. He was only a year younger than her, and his austere demeanor made it obvious he was friends with Royce—and that he shared the Sergeant's opinion of her. Hell, they practically had the same history: U.S. Marine service, deployment in Iraq, followed by thirteen years as a cop in Miami—interestingly, it was something he always brought up when talking with the other officers when she was nearby, like he wanted her to hear it.

The orange flame danced in the distance, the boat slowly pushed north by the current. Its reflection stretched for hundreds of feet in the water, almost giving off the appearance of an illuminant circle that surrounded it.

"Anybody see it happen?" Silvia asked.

"Just a couple neckers over there," Zirke said, pointing at a young couple sitting on a bench nearby. At most they were college age, and only their first year. They stared at the water, completely stunned.

"They were the ones who called it in?"

"No, that must've been somebody further inland," Graft said. Flashing lights caught Silvia's attention as Royce's Interceptor raced into the lot behind the tiki bar and parked next to her truck. He left them on as he got out. She could hear him muttering something before he hustled out onto the beach.

"Thought you were heading home," he said to her.

"My radio was still on. I heard the call," she said. She realized after she spoke how she sounded like the subordinate having to justify herself. Royce approached the shore and gazed at the burning vessel.

"Dispatch. What's the ETA on Maxwell Fire Rescue?"

"Units have been dispatched for Harbor Response. They'll be arriving any minute."

"Copy." Royce clipped the microphone to his shirt, then turned to the two officers.

"God, that thing's really burning," Silvia said. "How big is that boat?"

"Big enough to be seen from here," Royce said. His voice lacked the astonishment she had. "Probably a couple idiots playing with fireworks and set off a spare fuel drum." He turned to his officers. "Did they witness it?"

"Yeah," Zirke answered. The teenagers stood up as the muscular cop and the brunette walked up to them.

"Hey, kids," Royce said, his demeanor suddenly a friendly one. "Probably not the kind of fireworks you were hoping to experience." The boy laughed.

"No, no sir."

Silvia withheld her desire to scold the Sergeant. *These kids aren't supposed to be here at all...much less doing God knows what to each other.* Their clothes were wrinkled and there was plenty of sand stuck to the girl's shirt. Didn't take much imagination—and if the night patrol would actually check the beaches...

There were more important things to worry about at the moment.

"So, what happened? What did you see?" Royce asked.

"It was loud. Whoever was on there, they were shooting off fireworks. We didn't think much of it. We were walking on the beach when—" The boy mimicked an explosion with his hands. "It was like, I know it's a cliché comparison, but it was like a movie. The boat just blew up!"

"Did you see any other boats nearby?" Silvia asked. The boy glanced at her, then back at Royce as he answered.

"No. Not that we could see. Then again, it's nighttime. We couldn't see that boat until, well..."

"I get it," Royce said. "Thanks for your help. Remember, beach is closed after ten."

"Okay." The teens started heading up the hill to the gate.

"Wait, one more thing," Silvia said, stopping them. "Officer Graft, get their info for the report, please." Royce rolled his eyes, then glanced back at the kids.

"We uh, don't have our IDs on us," the girl said.

"Just give the officer your names, dates of birth, and phone numbers," Royce said. "Just in case we need to ask you anything more about what you saw." He then walked with the Chief over to the shoreline. "You wanna type this one out, or should I?"

"We'll need all the info we can get," Silvia said.

"Rather, the appearance of information," Royce said. "Name and DOBs from witnesses amounts to nothing but a little extra typing in cases like these. We're not gonna learn anything more from them. They saw a fireball, at night, when it's impossible to see anything that far out. And I somehow doubt they're the suspects."

"Just do your job, Sergeant," Silvia said.

"I am doing my job, *Chief*," Royce said. The word came out in a dull croak. He hated referring to her by the title, and not just because he wanted it for himself. When it wasn't her title, it was her last name. Never once had Silvia ever heard her first name uttered from his mouth.

"I've responded to apartment fires, car fires, hell, even a tanker fire. You can imagine how fun that one was. And I tell you, most people simply driving by when it happens usually say the same stupid thing: "I was going about my day when, kaboom!" That's the most you get, especially when it happens at night and it's hard to see anything. Anything beyond that is just more stuff to type on paper, which I suppose is suitable for someone eager to make it *look* like we've done our job. Might fool a Mayor, but it won't solve a case. We'll get a better report from the Fire Chief once the inspector gets to looking at the wreckage. Speaking of which…"

They saw flashing red lights strobing from the north, illuminating the silver and red hulls of two Fire-Rescue Munson vessels.

****

Purchased from the Greater Boston area, the island committee on Maxwell was able to supply their fire department with two thirty-four-foot Munson vessels. The Fire Chief had specifically outlined the specs, and demanded the boats be outfitted with Hale 1500 GPM fire pumps with bow and stern discharges and Class B foam system. To his surprise, it was a bit of a fight to get the funding for these projects.

Captain Maurice Peterman remembered being there at the meeting, and the burning contempt in his superior's face when the Chief Financial Officer told him, "Oh, this is a little island. It's not like you're gonna be putting out big oil fires. Just one boat should do it." The Chief was able to negotiate it to two, though he couldn't get the tugboat he asked for.

It would certainly come in handy tonight.

Maurice could smell the burning diesel as the Munsons approached the yacht. As they closed in at two hundred yards, he could see that the entire fly deck was gone. Every inch of the vessel from bow to stern was covered in thirty-foot flames. The air was black, and not because it was night. The smoke had blotted out the moonlight, while the flames glistened against the gentle ocean surface.

Not only that, but there was fire ON the water itself. Fuel had exploded everywhere, creating a hellish ring all around the approaching firemen.

The glow of orange reached the hull of Boat 1.

"My lord, somebody did a number on this one," Maurice said. He stood on the forward deck, accompanied by two firefighters who took position at the water cannons positioned on each side of the bow ramp.

They didn't need to await instruction. They quickly went to work extinguishing the flames in the water. That was the easy part. The boat on the other hand—

At six-hundred feet, they were well within range of the yacht. Water pumps beneath the hull suctioned up the Atlantic and jetted twenty-thousand gallons a minute at the seventy-foot vessel. The helmsman slowed, allowing the gunners to keep a forty-degree arch of water descending on the portside. As they assaulted the flames, the second boat circled around the bow, the starboard pump already going to work while the helmsman positioned the boat.

Maurice had seen ships burned with electrical fires before. He'd seen boats with owners barbequing so much on their decks that they accidentally added their own boat to the menu. These were either smaller boats, or smaller fires, or both. But one completely overtaken by flame? This was a first.

What concerned him more was that the call came in from witnesses, and not a 9-1-1 call from the people on board—which would at least indicate they were still alive. Looking at this flame, and given the caller's description of a loud *boom*, something in his gut told him he'd be scraping out some charred corpses.

"Boat Two, make sure you keep an eye out for anyone in the water," Maurice said.

"Will do," Boat Two's helmsman replied.

The pumps rained ocean water all over the yacht. Little by little, the flames started to shrink. They still had a ways to go; there was fire in the lower compartments that would be hard to reach from this angle. Boat Two now had both pumps hitting the forward deck. After a few minutes, the bow rail was visible, blackened by the hot flames. The deck itself was almost non-existent; what remained of it was a charred heap of battered steel and wood.

The outer hull seemed relatively untouched. The Lieutenant aboard Boat Two shined a spotlight under the starboard bow revealing the name.

"*Dream Wrecker*," he radioed Maurice. "Seems almost poetic."

"Keep hitting it. I'll have my crew take us around to the back to get the serial number," Maurice replied.

As the flames subsided, Maurice could make out further detail on the yacht's interior. There were enormous cracks running down the portside, which traveled up along the middeck. The ship was practically broken in two. The cabin interiors were completely ravaged. Worse, he could see the inside of the fuel tank.

"This thing blew up from within," he said.

"Could fireworks have done that?" one of the firemen asked.

"I don't see how. That thing should be protected by two-inches of steel all around. Unless there was a leak. It's all I can think of. Until the inspector gets a look at it, there's no way to tell." He continuously panned his spotlight down to the water in search of swimmers. "No sign of anyone."

"By the looks of it, they wouldn't have gotten off in time anyway," the helmsman replied.

"Probably not," Maurice concurred, reluctantly. He waited until the pumps diminished the flames on the portside. "Alright, take us around the stern. Let's see if we can get a serial number for Chief Remar."

"Think this is a tourist vessel?"

"Most likely. I don't recall seeing a *Dream Wrecker* docked in the harbor during the off-season," Maurice said. The helmsman took them around, allowing the men on deck to spray the back of the yacht down. Flames danced in defiance, evaporating the water into white steam. Flares reached out over the transom. The breeze carried its roaring sound. Maurice could hear something cracking behind that first wall. A piece of the interior collapsed in on itself, causing an impact heavy enough to rock the ship.

Soon, the flames began to shrink. Hot mist formed a tornado over the yacht. After a few more minutes, the only flames remaining were in the interior compartments.

Maurice aimed the spotlight at the serial number located on the upper right corner. *AQV-48381-B6-06.*

"Take us back around the side and get us closer," he said. As the boat came around the portside, he was able to get a better look at the large breach. The big crack ran well below the waterline. "Shit...Dispatch!"

"Go ahead."

"Yeah, get ahold of Kavon and tell him to get his tugboat out here on the double."

"At this hour?"

"Gotta get this yacht to shore now, or we'll be digging it off the seabed," he said. "It's breached below the waterline. Doesn't look like a big one, but the water we're adding to it is accelerating the situation."

"Ten-four. I'm on it."

Boat Two worked its way down the starboard side, raining water along the way, then came around the stern to line up with Boat One. All flames on the upper decks were completely extinguished, leaving only a few smaller flames below.

"Alright, take it down to one pump, Lieutenant," Maurice said. "I don't want to accelerate the flooding.

"All the same, we'll probably have to get some dive-crews in the morning," the Lieutenant replied. "If anyone was on deck, they were probably tossed into the water—and I don't see anyone splashing, so..."

"That's one thing I'm afraid of," Maurice sighed.

"Dispatch to Maxwell Command, just an FYI, Kavon Hayes is on route now. He says he'll be there in five minutes. Also, I've been getting calls from Mayor Marsh's staff asking questions about this."

"Great. Can't keep their noses out of our business," he muttered, then replied, "Let them know I'll get in touch with them as soon as I know more. The inspector won't be able to examine this until the morning."

"Already done, Captain."

"Thanks, Dispatch," Maurice let out an exasperated sigh. "Alright, Lieutenant, keep spraying it. Keep an eye on that waterline. Hopefully it'll stay afloat long enough for Kavon to get a tow-line on it."

"You think that transom is structurally stable?"

"Only one way to find out," Maurice said. "In the meantime, I gotta go see Chief Remar. I'll keep in touch." He patted his fist against the cabin and pointed to the flashing lights near the shore. The helmsman cut the wheel to starboard and throttled toward the beach.

****

Silvia and Royce waited at the lifeguard dock. The tall beach lights shined down on the Munson boat's hull as the firemen lined up behind the motorboats used by the beach staff.

"I see we're all working late hours," the Captain said, giving Silvia a quick wave before stepping up onto the dock.

"You saw nobody in the water?" Royce asked.

"Nobody," Maurice said. "Kavon should be arriving shortly with his tugboat. If we're lucky, we'll be able to beach it before it sinks. There's a big crack in the hull."

"What do you think happened?" Silvia asked.

"It blew up. Can't tell you how until the inspector gets a look at it."

"You'll have to beach it here?" she asked.

"Chief, that thing won't make it to the harbor. If that thing sinks, we'll lose a lot of evidence as to what happened," Maurice said.

"What about the flatbed?" Silvia said. "I can have Dispatch call up Eddie Hill and see if he can get this thing hauled near the station."

"He's out of town for the day," Royce said. "Won't be back until Thursday."

"Oh, great," she muttered. "The Mayor's gonna be up my ass about this."

"Yeah, she's already calling my office asking questions," Maurice said.

"I take it there was nobody in the water?" Royce asked. Silvia squeezed her eyes shut, absorbing the feeling of foolishness. That should've been the first thing she asked, but no, she was more focused on what JoEllen Marsh would ask of her.

"Nobody," Maurice answered.

"We'll have to get divers to check out the bottom," Silvia said. "I'll try and see if we can get anyone out here this morning."

"Did you get the serial number?" Royce asked.

"Got it here," Maurice said. He ripped the page from his notepad and handed it to the Sergeant. "Called the *Dream Wrecker*. Don't know if that name rings a bell or not."

"No, but that's what the databank is for," Royce said. "Thanks, Captain. I appreciate you thinking ahead on that."

"Just part of the job," Maurice said. "I'll stick around tomorrow when the inspector gets here. Just to let you all know, there's a chance there are bodies inside there. We'll take a look for what we can, but it'll be hard to do a proper job until daylight."

Now Silvia was really dreading her next conversation with the Mayor. JoEllen Marsh would not be pleased to know this boat would be beached in a public area during the busy season, especially considering the fact that it likely contained charred corpses. JoEllen was not necessarily an insensitive person, but she was very mindful of the dollars the vacationers brought in. And East Beach was a prime area where they gathered for recreation.

"Damn it," Silvia muttered.

"Problem, Chief?" Royce said.

"Nothing. Just prepping myself for the inevitable meeting tomorrow with the Mayor."

Royce scoffed. "She'll just have to get over it. She could either have it here, or spend a bunch of money to float it back up after it sinks."

"Yeah, I'm sure that'll go over well," Silvia said.

That's because you've always been an administrator instead of a real cop. He wanted to say it. The damn Chief would probably bend the knee to the Mayor, too afraid to piss her off and supposedly risk her job, since it was the only thing she had.

"Can't halt an investigation just because it gets in the way of a few knuckleheads that wanna try out their new speedos."

"Thanks for that image," Maurice said.

"It's an island, Captain. I'm sure you've seen it before," Royce chuckled.

"There are some things you just never get used to...especially when they're three-hundred pounds." The two men laughed. Royce noticed Silvia's glare. She didn't say anything, but might as well have.

He could read her mind like a fortune cookie: *"How can you joke around right now?" Jesus, has she ever had a real call in her life beyond citations?*

"Listen Chief, I got this," he said. "The fire's just about out. The tugboat's almost here. Go on home and get some shut-eye. I promise to dot my Is and cross my Ts in the report."

Silvia nodded, also understanding what he was really saying: *Get out of here so I can handle this.* Unfortunately, the crushing feeling in her back obliviated any desire to remain standing. Between stressing about the situation and the pain, sleep was gonna be near impossible tonight.

"Alright. Keep on it, Sergeant. I'll see you in the morning. Thanks for your help, Maurice."

"No problem, ma'am," the Captain said. Royce waved goodbye, his eyes never looking up from the boat's serial number.

The walk back to her truck was short but tedious. Even a slight uphill climb seemed difficult at this moment. Silvia struggled up to the lot and eased herself into her truck.

God, now of all times. Usually spring was the most difficult season on her back, but now it seemed the agony lasted all year long. She straightened her posture as best she could, while reminding herself not to get angry at the pain. It just wasn't fair. She hadn't done anything to deserve this. She used to run five-mile marathons, and now it was a struggle to go up a flight of stairs on some days. Stress made it worse—and she was feeling a lot of it now.

She started the truck and looked at the clock. 12:23. Great. She still couldn't put off the walk. Maybe the physical exercises.

As she backed from her spot, she heard Royce barking commands on the radio. Officers responded without hesitation or argument, and with a military-like discipline. He had something she didn't—respect.

Worse throbs came with the thoughts. She switched off the radio and headed for home.

CHAPTER 4

Miles Bren leaned against the edge of the cockpit, blowing multiple sighs of relief, while simultaneously watching the fiery glow diminish from afar. When he saw the flashing lights coming straight for him, he figured his vacation here on Maxwell Island was coming to a swift end. The Rustler 24 would easily be spotted against the flashing lights. Yet, the boats didn't even seem to notice him. After following their trajectory he realized they were fireboats, not police.

For several minutes, he watched the glow of the flashing lights combat with that of the big fireball. It was too far away to see the details, but it was obvious they were there to put out the flame.

The drugs in his system played with his vision. More than once, he swore he saw the fireball form a fist and raise the middle finger to the firemen. He would laugh at this, which would subsequently cause his date, Anne Lang, to laugh hysterically as well.

She had hastily put her bikini top on when she first saw the lights. It was tied sloppily, the left cup dangling low, hardly covering her breast. Her hair was a mess from her date's constant fondling of it. She found herself constantly running her own hands through it, oddly sensitive to the touch. It was her first time doing cocaine. Until now, the only high she ever got was from smoking weed, and that got her sleepy more than anything. This, on the other hand, felt like it gave her a burst of energy.

It was their first night together, though she had first met Miles during her last visit a year ago. He was exactly the same as now; talkative, energetic, suave, and not too hard on the eyes. She had a weakness for his faux hawk haircut, and his skin was the perfect shade of tan. Almost golden, likely from having unlimited access to the beach. From what she knew, he worked from home. Being his own boss granted him the flexibility to do basically anything he wanted. She envied that. She was a year out of high school, and already she was dreading the mundane existence of living day-to-day, with each life event needed to be worked around her job at Walgreens. Hell, just getting the time off for this vacation required switching shifts with co-workers and promising favors for others in exchange for coverage. And college...the first semester, she cried. Nothing interested her, at least not enough to endure the agony of being forced to take English, Sociology, and God help her, the algebra.

She felt the high starting to wear off. Really? It had only been twenty minutes! Thirty at most, and already it was fading? She wanted more. She looked around for the straw, using her iPhone as a flashlight. She stopped briefly to look at the text messages on the screen, and two missed-call alerts. It was her dad again.

God! For the whole first day of the family trip, she had to endure lectures about going back to school and bettering herself. Yada-yada-yada. Apparently, she wasn't good enough as she was. And now, during the little bit of time she managed to be on her own, he still wouldn't leave her alone.

"Where'd you go?"

"It's past midnight."

"Hey, kid. Look at your phone! Text me back or call when you see this."

Anne leaned her head back and groaned at the sky. *Jesus Christ! Does that asshole think I'm twelve?!* She considered texting back, but a rebellious nature prevented her thumb from touching the screen. She was nineteen, damn it! She ought to be out without having to feel monitored. She turned her phone off then let it drop into the cockpit.

She wasn't going to let anything rob her of this night. She had never felt so free. Hell, the only reason she was wearing anything at all was because they thought they were about to be caught. But the danger had passed, and the two returned to their relaxed state.

Lustful eyes examined Miles' trim figure as he dipped down into the cockpit. He came back up with a bottle of Red Chateau les Clauzots. He had bragged about how he had it shipped from France. He handed Anne her glass and filled it with the red liquid.

"Well, enough of that nonsense. Now back to you and me," he said, smiling.

"You got any more?" she asked.

"The whole bottle," Miles replied.

"No, the other stuff," Anne said. Oddly, she didn't want to use the word 'cocaine'. It somehow felt like an acknowledgement she was doing something bad. Not just bad—illegal.

Miles chuckled. "I do, but you don't want to go too crazy on the first time." Anne scoffed. A *responsible* drug user? What planet was she on?

"Come on, Miles. I've never felt so alive," she said.

"I hope that has something to do with me," he replied. She eyed his bare chest and wrinkly trunks again. *Ohhh, it has.* She leaned forward and dug her tongue into his mouth, a gesture he immediately reciprocated. The make-out led to Miles putting himself onto her, pressing her back against the edge of the cockpit. The glass tipped, spilling wine into the water.

"Oh!" she exclaimed.

"Eh, don't worry about it," Miles said. He grabbed her chin and directed her mouth back to his. Like sinking ships, they slipped below. Anne was on her back, eagerly allowing his lips to access her whole body. She wanted this to last forever. Maybe she would stay here after her family returned to Oregon. She hated that state. Hated the winters, summers were boring, as were the people. Plus, she'd be away from that overbearing father of hers.

The drugs and wine made her like putty. Every so often, she'd wonder if Miles had brought other girls out on his boat before. Charming man, well-to-do from his art and writing business, it was hard to believe she was the only one that ever caught his eye. Was she just a fling? No, she didn't want it to be true. The fantasy of staying here with him was too good—freeing even. She'd always been told to go to college and gain a prosperous career. But she hated working. Screw what other people thought. If being a simple stay-at-home housewife felt this good, then she'd take it for ten lifetimes.

Unfortunately, her mind couldn't repel the worry that she was just a fling to Miles. Just a good time, another person for him to get his rocks off with, then forget about the next morning. She needed to chase the thought away.

He was nipping at her midsection and working his way down. Though electrifying, it wasn't enough to distract her. She cupped her hands around his face and guided him back to hers.

"Just a little more," she pleaded in a sensuous whisper. "Please." Miles was breathing heavily, lost in the bliss of ecstasy. It was usually in that stage when a man would give a woman anything she asked for.

"Just a bump," he said.

"Yeah?" She nipped his chin and caressed his body, working down to his groin. "Only a bump?"

Miles stiffened, barely keeping it together. "A-Alright, a little more than a bump."

"I like that," she said, then kissed him. "Then, you can give me another bump, if you know what I mean." He did, and it practically had him leaping off her body for the cocaine. Anne got up on her knees and pulled her hair back as Miles poured a line of the white powder on a plate. He handed her the straw.

"Enjoy, darling."

"I will, and believe me, *you'll* benefit from this as much as I," she said. She lowered herself to the plate and took in the cocaine. She worked her way down the line, then leaned back, her dilated eyes wide open with delight. She held that pose for a minute, then the high finally took its effect. Suddenly, she wasn't worried about her father anymore. She wasn't thinking about lousy careers, school, the misery of watching everyone else succeed in the workplace, or whether she was just a fling for Miles. As far as her mind was concerned, he was hers forever.

And she was his.

She wrapped her hands behind Miles' head and pulled him back on top of her. They hit the deck with a tremendous thud. Their hands were all over each other, mouths connected, moaning their pleasure. Anne felt electrified, the drugs making her hypersensitive to her man's touch. The pleasure gave her new energy, and a desire for control. She flipped Miles onto his back, his impact shuddering the boat. She threw herself on him and kissed his neck and chest, her hands working their way to his trunks.

Miles smiled. *Two can play at this.* His hands ran up her inner thighs, as though intending to pleasure her womanhood, then suddenly he rolled her to the side and threw himself on her. She laughed and screamed, then continued the game.

Their vigorous foreplay continued, battering the deck with motion, sending vibrations deep below the waves.

****

The eel traveled along the seabed in search of shallow prey. As it traveled, it watched the alien red lights with caution. In the deep world it came from, such light usually indicated prey was nearby…or an enemy of equal size. However, it had never seen lights like these before. Most lights from the deep were static blue, or green, with some lifeforms illuminating mixtures of red, violet, and yellow. But these were much brighter, almost to the point of stinging its large eyes. Because of the strain, it was unable to gauge the size of the things emitting them. The vibrations in the water suggested something smaller than itself, and in normal circumstances, the eel would attack. However, it was in a new environment, swimming in light and temperatures it was not used to.

Even the moonlight seemed alien to it. It was adjusting, but gradually. It would be another day or two before its eyes were finally adjusted.

Until then, it would take few chances and chase easier prey.

It traveled northwest, grazing its belly along the soft seabed. It spotted a pod of flat-tailed creatures, which quickly darted out of view. It had never seen dolphins before, but their reaction to its presence immediately informed the eel that they were lower on the food chain. They were fast creatures, but like everything else in the ocean, they could not outrun its electric bolt. Three of the dolphins were stunned instantly, frozen by the invisible blow that stopped their hearts and singed their flesh. The only thing they felt afterwards was crushing pain, as the Eel's enormous jaws snatched them up one by one. The rest of the pod had no choice but to abandon their beloved members and flee, their sorrowful chirps echoing in the distance.

The beast finished its meal, leaving a cloud of blood and scraps floating to the bottom. It cruised the ocean at a relaxed speed. It was still hungry, but cautious, as it quickly learned in its journey that it wasn't the only large creature lurking in these waters. It had met the mighty sperm whale several miles back. Their encounter resulted in a tense standoff, where the beasts circled each other. No clash resulted, and the leviathans eventually distanced. Had it been a few days later, the eel wouldn't have hesitated. It was still learning, growing bolder with each day in this environment.

It had been king of its previous world, a leviathan that all other creatures were quick to avoid. Anything that tried to escape, failed, as nothing could escape its electrifying bolt. But now it was a stranger in an alien land, teeming with alien creatures. The land-dwelling creatures were the most bizarre. The boats were the most bizarre, as they were not alive, yet they moved similarly to living things. But tonight, the eel learned that the land-dwellers were as edible as the squid and fish it fed on in the deep. Still, it was cautious.

However, though caution was the thing keeping it alive, it was now depleting its energy. The land-dweller and the three dolphins it gorged on only intensified its hunger. It searched for other signs of prey. Still weary of the meaning of flashing lights, it searched for safer prey. Its sense of smell was compromised from the cloud of blood from its attack on the dolphins, thus, it relied on sound and electromagnetic waves from nearby vibration.

It detected a faint drumming sound from up above. The eel ascended for the moon-lit surface.

A single floating object drifted above. It was smaller than most it had seen so far. The sound was originating from its belly. There were no lights, nothing to threaten it.

As it got closer, its nostrils picked up a strange scent dripping from the creature. It wasn't blood, but it was certainly organic of some kind. Whatever it was, it emboldened the eel to investigate. There was no attempt by the object to escape or attack. The eel would save its energy, and rather than strike with its electric charge, it would attack head-on.

With a wave of its tail, the beast moved in. Its jaw opened to nearly one-hundred-eighty degrees, then like scissors, they closed down on the target.

****

Anne and Miles both screamed as the walls imploded in large shards. Huge pointed objects, like knives made of bone, reached in through the gaps. The hull shook, as though succumbing to intense pressure.

Their screams intensified as the boat rolled over to its side. A raging river of ocean invaded the boat from the breaches and cockpit, drowning out their cries. Adding to the confusion was the sensation of being tossed around. It was like they were trapped inside a giant pepper shaker. They flipped head over heels, completely submerged, bumping against the walls.

Miles threw his arms out, trying desperately to find his buoyancy. The world around him was dark, the light having burned out by the water. He felt fragments of his boat bouncing off his body. There were crackling sounds from imploding hull.

Suddenly, he was surrounded by moonlight. The boat fell away around him, broken into numerous fragments. He looked straight ahead, his eyes fixed on his own air bubbles. He was face up, sinking, the surface directly ahead of him. His body kicked into action, using whatever strength he had left to shoot for the surface.

Then he saw something passing between him and the moonlight. At first, he thought it was a boat, then noticed its long, squiggly shape. The moonlight gave a silver glow to its huge black eyes. The thing looked down at him.

Miles gasped…then gagged after accidentally filling his lungs with seawater. The creature lunged for him. Pointed teeth punched through his body like spears.

The eel thrashed its head side to side, mashing its victim between its jaws. Teeth mashed Miles into an unrecognizable lump of flesh. Pieces of meat broke apart from the body. A hand, detached from the forearm, spun like a falling leaf as it sank beneath the waves, followed by a foot. The creature swallowed its victim, then searched the water for more. Vibrations drew its attention to the surface, as another land-dweller tried paddling for safety.

It was only by pure luck that Anne made it to the surface. After the boat split apart, she started swimming with her eyes clenched shut, with no sense of direction. Luckily, that direction was up. She screamed, thrashing her arms in the water.

She struggled to stay afloat. Her head dipped under again and again. It had been a long time since she had last swam, and that was in a six-foot deep pool. Here she was, floundering in the ocean, with no sign of the man that brought her out here.

"Help me!" she screamed, spitting seawater. Her palms slapped the water in her attempt to remain afloat. Finally, she struck something solid. A piece of hull bounced in the waves. She pulled her upper body over its edge. It sank a couple of inches, but otherwise was sufficient in keeping her afloat. She rested her head on the side and caught her breath.

After a few seconds of levity, she looked around for Miles. She called his name but got no response. As she searched, her eyes spotted lights coming from the island. The desire to find Miles dissipated in favor of her own survival. Holding tight to the chunk of debris, she kicked for the shore. It was hard to tell how far away, but as long as she was heading in the right direction, she'd get there eventually.

She still didn't fully grasp what had happened. All she saw were the walls caving in, and the big things poking through…like *teeth*. Impossible! It had to have been the drugs. Maybe they hit another boat, or…

Anne saw the water swirling up ahead. Something was moving…something HUGE. At first, she thought it was a whale. It was certainly big enough. But whales didn't move their tails side to side.

The creature dipped, its tail generating a small splash before disappearing. A moment later, she felt herself rising with a swell. There was a mass underneath her, pushing the water.

Anne looked straight down and saw the teeth glistening under the moonlight. She kicked her feet in a futile attempt to scare it away.

All that did was entice it.

The enormous jaws snapped shut, the front teeth intertwining over her midsection. With the pain came pressure, then a sudden *crack*. All of a sudden, she was free, carried away by another huge swell.

She tried to scream, but her lungs had deflated. Rapid blood loss triggered lightheadedness, then permanent blackness. Her last sensation was the sting of saltwater on her exposed organs as her severed torso drifted with the waves.

CHAPTER 5

The morning sun peered over the horizon at 5:48 a.m. It was July 1st, the start of the busiest month on Maxwell Island. At 7:00, the beaches were officially open. The early birds set out to enjoy the sunrise, while taking advantage of the small window of relative quiet. Breakfast stands set up for business and served lines of customers all over the north, south, and west beaches.

However, the businesses on East Beach opened up on an empty stretch of sand, with nobody but police and fire personnel. The few tourists that ventured nearby were deterred by the long stretch of caution tape strung around a large yacht.

"Yeah-yeah, I'm working on it," Sergeant Royce Boyer said to the angry owner of *Kirk's Food & Beverage*. He already had his breakfast items set out in the kitchen, ready to be prepared. But he couldn't waste his supply when the beaches were empty, yet at the same time, he couldn't keep everything frozen and locked away when the crowds could arrive at any moment. It took time to prep some of his signature recipes, and usually, he tried to get a head-start in order to get people served quickly and efficiently.

"Whose bright idea was it to drag this thing up on a public beach?" Kirk grumbled. "And *leave* it here, no less?!"

"Bad luck and circumstance," Royce said. "But I'm pulling some strings. I should have this thing out of here in an hour. In the meantime, why don't you make me up a double omelet with mushrooms and tomatoes, and a side of hash browns."

"Well, um…" Kirk's demeanor softened. "I would, but I can't fire up the stove for just one order…"

"Oh, no. Not just for me," Royce said. "Take orders from my officers and firemen here. All on me. And while you're at it…you got any coffee going?"

"Hell, I'll throw it in for free," Kirk said. He was now the complete opposite of the angry forty-year old former Navy chef he was thirty seconds ago.

"Oh, you don't have to do that, Sarge," Captain Maurice Peterman said.

"No arguments. You guys have been busting ass all night. Besides, I've been making a killing with the overtime lately," Royce said. Maurice looked at his empty thermos, having depleted his coffee over an hour ago. His shift technically had ended, but he still needed to wait with the officers in order to brief the Fire Chief and preserve the scene.

"You're a stand-up guy, Royce," Maurice said, then got in line to take breakfast orders from Kirk.

Royce felt his phone vibrating. He recognized the number and eagerly accepted the call.

"This is Sergeant Boyer of Maxwell Island Police Department."

"Yes, Sergeant. I spoke with my boss, and we can get a truck to the ferry in about twenty minutes. It'll probably take another thirty or so to get there."

"Perfect," Royce said. "Thank you very much. I'll have a man there to meet the driver and he'll direct him to East Beach."

"You got it."

"Call me if you have any other questions."

"Will do."

Royce hung up the phone and started dialing another number. The line rang once before someone answered.

"Mayor's Office."

"Hey, Stefanie. This is Royce, over on East Beach."

"Oh, hey, Royce. I'm glad you called. What's going on with that boat over there? I've only been in the office for fifteen minutes and already I've answered four calls about it."

"That's exactly what I'm calling to tell you about," Royce said. "It won't be here longer than an hour. I was able to get a truck ferried in from the mainland to take this boat over to the fire station."

"Oh, good. I'll let the Mayor know."

"Appreciate it, Stef. Talk to you later. Bye." As he clipped his phone back to his belt, he saw white pickup trucks pulling into the parking lot. Fire Chief Stan Rolling and Fire Inspector Brandon Webster got out and headed down to the *Dream Wrecker*.

Stan Rolling walked with a confident stride, his physique clearly showing a lifetime of fire training and execution. He had transferred to Maxwell Island five years ago—around the same time as Royce. Both came from big cities, and both had transferred due to pestering from their spouses about wanting to move to a quieter setting. Now at 58-years old, Stan was only a couple years from his intended retirement, but now he wasn't sure. He loved the job and the island, which provided just enough work to keep him busy, but with significantly less stress overall.

"Oh, that's not good," he said, looking at the charred deck and structure. The hull was mostly clean from what he could see, though most of it was obscured by the beach. He glanced at the huge crack in the side, which seemed to run underneath the ship. "Yeah, I see why you needed to beach this one quick, Captain."

"Yeah," Maurice said. "I tried getting a look inside, but frankly, it's a mess, Chief. There was almost nothing left of the two bodies in the cabin. I think they were in the pilothouse. When the ship exploded from under them, I think the structure collapsed down to the lower levels with them on it. With any luck, the blast killed them instantly."

"Can't even tell if they're male or female," the Lieutenant added.

"Shit. So we have no clue who they were?" The Inspector asked.

"I ran the number. Boat belongs to a gentleman named Jonathon Stevens. His residence is over on the Georgia coast. I've alerted local police in his area and they've reported back that he's alive, and that he had a son, his girlfriend, and a college buddy."

"Three individuals?" Stan said. He looked at Maurice. "And you said you only found two?" Maurice nodded.

"Hate to say it, Chief, but we're gonna have to dredge the area," Brandon said.

"Took the words right out of my mouth," Stan replied. Inspector Brandon Webster took a quick walk around the yacht.

"Yeah, the fuel tank definitely exploded," he said. "Can't really say how without climbing in and getting a closer look." He found the diving port near the portside, put on some gloves, and climbed up onto the main deck. The pilothouse had been blown wide open. He could tell by the pieces of bulkheads pointing straight up like teeth that there had been a fly deck on board. He checked as best as he could, but there was no sign of a third body.

"Gosh, the Mayor's gonna be up in our asses if we keep this thing on the beach," the Fire Chief said.

"I got a transport on the way to take it to the station," Royce said.

Stan blew a sigh of relief. "Good thinking. Eddie picked a hell of a day to go out of town."

"Hey, Maurice?" Kirk the restaurant owner called. The smell of eggs and bacon wafted right into the Chief's nose.

"What's all this? Having a breakfast party?"

Royce chuckled. "No. I ordered breakfast for everybody." He whistled to get Kirk's attention. "Hey, go ahead and get orders for these guys when you get a sec, please."

"You got it, Sarge."

"I suppose I don't have a choice in this matter, huh?" Stan said, jokingly.

"Shit, I can think of a worse scenario," Brandon said. He quickly climbed down the yacht and walked up to Kirk's little eatery. Stan chuckled then followed the Inspector.

On the ball with the Mayor's Office, keeping the locals as happy as possible, keeping morale up, and thinking ahead as always. Why the hell was HE not appointed Police Chief?

He glanced down at his watch, then looked back at Royce.

"By the way, where's Chief Remar?"

Royce checked his own watch, then answered, "Probably back at the office."

Stan simply replied with a 'Hmm' and a nod, then proceeded to go see Kirk. *Interesting she's not here. Probably got loads of other duties on her plate, I'm sure.*

CHAPTER 6

"Thank you for your patience. Please hold until one of our operators is available."

It was the third time Silvia had listened to that stupid artificial voice. She tapped her fingers on her desk, while staring at her computer monitor. She was afraid to move. Even the slightest twitch would cause one of those horrible spasms. The only thing worse than the pain was the *fear* of the pain. It created an almost obsessive focus on literally every move she made, which made concentration difficult.

Her office phone rang.

Damn it! She didn't want to set her personal phone down while on hold and risk the schedule clerk finally answering, only to get no response. Then again, she didn't want to hang up, only to call again and essentially be at the back of the waiting line. Unfortunately, she knew it was the Mayor calling, and it was a call she couldn't miss.

"This is the Chief."

"Good morning, Silvia," Mayor JoEllen Marsh replied.

"Good morning, Mayor."

"Well done on that boat fire last night," the Mayor said. Silvia was surprised to hear this. She was expecting a rant about it being July, and how she needed to keep the beaches open. Silvia had stressed about it all night, her mind interrupting her sleep as it worked to come up with explanations and solutions.

"Oh?" Her surprise escaped vocally. "I, uh, appreciate that, JoEllen. I'm right now in the middle of figuring out what to do about getting it off the beach." She held her ear to her iPhone to make sure she was still on hold.

"My secretary received notice from Royce this morning about moving the boat."

"She has?" *Why am I learning this from her?* Silvia checked her desk, but hadn't seen any notice from Royce. On top of that, she hadn't seen Royce in the office at all since she got in. Had he been at the beach all night? "How's he—" she stopped herself, realizing how she was about to sound. A good Chief was on top of things, and she couldn't make it appear she didn't know how things were going in her own department. She corrected herself with, "That's right. We'll have it taken care of." She could hear it in her own voice that she was trying to get JoEllen off the line as quickly as possible.

"So, I haven't received your report about the Vic Pally case," JoEllen said. Silvia felt herself clamming up.

"I'll have it to you by the end of the day," she promised.

"So, what was the deal about that?"

"Just a report of suspicious activity near the hotel. I had my people check. There was nobody in the hotel lot. The clerk didn't see anything."

"Steven Pack claimed he saw someone with drugs," the Mayor said.

"We found no evidence of that, Mayor," Silvia said.

"Alright. Do me a favor and have a couple officers stationed there for the next few nights. Say...between 9:00 p.m. until 7:00."

"I'll, uh..." Silvia wanted to explain that she was low on manpower already, and that the department couldn't properly do their jobs if they were spread thin performing specially assigned tasks for special interest groups.

"Is there a problem?" Silvia was immediately aware of how quickly the Mayor's friendly demeanor disappeared. *"Silvia? Do I need to remind you that Steven Pack brings a lot of business to our island? I don't want him thinking this place is turning into San Francisco."*

"No need to worry about that. I'll get on it," Silvia said. How? She didn't know. She could hear Royce's voice in her head: *"Gotta keep those sponsors happy, or else she'll have to find a new way to fund her next campaign."*

"I appreciate it," JoEllen said.

"Mayor, on that note, I wanted to discuss hiring on a few more officers," Silvia said. "My staff is stretched pretty thin with all the activity around the island and we could use a few more personnel to help with the extra load."

"I can probably get funding for additional overtime. But more officers?" JoEllen chuckled. *"There's no point really. The only time we'd need the extra manpower are June, July, and August. Mostly, it's July when things get really hectic. And besides, hardly anything major ever*

happens here. Hell, that boat fire is probably the busiest moment your department has had in over a decade."

"I suppose," Silvia said. Overtime was not what her staff was hoping to hear. It would not be pleasant when she presented the news. "Mayor, has there been any update on the Belanger Fireworks Show?"

"Yes, they're requesting at least seven officers patrolling the beach, with two units on boat patrol. Hours are still the same. It'll kick off around 7:00, but the actual show won't start until 9:30 or so, when it gets dark."

Silvia rubbed her forehead. With only six officers on afternoons, and five on midnights, it was clear she'd have to mandate overtime again. It was clear that the Island government would rather pay time-and-a-half than spend money on new personnel. For three nights in a row starting tomorrow, she'd have to stretch staff out between the firework festival, the hotel standby, and general patrol. Silvia was hating herself right now for not pursuing this issue a few weeks earlier. Of course, with all the distractions, it kept going to the backburner, and now she was paying the price. Or rather, her staff was paying the price.

"I'll do the best I can," Silvia said.

"That's why I hired you," JoEllen said. She made it sound like a friendly compliment, but it only furthered that shrinking feeling in Silvia's gut.

Yeah, you hired me because I've got no backbone.

Speaking of backbone, Silvia was practically squirming in her seat. She needed to stand and move around.

"Alright, Mayor, if there's nothing else, I better get to work on scheduling all this fun."

"Thanks, Chief. I'll be meeting with some of the businesses coming into town today. That includes Steven Pack, so don't forget about that report please."

"It'll be done. Bye." Silvia calmly hung up, though her raging brain wanted to slam the phone down like a gavel. She then heard somebody speaking. It sounded far, but near at the same time.

"Hello? Hello?"

"Who the hell?" Silvia glanced at her iPhone. "Oh shit!" She snatched it up. "Sorry I'm here. Hello?" She was too late. The scheduler had hung up, leaving Silvia with a bobbing dial tone. Now, she hit the desk. "Damn it!"

She dialed the number again, and again, she endured the mechanical voice. *"Thank you for your patience. Please hold until one of our operators is available."* Silvia paced around the room while listening to the dull generic music that played in the background. *God, this crap would put someone to sleep. Maybe I should play it tonight.* She had already drained her second cup of coffee, and it only did a little to help. She had walked with her back brace on for an hour last night. It dulled the pain a bit, but by the time she was done showering it was almost back in full force. On top of that, she only got three hours of sleep, and even throughout that, she felt like she woke up a hundred times.

Christ, she needed a sick day; just a twenty-four hour period of nothing but physical therapy to work the disc back in. But how could she do that when she wasn't allowing time off to her own staff? Sure, it was medical, but most of them didn't know that. Those who did didn't understand the severity of it. To them, it just sounded like 'Oh, my back hurts.' Most people didn't unless they experienced it.

As she paced, she realized she hadn't checked the mailbox. She stepped out into the briefing room and went to the assorted mailboxes. There were several reports, brochures, and other junk she would have to either submit or toss away. There were a couple of time-off request forms she would likely have to deny.

"Gosh, won't these people get the hint?" she muttered. She flipped through the papers, then stopped at a typed letter addressed to her from Lieutenant Adam Henry.

Adam Henry
600 Sterns RD.
Maxwell Island, GA 92842

06/31/2021

HR Management
Silvia Remar – Chief of Police
JoEllen Marsh – Island Mayor.

Maxwell Island Police Department
E. Huron River Dr.
Maxwell Island, GA 92842

Please accept this letter as notice of my resignation from my position as Police Lieutenant. My last day of employment will be 07/17/2021.

I received an offer to serve as a Task Force Sergeant in the Texas Border Patrol. I'll be leading a task force to investigate cases regarding kidnapped children being shipped in and out of the country. While I appreciate the relatively low-stress nature of serving Maxwell Island, this new position is more in line with what I originally intended to do when I decided to become a police officer.

It has been a pleasure working for Maxwell Island Police Department over the past ten years. One of the great highlights of my career has been working with Sergeant Royce Boyer, who has proven himself to be an excellent officer with excellent experience, as well as my time with Chief Engler.

Thank you so much for the opportunity to work with MIPD. I wish the best for all my fellow officers, the Chief, and the island residents.

Sincerely,

Lt. Adam Henry

Silvia sighed. It was only a matter of time. Once again, JoEllen got what she wanted. It was no secret she wanted to do away with the lieutenant position, since much of the work was completed by the shift sergeants anyway. For the town, it was fifty-five grand a year they'd save, not to mention the medical benefits.

She couldn't help but read that last main paragraph over again. Though Adam certainly didn't intend it as a jab at her, it still caused her to question her leadership competency. Or maybe she was jealous that she got to watch another person go on to do bigger and better things. Hell, this was technically a demotion too! But it clearly didn't matter to him because he was pursuing a goal, and goals meant more than rank.

A sigh escaped Silvia's mouth. She was jealous, and ashamed to be. She should've been happy for Adam. Instead, all she could focus on was her own misery. She was a crippled woman, working a job she wasn't qualified for, supervising people with more real experience than she'd ever see in her lifetime. The worst part was that it seemed there was nowhere to go from here.

Still on hold with the pain management clinic, she placed the paper on her desk. Any minute now, they'd be answering.

The radio blared.

"Dispatch to all available units, we have a report of an overturned boat over by Wesco Peak. Fire and Rescue has been notified and are en-route to the scene."

"Zero-One copies. En-route," she replied. She hung up the phone and hustled out to her truck. Two boat accidents, less then twelve hours apart? Well, it was a full moon last night...

CHAPTER 7

It was nearing 8:00. It was a beautiful Wednesday with a forecast of clear skies with light breezes, and a high of ninety-two degrees. The population, both local and tourist, were pouring out onto the streets. The town area was alive with thousands of people walking the streets to get breakfast, make their spa appointments, make boat rentals, and enjoy the festivities the island had to offer. Jet skiers and speedboaters took to the water. Charter boats took on their first appointments, taking people out to the Malcom Sand Atoll two miles to the east, and Tree Island, located a mile north of that. Tree Island lived up to its name, as it was literally a speck of land with a single tree growing in its center, like something drawn in a cartoon. The air was full of whooping screams as boats pulled water skis along the waves.

However, no festivity matched those offered by the beautiful beaches. Even when crowded, it still served as a perfect place for relaxation. Almost the entire manta ray-shaped perimeter of the island was white tan. The only exception was Wesco Peak, otherwise known as the tail of the manta. It was the site of the lighthouse, which overlooked a small string of rocks and atolls on the northwest corner of the island. It was a spectacular site that served as another attraction for visitors. Though lifeguards were present, there was hardly any risk at Wesco Peak. The water here was shallow. A full-grown adult could walk a hundred feet out and only be waist-deep in water. It was the perfect place for people with small children to spend their time. Kids splashed in the shallow water and searched for small crabs while their parents formed lines at the breakfast cafes.

But when the crowds arrived on the morning of July 1st, they found strobing red and blue lights lining the shore near the lighthouse. Instead of children wading out into the water, it was a team of firemen and police officers, headed toward a half-submerged speedboat.

Royce had to scoop the few remaining bits of his omelet once the call came in. He was the first on the scene and first into the water. Maurice was with him, as was the Fire Chief and several firemen from the next shift. If somebody was injured, they couldn't wait on the motorboats, which would have to carefully maneuver around the manta's tail, as well as the less visible rocks that were barely small enough to be hidden under the surface.

The boat's underside faced the shore, making it impossible for the first responders to see if anyone was inside. The bow was pointed up at a 45-degree angle, the starboard quarter embedded in the sediment beneath. Clouds of silt had sullied the normally crystal blue water, stirred by the submerged outboard motor before it died. The water was up to the Sergeant's armpits now. He worked his way around the bow to look into the cockpit. He instantly recognized the faded plaid shirt and Boston Red Sox cap worn by George O'Mara, a local charter. He was slumped in the cockpit, his face painted red by rivers of blood streaming from a gash in his forehead. It was obvious he had collided with the dashboard when he crashed.

Royce propped himself up on the submerged edge of the cockpit in order to reach O'Mara. He placed two fingers on his neck in search of a pulse.

"He's alive!" he called to the others. Maurice and three firemen gathered at the cockpit, while Fire Chief Stan Rolling checked for any fuel leakage near the motor. From what he could see, the engine was fine, but the draft side of the hull was breached at several points.

Stan knew George. The man could travel the waters with his eyes closed. Every day, he was chartering his speedboats and fishing boats out to tourists. How the hell did he manage to speed his way into this shallow area? In broad daylight, no less?

Then it hit him—if George was operating his speedboat, it was likely there was one or more persons with him. Tourists.

Oh, shit.

He looked out at the surrounding water, hoping to see someone splashing. Other than minor swells, the ocean was as calm as the sky above it. Stan looked toward the beach, but saw nothing but curious onlookers. Anyone who had just lived through a crash would easily stand out in the small morning crowd.

"Oh, hell! Guys, we need to branch out. There's someone else out here," Stan said to the others.

"We gotta get him out first," Royce said. He pulled himself all the way into the cockpit and undid O'Mara's safety belt. Maurice and another fireman was there to catch him before he slumped into the water.

"Where the hell is that ambulance?" the Captain radioed.

"Any minute, sir."

"Alright. I want two men to carry him to shore. The rest of us, branch out as far as you can. See if you can find anyone else."

More flashing lights appeared on the shore. Chief Silvia Remar brought her truck to a screeching halt, then stepped out as fast as her spine would allow her. By now, several more curious onlookers were gathering. Silvia stepped to the water's edge and saw the firemen bringing the victim in. Further out, she saw Royce wading further with Stan, Maurice, and a few others. Royce saw her and waved.

"What's the status, Sergeant?" she said.

"We've only found George O'Mara. We're pretty sure he had at least one person with him. He has a ski rope attached to the boat, but nobody on it," he replied.

"Oh, Jesus," Silvia whispered. *What the hell happened?* She turned around and addressed the crowd. "Did anyone witness what happened? Anybody?" Almost every head shook no. Further up the hill, a pudgy figure raised a hand. Of course, he didn't want to leave his food stand, forcing Silvia to struggle her way up the slope. She grimaced with each step, gasping once from a nerve spasm. She could feel herself starting to sweat, and it wasn't just the heat. She couldn't help but notice the stares. The expressions were a mix of '*This* person's in charge?' and 'What the hell's wrong with her?'

Silvia struggled to remember the businessman's first name. Joe!

"Hey, Joe. What happened? What did you see?"

"I was just getting set up when it happened," Joe said, brushing his hands over his grease-stained apron. "I could hear the motorboat while I was thawing out some of the perishables. Didn't think much of it at first. It's summer, after all. Everyone and their brother is out on a boat. Then I heard two, uh—" he paused, trying to think how to describe it, "two different noises. One sounded almost like a, uh, it sounded like an explosion. At the same time, there was a loud splash...like a *big* one, like when a whale breaches. I looked to the window, and suddenly the speedboat is flipping over like a pancake. It rocked and settled where it is now."

"Did he come from that way?" Silvia asked, pointing over at the rocks.

"By the time I laid eyes on it, it was already crashing. I didn't see what led up to it. There was nobody else out here at the time, either.

People don't normally start coming over to this side of the island until 9:00 or so. All I can say, and again, I didn't see the whole thing, but it *looked* like he was coming in from straight out that way." He pointed out to the open water dead ahead.

Silvia used her imagination to simulate a path based on what Joe had told her. It didn't make sense. Aside from the famous 'manta tail' there were no rocks further out than where the officers were wading. At least, nothing large enough to cause a speedboat to flip over as described.

"He had to have been coming from the east," she said. "There's nothing out there. Had he hit the submerged rocks at such a speed, the momentum would've placed him on the shoreline."

"Hey, that's your department," Joe said. "I'm just telling you what I saw. Though I will say: If he hit those rocks, he'd have been rolling *that way*," he pointed to the left, "but no, the boat was rolling directly toward me. Maybe he hit something. Maybe he made a really sharp turn he couldn't handle. But he did not hit those rocks, because I guarantee you, at the speed he was going, that bow wouldn't be so intact."

It was a good point, one that she would've made herself with the right attention to detail.

"You said it was already crashing by the time you looked. I'm assuming you weren't able to see if anyone else was on the boat?" she asked. Joe shook his head, frowning.

"And nobody swam to shore. I would know. I've had my eyes glued to the scene since I made the call."

"Thanks, Joe," Silvia said.

"Good luck, Chief," Joe replied. Silvia made her way back to the shore. By now, two ambulances had arrived. The two Munson Fireboats came in from the northeast, along with one of the Police Department's patrol vessels. Royce and the others in the water had spread out for several hundred feet in search of any other persons in the area.

The Sergeant's voice came through the radio. "Chief, we're probably gonna have to get divers out here."

Silvia closed her eyes and slowly exhaled. She couldn't sigh, or show any kinds of distress around all the onlookers. Or the first responders, for that matter.

"Zero-One to Zero-Two," she radioed.

"Zero-Two. Go ahead."

"Hey, give me a TX on my personal." Silvia waited a moment, then felt her phone vibrating. She answered the call and raised it to her ear. "Hey, Adam."

"Everything alright over there, Chief?"

"Actually, no," Silvia said. "I know you're on standby over on South Beach, but I'm gonna need you and Officer Fahley to get in your dive gear and meet us at Wesco Peak. We, uh," she walked away from nearby tourists trying to listen in on her call. "We might have a deceased person. In the water. Boating accident. Speedboat was clearly towing a water-skier and, well, there's no water-skier."

"Oh, that's not good. I'll be there ASAP, Chief."

"Thanks a bunch, Adam," she replied. She hung up the phone and dialed the number for Kavon Hayes.

"Hello?"

"Hey, Kavon. It's the Chief. How are you?"

"Not bad. What can I do for you?"

"Can I ask you to bring your truck and trailer over to Wesco Peak?"

****

"Okay, okay, just a little further," Royce directed Kavon as he towed his trailer out to the crash site with a small tugboat. He pulled it along, slowly lining up the ramp with the bow. "Watch out. Rock right ahead of you. Move ten degrees to the right."

"Thanks, Sarge," Kavon said. "Hate to add one of my boats to the list of sinkers today."

"No shit," Maurice added. "What the hell's going on?"

"Don't know. Our Lieutenant will be here any minute to start diving. Problem is, we don't know where exactly to start. He'll have to start with broad strokes," Royce said.

"You'd think that person would be wearing an inflatable vest," Maurice said.

"Which I find odd," Royce said. "I've chatted with George O'Mara plenty of times. He usually has a strict policy of making his clients wear safety gear on his boats. And there's something else that's bothering me." He looked out at the shore, then out into the ocean. "Why haven't we found the ski board? You'd think that would've washed up on shore or something."

"That's...a really good point," Maurice said, the realization causing him to glance all around. Kavon finished lining up the trailer with the boat.

"How's that?"

"That's about as good as we're gonna get it," Royce said.

"Alright, let's hook the cable onto the bow, and I'll see if I can drag this thing onto the trailer. Ohhhhhh, boy. This is gonna be—not fun."

No, it won't. Royce waited while Kavon pulled his boat as close to the bow as he could, then found a cleat for him to hook it to. Unfortunately, the boat was wedged at a perfect point where it was too deep and too far out for a crane, but too shallow for a larger tugboat or utility boat to lift it, forcing them to improvise.

Kavon took his boat to the shore, tossed a line to one of the deputies to keep it from drifting away, then climbed out. Water climbed up to his ankles as he approached his pickup truck, which he parked at the shoreline. He hooked up the cable and got inside. Before he slammed the door, he waved to Silvia.

"Chief, I'm gonna need you to be my eyes and ears," he said.

"You got it," Silvia said. She held her radio up so they could both hear Royce. "Sergeant, you ready?"

"As ready as we'll ever be."

"Alright, Kavon, go ahead."

Kavon shut the door and rolled the window down. He pushed his dreadlocks back and took a nervous breath.

"Here we go." He eased on the accelerator. The line went taut, tilting the speedboat toward the trailer.

"Steady," Royce said. "Keep it going…Keep it going…a little more."

The tires kicked wet sand as he applied a little more pressure. The truck bumped forward, gaining some traction.

"Whoa, slow down a bit," Royce said. Kavon watched his rear-view mirror. He could see the boat halfway up onto the ramp. So close. He just needed to keep from pulling it too far. Should he accidentally pull the boat even partially over the forward rim, it'd be a real pain to re-attach the cables to the transom and pull it back.

"Almost there," Silvia said. Kavon inched forward, nudging the speedboat further onto the ramp.

"Good!" Royce said. The Sergeant leaned down as far as he could to attach the cable to the neck of the trailer. Maurice held his radio for him to keep it from getting wet. Royce stood straight, spitting saltwater, then gave Maurice a thumbs up.

"Alright, go ahead," the Captain relayed for him. Kavon tapped the accelerator again. This time, he was able to apply a little more pressure. He started off easy, while the deputies made sure everyone kept clear of his path. Slowly, but truly, the trailer shallowed. Sand bunched at its wheels as it finally made it to the shore.

"Voila," Kavon said. "Alright, Chief, that's enough boats for one day."

"You're telling me," Silvia said. She walked to O'Mara's speedboat and waited for Royce and the others. The Sergeant squeezed his sleeves, drizzling thick streams of water. His duty belt and outer vest were the only dry part of his outfit, as he had taken them off before hurrying into the water.

Silvia noticed that the speedboat was heavily leaning on its starboard side. She knelt down to look under it, and immediately saw a breach.

"Well, there's no denying it," Royce said, shaking the water from his pantlegs. "George hit something. Though, I can't believe he was foolish enough to travel this close to the peak."

"I guess so. But what's *that*?" Silvia asked. Royce stepped up alongside her and knelt down for a look. There was a second breach near the stern. The hull around it was discolored. Dark.

"Residue from hitting a rock?" he guessed.

"I don't know. That looks more like a burn," Silvia said. Royce checked the outboard motors. They were fine by the looks of it. Maybe beat up a little bit, but no breaches, and certainly no signs of fuel leaks or fires. He took another glance at the strange markings.

"Hmm." He could not deny it resembled a burn of some kind. "Hey, Mau? Stan? What do you guys think of this?" The Fire Chief and Captain walked over and knelt to examine the boat. "Anything you've seen before?"

Stan brushed the remaining droplets of water from his bald head and shined a light under the hull. The discolored section was inside a large cavity, meaning whatever had caused it, was the same thing that caused the breach.

"Hard to say," Stan said.

"Almost looks like a lightning strike," Maurice said. Stan nodded. He had seen metal trucks and posts that had been subject to lightning strikes during thunderstorms. The black and brown scorch marks were admittedly identical to what he was looking at. Then again, lightning didn't hit with the force of a battering ram.

"Still doesn't explain the breach," Stan said.

"I wonder why there's no damage to the front," Silvia added.

"He might've been doing some sort of sidewinder, tight-circle maneuver-thing," Royce speculated, mimicking the motion with his hand. "Of course, you'd think George of all people would be smarter than that. But I can't think of anything else that makes sense."

Another police truck pulled up along the shore. A man in his thirties stepped out. Black diving gear hugged his muscular frame, leaving only his tan-skin face and brown eyes visible.

"Lieutenant Henry," Silvia greeted him.

"Chief," he said, then looked past her at the Sergeant. "Royce! What did I tell you about swimming while on duty?"

"Couldn't help it, Adam," Royce bantered. "Couple hot senoritas wanted to play Marco-polo. Mayor wants us to keep the tourists happy, so..."

"Well, I always knew you were dependable," Adam joked. His fellow officer, Fahley, stepped out of the passenger side. He was younger, only in his early twenties, but already had more certifications than most of the senior staff, who jokingly referred to him as 'Book Nerd'.

"Looks like they did a number on this one," he said.

"I'll say," Adam replied. "Where did you pull it from?"

"About two-hundred feet out. Straight ahead," Royce said. "We were just speculating which direction he was coming from. Unfortunately, we don't have any solid suggestions on where you guys would want to start."

"Well, we'll start near the rocks and work our way out from there," Adam said.

"You're going in from the shore? You don't want one of the boats to take you out?" Silvia asked.

"Best way to do this is to start in the shallows and work our way out, since that's where you found the boat," Adam explained. "Just have one of our boats on standby out there in case we have to go deeper, which we probably will." He checked his rebreather and goggles, then glanced back at Fahley. "Ready, kid?"

"Whenever you are."

"Oh, by the way, Lieutenant?" Silvia said.

"Yeah, Chief?"

Silvia lowered her voice, unsure if Adam wanted his personal business known to anyone else yet. "Just wanna let you know I got your message. We'll talk about it later when we get a chance."

"Appreciate it, Chief," he said. He tapped Fahley on the shoulder, then pointed to the water. "Let's go." The two officers waded into the water, their suits, goggles, and flippers giving them the appearance of humanoid amphibians. The water climbed to their waists, then up above their shoulders. The patrol vessel steered close, the officer on deck keeping a close eye on the divers as they went under. Meanwhile, the two Fireboats branched out in an attempt to spot anything unusual in the visible seabed.

"Well, I suppose I may as well go home and get into a drier uniform," Royce said. He untucked his shirt and scrunched handfuls in his fists to wring the water out.

"Go ahead," Silvia said. "I'll keep an eye on things here."

"It probably wouldn't be wise to leave," Royce stated. Silvia wasn't sure what he meant by that. Was it a snide remark? Was he just trying to be funny? Or both? Then she noticed him pointing a finger past her.

Silvia turned and saw the Mayor's brand new 2020 Honda CR-V, a gift, no doubt from one of her sponsors. A well-dressed woman with short almond-colored hair stepped out. She was just a couple of years older than the Chief, and stood three inches taller.

"Hi, JoEllen," Silvia said.

"Chief," the Mayor greeted. She smiled, a gesture Royce always described as fake as a 3-dollar bill. That smile was fast to disappear as JoEllen Marsh looked at the speedboat and out into the bay. "What's all this? What's happening?"

Silvia took her aside, away from the spectators.

"We're not sure," Silvia answered. "It belongs to a local charter. Got a report that it flipped over, but nobody actually saw what led to the actual accident."

"Idiot probably hit a rock," JoEllen said.

"We don't know," Silvia said, not wanting to debate the issue.

"Why's the boat still there?"

At that moment, the radio blared. *"Dispatch to Zero One."* Silvia ignored it in hopes to quicken her interaction with the Mayor.

"We literally just got it out of the water," Silvia said. "We have to inspect the damage to see what happened."

"Look behind you," JoEllen said, subtly nodding toward the tourists gathering around. Many of them had small kids, clearly intending to enjoy the shallow area without all the wild swimmers. Some stayed and watched, while others left. "We can't have this thing on the beach like this. It's hurting the businesses."

"We have to investigate," Silvia said. Her words came out as a croak; a half-restrained effort to push back against the person who gave her this position. Silvia sighed, then looked over at Kavon. "Could you take the boat to the station, please?"

"Sure thing," he said. He got in his car and towed the boat onto the main road. Silvia couldn't help but notice a smirk on Royce's face as he got into his Interceptor. He shook his head and drove off. As usual, Silvia had caved to the Mayor. They hadn't even finished inspecting the boat. Who knew what clues they might have found. Belongings? Fingerprints? The interior wasn't completely wet, so it was possible some DNA evidence might've survived. But all that would have to be delayed so JoEllen could be happy.

"So, what are they doing?" JoEllen said. Her tone was only on the verge of confrontational, as she *usually* waited to have the facts presented before issuing her demands. Usually.

"As I said, George O'Mara, the owner of that boat, is a charter. We think he might've had at least one other person on the boat."

JoEllen's expression became serious.

"Oh, hell. Do we know if they were tourists, or locals?"

"I would guess tourists, but don't know for sure yet. Nothing's washed ashore, and nobody has seen anyone else. Only George was in the boat. There's not even a waterski."

"No?" JoEllen said. "Well, maybe he was out on his own, then."

Dispatch radioed again. *"Zero-One? Chief?"*

"Stand by," Silvia answered, then returned her attention to the Mayor. "I hope so, but we don't know the facts. I have to have people search the shore area in case anything washes up."

"Anything...like belongings?" JoEllen asked.

Silvia checked again to make sure they weren't being overheard. "Or a body."

"Was it that bad?" JoEllen said, covering her mouth.

"Witness said it flipped repeatedly," Silvia said. "God only knows what happened before that. The driver's unconscious, so we can't get anything out of him at the moment." It was difficult for her to stand still. All Silvia could think about was laying on a foam mattress. It was the closest thing to relaxation she would ever get.

"Damn it," JoEllen muttered. As much as she didn't want these first responders deterring tourists from enjoying the area, it was inevitable until they got answers. JoEllen often set her priorities on the tourism—or rather, the money they brought it, but she wasn't so cold as to prevent an active police investigation. Maybe hinder it a bit, but not entirely obstruct it. She was still happy to have the boat moved. In her mind, it gave an impression that Wesco Peak, and Maxwell Island in general, weren't the safest of places to boat when she knew the opposite was true. "Alright. Have them search, but PLEASE, have them appear as though they're simply doing their rounds. I don't want people worried or asking questions. I've already got two complaints from other charters about cancellations because of the activity going on here. Hence, why I stopped by."

"Believe me, Mayor, nobody wants this taken care of more quickly than me," Silvia said. JoEllen smiled.

"I knew there was a reason I liked you. By the way, how's it going with that yacht? Any clue as to what happened?"

"Fire Inspector's looking at it now," Silvia said. "I'll meet with him later on to see what his analysis is, but we're pretty sure it was a fuel tank explosion."

"Terrible," JoEllen said. "Well, at least it's off the beach. Truck took it away a few minutes ago. Good job on being so quick on that."

"Um...well actually—"

"Dispatch to Chief?"

"Jesus!" Silvia grunted, annoyed. "Uh, I appreciate it, Mayor."

"I'll stop holding you up," JoEllen said. She turned and approached the crowd, who stood behind a line of caution tape set up by some of the deputies. Silvia took a breath, then walked to the shoreline. She could hear the Mayor apologizing for the inconvenience and informing them about other shallow pools, and making promises about directing bus traffic to this area.

"Sorry, Dispatch. Go ahead," Silvia said.

"Chief, I've got someone here who wants to speak directly to you."

"I'm a little busy right now. I'll send one of the deputies over."

"They're specifically requesting you, Chief. It's about a missing person."

Silvia dropped the mic to her side and looked to the sky. *What in God's name is going on?*

She sighed, then lifted the mic back up. "I'm on my way."

CHAPTER 8

The glare of the computer screen glinted off Dr. Martha Cornett's oval lenses. Usually, she'd spend no more than a half-hour in her office to enjoy some morning coffee while catching up on articles from her institution. But after ninety minutes, the beverage had gone cold and untouched, and Martha's eyes were still glued to the screen.

The article she was reading HAD to be a hoax. That, and the half dozen others she came across sharing a similar story. The article showed a Florida fisherman holding up a seventy-pound anglerfish. Its open mouth displayed rows of needle-like teeth. The article went on, describing the two-hundred-plus species of angler fish, and how most live in the shallows, but some lived deep below the sea. There was no doubt that this one was one of those. Its esca dangled from its snout like a bent fishing rod. In life, its luminescent tip was used for attracting prey in the deep. The article continued to explain how the species grew up to seven-feet in length.

"Wrong," Martha groaned. They didn't get much bigger than a meter. Still, it didn't explain what that little sucker was doing all the way up here. She looked up at the printed photos of recent anomalies. Pinned to the wall were images of dead colossal squid washing up on the shores of the Bahamas. To the right was a record size *Architeuthis Dux*, in an image taken at five-hundred feet.

Before reading this article, she had scoured reports of viperfish suddenly appearing along the southeast coast of North America, along with Pelican eels, macropinna microstoma, with its dome-shaped head still luminescent.

"What the hell is going on?" Martha muttered to herself. At first, there were only a handful of stories. While rare for a deep-sea species to turn up, it wasn't unheard of. But in this quantity, in such a short span of time? Something was going on, and Martha was willing to bet her dwindling budget it had something to do with the reported seismic activity in the Puerto Rico Trench. Located between the Caribbean and North American Plates, each moving against each other, the Puerto Rico Trench served as a boundary. For seventy-million years, the plates had grinded against each other. A recent report indicated that Puerto Rico had been hit with several-dozen earthquakes of varying magnitudes since the meteor landing.

The numbers were increasing, as well as the magnitudes, and marine biologists were beginning to speculate the effects on the marine life living in the twenty-seven-thousand-foot depths.

Her phone pinged with an alert. She looked at the screen. *Temperature alert*—Buoy Three.

Ah, I got that yesterday. Probably just a malfunction— "Wait a sec." She looked again. Buoy Three. The last alert she received was from Buoy Five, over on the northeast corner of the island.

"Okay, that's not normal," she said out loud. The temperature had been steady at fifty-eight degrees. Sometimes the surface temperature would spike to sixty-one, but that's not what the buoys were telling her. Buoy Five had a reading of an increase of nine degrees Fahrenheit at 10:04 p.m., last night. Now, Buoy Three was showing an increase of eleven degrees.

She rolled her chair to the end of her long, crescent-shaped desk and flipped open her laptop. It took a moment to load before finally bringing up the GPS locator on her tagged specimens out in the ocean. She spotted Marker-00281, a sperm whale she had nicknamed Sly. A year ago, she had untangled him from a fishing net, and good ol' Sly seemed to hang around the island, migrating every so often to hunt, but always managed to hang around Maxwell Island. In the past few days, she had noticed strange readings in his vitals. His heartbeat had gone up on at least two occasions, and suddenly, as though he encountered a threat. Now, the fifty-eight-foot sperm whale was lingering ten miles further to the east. Normally, she would chalk this up to just another of his hunting dives. But now, she suspected otherwise.

"You're avoiding something, aren't you?" she said. Was there something in the water causing a rapid increase in temperature? First thing to do was to go out there and get a manual reading, and inspect both buoys.

Martha brushed her short butterscotch hair back, then scrolled through her short list of contacts.

He answered with an enthusiastic *"Hey!"*

"Good morning, Andy," she said.

"Thought you were taking a sick day. I've never seen you stay in this late in the morning."

"Don't worry, there's enough work to make up for it," she said. "Meet me at the dock in twenty. I'm getting another odd temperature reading, and I want to check it out."

"The same buoy? Or a different one?"

"Different one. Buoy Five. Just got the alert. I wanna stop there first. Maybe we'll figure out what's going on."

"Okay. I'll be there."

"Thanks." Martha hung up and stepped into her bedroom. She couldn't believe herself. 9:30, and she was still in her cami and sweats. For the past twenty-years—since graduating from the University of Florida with her doctorate in Marine Biology, she was always out the door no later than 7:30, unless there was a hurricane. She preferred to work outside, as she hated enclosed spaces, with the exception of the cockpit of a Triton submersible. That was part of the gift of tracking whales; she always got to be outside. If Martha could help it, she'd spend most of her life underwater with the creatures she loved most. But by the very nature of her human existence, she was bound to the world above, no matter how hard she tried.

She switched into a set of khaki shorts and a white tank top, then threw a thin denim jacket over it. Despite running late, she couldn't help but take the time to neaten her sleek crop hairstyle. She was going out with Andy, after all. Even after years of living and working together, she still wanted to look good for him. At least tolerable, she had no idea how good she actually looked in these field outfits. Knowing Andy, he'd say she looked great, and would probably suggest they 'take a break' in the cabin a half-hour after departure.

A smile came over her face, thinking of the times she agreed to the idea. Her phone pinged again, ending the moment of bliss, and reminding her of the task at hand. She slipped into her shoes and went out the door.

****

The research yacht *Infinity* was prepped and ready to go when Martha arrived at the dock. Being the control freak she was, Martha took the helm. It was a three-mile trip to Buoy-3. Immediately, she wished this had happened in May or September. Hell, even late August. Navigating the waters was simple, as she knew the island by heart. It was navigating all the boaters that was the struggle. So many hulls slashed the water in July, she sometimes felt like she was crammed in a small lake. The busiest of activity went on for about a mile, after that it was mainly fishermen and sailboats.

Twice, she found herself in the path of a group of jet skis, their riders flipping her off as though she cut them off on the highway. Despite the vast activity, the *Infinity* crossed the busy-mile untouched.

Martha put the side windows down and took in the smell of the open ocean. The moment she was no longer on dry land and out on the big blue, she felt as small and insignificant as humans really are. The water was an oasis of endless fascination for her, whether she was above or below the surface. Twenty years as a marine biologist, preceded by ten years of study, and a whole childhood of going out on boats and diving, and it still didn't get old for her. Few people were ever so lucky to have such a thing.

During the trip, she flipped open her laptop to check the other buoy readings. So far, everything was normal. Including Buoy Five.

"Huh?" she muttered. It still read sixty-one degrees, slightly higher than the others, but significantly lower than the previous night. It wasn't consistent with a malfunction. If it were a malfunction, the numbers would be skewed with no pattern. This reading made it seem that that area was gradually *cooling*.

Her thoughts were interrupted by the swift opening of the pilothouse door. In stepped her husband, Andy Cornett.

"You know, I never got my good morning kiss," he said, faking a grouchy tone. Martha chuckled and looked over her shoulder at him.

"I guess I'm just dropping the ball all around today," she said. She scrunched her lips, and Andy returned the gesture. Of course, he wouldn't do with just a peck. It had to be a long, drawn out moment with a bit of tongue. "Alright, alright, beast," she laughed, playfully slapping his hand from her ass.

"Just checking for any other unexpected rises in temperature," he joked.

"I'm sure you are."

After a few more minutes, she entered the zone for Buoy Three. There were only a handful of other boats in the distance. She could recognize the distinct markings on some of them. She could see the black pirate flag on the trawler *Red Machete* to the northeast. Far to the west was another trawler she thought she recognized. The *Underwater Kingdom*, if she remembered correctly. She had met its captain, Brock Giler, on a few occasions. They had first met when she had rescued Sly from the drift net that nearly drowned him. In the three years since, he checked in to see how his new 'buddy' was doing.

She kept her eyes on the ocean. Finally, she spotted the orange floatation device a few hundred yards to her starboard bow. The device resembled a radio-tower balancing on a floatation device. It stood three-feet high, its antennae adding another two feet.

"Found it," Dr. Martha Cornett said.

"You know it's probably just a malfunction," Andy replied.

"Normally, I'd agree," Martha told him. "But this is the second buoy to show a spike in temperature. After we bring it in, I want you ready with that thermistor. I want to find out what's going on around here."

"How deep do we want the reading?"

"The buoy probe measures temperature one meter below the surface. I wanna see if there's a similar increase at twenty meters."

"You're the boss, Boss," Andy said.

"Damn right, I am," she quipped. She guided her seventy-foot research yacht to the buoy and stopped as close as she could. Her motor yacht rocked gently with the swells while the sun continued its climb into the summer sky.

Martha stepped out onto the fly deck and gazed to the south. Maxwell Island was barely visible to the naked eye, the curve of the planet making it look like a thin grey line on the horizon. On the aft deck below her, her husband stepped onto the dive ramp behind the transom. He was the same age as her, and to her appreciation, aged gracefully. His open red Hawaiian shirt displayed his fit physique that the sun had touched even more than his wife. Even at forty, the man still had the body of his college wrestling days, which happened to be when she first met him.

He screwed together the two halves of a steel pole with a hook at the end of it, then reached out for the buoy. It took a couple of tries, but he was able to get the hook through a loop on its dome. He pulled the buoy up onto the deck. Trailing behind it was a two meter probe.

Andrew examined the device, then shook his head at his wife.

"Doesn't appear to be damaged. I'll run tests on the probe, but so far, there doesn't appear to be anything wrong with it."

Martha climbed down to the aft deck and uncoiled the black cable for the 109SS probe. At its end was a thermistor encased in a sheath made from grade 316L stainless steel, designed for harsh conditions. White markings on the cable labeled depth for the operator. Andy dipped the probe into the water, carefully watching the markings until he lowered the cable to twenty meters. They needed a couple of minutes for an accurate reading.

"You know..." he winked at Martha, "We can kill time by..." He tilted his head toward the cabin.

"Good to know your mind's always on the job," Martha replied.

"There's more to life than work," Andy said. Martha smiled. Indeed, there was. She wanted to say yes.

Her laptop pinged. She gazed at the monitor, squinting to see through the sun's glare. *Temperature alert. Buoy Two. 69-degrees.* By this point, even Andy was puzzled.

"Okay, now I admit something's off about all of this," he said. "What's our probe reading?"

Martha checked the reading. "Sixty-seven degrees."

"Okay, so it's definitely not the buoy," Andy said.

"But there's something else," Martha said. "I got a new reading from Buoy Five. It's gradually returning to normal."

"Wait…that one had a rise, and is returning to normal. Then this one gave us an alert this morning, and by the looks of it, is now cooling. You said the buoy gave a reading of seventy-one, right?"

"Correct."

"And now, we've got a buoy on the west side of the island giving off readings of a temperature rise. Am I sensing a pattern here?"

"None of the other buoys around the island are giving off alarms, nor are any of the institution's buoys that are scattered further out. These spikes are scattered, and taking place in condensed areas." Martha gazed out into the water. "There's something out there. It's moving, and hot enough to trigger all of our buoys."

"You think that's why Sly had moved far out?"

"That, and I think it explains his heart reading from the other day," Martha answered. "I think he encountered something he didn't like. And if something makes a sperm whale nervous…"

"Perhaps we should notify the Police Chief," Andy said.

"I would, but we don't even know what it is we're reporting on," Martha said. "Besides, from what I've been hearing, it sounds like the Chief has enough on her hands to worry about a literal moving spike in water temperature."

"But that's what I mean," Andy said. "You heard about that explosion yesterday. Do you think there might somehow be a connection?"

"Let's not get too carried away," Martha said.

"Martha, there's something moving under the water causing temperature spikes high enough to be registered by our equipment. This isn't normal. And this is happening at the same time these incidents are occurring. Doesn't it seem odd to you?"

Martha nodded. She couldn't deny the timing was questionable.

"Too bad neither of us speak whale," she joked. "I'd just ask Sly what the hell's going on out there."

"Maaaaybe I dooooo," Andy joked. Martha facepalmed her forehead, then glared at him. She should've known she was setting him up for a *Finding Nemo* impression.

"Why the hell did I marry you?" she muttered.

"You've always said it was the abs, baby," he replied confidently.

"Certainly not your brain."

Andy obnoxiously mimicked the swimming motions of a whale.

"Yoooouuuu knoooooooow? Speeeerm whales haaaaaave the biiiiiiiiiiigest braaaain mass of anyyyyy aaanimal."

"Stop," Martha laughed. "God, I'm married to a forty-year-old teenager."

"Well, fine then," Andy said, faking offense. "Why don't we drop this buoy back in the water and go check Buoy Two. Whatever caused the spike might be there right now."

Martha nodded. Once in a while, her hubby had good ideas. Work-related, that is. She reached to help him lift the buoy, but like his typical self, wanting to look good for his wife, Andy did it himself. He set the buoy in the water and waited a moment for the reader to send a signal to Martha's computer.

"Okay, it's back up and working. Let's go check out the west side."

"Red Machete to Infinity. Is that you back there, Doctor Cornett?"

Martha climbed back up to the pilothouse and got on the radio.

"That's me, Captain. How's your day going? Better be catching some mackerel. I've been craving tuna lately."

"Got plenty of that and then some. But I've caught something else that might hold your interest."

"You found Kip Moore over there?!" She looked down at Andy and made an obnoxious smile.

"I tried, but no luck. Maybe next time. But seriously though, if you can, bring your boat up over here. No joke—you'll want to see this."

"Care to tell me what it is?"

"It's simpler if you come take a look for yourself."

"Alright then." Martha glanced back at Andy. "You think our investigation can hold off?"

"He sounded serious to me," Andy replied. Martha stepped to the console and throttled the boat northeast.

Captain Sean Bradley stood on the fly deck of the fishing trawler, watching Dr. Cornett's yacht approaching from the southwest. Down on the main deck, his two crewmen wore the same puzzled expression as he, gazing at the dead fish at their feet.

The doctor lined up the *Infinity* with the *Red Machete's* portside. Bradley's pilothouse towered ten feet over that of the yacht.

"Good morning, Doc," he said. Martha stepped out onto her fly deck and gazed up at the Captain. He had a cigar clutched between his teeth, his red shirt almost grey from all the ash that had fallen on it in the years of smoking.

"Good morning," she replied. "What's going on? What's the big surprise?"

Captain Bradley snapped his fingers at his two crewmen, who proceeded to lift something off the deck. Martha stared in silence, her eyes absorbing the distinctively flat snout of a ten-foot goblin shark. Its mouth hung open, fully extended to the end of the snout. It still had its pink color, meaning it had only died recently. Within a couple hours, its color would fade to a dull grey or brown.

"We have two of 'em," one of the crewmen pointed out.

"I think they were trying to go after our catch. They got hung up in our net and strangled," Captain Bradley explained. "One was dead right away. We tried to revive the other, but we don't have the right equipment."

"Wow," Martha said. This day was getting more fascinating by the minute.

"I know these bad boys are rare, so I thought you'd wanna take a look at 'em," the Captain said.

"Please!" Martha exclaimed. "How much do you want for them?"

"Oh, give me a break," Captain Bradley laughed, waving his hand. "You don't owe me anything. Consider it my contribution to science."

Andy tossed a line to the crewmen to help keep their boats together for the transfer. They carefully closed the distance until the hulls were almost touching, then placed a board across the two railings to slide the dead sharks over.

"How much are these guys worth?" one of the crewmen asked.

"From what I hear, the jaws go for a thousand bucks in the U.S."

The two crewmen glanced up at their Captain. "Damn! We should've held on to 'em."

The group shared a laugh and slid the second dead shark over to the *Infinity*. Andy gave the specimens a quick inspection. One was ten feet long, the other eleven feet. Even in death, they looked like possessed demonic spirits ready to slaughter anything that dared to come within reach. Hence, their infamous name.

"So, they were just here?" he asked. "How deep were you trawling?"

"About five-hundred feet," Bradley answered.

"These guys were probably struggling to begin with. The temperatures up here are different than what they're used to. They're used to much deeper waters."

"You should talk with Captain Dan Hahnlen," Bradley said. "He radioed in last night and said that he had a dead viperfish. Nine feet long!"

"Did he say where he caught it?" Andy asked.

"A few miles to the east, I think," Bradley said. Martha climbed down to the aft deck and conducted measurements of the fins and jaws, then jotted the information down on a pad.

"We need to get these to the lab," she said. "I want one on ice before it deteriorates too badly, and I want to cut the other one open."

"Hell, we could've done that," one of the crewmen joked.

Martha smiled. "Not exactly what I had in mind." She turned to Andy. "I have a hunch about something. If these guys have eaten anything in the past couple of days, we might get an idea where they came from."

"Where *do* you think they came from?" Captain Bradley asked.

"I can't prove it yet, but I'm wondering if these sharks, and several other species, are vacating the Puerto Rico Trench. Or at least a portion of it, possibly due to the seismic activity that has been recorded there recently. If the sharks have eaten anything prior to ascending, it could lend evidence to my theory."

"That's a short window," Andy said. "We have no idea how long they could've been up along the surface. On top of that, it's over two thousand miles from here to the trench. I'm shocked that they've made it this far, considering the temperature is thirty degrees cooler than down there."

"Unless they were following a certain heat bloom," Martha said.

"Heat bloom?" Andy looked at her questioningly. "You think that whatever caused our readers to spike came from the trench?"

"What do you think?" she asked. Andy let out an exacerbated breath and brushed some sweat from his brow.

"I think it's been a weird day, and it isn't even noon yet."

"Let's go," Martha said. She was clearly eager to get to the lab.

"You sure we don't want to check out the other buoy?"

"We have to get these guys on ice. I wanna get the operating room set up so I can get samples. We'll probably get more readings if the pattern continues."

"Okay," Andy said. He didn't agree, but he wasn't the one with a doctorate. He had simply trained to get his bachelor's degree in marine biology, content with becoming an assistant. Little did he know he'd be his own wife's assistant. Despite the jokes, it never bothered him. Rather, he felt lucky that they could spend so much time together and not get sick of each other. Deep sea organisms could potentially provide rare samples, including newly discovered bacteria, so it was understandable why she wanted to get back.

"You're the boss," he said, intentionally stroking her ego. She smiled, feeling the intended effect, and knowing his ulterior motive.

"Knock it off. We're busy," she said, half-playfully.

"Take a lunch break," he joked. They waved goodbye to Captain Bradley and his fishermen, then circled back for Maxwell Island.

CHAPTER 9

"What the hell do you mean you can't list her as missing?!" Kenneth Lang's voice bounced off the office walls. He was visibly agitated, his face almost purple. His shirt was wrinkly, having been worn through the night. His eyes were baggy from lack of sleep. Silvia wasn't a parent, but she could understand the father's frustration from not knowing where his daughter was.

"Mr. Lang, she's nineteen," Silvia said. She spoke softly, sympathizing with his anxiety. "Legally, she can spend the night anywhere she wishes, and I can't do anything about it."

"How long does she have to be missing before you *can* do something about it?" Lang said.

"Legally, I can do it now," Silvia said. "I can list her as missing, and I can instruct my people to keep an eye out for her. I'm just letting you know that it hasn't even been a day yet, and there are several places she could be on this island."

"Do it. Don't feed me this crap about her being nineteen and legally an adult," Lang demanded. His arms were crossed. He was rocking side-to-side, tired and uneasy, while also getting increasingly agitated. It was clear his faith in the Chief was dwindling by the second.

"Do you have a recent picture of her?"

"I do. On my phone."

"Are you able to email it to this address?" Silvia wrote down her police email on a pad and handed it to him. He took it and nodded, immediately getting on his smartphone to complete the task. "Do you have any reason to believe she's at risk?"

Lang spoke combatively. "Other than the fact she didn't return last night? That she's copping attitude with me every chance she gets? That she won't return my calls or texts? No."

"Did you guys have an argument?"

"I don't see how that's relevant."

"It is, Mr. Lang, since it might pertain to why she's not responding. We need to know these things to help determine why she might be missing."

"We've been arguing for the past month," Lang said. For once, his voice lacked the combativeness. "Kid dropped out of school, and now she expects me to coddle her for the rest of her life. I say, hell no to that. We all came here, like we do every summer, and I thought it'd at least be a break from all the drama. But no. We argued on the plane. On the boat ride here. About anything, even though the real issue is her career." There was regret in his voice. Silvia felt awkward. The man had rapidly switched gears. Silvia now felt like a counsellor serving as a sounding board for someone with baggage, rather than a cop trying to solve a case.

"Mr. Lang," Silvia paused, not wanting to invoke any further anxiety. Lang likely wasn't aware of the boat crash, so she had to be delicate in how she asked the next question. "Did Anne have any appointments that you are aware of? Has she chartered any boats? Waterskiing trips? Anything?"

"Not to my knowledge," he replied. "She does have her wallet and ID…and my credit card. There haven't been any purchases made with it yet."

"But she could've paid for one with her own money, perhaps?"

"I doubt it," he said. "She's never skied in her life. I doubt any boater would simply take her on."

Silvia looked at the picture as it came though her email. She frowned, looking at Anne's petite figure. Lang was right, in the sense that any professional boater wouldn't take her on. Unfortunately, not all the boaters on the island were professional, and they came from all over the country. With all that in mind, taking into account Anne's age and alleged behavior, it was possible she wasn't paying simply in cash. Of course, she wasn't going to mention that to her father.

Then again, George O'Mara was definitely a professional who wouldn't have taken anyone he didn't consider able to handle the waterski. The likeliness that Anne was on his boat was starting to deteriorate in her mind. Still, it was odd that she went missing around the same time as the boating accident occurred. It was too odd to be a coincidence. So far, nobody else had been reported missing. It was the closest Silvia would have to a lead until she could speak with George directly.

Her phone buzzed. She glanced at it. It was the Fire Inspector, shooting her a series of texts.

"Hey Chief."

"Found something on yacht."

"Stop by if you get a chance."

Silvia proceeded to get Mr. Lang's contact information, then closed her notepad.

"I'll get started on this right away," she said. "Mr. Lang, I would appreciate that you give us a call immediately if you get in contact with her."

"Will do," Mr. Lang said. His voice was dry. He was openly displaying his lack of faith in her. He had the look of someone who felt he had wasted his time, as well as someone who had questions. Why was she asking him about speedboats and waterskiing? What was she getting at? Did something happen? He left without saying anything further.

His absence brought a fragment of relief. Silvia took a breath, organized her notes, then walked into the dispatch room. There were four dispatchers, two full-time, the others seasonal workers. Silvia copied the basic info for Anne Lang and tore the sheet from the notepad. She placed it on Cindi Patrick's desk.

"Hey, Cindi. Get this to the officers, would ya?"

"Sure can," Cindi said. "Missing person?"

"Correct."

Cindi looked puzzled. Almost every call made regarding missing people turned out to be false alarms. The island was jampacked with people, all competing for the festivities the island had to offer. Cindi was the one who got the call about George's speedboat, and it was clear to her what was on the Chief's mind.

"I'll do it, but for what it's worth, Chief, I don't think she was on that boat," Cindi said. "The timeframe doesn't add up. She went missing last night. The incident occurred this morning. And I somehow get the impression that George wouldn't have taken this little doll on board."

Silva exhaled slowly. Cindi was a good person and a great dispatcher, but she had an annoying tendency to speak her mind straightforwardly. Maybe Silvia found it annoying because she felt like she was being judged.

"Probably not, but I wanna keep an eye out for her just in case," she said. She waited for the pinch in her back to let up before leaving. It didn't. She stepped back into the hall and got on her radio. "Zero-One to Unit-Five. Any update over there?"

"Lieutenant's still searching, Chief," the officer replied.

"Ten-four." She clipped the microphone, then muttered, "damn it." Her phone buzzed again. This time, it was Royce.

"Hey. Brandon Webster texted me. Gonna be heading to the Fire Station."

"Christ," Silvia said, annoyed. They had personally called him. It was in that moment that she realized that Brandon Webster had texted her as an afterthought. 'Oh yeah, better let her know too.' It was almost as if they forgot she was the Chief, and not Royce Boyer.

She looked at the missing person notes. Probably nothing. People went their separate ways all the time. And nothing pointed to the likeliness that she was on George O'Mara's speedboat.

Silvia tapped the screen to reply to the Fire Inspector's message.

"On my way."

CHAPTER 10

Freshly showered and dressed in a dry, ironed uniform, Royce parked his Interceptor in the fire garage's parking lot. Right away, Brandon Webster was standing in front of the building to greet him.

"That didn't take long," the Sergeant said. "You trying to make it into the Fire Inspector Hall of Fame?"

Brandon chuckled and shook his head.

"I'm gonna be busy through the next week looking at this thing, but this detail stood out like a sore thumb. Come inside and let me show you." He held the staff entrance open for Royce and followed him inside. Royce had only been in the fire garage a handful of times. It was divided into two main sections; one for the first responder vehicles and supplies; and this one for conducting inspections that had to be removed from the site.

The yacht took up a fourth of this section of the garage. It was lifted up on stilts, much like a car when getting its tires changed. There were two hydraulic lifts parked near it for Brandon's use.

Chief Stan Rolling turned around and greeted the Sergeant.

"Here to buy me lunch too?" he quipped.

"I was, but Brandon said he'd do it," Royce replied.

"Oh, gee, thanks," Brandon said. "Now he's gonna expect it."

"Damn right," Stan said. The three men gazed at the boat. Judging from the extensive damage, Royce would've thought the boat had blown apart by C-4. Whatever was left of the cabin had collapsed inward during the towing. All of the components holding it together had either burned away or melted. In this condition, it resembled a giant canoe with a large crack down the side.

"What do you make of it?" Royce asked. "Were your suspicions right? Fuel tank rupture?"

"Yes, definitely the fuel tank," Brandon said. "But, that's not why I brought you here. Come over here, please." He led the Chief and Sergeant under the stern of the boat. "Aside from the coaming and everything above the waterline, the draft area is mostly clean."

"Well yeah, probably because the water protected it from the burns," Royce said.

"Yes. Except for here." Brandon led them to the starboard quarter and pointed at a small, jagged hole two feet inward. It was heavily charred, almost as much so as the deck remains.

Royce nodded, though he wasn't yet convinced it was anything completely noteworthy.

"It's a hole," he said bluntly.

"Yes, smartass," Brandon said. "It's the burns that interest me."

"The fuel could've cracked the underside, and could've been hot enough in that split second before the ocean put it out."

"That's what I thought at first," Brandon said. "The interesting thing is that there's an inward crease. The blast would have bent the edges outward, since it exploded from within."

"Hang on a sec. You think something hit this from the outside?" Royce asked. Brandon nodded, his expression as puzzled as the others. Royce scoffed, unsure whether the Inspector was playing a joke.

The sound of the door opening drew their attention to the front of the garage. Silvia stepped inside. She could tell they were already in the middle of going over Brandon's findings.

Thanks for waiting for me.

She faked a smile and walked over. "Sorry I'm late. What'd I miss."

Royce pointed up at the ship. "Apparently something stung the ship like a bee and ignited the fuel tank."

"You're shitting me," Silvia said. "From *underneath*? Like what?"

"Whatever it was had to contain heat," Royce said. "I would still consider the fireworks a possibility. I've seen videos online of people setting them off underwater. Maybe that's what they were doing and it ended up biting them in the ass."

Silvia shook her head. "I just don't see how any fireworks could've busted through that hull."

Royce scoffed. "You kidding? They make all kinds of hot shit. It's almost the Fourth of July. These kids were probably fooling around, drinking, *probably* smoking weed, and seeing what tricks they could pull off with the fireworks. We already know for a fact they were shooting them off the deck."

"It is possible," Stan admitted. "Unfortunately, we have no way of knowing. The ocean would've washed away any residue. However, what Brandon and I really find interesting is the type of burn on this hull. It's consistent with damage from high-voltage electricity."

"Like it was struck by a bolt of lightning," Brandon added. Royce glared. These guys had a good sense of humor. They HAD to be pulling his leg.

"You're telling me this is *electrical* damage?"

"Just telling you what it resembles," Stan said. There was no hint of humor in his facial expression. He dug out his smartphone and got on the internet, then held the screen for them to see. "This was during Hurricane Maria. Lightning hit the side of a house."

On the screen was a close up shot of burnt scarring in the side of a garage.

"Interesting. Lightning is hot, concentrated, and instantaneous," Silvia said.

"Correct," Stan said. "The most damage to property is from the resulting fire, if the lightning hits anything that can burn."

"Okay, that's interesting…until you explain to me what could've hit that boat with such a concentrated dose of electricity underwater," Royce said. "The power cables are on the other side of the island. This yacht went ablaze on the east. We've established that the breach there was from an outside impact, and we know for a *fact* they were messing with fireworks."

"True," Brandon admitted.

"Listen…" Royce took a breath, making sure not to sound too harsh, "I don't think this would normally happen. Fireworks can detonate underwater, but I wouldn't typically bet they would damage a boat hull, especially considering the angle of the breach. But nothing else makes sense. I believe you guys know your stuff, and yes, that resembles an electrical burn. But really? Lightning strikes? Unless there's a storm cloud under the water…" He sighed. "No offense."

"None taken," Stan said. He understood the Sergeant's frustration was not aimed at the firemen. Bizarre complications to any investigations were very frustrating for all involved. Knowing the Mayor, she'd be wanting answers to this straight away, as well as the families of all those involved.

Royce thought for a moment. None of this made sense, but he didn't want to write off the Inspector's findings. After all, he'd seen bizarre things his entire career.

"Listen, we need to get divers over there pronto anyway. Remember, there were three people aboard that boat, and you only found two. Right?"

"Right."

"Have your divers searched that area this morning?"

"They have," Stan answered.

"And…"

"Nothing. No body. If it's down there, the current's swept it away. It could be anywhere at this point."

"What about electrical equipment? Did they see anything—anything at all that could produce a charge?"

"Not that they could see," Stan said. "Basically, your fireworks theory is the only lead we have."

"And we still have nothing on George O'Mara's incident. Two unexplainable accidents, within twelve hours of each other," Royce said.

"You suspect a connection? They were different kinds of accidents on different sides of the island," Brandon said.

"There is a connection." Royce pulled out his phone and displayed the image of the burn mark in the vessel. "You're the expert. Would you say that's the same kind of burn as that?" He pointed to the yacht.

Brandon took the phone and zoomed in on the image.

"Jesus. It's similar. Where is the boat?"

"In our lot," Silvia said.

"I'd like to get a look at it," Brandon said.

"Be my guest," Silvia replied.

Royce looked at his watch. "It's been over an hour since the ambulance took O'Mara to the hospital. I'm gonna go see if I can talk with him."

"He might not be able to speak," Silvia said.

"Chief…" Royce had to temper his tone after almost forgetting she outranked him, despite having the knowledge and thought pattern of a rookie, "…if there's something dangerous in the water, we need to know. Right now, he's our only witness. And we need answers. We don't even know if he was alone on that damn boat, or why he was speeding toward land like the devil was after him."

Silvia nodded.

"I'll go with you." She waved to Stan and Brandon. "Thanks for your help, gentlemen."

"Not a problem. I'll get a look at that boat," Brandon said. They watched the two officers exit the building and listened to the rumble of their engines. Brandon noticed the Fire Chief's eyes pan toward him.

"So! About that lunch?"

Brandon squeezed his eyes shut. *I'm gonna kill Royce.*
****

The hospital check-in clerk turned pale, intimidated by Royce's sharp tone, towering stature, and most of all—that piercing glare. Twice, he had demanded to know which room George O'Mara had been checked into, and the clerk could sense a third.

"Officers, you know the rules. Confidentiality prevents me from giving away private information such as this."

"Listen, you little twerp," Royce said. "We need to speak with him pronto. There could be a life at stake. I don't give a crap about confidentiality!" The clerk turned his eyes to the Chief. Oddly enough, she almost seemed as intimidated as he.

Silvia was conflicted. They could be wandering into some bad territory here. The hospital could easily report this to the Mayor's Office as a violation. As frustrating as she found Royce, she didn't want to risk losing him. That thought made her cringe. Right now, she was *dependent* on Royce, and she hated it.

"What about a doctor?" she asked.

"He was seen by an ER doc. That's all I'm allowed to tell you without a Judge's order," the check-in clerk said. Silvia noticed the look on his face. It was too damn familiar—the poor twenty-something year old wanted to help, but he was too damn scared about losing his job.

"Where's he at now? Or she?" Royce asked.

"Back in one of the rooms looking at a patient."

"Life threatening? You can tell us that."

"Uh…no."

Royce watched the doors swing open as a nurse stepped in to call the name of one of the patients waiting in the lobby.

"Good." He marched for the doors, catching them before they could latch and be secured by their automatic lock.

"Royce!" Silvia darted for the doorway, passing the dismayed nurse and a couple of other staff members.

"Hey, are you supposed to be in here?" another nurse said to them.

"This is an urgent matter," Royce said, his tone softened as to not overly concern them. "A man named George O'Mara was brought in over an hour ago. I need to speak to the doctor who's treating him. It's very important."

At that moment, one of the doors opened from the back of the hall. A woman in her mid-forties dressed in a doctor's coat stepped out. Like the police department, she was at her busiest this time of year. But today looked as though it had been particularly stressful.

"I'll speak with them," she told the nurse. Royce and Silvia approached the doctor, each taking a moment to look at her tag. *Dr. Renee Cobb.* "I guess it's been a real fun day for all of us."

"That's an understatement," Silvia said.

"I take it you treated Mr. O'Mara when he first came in?" Royce asked. Dr. Cobb nodded. "What's George's condition?"

"In and out of consciousness," the doctor said. "He's got severe trauma to the brain. He must've hit his head pretty hard during the crash. Our scans detected bleeding and we need to relieve the pressure. Our neurosurgeon is out today, but we've given him a call. He should be arriving within the hour."

"Can he talk?" Silvia asked.

"Probably nothing coherent," Renee said. "We're getting him prepped for the OR, once Dr. Santage arrives. The longer this bleed goes on, the more likely the patient will slip into a coma that he may not come out of."

"Oh, Jesus," Silvia said.

"I have to try and speak with him," Royce said.

"I'm sorry, Officer, but you won't get anything out of him. We need to reduce the stimuli to his brain in order to prevent seizures, and otherwise worsen the condition. Even so much as having a light on will strain him at this stage."

"Damn it," Royce muttered. So much for their lead. George would be in surgery, and probably in recovery for the next day or so. "You said he woke up a couple times?"

"Correct."

"Has he said anything? Particularly about the crash? We're trying to figure out if there was anyone else on that boat with him."

"Nothing that's made sense."

"Like what?" Silvia asked.

"Uh," she paused, thinking she was wasting their time relaying George's mumbling rants, "he's been *repeatedly* rambling about a monster."

Royce shook his head. Was this case in a personal competition with itself to get any weirder?

CHAPTER 11

As the clock struck noon, the beaches all around the island were alive with activity. Cash registers sprung open as the shop owners conducted their business. Many called it the golden time of year for the weather and skin tones, but the people of Maxwell Island that used the phrase referred to the bucks they brought in. The smell of freshly cooked burgers, hot dogs, and nachos were starting to waft through the air, stirring hunger in those around them.

Chuck Tate had been swimming for the last couple of hours, but the water was getting so crowded, he couldn't go anywhere without being shoulder-to-shoulder with someone. He loved swimming, but he couldn't even really do that. He was just wading past one moving body after another. After a while, it became more frustrating than relaxing. So now, he was stuck on shore, forced to take in the series of enticing aromas.

Poor Chuck couldn't even breathe without smelling French fries, hot dogs, and whatever else people were carrying onto the beach. He had eaten a light breakfast, as he never had much appetite in the morning. An hour ago, his stomach had started sending signals, but he had remained distracted enough with his swimming to put it off. But now, as he sat on shore, he couldn't help but take notice of all the delicious smelling goodness all around him.

"Mom, I'm starving," he said. His mother sat in her beach chair, her eyes barely lifting from her tablet.

"We're meeting your father and sister at Hankey's at 1:00. You'll just have to last until then."

"Ugh! But I'm wasting away," the twelve-year old said dramatically. "I'm practically a skeleton right now."

"Yes. Clearly," his mother said, poking his stomach with her toe.

"Hey!" Chuck complained, swatting her foot away as though it was a mosquito. She laughed, then returned her eyes to her e-book.

"Sorry, Chucky," she said.

"Don't call me that!"

"Right, *Chuck*. Anyway, I don't have any money to throw your way. You're just gonna have to wait until your dad and Megan get back from their boat ride." Her eyes returned to her tablet. With an exasperated groan, Chuck laid back in the sand and stared at the cloudless sky. Now food was all he could think about. The next hour was going to drag. He needed something to distract his mind. Of course, Mom wouldn't let him have his smartphone. Yet, there she was goofing around on her tablet right in front of him. Instead, she made him pack a couple of books for their vacation. One was interesting, the other boring as hell.

Chuck picked up the more interesting book. Sword and sorcery was a relatively new discovery for him. Most of his friends who recommended fantasy always suggested *J.R.R. Tolkien* or *George R. R. Martin*, but he was always intimidated by the monster-sized blocks of pages that those books were. A slow, easily distracted reader such as himself would never get through them. That's when his father suggested *Robert E. Howard*. Classic pulp fantasy. Shorter, and much more to Chuck's liking. Of course, his mother wanted him to read "nice" like *Mary O'Hara*. What the hell was she thinking? The only horses he wanted to see on the page was the one *Conan* was riding on before he cleaved somebody with a sword.

He tried reading, but couldn't get more than a couple of paragraphs. It was like the crowd was intentionally torturing him! Even the tiny bit he read he didn't retain, as food was the only thing that mattered to his brain at this point. He needed something else to take his mind off the torture. Lying here, surrounded by people eating lunch wasn't helping. And his mother wasn't going to do anything. As he looked around, he noticed more people were sitting on the beach. He sat up and looked out into the water. Half the crowd had come ashore for lunch, making the water much more spacious. It wouldn't last long; most would likely head back out as soon as they finished eating. But hey, even just a few minutes of swimming would take his mind off his rumbling stomach.

"I'll be in the water," he told his mom.

"Okay. Don't go too deep," she replied.

"Ha!" he said. His mother should've known better, telling him not to do something. Might as well have said, 'Hey! Swim to the bottom of the drop-off!'

The ocean splashed under his feet. As he went in, a few other kids followed. They were a little older than him. Already, he noticed a couple of stares, as if he was impeding on their personal space. It didn't matter, he was gonna go out further than they would anyway.

Chuck was now chest deep. The water was the perfect temperature, warmed by the hot sun. Had it not gotten so crowded, he'd have never left. He threw his arms over his head and dove, arching like a dolphin under the surface. He swam underwater for several seconds before accidentally bumping into someone.

"Hey!" the woman snapped. Chuck emerged up top, embarrassed. He had touched the rear end of someone old enough to be his grandmother. Unfortunately, it didn't look like she had a good sense of humor about it.

"I'm sorry," he said, immediately changing course. He glanced back, terrified he'd suffer his mother's wrath. Fortunately, she never bothered to look up. Must be a good book.

Before he turned back, he noticed an army of people approaching the shoreline. He sighed, realizing he had waited too long to enjoy the spacious ocean. Already, the annoying crowds were returning, some of them racing as though leading a cavalry charge. Grown adults screamed at each other, lifting each other up and slamming them into the water like professional wrestlers.

Chuck was a couple hundred feet out, but he knew it was a matter of minutes before he'd be trapped in a barricade of swimmers. Half of them would stay where their feet cold touch the ground. Another fourth would branch out a bit further, where he was now. His best bet was to go swim out near the shark nets. It was about thirteen feet deep there, and he didn't have any floatation devices. Luckily, he was an excellent swimmer…and his slightly large midsection helped him to float naturally.

Screw it; he wasn't gonna let himself get crowded. Plus, it was good exercise—something that was on his mind since his new fascinating interest in girls mysteriously crept into his brain.

The sensation of water splashing his face had successfully deterred his brain from lunch. He was now deep enough where he had to paddle in order to stay afloat. He dove again. The seabed was six feet deep now. He touched the bottom with his hands and continued holding his breath. Unfortunately, he wasn't quite used to the sting of saltwater. Normally, he swam in pools or in freshwater lakes. With his eyes clenched shut, he rose to the surface. Immediately, he felt the thud of another body.

"For the love of God!"

It was that elderly woman again, her eyes shooting at Chuck as though he was the devil himself. Immediately, he heard the plop of something falling into the water. He caught enough of a glimpse to recognize its shape. It was an iPhone.

"Uh…" Chuck stammered.

"Damn it, kid! You're a real pain in the ass," the woman said. She bobbed on her inflatable ring, resisting the urge to smack the kid.

"Sorry." He didn't know what else to say. Part of him wanted to chastise her for thinking she owned the damn water. Apparently, she could occupy any space, and to hell with anyone who got too close. Plus, what idiot would bring their electronic device this far out? Unfortunately, it didn't change the fact that he knocked her phone into the water. And knowing his mother and her love of devices, she'd probably take the lady's side in this argument.

"Sorry's not enough. Go down there and get it."

"Well, it's in the water now. It's broken," Chuck said.

"No. It's in a waterproof case," the lady said.

"Oh!" Chuck was relieved. All he had to do was go fetch it. Much better than explaining to his mom that they needed to replace someone's phone. "Okay. Let me go grab my goggles and I'll be right back."

"Well, hurry up!"

Gosh, she must be a joy to be around. As Chuck went to shore, he didn't notice anyone who looked as though they were here with her. Probably one of the reasons she was so grouchy. The hag should've rented a private cabin instead of visiting a public beach if she detested the presence of other people.

Chuck hurried to his bag and started digging out his goggles.

"Whatcha doing?" his mother asked.

"Oh, just helping someone find something they dropped," Chuck replied.

"Aw. That's nice of you, hon," she said. Chuck grinned. At least he was able to spin the story to make himself look good. He found his goggles, which were still in the plastic. Damn, those manufacturers. By the way they tightened the seams in this case, you'd think they were securing the *Cross of Coronado*. He glanced back to the shore. More and more people were invading the water, splashing and conversing. Behind the smiles and faces was the gravelly expression of that lady. She glared at him, then threw her hands up. *What's taking so long?!*

He finally got the plastic off, then started wading into the water past the crowd. There was no way in without bumping into others. This was the very thing he hoped to avoid. At least none of these people seemed to take issue with his presence, unlike the one person he was swimming out to.

Chuck maneuvered through the crowd and swam out. The lady's glare turned uglier.

Is she trying to turn into the Medusa or something?

"Sorry. New goggles. They were still in the case," a nervous Chuck said.

"Just get my phone. Even in its case, it's not gonna last down there forever!"

"Hang on." Chuck pulled the goggles over his eyes, then dove to the bottom. The seabed here was not as attractive in appearance as the sand closer to shore. There was more weeds and silt in this area. And no phone. He touched his hands along the sand, praying that the phone didn't get caught under some seaweed, or buried under some silt. He'd be down here forever! Suddenly, that hour until lunch that was dragging by seemed too short.

He came up for a breath. Several other swimmers were branching out. The lady cocked her head at him. "Well?"

Without saying anything, he went back down for another look. It had to be somewhere. It fell right beneath them, for crying out loud! He searched around, succeeding only in stirring up more silt. *Great. Making it more difficult.* He came up for another breath, not bothering to glance at the lady. Unfortunately, he could not escape her verbal assault.

"Boy! If you don't find that thing, I swear I'll break you over my leg!"

Lady, you're more likely to break your leg.

Chuck went for another try. This time, he crawled further out. His eyes went left to right, like a security camera. He studied the shape of every weed, every piece of gravel. Every—there!

A few feet ahead of him was the blue case. Finally! He could get the stupid thing back to the hag and get the hell back to shore. With the busy crowds, and the phone's pestering owner, he craved to go back to reading about *Conan* slaying enemies with his broadsword.

He realized the phone was propped against something. Initially, he thought that 'lump' in the seabed was just a clump of sand. But it was something different. It was rigid! Like part of a boat!

Chuck closed in and picked up the phone. Curious, he touched the object. It was definitely some kind of steel. It was only a few feet long, rounded like the underside of a boat. Wreckage? It could have been part of that fire he heard about—that boat was big. This was way smaller, maybe only enough to fit a couple of people. He lifted the edge.

A pinkish mass raised out, its arms waving like tentacles. Even in the water, he felt their slimy texture. Chuck's scream exploded into a series of air bubbles. He pushed the thing down and shot for the surface.

He arose with an enormous splash, his scream drawing the attention of the entire shoreline. Hundreds of eyes turned toward the frightened twelve-year old. The first person to respond was someone completely unconcerned with his distress. As far as she was concerned, he was just a stupid kid who lost her phone, and now he was playing a game to get out of finding it.

"Now what's your issue, you little twerp?" she said, paddling closer. Suddenly, something rose to the surface. Bloated limbs flopped onto her inflatable, the slack-jawed head plopping against her belly. Wiry hair spread across the rubber. The lady sucked in a breath, seeing the ballooned face of a woman. She had been torn in half, her shoulders, neck, and breasts deflated, yet, extended. The skin was a pale pink, the left eye eaten away by fish.

The woman's screams were the first of hundreds. Nearby swimmers saw the corpse and panicked, which led to a chain reaction that traveled down a mile of shoreline in each direction.

The screams traveled far inland as an exodus of swimmers raced to shore.

Chuck paddled as fast as he could. His appetite was gone. Probably would be for a while. As soon as his feet touched the bottom, he ran, his swells crashing against those generated by the terrified swimmers around him.

On shore, he found his mother in the crowd. She hugged her son, completely confused, yet equally terrified. In less than a minute, the water had emptied. A moment later, a handful of lifeguards raced in to rescue an old lady keeled over in her inflatable, suffering from what appeared to be a heart attack.

Behind her, the corpse bobbed in the water, its one intact eye pointed at the approaching lifeguards.

CHAPTER 12

Martha Cornett put the mask over her face, then washed her hands for the third time. The operating room was cold and bright. The first of the two sharks was laid out along a twelve-foot table, the other frozen in storage. On the side of the table near the caudal fin was a tray containing forceps, syringes, scalpels, tweezers, and scissors. To her left was a machine with suction hoses for drawing fluid and siphoning blood. To her right was a wheeling table, with a setup stand for glass vials. Behind her was another long table, equipped with sample trays, microscopes, computers for analysis, and clipboards for physical notes.

Andy walked into the room, then shivered. Autopsies were his least-favorite part of the job. Despite being around fish all his life, he never got used to the smell of their guts—something his wife often poked fun at him for. He put the mask over his face and pulled his gloves over his hands.

"Alright, I'm ready to start whenever you are," he said.

"Let's get this party started," Martha said. She grabbed the scalpel and began cutting across the shark's underbelly. The carcass wiggled slightly with the motions, giving the impression that it was still barely alive. She cut in a straight line, then used the forceps to peel back the skin. "Alright. Now to find out what this bad boy has eaten recently."

"Canoe," Andy joked.

"Probably not. But if you keep up with the jokes, I might find *you* inside the next one," she retorted. She sliced at the inner layers of tissue. The smell of dead fish filled the room. Martha widened the wound, exposing intestines, the liver, and the u-shaped stomach. She switched to the scissors and tried pushing the tips through the thin tissue. There was something off about it. Normally, stomach tissue had a pinkish-white color to it. But this was a darker red, and much tougher than normal. Something was wrong with it, but now was not the time to figure out what. She punched the blades in and proceeded to cut a long slit.

Thick fluid spilled onto the table, carrying a fragment of a small tuna.

"Not from the trench," Andy said.

"You're not helping. Here, help me siphon up some of this blood, will ya?"

"Alright," he said, imitating the voice of an annoyed child who was told to turn off the TV and do his homework. Knowing that she would want samples, he used a syringe to draw some of the stomach fluid and filled a couple of the vials. He then took samples of the blood, then proceed to siphon the rest, allowing Martha to see what she was digging out.

She pulled forceps and reached in. There was something hard inside the shark's stomach. Whatever it was, it was definitely something that had been ingested.

"Damn," she muttered. She pulled back, then used her instruments to widen the slit.

"What is it?"

"Crustacean of some kind," Martha said. She pulled harder. She could feel small, spindly legs attached to a much larger body. It didn't feel proportionate enough to be a crab. She grabbed it with both hands and pulled. The shelled organism rolled out onto the table.

"Jesus!" Andy said. The creature looked like a giant parasite. Its shell had turned a shade of grey, its remaining legs bent into a half-clutched position. Much of the underbelly had been dissolved from the goblin's stomach acid. The creature itself was about twice as large as Martha's fist.

"Isopod," she said. "Not quite a mature size. Still, the shark must've swallowed it whole."

"Considering how solid that shell is, and how much is left, he's been carrying this thing around a while," Andy added. "These guys live super deep. Like, *really* deep."

Martha's smile was unfortunately concealed behind her mask. It was her husband's way of admitting she was right. And Martha *loved* being right.

"Only one spot near here deep enough for these guys to reside," she said.

Andy nodded. "The Puerto Rico Trench. Which means, that's where these sharks came from."

"And they followed that heat bloom. It's the only way they could've survived the change in temperature for so long."

"So, we have a theory," Andy said.

"It's gotta be what happened," Martha said. "Had to. It can't be a coincidence that these things popped up around the time we discovered that heat bloom. And all these reports of deep sea organisms coming to the surface. There's a connection."

"But what the hell can create heat that significant? Whatever it is, it'd have to be big!"

Martha nodded. "There's nothing recorded that I know of. But there's all kinds of things living down there that haven't been discovered yet. And with the geological conditions, it's possible that something might've been driven to the surface."

"You're suggesting it's a *living* thing?" Andy asked, to which his wife nodded. Conversely, he shook his head. "Babe...we're really reaching here."

"I don't think so," Martha said. "We need a research team sent here to help us track down whatever's causing this. And also, we need to find out if there have been any dives into the trench, and what the latest seismic scans have indicated."

"The institute will be fascinated by this find, but if we tell them we suspect there's something swimming around out there raising the water temperature to nearly eighty-degrees, we'll find ourselves conducting research in Antarctica."

Martha shrugged. "I have always wanted to go there."

"You can go alone. I'll find a new wife down here," he joked. "I've had over a dozen women wink at me in the past week alone! They all wanna climb Andy's Mountain."

"Well, I hope they enjoy a short, bumpy ride!"

Andy laughed. "Way to turn it around on me, babe. But seriously, I do think we're getting a little bit ahead of ourselves."

Martha sighed. This time, *he* was right—and she hated when he was right. But it was true; she was letting the excitement of a potential new discovery get the better of her.

"Well, then we need to conduct more research," she said. "What's the latest reading on Buoy Five?"

"I don't have my phone on me. I need to go into the other room to check," Andy said. He took off his gloves, washed his hands thoroughly, then exited through the back door. As she waited, she proceeded to slice extremely thin samples of various tissue, then placed them on slides for the microscope. She placed a slide containing some of the discolored stomach lining.

The image was a dark red. Some of the cells had been completely eradicated. Burnt.

"What the hell?" Martha checked another piece of tissue under the microscope. It was the same thing. It was as if a fire had lit inside the fish. She widened the incision, intending to remove the entire stomach. First, she needed to remove any other contents inside. She pinched her fingers along the stomach walls. The whole front side appeared to have burn marks. She reached in, finding another piece of tuna. Then a bone of some kind that she didn't recognize. She held it up. It was long and pointed—a tooth!

"What the hell did you eat?" She used the forceps to pull the stomach completely open. There was something inside it, partially digested. It was curled into a tight loop. Moray eel, perhaps?

Martha reached inside and pulled it out. The skin was tough and leathery, the head elongated. It was roughly two feet in length, with a single large fin running down the length of its body.

She held it up over the table, then turned it for a view at its head.

An eel of some kind. I wonder where—

The creature shifted its body. Its mouth opened, baring jagged teeth. Suddenly, Martha's entire body jolted as an invisible force surged through her. With a brief yelp, she dropped the thing and reeled backward, hitting the table leg behind her.

Andy rushed back inside. "You okay?!"

Martha nodded, her face almost purple. Her hand clutched her chest, her left curled tight against her ribs. With his phone in hand, Andy started to dial 9-1-1.

"No, no—I'm good. I'm fine," she said shakily. "Caught me by surprise, was all."

Andy looked at the dying serpentine thing wiggling about on the table. Its jaw snapped repeatedly, biting at anything it could get ahold of.

"An Eel?"

"Looks like it," Martha replied. Andy knelt down by her and held her hand. Her muscles were still tense, but gradually loosening up.

"What the hell did it do to you?"

"Shocked me," she said, gasping. "Electric shock."

"Electric shock? But that's not..." He took another look. "That's not an electric eel. They don't live in the ocean."

"I know, dufus—I'm the one with the Ph.D." Martha reached out a hand, and Andy carefully pulled her to her feet. He kept his arms around her waist, letting her lean against his strong frame. He could feel her body quivering as it came down from the surprise and literal shock.

"You sure you're okay?"

"Yes. I promise." She looked at the thing again. It wiggled slightly, then tensed before lying limp on the table, finally dead.

"How the hell was it still alive?"

"Eels can live up to fourteen hours out of water. At least, the known species can," Martha said. Her color was gradually returning, her hands steadying. "And this one ended up in the belly of this shark. I guess, he wasn't too keen on being swallowed. He shocked the bastard from the inside."

"But where the hell did it come from? The trench?"

Martha nodded. "Had to."

"That shark didn't eat it down here," Andy said. "By the looks of it, that thing's been thrashing about in its belly for a few hours. Which means, it had to be swimming around somewhere out in our waters." He thought about it for a moment, then smiled with a grand realization. "It this thing could generate heat from its electric shocks, it could survive the change in ocean temperature and adapt naturally."

"You believe me now about a new species?" Martha asked.

"More importantly, I think the institute will."

"It burned the hell out of the goblin's guts. There's got to be a connection between this sucker and the heat bloom."

Her husband chuckled. "I'm not sure one of these guys would start a massive heatwave under the water," Andy said. "It would take a whole pack of them. Or one big momma." It was meant to be a joke, but even he didn't find it funny. Instead, his eyes widened as a new realization flooded his mind.

He pointed at the eel. "*If* this is a baby...how big would its mother be?"

Martha shrugged, still a bit jittery from the jolt.

"There's no way to tell. We don't even know if this species is birthed live or by eggs."

"Say there was a really big one—like, as big as a boat, would it generate an electric voltage strong enough to, say...ignite a fuel tank?"

Martha started to chuckle. Kind of an odd question. Except, it wasn't. She put a hand to her mouth.

"The yacht! Oh my lord." It was so obvious now. "We need to get in touch with the police and fire department. They need to be made aware of this. But first, we need to figure out how to tell them. If we just say there's a goddamn giant electric eel swimming around our island, they'll laugh us out of town."

"Also, I think the Chief might have her hands full," Andy said.

"What do you mean?

He went back to his phone and switched on safari. "This was why I was taking forever in the other room." He handed her the device. She read the article.

News alert! Northeast beach. They found a body, torn in half. Witness claims that the mother of all sharks must've gotten ahold of the victim, who has yet to be identified.

"Good lord." She looked at the time posted on the article. "Jesus, this JUST happened."

"You think there's a connection?" Andy asked.

"There's no way to know unless we can get a look at the body," Martha answered.

"I'm not sure that they'll let us. We're not medical examiners for a police case."

"They often reach out to specialists for formal opinions, and they'll want a marine expert to tell them whether a shark killed that person," Martha said. She was finally able to stand without leaning on him. The shakes were gone, and the only discomfort that remained was a small knot in her stomach. That would likely be gone in a few minutes. She gazed at the specimen and the numerous samples.

"First, we need to preserve this thing. Help me get tissue samples, then we'll need to get an X-ray scan."

"Okay," Andy said. He watched his wife start to reach for the dead eel. "Ah-ah!" Martha stepped back, alert, then noticed her husband's strict expression. He pointed at the eel. "Don't you think we should get rubber gloves before handling that thing?"

She smiled. It *almost* seemed like a joke. Except, it wasn't.

"Once in a while, you have good ideas, babe."

"Damn straight. You didn't marry me for just my good looks, you know. Well, maybe you did. But still." Martha tapped his face playfully, shutting him up. He smiled then went to dig into one of the back drawers for gloves. "You *sure* you're alright?"

She nodded. "Just glad I used the bathroom before starting this."

"Yeah, me too. Knowing you, you'd make me clean up the mess. Your hair's standing up by the way."

Martha shook her head. *Smart ass.* Her eyes went back to the eel. It was on its side, its grey eyes as large as silver dollars. She paid close attention to its teeth. Just the sight of them made her shudder. They were two centimeters long, and were very sharp. She was lucky those jaws didn't snap shut on her hand. She began to wonder, if this was a baby, and it was this vicious, how bad would a big one be?

She gave one last look at the article. At the bottom was a link for another news alert.

Police search for missing body of possible water skier after unexplained speedboat crash.

CHAPTER 13

As the clock struck 1:00 p.m., every single person on Maxwell Island knew of the horrible, half-eaten corpse. The news had spread like wildfire, and its destruction was evident in the beaches. With the news came rumors, and those rumors quickly concerned the mind of every tourist intending to enjoy the water. With the grisly details of the corpse, it didn't take much imagination for anyone to envision a killer shark lurking beyond those shores. That imagination instilled fear, which stultified any desire to enjoy the beaches.

The news also brought attention to another incident which had occurred that morning. Tourists and residents started asking questions about a speedboat that mysteriously ran aground at Wesco Peak. Residents who knew the driver added to the confusion, adamantly stating his competence as a boater and the unlikeliness that it was a simple mistake.

The domino effect of news soon made its way to the Maxell General Hospital, where reporters demanded to get information from the staff. The only reply reporters received was that the patient was undergoing surgery, and to relay all questions to the Police and Mayor's Office.

Thus, the police dispatch station was flooded with phone calls. People expressed their fears of going into the water. Additionally, business owners located near the beachlines demanded something be done, as their main source of revenue moved inland. Among the businesses suffering losses for the day were charters. The incidents with the speedboat and exploding yacht had even made people afraid to go out on boats. Even reservations for the upcoming days were rapidly being cancelled.

For Mayor JoEllen Marsh, the most concerning piece of information was the fact that hotel reservations were being cancelled. This meant that the information had already gone beyond Maxwell Island.

She had already advised security to have the gates ready to let her in through the back entrance. No doubt, there'd be a few reporters waiting at the front of the building. JoEllen knew avoiding the cameras was no option. She needed to radiate confidence to ensure the people that the problem was being looked into. The most important thing was to stop the bleeding of cancellations. The businesses could easily bounce back from the revenue lost from cancelled activities, as people currently residing were not going to leave just yet. Early departure would result in wasted money for them, as hotels and beach houses would not allow refunds at this point. But cancelled reservations was certain financial loss that was less likely to be regained, especially this far into the summer.

JoEllen passed through the gates and parked in the back lot. Her secretary, Stephani Vogel, met her at the door. The worry lines on her face were indicative of a flood of phone calls.

"Any word on the police investigation?" JoEllen asked.

"Chief Remar is there right now," Stephani replied. "I just saw her on the television. She did pretty good letting everyone know that the situation is being handled." The twenty-four-year-old brunette could tell her words did little to alleviate the Mayor's concerns.

They entered the building together and walked through a series of halls before reaching the privacy of her office. Right away, JoEllen broke out her makeup kit and started getting right to work freshening up.

"How bad are the calls?"

Stephani chuckled nervously. "When I get back to the desk, I guarantee I'll have a couple dozen angry messages."

"Has Mr. Belanger called?"

"Yes," Stephani said. "I had to listen to his rant about how he's spent thousands of dollars on boats and crew and fireworks, along with reserving the beaches. It's like he thinks we deliberately had these incidents to inconvenience him."

"He's nice as long as things are going his way," JoEllen said. "I'll let him know the show is still on."

"You'll want to talk with Chief Remar," Stephani said. "It's unclear, but I think she's considering closing the beaches."

"She has to go through me to do that," JoEllen said. "Is she still there at North Beach?"

"Yes."

"Good. News cameras still there?"

"As far as I'm aware."

"Perfect. Let me get finished getting fixed up and I'll head on over." JoEllen fixed the imperfections under her eyes, then dabbed her cheeks.

"Ma'am, it's not my place, but don't you think it might be safer to close the beaches for one day?"

"Maybe if it was August," JoEllen replied. "But right now, there's too much business we can't afford to lose right now. The islanders will have my ass. I'll never hear the end of it. We have hundreds of thousands of visitors every year. We can't suspend all activity because of a few accidents. Besides, Silvia will listen."

"It's not actually her I'm worried about," Stephani said.

"Who, then?"

"That Sergeant...Boyer, I think his last name is. A lot of people think he's running things. I think he's putting the idea in her ear that closing up the beaches is the best idea."

JoEllen shook her head, frustrated. That damn Sergeant was always too outspoken for his own good. Hence, he didn't get the promotion.

She felt her phone buzzing in her purse. JoEllen snatched it out, immediately recognizing the number. Looks like Mr. Belanger was tired of waiting for her to return to the office.

"Mayor Marsh speaking."

"Hi, Mayor. My apologies for calling you on your personal phone. I know you must have your hands full right now, but I can't really afford to wait."

"No, no, it's okay, Mr. Belanger," she said. "How can I help?"

"Well, I need to know what's going on with the beaches. Not to sound like I own the island, but I've already accepted an offer from the administration in Simone Bay. They've even got an ad campaign ready to broadcast. I can get my crew and equipment over there pronto, but I'd have to get started now."

JoEllen took a moment to prepare her answer. At first, she thought he was bluffing, then remembered that most of his crew had been scheduled to arrive tonight around 7:00 p.m. If Simone Bay had some hotels on standby, all he would have to do is divert his people there, and only lose his deposit for the island hotels.

She would never hear the end of it, as his show brought a lot of revenue to the island. Also, what if he did great business there? There was a stronger population, thus more opportunities for tickets. Hell, one of the main reasons he did the show on Maxwell Island was for tradition. Specifically, it was where he started. But money was often the slayer of such things.

No, she couldn't afford to lose his business.

"Please don't worry, Mr. Belanger. I'm already working on it. I've got my secretary prepping a press statement." Her eyes turned to Stephani. "I've already spoken to the Police Chief, and she's already prepared to have her staff out on patrol during your event. Just for protection, we've got shark nets that we'll be placing around the beach area, but those are common use anyway. Also, I'll get in touch with our marketing department to help spread awareness of your arrival. Perhaps I'll get word to the mainland, and maybe arrange a discount for the ferries to bring in ticket buyers."

"*Hmm...*"

JoEllen held her breath. It was clear he was thinking it over. The Simone Bay offer must've been a tempting one.

"*Alright. Sounds good.*"

"Thank you. I'll be in touch." She hung up the phone and blew a sigh of relief. "Oh, thank God."

"I'll get started on that press release," Stephani said.

"Inform the public there's no danger, that the beaches will remain open, and are completely safe. We need to eliminate all doubt."

"But ma'am, what if they aren't?" Stephani asked. JoEllen rolled the question over in her mind. Her initial reaction would've been to scold her secretary for daring to ask such a dumb thing. But it was a legitimate concern, and she didn't get to her position by being a pushy bitch.

"It's a shark attack," she said. "You're more likely to get struck by lightning. It's an island—it was bound to happen at some point, despite how unfortunate the incident is."

"But the boat incidents?"

"Mr. O'Mara probably saw the shark and panicked. The body they found was probably his client. As for the yacht? That's simple. Fireworks accident. Just *Google* it. You'll find all sorts of incidents that dumb people have done over the years."

The Mayor finished touching up her makeup, then opened her closet for a new outfit that wasn't marred by sweat stains.

"Now, if you'll excuse me, I'm gonna change, then head over to meet the Chief."

"Yes, ma'am." Stephani closed the door on her way out, then hurried back to her desk. Thirty messages on the machine. She had a busy day ahead of her.

CHAPTER 14

It was a rare sight to see such a long stretch of vacant beach on a bright summer afternoon. Many of the vacationers had packed up and left for the center of the island, several in hysterics. The ambulance had left to take an elderly woman to Maxwell General for her heart condition, while other first responders treated those who suffered minor injuries during the panic.

The Fire Department's Munson boats cleared a path in the shark nets, allowing for Kevon to bring in his tugboat. Lieutenant Adam Henry was in the water, ready to hook up his cable to the wreckage beneath.

Another ambulance drove down onto the beach. A minute later, the paramedics came by with a stretcher to remove the body, which had been pulled up onto the waterline and wrapped in plastic.

Silvia Remar forced a blank expression as she watched the first responders place the wrapped carcass in a body bag. It was a young Caucasian female, judging by what little remained of her. However, there was one particular detail she did notice: the stretched, blotted remnants of a tattoo on the back of her neck. This was the missing woman she had taken a report on just a couple of hours earlier. She felt the spiral notebook in her pocket. There was only a handful of times since her rookie days that she had to make a phone call like this, and most of those occasions were during her brief stint in Miami. Also, it was the first time since Miami that she'd seen such a corpse so mangled. She had seen corpses that were dead in swimming pools, a homeless person who'd been hit by a semi, and one murdered and stuffed in a trash can to rot—that was probably the only one worse than this.

"How am I going to explain this to Mr. Lang?" she muttered to herself. Royce, who was standing a few feet to her right, turned to face her, thinking she was speaking to him.

"You know how to contact him?"

"I have his info."

"Well, don't spill the beans over the phone. Call and tell him to meet you, then tell him in person. He'll probably know by the nature of the call that it's bad news. Not that it matters much, but it may help brace him for what's coming."

"Right," Silvia said. Royce watched her facial expression. Something was wrong with her, though he wasn't sure what. He suspected an upset stomach from seeing the body.

Wouldn't be surprised.

Silvia really needed to sit. More specifically, she needed to lay back. What she *really* needed was surgery, but that wasn't an option right now.

"You alright there, Chief?" Royce asked.

She grimaced from the damn sciatica. It felt like an invisible hand was grabbing the insides of her calf muscle and pulling them into her thigh.

"Just thinking," she replied. Out in the water, Kevon's tugboat lifted the wreckage from the water.

"Is it just me, or are they lifting out multiple pieces?" Royce said.

"It's like it exploded," she said.

"Seems to be a habit with boats around here this week," Royce replied. They waited as the men retrieved all the available fragments. Whatever was there only measured ten feet at most, put together.

"Ready to go, Chief," Adam said.

"That's it?" she replied.

"That's all there is. There's gotta be more, but it all must've drifted apart after—whatever caused it."

"Bring it to the dock," she radioed. She saw the Lieutenant wave at her, then climb aboard the boat. She proceeded to walk the half-mile distance to a dock located at a small extension of the shoreline. The walking felt good, even if she was walking on lumps of sand rather than a treadmill.

"You do realize we'll have to close the beaches, right?" Royce said. Silvia sighed. This was not the conversation she needed right now. JoEllen would kill her for even considering it.

"That might not be necessary," Silvia replied.

"You're kidding, right?"

"Sergeant, it's an island. Boat accidents happen," she replied.

"Sounds like Marsh, but is dressed like our Chief," Royce said. She stopped, then faced him.

"You care to repeat that?"

"It *sounds* like Marsh, but is dressed like our Chief," he repeated.

"How 'bout I fill the midnight vacancy with you?" she said.

"Fine. Have fun managing this island without me, especially with Adam being gone," Royce retorted. Silvia didn't reply. The jerk had called her bluff. Worst of all—he was right, though she wouldn't admit it.

"What's your issue?" she replied.

"My issue is that repeated accidents like this *don't* happen," Royce said. "Three boat accidents...THREE," he held up his fingers. "In sixteen hours. That doesn't happen unless it's 1944 in the Pacific!"

"You think somebody is doing this deliberately?"

"Either somebody, or some*thing*," Royce replied. "Normally, I'd discount talk of sea monsters, such as what George O'Mara was apparently mumbling to his docs, as garbage. But these boat accidents aren't making sense. And, I'll tell you one thing—that was no propeller that chopped up that chick."

"Shark, then?"

"Hard to say. Can't imagine George fleeing from a shark unless it was the size of an eighteen-wheeler. Still, I think there's something out there that doesn't belong here."

Silvia snickered. This was the kind of talk she'd expect Royce to mock, not state seriously.

She proceeded to walk to the dock.

"What's so funny?" the Sergeant asked.

"It's probably just a shark," she replied.

"Yeah, I don't get my info of sharks from B-movies," Royce replied. "Such, I know that they don't actually crack boats in half."

"What do you want me to do?"

"Close. The. Damn. Beaches! Oh, and tell the boats to come in."

"Boats?!"

"Yeah! All of them."

"That's half the revenue in this town."

"Chief, I don't know if your eyes are closed, but these are *boat* accidents! Assuming they're even accidents. There's something going on here that isn't adding up."

"You seriously think we should call them in? How the hell do you expect me to do that?"

"By getting on the damn radio and instructing them to come in. There! It's that simple."

Silvia's nervous laughter had ceased. This all seemed a little too unbelievable for her to accept. Was Royce correct? Even if the fishing was shut down for a day, the backlash would be enormous. She'd have riots in front of the police station and Town Hall. Not to mention the message that would send to vacationers. Nobody would think their waters were safe.

Safe from what? None of this made sense.

"You guys coming?"

She saw Adam standing on the dock, waving at her. She waved back and continued walking the remaining hundred meters.

Her lips were tight, hiding the fact that she was clenching her teeth. Too much pain, too much stress, all at once. It was hard to maintain a coherent thought. There were too many factors to consider, each counterproductive to the other. What was the right call? There was a pattern of boat accidents occurring, but it still seemed like overkill to ban vessels from going out. With that in mind, if another incident happened, then she'd be to blame for sure. Of course, the economic crisis would also be pinned on her.

The self-doubt was strong today. She couldn't even hide it from herself. She was never ready for this job. That reality stung more than any nerve pain. She had hoped, despite her better judgement, that being Chief here on Maxwell Island would be mostly sunshine and rainbows. Hell, that's how it was the vast majority of her career here. But, in the back of her mind, she always wondered how'd she handle a potential crisis. Now she knew: she was falling apart like dried leaves.

Adam helped Kavon secure his boat to the dock as she approached. Water dripped from his wetsuit. He took his goggles and flippers off. His air tank had been completely drained in the search.

"Damn it, Chief. I said no more boats for today," Kavon said. Her lack of response triggered a slight feeling of guilt. *Probably not the time to be kidding around.*

"Hell, if you can call it a boat," Adam said. Most of the wreckage had been tossed into the tugboat's deck. There were several loose scraps scattered about. At this stage, it was impossible to tell what segment of the boat they were attached to. The only part that was identifiable was the bow.

"Judging by this, I'd say we've got half of the boat," Kavon said.

"Any guess on what happened? A crash?"

"I don't think so," Kavon said. "This is the front, and it's relatively unscathed. Look at how the hull caves in along the middle section—what remains, that is."

"Both sides too," Royce pointed out.

"As you've asked, and I'm just guessing, but I think this bad boy came apart around the center. We'll know more if the stern ever washes up." Kavon had a mild look of excitement, as though he had discovered the answer. "The speedboat! Maybe that guy struck this one, panicked, then accidently ran aground?"

"No. That body is several hours old," Adam said.

"And the markings on O'Mara's speedboat aren't consistent with this kind of crash," Royce added.

"Besides. It almost looks like something grabbed this thing and squeezed, judging by the way these sides are caved in. And what the hell are these?" Adam pointed to a couple of perfectly shaped holes along the underside. The edges were jagged and caved inward.

"Looks like somebody tried to drive a stake through it," Silvia replied. "Maybe it hit something on the seafloor after it sank."

Royce stepped around her, intentionally making his upcoming exchange with the Lieutenant front and center.

"Lieutenant, obviously it's up to the *Chief*, but I'd like to hear your opinion. I think it's important that we close the beaches temporarily, and suspend all boat activity until we figure out what's going on. We've had three boat incidents, one of them a large yacht. I'm having a hard time believing this to be a coincidence."

Adam nodded.

"The problem would be explaining it to the public," he said. "We don't have any suggestions as to what might be causing this. Sharks don't attack boats like this. Though something did tear up that girl..."

"And there's still that missing water skier," Royce pointed out.

"But what could be doing all of this?" Adam said.

"This is all speculation," Silvia said. "We have nothing to go on. We don't even know that there's a person missing. There's been nobody reported missing other than Ms. Lang. And I can't think of anything out there that can do this kind of damage."

"There's that whale that swims around," Kavon said. All three officers looked at him.

"Whale?"

"The sperm whale Sly. You know of him. Everyone's seen him one time or another," Kavon said.

Adam shook his head. "It doesn't add up. Whales don't devour people, nor do they go out of their way to attack boats."

"Ahab might disagree," Royce quipped.

"Well, Sly's no albino, and he's not in battle with whaling ships," Silvia said. "He's fairly docile, from what I know. And it's a bit of a stretch to put all of this on him."

"I agree with you there," Adam said. "But I think we do have grounds to close the beaches and suspend boating activity. At least for a day."

Damn you, Royce.

"I'll have to run it by the Mayor," Silvia said reluctantly.

"You can do that right now," Adam said, pointing up along the beach to the left of the dock. Silvia looked and saw JoEllen's vehicle. She didn't bother hiding her frustration. She was on the spot now. It was bad enough that the department's confidence in her had bottomed out. If she didn't do anything here, it'd be much worse. She needed the respect of her team. The problem was earning it seemed impossible.

She stepped off the dock and approached the Mayor, who was already talking with several reporters.

"Yes, please rest assured that Chief Remar is on top of the situation. Also, let me assure you that the beaches will remain open. From what we know, this was just a simple accident. It's a terrible thing, and our hearts go out to the victim's family. But regarding a possible danger, we believe there is none. I'll let you know once the investigation is concluded."

Silvia wanted to scream. She knew exactly what JoEllen was doing. She was ending the argument before it even began. She glanced back, seeing Royce's 'So what, go in there!' expression. Maybe he was actually trying to get her fired. He probably wouldn't mind it. Adam? Hard for her to tell what he thought, but judging by his resignation letter, he wasn't the most impressed with her either, though his personality was much more respectful. He had been offered the position before it was open for hire, but he turned it down, not wanting to tie himself to this department.

After answering a few more questions, JoEllen thanked the reporter, then approached Silvia.

"Chief. Sorry we have to see each other again under such circumstances."

"Mayor. I think we've got a problem," Silvia said straightforwardly. "My officers and I suspect there's a danger in these waters. The decision to not close the beaches may not be a wise one. We've got four people confirmed deceased, one of those has never been recovered, and a possible fifth person missing. God knows what else is going on that we aren't aware of yet."

"Chief, you understand the damage that would cause economically?" JoEllen said.

"Believe me, I don't say this lightly. But we suspect there might be something out there causing this. We can get in touch with the Coast Guard and ask for a sweep of the area. They can map the whole seafloor around Maxwell Island in a day."

"You seriously think that's necessary?" JoEllen said. "What do you have to go on?"

The Chief sighed. "Nothing. Just a string of incidents, each containing its own bizarre set of clues. None of which make much sense."

"Yet you want to shut down our major tourist attractions?"

"Mayor, you've got to admit there is a pattern," Silvia replied. "We need to call in all vessels before we find another one in pieces."

"Bring in—" JoEllen stopped to prevent herself from raising her voice. She inhaled, relaxed, then spoke gently, but firmly. "You realize we'd have a riot on our hands if we did that? The fishing industry is struggling this year as it is. And if we get Coast Guard ships out here, you don't think that reporters won't plaster stories all over the internet. Doesn't inspire confidence in consumer spending. We've already lost several hotel sales, as well as sales for the fireworks festival."

Silvia nodded. The Mayor only reinforced her concerns. Still, they had multiple deceased persons in less than a day. The stress was taking its toll on her physically. With Marsh promising the local news that the beaches would remain open, that put the spotlight directly on the Chief. Any economic consequences would be put on her shoulders. Already, she felt like its weight was crushing her. The backlash would last months, especially if the investigation came up with nothing, as she suspected it would. And how would she present this to the Coast Guard? *"Hey, we might have a sea monster in our waters. Can you confirm?"*

"Can the fireworks festival be delayed, possibly?"

"No," JoEllen answered. "They're in the process of getting everything set up. These are big boats that they shoot this stuff from. I've gotten word that six-thousand people might be coming in tomorrow night alone. And that won't come close to what we'll have on the 3rd, and especially the 4th. We're talking over a million dollars of revenue for them, and probably an equivalent of that in local business those people will bring here."

"Shit," Silvia muttered. She wanted to bang her head against the wall.

"Have your divers found anything other than wreckage?"

"No."

"Well, they were probably just accidents, then," JoEllen said. "And come on, think of it. Look at that out there." She pointed to a large fishing trawler in the distance, traveling to the east. From where they stood, it looked no bigger than a bean. Considering that it was nearly a mile away, it had to be at least a hundred feet long. "You really think ships like that are in danger? I'm pretty sure there's no Kraken out there about to get them."

Silvia faked a laugh, though none of this was funny to her. However, it did seem ridiculous to call in the boats, especially the larger ones.

"I want patrols out on the shores," she said. "I'll tell the public it's just routine."

"That's fine," JoEllen said. Her posture became much more casual. Her hands came out from behind her back, her eyes fading out from that stern, narrow gaze. Suddenly, she had the demeanor of someone simply hanging out with one of her girlfriends. "You're doing good, Silvia. I know it's been a stressful day for you."

"Hasn't been fun, that's for sure."

"But that's why I chose you for the job. Because I trust you to take everything into consideration. Not a stupid 'ends justifies the means' approach. You're willing to take our residents into consideration with everything you do."

The ego boost had worked in the past, but didn't do much this time. Usually, all her issues were just a matter of shifting manpower and mandating overtime. Now, it felt like there were bad consequences no matter what she did. And judging by the glaring look on Sergeant Boyer's face, it was clear she had chosen the path of least resistance.

Royce turned and started walking inland, disgusted with the conversation he had just witnessed. He glanced back to his friend, Adam.

"You're wise to be getting out of here," he said. Adam shook his head slightly, making sure not to be too obvious. He felt a small degree of pity for the Sergeant. The only reason he was here was because his wife got a transfer. Not that he didn't enjoy the scenery, or the laid back nature of the job, but it was hard to watch the department go from a confident leader like Chief Engler to Remar. Belanger would've fought JoEllen on this issue. And Silvia had started so well in that conversation—he nearly gained a new respect for her, until she buckled and collapsed at the slightest pressure.

Silvia noticed him walking away as well. Normally, she'd brush it off as him being a jerk, but now she wondered if he was right.

JoEllen had walked off to speak with another reporter. The Chief could hear her spreading word for the fireworks show, letting everyone know to buy tickets and be at the south beach at 7:00 tomorrow night. It was by far the largest beach with enough room to hold over ten thousand people across.

Silvia saw the flashing lights from the ambulance as it drove off the beach and onto the road. Its next stop would be the coroner's office.

It was time to inform Mr. Lang that his daughter had died.

CHAPTER 15

Not since High School did Martha Cornett feel any apprehension about dissecting a specimen. However, the sudden, unexpected jolt from the strange eel had left an impression. The muscles in her arm, particularly her right, were still sore from the attack, and the adrenaline rush that came with it had depleted her energy.

She and Andy completed their X-ray scans of the specimen, getting a complete layout of its skeletal structure. Martha wished she had an MRI machine for better images, as she *really* wanted to get a look at the insides. Despite the loss of physical energy, her mind was still racing. She had found a new species, which was an increasingly rare feat, even with present technology.

After putting the specimen on ice, she and Andy proceeded to start an autopsy on the second goblin shark. Originally, she intended to preserve its corpse, but considering it had likely ingested one of the eels, she didn't want to risk a second specimen deteriorating further.

The gamble paid off. The goblin shark had also eaten one of the eels. In separating it from the shark's stomach contents, she quickly realized this one did not fare as well as its brethren. As opposed to the other, which had been swallowed whole, this one had been completely ravaged in the jaws before being ingested. Some of the goblin's teeth were even still lodged in its back and side, the stomach and torso completely torn open, exposing its many innards.

Both scientists quickly concluded that it must've had just enough life in it to zap the shark from the inside before it died.

Andy snapped several pictures as his wife extracted the specimen.

"Hey, don't forget to pose!"

"You're obnoxious," she replied.

"Come on! Do it for me. Look sexy!" Andy joked. He heard an exaggerated sigh through his wife's facemask before she turned to face him. In her hands was the gutted eel, ready to have its organs extracted and preserved. "Oh yeah! Love it, girl! You rock those scrubs and guts!"

"Thanks," she replied. "Maybe I'll end up in a magazine."

"Hell, babe! Let's get your bikini out, take the other specimen to the beach, and I guarantee we'll make it happen! Science articles will become popular again, that's for damn sure."

"Glad to know your brain's on the science," Martha chuckled. She finished a few measurements of the shark and eel, then placed the latter in a large glass container. It was exactly the same size as the other, except with mass lost due to its violent encounter. She checked the shark's mouth and throat.

"It zapped him while it was being torn apart," she said. "If I had to venture a guess, I think it started a seizure, which accidentally caused the shark to clench tighter and convulse."

"Oh," Andy said, wincing. "And with the thing still in its mouth. No wonder it looks like it had a buzz-saw taken to it."

"The injuries probably made it stop shocking. The shark recovered, swallowed it, only to get one last zap from the inside. Then struggled with its buddy for some time before getting scooped up by fishermen."

"Ladies and gents, I present to you *Sherlock Holmes of Marine Biology!*" Andy announced.

"You're all about stroking my ego today, aren't you?" she replied.

"Hey, it works better than flowers and chardonnay. If you know what I mean," he replied, winking.

"It's never a mystery what you mean," she said. "First, I need your help carting our shark off, so I can start dissecting the specimen."

"You want to do that *now?*" Andy said. "Don't you want to take a break? You've been at it all day, it seems."

"I want to get records of their anatomy," she replied. "This stuff might even end up in books that'll be taught in graduate schools."

"You're like a kid with a new toy," Andy said. "But what about the buoys?"

"We'll keep an eye on them. But this is more important. We know now that two of these things exist. It's highly possible that they travel in a pack, and if so, their combined electrical charges would account for the temperature spikes we've been detecting. Considering that the goblin sharks were probably swimming in unison, they were probably following this pack until they tried to have a couple of them for lunch."

"That makes sense in theory," Andy said. "But what about Sly? You really think he'd back off from a swarm of these eels? Assuming you're right."

"If they're letting off all kinds of electrical charges, then it's possible," Martha said.

"I mean, it's possible, and I still know too little about these things to make guesses. All I can do is relate to current species that conduct electricity. Electric rays. Electric eels in South America. Yeah, they can shock people, but I don't think they're shooting off electrical charges every time they swim upstream. For that to be happening, these things must be carrying an electrical charge that they can't contain. Like an overloaded battery. And wouldn't their discharges affect the others in the pack?"

"Hmm..." Martha was lost in a world of thought. It didn't take long for her theory to get shot down. Andy was right, however. Freshwater electric eels frequently shock *themselves* as much as anything else. They often would shock other electric eels by accident. So, if a pack of these creatures was traveling in unison, emitting all kinds of electrical charges, they'd likely be zapping each other.

"Hence, the reason I want to get a look at the inside of this bad boy," Martha finished her thought out loud. "I can run a few tests. Maybe put a little current through this guy. Wouldn't be the same as if he was alive, but it might give me clues."

"Why? To see if electricity can harm his tissue?"

"Precisely. All kinds of species adapt to remarkable environments and conditions. Hence, fish that live in the Mariana Trench don't get crushed—because they don't have air sacks like fish that live above. That's why fish that live in darkness produce lights. There's all kinds of neat shit out there. I'm not willing to put it past nature to produce a creature that can withstand electrical charges."

Andy leaned against the wall and smiled at her.

"You know, you're so hot when you talk marine science."

Martha rolled her eyes. "Here we go again." She giggled. Despite her reactions, she enjoyed the random flirting attempts, even the obnoxious ones.

"Seriously, though. You want to do this today? You've been at it for hours. You're not an OR doctor giving emergency surgery. Why don't you take a break? Take your images and look them over with a nice hot cup of coffee. And probably inform the institution of what we've found before doing anything more."

"Not yet on that," she answered. "Forgive me for having a little ego, but I want everything here to be from me as possible."

"Damn! I don't get a little credit?" Andy said. Martha cringed. Sometimes her ambitions led to moments of selfishness. She often inadvertently neglected to credit Andy for his expertise and assistance. Though not a Ph. D, he knew the ocean extremely well, and often challenged her hypotheses and theories. Hell, he did that today by pointing out a fallacy in her theory of an eel pack.

She turned around and leaned back against the table, then graced him with a smile.

"You know I love you, right?" It was her way of apologizing.

Andy moved in and planted a kiss on her lips. It was his way of forgiving, if he was even offended in the first place.

"Babe," she giggled between kisses. "I'm covered in shark guts."

"Mmm. I guess I have a new fetish," he joked.

"Eww," she pushed him away playfully.

"You know, I'm also an expert of conducting electricity," he joked. "Two objects...moving against each other..."

The stud was not gonna give up. Then again, Martha's 'annoyances' were a façade. In reality, she loved his attempts at wooing her.

"I'll make you a deal: help me take these images and complete an initial inspection of this eel. I'm gonna have to separate its organs anyway. Then, I'm gonna have to take a shower—I could use a little help with that." She smiled, though not as enthusiastically as her husband.

"Where'd I put that damn camera?"

CHAPTER 16

As the afternoon pressed on, roughly half the crowds had quelled their anxieties and returned to the water. North Beach, however, was nearly vacant, especially near the eastern corner where the body appeared. Even if people weren't afraid of something potentially lurking in the waters, the thought of swimming in an area where a body had been rotting for God knows how long did not sit well.

Silvia sank in the cockpit of her patrol boat and watched the long stretch of sand, unobscured by the usual blur of moving bodies. Some of the businesses in this sector had thrown in the towel and closed up for the day. Surely, JoEllen would hear about this. The only area on the northside with a hint of activity was Wesco Peak, where parents played with their young children.

Silvia patrolled to the west, listening to the giggles of toddlers and preschool aged kids splashing with their siblings and parents. Such laughter could brighten anyone's day, even Silvia's.

Patrolling the waters served two purposes for her. Right now, she needed a little peace and quiet. It was never an easy thing telling somebody a beloved family member had passed away. It was doubly hard when it was somebody's kid. Though she tried to keep the details to a minimum, Mr. Lang discovered the horrific extent his daughter had been disfigured. Had it not been for the tattoo he so adamantly hated, it would've been impossible to know it was her. Seeing such a hardened man crumble with such sadness haunted her mind. She had to make such appearances in the past, usually for fatal car accidents, and it was never easy.

She checked her phone. The medical examiner should be contacting her any minute to provide his analysis on Anne Lang's cause of death.

Which was the second reason she was out. Silvia's mind was in conflict. On the one hand, it seemed implausible that a living thing could be causing all these problems. However, she did look at that body, and couldn't deny how everything below the waist had been torn away. She'd seen a few propeller accidents, and it's unlikely the uppermost part of Anne's body would've gotten away clean from the blades. All she could think of was a shark. Regardless, it generated a feeling of anxiety…and guilt…for allowing people to swim despite a possible danger.

Her phone chimed. It was Brandon Weber.

Hey! Completed my examination of O'Mara's speedboat. Yes. Burn marks are same as yacht underside. Reminiscent of lightning strike.

It chimed again.

Not saying that's what it is, but definitely a burn. Not a friction burn from grazing rocks. No explanation at this time until I can get a look at the area.

Another text came through, with Sergeant Boyer's name over it.

Thanks. We'll keep in touch.

Something about seeing his name irritated Silvia. Not a distain for the guy himself, but for how the community saw him. Nobody consulted specifically with Royce when Chief Engler was in charge. Why? Because they were confident in him. And now, that's how they saw Royce, instead of her.

She typed in a quick response.

Noted. Thank you. We'll talk soon.

Next, she got onto her contacts and searched for Royce's number, then sent a call. It rang twice before he answered.

"Yeah?"

"Royce, really quick before you get out for the day: have you completed the report on the Vic Pally case?"

"Had it done around 2:00. I printed it out and put it in your mailbox. The O'Mara, yacht, and northeast beach reports are all filled out too. Just the way you like it. I would've become a novelist if I knew I'd be doing so much writing."

It was the closest he'd come to verbalizing his thoughts on Silvia being an administrator rather than a cop. To her face, at least. However, he was more clearly irritated with her phone call than usual. It suddenly hit her that she'd been out for a while. She checked her watch. 4:00.

Silvia had completely lost track of time, and she had just phoned Royce when he was off the clock—something he absolutely *hated.* On top of it all, she did it to ask about a report that he saw as nothing but catering to JoEllen's special interests.

"Appreciate it, Royce. See you in the morning."

"Yep." He hung up. Yeah, he was pissed. Then again, when was he not pissed at her? Except, Silvia struggled to get used to his attitude, probably because it affected the rest of the officers in the department.

"Whatever, dude. I'm the Chief, you're not." *Interesting how I can't say that to his face.*

She drove her boat around the northwest corner of the island and proceeded south. As she moved along the west beach, she saw a little bit of increased activity. People splashed in the shallows, though hardly anyone branched out more than belly-deep. A few of them were nice enough to wave at her. She put on a smile and waved back. Luckily, they wouldn't be able to see the back brace from this distance.

Her window of opportunity to make a pain management appointment was closed now. She would have to try again at 8:00. On top of that, she'd have to figure out when she could squeeze in time to even get it done. What bothered her was the hardened rule she created of no time off during the busy season. Yeah, this was medical, but to everyone she met who never experienced spinal pain, it didn't seem like a big deal. They always assumed it was like muscular pain, or joint pain. If Silvia had a dollar for every time somebody tried to relate by saying "Yeah, I messed up my knee," she'd no longer need this job. Yeah, they meant well, but they missed the point. Knee pain wasn't nearly as debilitating as a degenerated lower disc, especially with arthritis added to the mix. It affected drive, focus, especially attitude. She was always quick to get angry and bitter, and all the little problems she saw in others were magnified.

And all she could think of right now was how everyone looked to Royce for guidance and not her.

She focused on the water and the sunny sky. Its calming effect managed to help a little. Before transferring to Maxwell Island, the thought of living on an island seemed like an impossible feat. Despite despising the reasons for coming here, she couldn't deny how lucky she was to be living in a beautiful community. A cool breeze swept over her. She watched the little swells roll away from her portside toward the beaches.

Further to the south, the crowds were a little bigger. Still smaller than average, though. Those people were not who she was concerned about at the moment. Her gaze panned right to the sailboats and kayaks scattered across the ocean. So far, there didn't appear to be anything wrong. The jet skiers were clearly the least anxious of the crowds. They kicked up huge jets of water, zigzagging in tight arches as though trying to impress a bench full of judges.

She heard a scream to her right. Silvia turned and saw the big splash, water skis flinging upward. The speedboat made a sharp turn, then circled back. One of the people on deck gazed over the side.

"Terrie? Terrie? Where are you?!"

Nobody popped back up.

Oh, God! Silvia cut the wheel and gunned the throttle. The person was still nowhere to be seen. Suddenly, the ocean didn't feel so calming and peaceful anymore. It was now the architect of her nightmares. Already, she could hear Royce's voice in her mind.

"You've should've fought harder to close the beaches!"

She flashed the lights and pulled up near the speedboat. She raced back onto the main deck and looked into the water. However, she wasn't just looking for a person; she was looking for a mass. If George O'Mara's monster was real, then it was probably here. Her hand rested on her pistol grip, ready to draw and fire at anything that rose to attack.

A splash erupted between the two boats. Silvia gasped, her gun half-drawn. The two girls in the speedboat broke out in laughter at his stunt.

"Whoa!" the skier yelled triumphantly. "Went all the way to the bottom! It's gorgeous down there!" He realized his friends on the boat were looking past him. He turned around and saw the Chief standing there. "Hey, Officer! Wanna take a turn?"

Silvia breathed a sigh of relief, then let a chuckle slip through.

"I'm good, thanks. Just don't scare me like that," she replied. She turned off the flashers.

"Is everything okay, Officer?" The girl in the back seat raised her hand. "I heard they found a body earlier today. Are there sharks or something in these waters? We were told it was safe, but I've seen more police boats than usual today. Should we head in?"

Silvia hesitated before answering. She wasn't sure what the right answer was. Either tell them no, and potentially start a panic and hurt the island economy, or say yes and run a gamble with their lives, based on a seemingly connected series of boat accidents.

"No, it's perfectly fine," she said, gracing them with a warm smile. "Go on, and have fun. I just got worried he might've gotten hurt, was all."

"See Mike, quit with the stunts," the girl at the helm said sarcastically.

"Thanks, Officer. God bless," the skier, Mike, said.

Silvia cut the wheel to port and steered closer to the beach. Of course, she couldn't help but wonder what the relationship between those three were. Girlfriend and sister? Two sisters?

Silvia laughed at what her mind settled on. *Two very open-minded chicks. How do those dudes do it?*

Up ahead, she saw another police boat. It was Adam. The Lieutenant's shift didn't end until 5:00, and like her, he wanted to spend the rest of his day keeping an eye on the activities in the water.

He was a thousand feet up ahead, slowly drifting in her direction. All of a sudden, he made a sudden turn to port and sped up near a small motorboat. From what she could see, there didn't seem to be anything wrong. However, she could hear commotion. There was a woman and a child on the boat, and the child sounded upset.

Again, Silvia's mind went into overdrive.

Did they see something? Should I call everyone in?

She throttled the boat and quickly crossed the distance, slowing to a drift behind Adam's boat. He was leaning over the side rail to speak to the mom and child. The kid was five years old at most. He had tears rolling down his face. His mom looked upset too, but not from fear, but from guilt.

"I'm so sorry," she said to Adam. Suddenly, it made sense. The *kid* flagged Adam down, not the mom.

"It's okay," he said, smiling gracefully. He leaned on his elbows on the rail to focus on the little guy. "Hey, little man? Why the wet face?"

"I'm scared," the boy mumbled.

"You're scared? What's there to be scared of?"

"I heard somebody say there's a monster in the lake," he said. Adam resisted the urge to laugh at the kid referring to the ocean as a lake.

"A monster?!" he said enthusiastically. He looked around. "I don't see any monsters."

The kid's expression changed.

"Well, it's an underwater monster. You can't see it."

"Oh, right, I forgot," Adam said.

Silvia found a moment to chime in. "Hey, kiddo. What's your name?"

"Billy."

"Well, Billy, you know who else goes underwater?" The boy shook his head. Silvia pointed at Adam. "*He* does!"

Adam pulled his smartphone out and put a photo on his screen taken during a hundred-foot dive. He reached across and handed it to the boy, who looked at it with amazement.

"See this? I dive all the time. I was actually in the water today, and I didn't see any monsters. Lots of fish! But no monsters."

The boy watched the image, mesmerized by the blue ocean, kelp, and fish that he thought only existed in cartoons.

"Cool," he said. The tears were gone now, and the sun was already drying up his face. He handed the phone back to Adam.

"Believe me, buddy, there is nothing to be scared of," Adam said. "I'm always watching the water to make sure. That nice lady right there is our Chief. If she thought anything was really wrong, she and I would do anything to make sure you were all safe."

The boy glanced over to Silvia, then smiled.

"Okay!"

"Alright. You behave now," Adam said.

"Enjoy your vacation," Silvia added. The boy took a seat, while his visibly relieved mother leaned over to the two officers and mouthed "Thank you so much!" before taking to the helm. She steered away to the north where the waters were quieter.

Silvia chuckled at Adam. "She probably won't be thanking you after a month. You probably just started a new obsession!"

"Hey, diving's a great sport. I still think you should get into it," he replied.

"I wish," she said.

"You always say that when people suggest new stuff for you."

Silvia shrugged. He wasn't wrong. "I guess I'm afraid to try new things."

"Don't let life get you down," Adam replied.

Silvia nodded. Best not to respond, as anything she'd say would be negative. She wasn't sure how to be positive when she was in pain all day, and second guessing literally every physical movement she made. Best thing to do was to change the subject.

"So, I wanted to congratulate you on your new job," she said.

"Oh! Thank you, Chief," he said.

"It'll definitely be a change of scenery."

"Yeah. It'll be much hotter with a lot more farmland. I won't lie though; I will miss this. I see myself doing that for ten or fifteen years, then coming back to something like this if it ever opens up."

"Gosh, you'd be at retirement age by then," she said. They were roughly the same age. In fifteen years, she would likely retire. At least she had that going for her.

"I like working," Adam said. "I have a lot of goals I want to pursue. It's gonna be a tough job, and it'll definitely age me, but I'm eager to do it. Human trafficking was one of the key things that drove me to pursue law enforcement."

"That's great, Adam. I'll make sure we make time to throw you a goodbye party. And hey, since I'll probably be retiring around that same time, hit me up if you're thinking about coming back. If you're still interested in working at that age, you'd make a great Chief for this place."

"Thanks, Chief," he replied. "Don't sell yourself too short, though." He was speaking as a friend now, rather than as a fellow officer. He was aware of her ambitions, and knew of her injuries, which was why he had a little more sympathy toward her than the rest of the department. She knew of her attitude toward this job. Yeah, she appreciated it, but she didn't see it as anything dauntless. It was a pretty easy location, with the summer being the only busy season. And even that, in comparison to many departments, was laid back.

"You have any advice for me?" she asked. She was afraid to hear the answer. He thought for a moment, then looked her in the eye.

"Don't feel like you have to micromanage," he said. "Trust your officers to do their jobs. Also, don't be afraid to stand up and fight for what you know is right. Just because the Mayor wants something, doesn't mean you have to follow through exactly. Especially if you suspect there to be a danger to the public."

Silvia looked into the water.

"You think there's a danger now?"

Adam shrugged. "You know? That's a really tricky one, even for me. None of these accidents add up, and the explanations we've come up with are...how do I put it? To quote *Lethal Weapon*, they're "Thin. Very Thin.""

"Anorexic," Silvia added. They shared a laugh.

"All I can suggest is go with your gut," Adam concluded. "But if you *know* there's a danger, you fight to protect the people from it. Don't let JoEllen's ambitions cost lives. She's a nice person, but she's granting too many favors to these big companies. She feels she owes them something, probably because they backed her up when nobody else even knew who she was. And everyone knows she plans to run for governor in the future, and she'll definitely need the backing of these people."

Silvia nodded.

"Thanks, Adam."

"No problem."

She was just starting to cut the wheel when their radios crackled.

"Dispatch to any available unit, we have a situation at the General Hospital, Emergency Department. They're reporting a disorderly visitor trying to gain access to a patient's room, and refuses to leave."

Silvia glanced back at Adam.

"Right as I thought the craziness was winding down..."

CHAPTER 17

It was January 6th when Timothy Rominski and his fiancé made their reservation at the Windle Beachfront Resort, house number two on Maxwell Island. It was to be their last vacation together as an unmarried couple. The wedding was to take place in September, on the exact anniversary to the day they first met.

At that time, Tim had just started his senior year of college. Most of his requirements had been fulfilled, leaving a handful of electives to finish up. Naturally, he wanted easy classes to wrap up his four years and get the hell out. He always had a minor interest in culinary school. He was never much of a cook, but he was good with money, and had enough self-awareness to know he didn't want to boil every meal or order takeout every night. So, he figured, 'what the hell?' and signed up.

Initially, he had regretted his decision. The class had little to do with cooking, and more to do with terminology. He spent his initial hours salivating over the thought of takeout pasta, seafood, and burgers that he desperately wanted to avoid.

Then he noticed the pretty girl that sat next to him every single day. She was a brunette, loved to wear denim—which scored a point in his mind as he grew up around horses and cows, and something about the cowgirl attire was an instant winner for him. Even without it, though, she was more gorgeous than anyone in the room, and her flamboyant personality only added to that. She told better jokes than most of his buddies, and always seemed to have a quip on hand.

Normally, he had no reservations about getting to know a pretty girl, but this time, even asking her name seemed daunting. Eventually, he did. Rachel Hollins. She asked him his. A good sign. It was her senior year. Unlike him, she had a vast interest in culinary school. Thank goodness, because she was able to tutor him through the class. It didn't take long for him to know he wasn't cut out for the world of cooking. Even basically. Yet, the class had served its purpose in a way. He wouldn't have to cook his meals, not when the love of his life could do it for him.

He graduated that year and started his career as an account manager for, ironically, a food distributer. However, while not good with food, he was great with people, and knew how to sell his product. Meanwhile, Rachel flew through her classes, completing the four-year program in only three. It was a passion, and unlike most other students, it was not a chore for her to get through the program.

She graduated and immediately landed a job at a high-paying restaurant in Cambridge, Massachusetts. There, she was in charge of a vast menu involving pasta, seafood, beef, chicken, Italian, Greek, and so much more. Despite their busy lives and lavish careers, the two lovers had no problem finding time for each other.

On Christmas Day, he proposed. Less than two weeks later, he surprised her with reservations to Maxwell Island, set for them to arrive on June 30th. One week seemed too short, two weeks felt like too long, plus they needed to reserve some time for the honeymoon later that year. So, Tim settled for something in-between. It would be ten days and eleven nights of sunbathing, waterskiing, bungee jumping, whale watching, and anything else they could think of.

The coming of summer intensified the excitement for vacation. Within a week, they were already packed. Plane tickets were prepared. Already, they were enjoying fantasies of having cocktails together on the flight. Then Wednesday came.

A new distribution center was opening up in Green Bay, Wisconsin. A manager had been hired, trained specifically by Tim, and was all set up for the opening of the store. Then, on Sunday came a phone call. The manager, Brock Wey, had to be rushed to the hospital with symptoms of a high fever. The store was literally about to open that Friday, and the other managers were preoccupied with other staff. The good news was that Brock only had heatstroke and was already improving. The bad news was that he would not be released until Tuesday afternoon.

With no other managers available and the opening already marketed to open on Monday, June 29th, the CEO Mark Zion asked on bended knee for Tim to oversee the opening until Brock could be released. With a promise of a second week's paid vacation and a three-thousand-dollar bonus, Tim reluctantly accepted…after he was able to find a flight that would take him directly to Brunswick Golden Isles. From there, he'd be able to catch a boat to Maxwell Island on Saturday morning, and arrive right as Rachel would be getting out of bed.

She had taken the news with the expected amount of disappointment, but overall had a fairly good attitude about it. They had already made a couple of reservations by phone for breakfast, waterskiing, whale watching, and the spa. Tim's response was simple: "If I can't make it, just go on your own and have fun. I'll still be there to enjoy the rest of the festivities."

Disappointing, but things could be worse. Plus, now they had three grand extra to blow.

The store opening went as planned. As Tim oversaw the operations, he managed to open a few new accounts in the Green Bay area. By the time Brock came back to work, he already had four new clients, all pizzerias. It was a grand opening for a store that promised to bring in much revenue, as long as no other medical emergencies should appear.

By Tuesday afternoon, Brock was fully recovered from his brief setback and was eager to take over. All was looking well…until Tim found out that his stupid flight was being delayed. Having checked out of his hotel by 11:00, he had nothing to do but hang out at cafés until he could finally catch his flight.

By 4:00, he was receiving text photos from Rachel. The sight of the crystal blue waters and white tan beaches made all the inconveniences all the more frustrating. He wanted to be there, damn it!

From what he could gather, the delay was caused by an engine inspection. Surprise inspections like these always took their time. Tim tried not to be pissed off about it; better to get there late and in one piece than leave on time only to see smoke coming out of the wing. As it turned out, issues with the shaft and rotors were reported. A new plane was being flown in, but the flight would not be until 9:00 a.m. Wednesday morning.

"Hey babe, I guess you'll have to get started without me. Maybe I'll manage to get over there before we both grow old," he said in a phone conversation with Rachel.

"I feel strange going out without you," she replied.

"Babe, the stuff's already paid for," Tim said. "The reservations are made. I'm stuck over here whether I like it or not. If you don't do the appointments, then the money's gone to waste."

"Yeah, that's true," she said.

"It's fine, sweetie! Just go ahead without me and enjoy yourself! I'll be there soon, and we'll enjoy the rest together!"

"Okay."

"I'll let you know when my boat's coming in. Hell, with the luck I'm having, I'll probably hit an iceberg on the way there."

"If you get here before 2:30, then you can come to the spa with me!"

"At this point, I'll take anything. As long as I'm on an island with a drink in my hand," Tim said.

"We'll do that all the way through next week, I promise. I'll meet you at the port when you get here."

"Alright, babe. See you when I get there."

All night, Tim had a gut feeling that something was going to go wrong. Maybe it'd be a boat problem, maybe a problem with the beach house, or another delay in the flight. It was all speculation, but it was enough to keep him awake all night.

Nine o-clock arrived, and Tim boarded his flight. To his relief, it departed on time with no complications or further delays. Finally, he was on his way to Maxwell Island.

Two hours and twenty minutes later, the plane landed at Southwest Georgia Regional Airport. What followed was an hour-long drive to the harbor, where Tim would have to wait an additional thirty minutes for a boat. By one in the afternoon, the mainland was behind him. Up ahead was nothing but ocean, and one gorgeous island, where the love of his life waited. After a few miles, he could see it up ahead.

He pulled out his phone and made a phone call. She didn't answer. So, he left a voicemail.

"Hey babe! Guess who's about to make landfall! I'll see you soon!"

The spa wasn't until two-thirty, so he had time. She had been waterskiing and was probably enjoying the beaches in the meantime. Maybe she was showering right now. He sent her a text just to be extra sure she knew he was coming.

The boat docked in the west harbor. She wasn't there.

Hmm. Perhaps she was on her way? He tried calling again. Still, no answer. After twenty minutes, he grew tired of waiting. *Probably taking a nap.* Luckily, a clerk at the harbor was able to get him a shuttle to take him to the Windle Beachfront Resort.

But when he got there, Rachel was nowhere to be found. He was definitely in the right house. Her stuff was everywhere. There was a small beach in front of the house, but she wasn't there either. He tried calling again, without an answer. This time, his voice message was a little stricter. "Where are you?"

For the next hour, he waited at the house.

It was odd now. He had a perfect phone signal, and they both were on the same phone plan, so hers should've worked. Her wallet and cards were there. Her license and swimsuit were the only things that appeared to be missing. At the beach, maybe?

The days of frustration, bad sleep, and anticipation were accumulating into one big storm. Tim had hoped he'd arrive to a nice lunch and possibly a good celebratory time in the bedroom before enjoying the spa and other attractions. But no, he was spending the next hour and a half searching for his fiancée. There was no sign of her near the beaches. And she'd be easy to spot, as the beach areas were not nearly as busy as he expected them to be. Realizing it was already past 2:30, he went to the spa they had booked. The woman at the desk shook her head when asked if Rachel Hollins had checked in.

Now, Tim had gone from irritated to worried. The spa was something Rachel would definitely not miss. His heart was racing. Something was wrong. *Very* wrong!

The next hour was spent going through a series of cafes and diners, again with no sign of her. As he conducted his sweeps, he had gotten word of certain strange events that were occurring around the island. There was talk of an exploded yacht, which didn't concern him too much. Rachel didn't know anyone here, and she wasn't the type to go partying with anyone she didn't know. But then he caught a glimpse of a local news broadcast.

"Police are still investigating the mysterious circumstance of a boat crash that occurred over by Wesco Peak. The boat owner, George O'Mara, was rushed to Maxwell General Hospital with severe injuries. Police have not had an opportunity to question him about the events. So far, they have not found any evidence that anyone else was on the boat with him."

That name—George O'Mara! *Wasn't that the guy who we scheduled to—*

Tim rushed home and dug his receipts out of Rachel's bag.

"No. Don't tell me that was the charter," he prayed as he tore through the various sheets of paper. Finally, he found the familiar red and blue logo of *O'Mara's Boating.*

They had a 7:30 arrangement.

"It's fine, sweetie! Just go ahead without me and enjoy yourself! I'll be there soon, and we'll enjoy the rest together!" he had told her.

The report had already stated that the police and fire department had not found evidence of anyone else being there. Notifying them would not get him anywhere. Tim needed answers, and he couldn't afford to wait for a police investigation to take weeks or even months to get those answers!

Maxwell General Hospital, the reports had said. He would go and speak with this George O'Mara himself!

Tim entered the ER front doors, immediately drawing the attention of the security staff with his stern demeanor and fast pace. The man had entered this building with intent of some sort, and somehow, they knew it wasn't medical.

For the young man at the check-in desk, George O'Mara might as well have been a celebrity. He had turned away cops, reporters, a few curious bystanders, all wanting to know what led to the accident. But other than the Police Sergeant who had come in that morning, this guy took the cake.

"George O'Mara! I need to see him right away," Tim demanded. "What room is he in?"

"Sir, are you related to him?"

"No. He knows where my fiancée is. I need to speak with him asap!"

The officers crowded around him.

"Sir, let's step aside and—"

"Get away from me," Tim said, spinning out from between them and the desk.

"Sir," the desk clerk said. "Please, calm down and let us help you get…"

Tim ignored him and rushed for the double doors, but the electronic locks prevented him from pulling them open. One of the security officers moved around the desk to phone the police, while the others attempted to deter Tim, despite their strangulating rules about no contact. Only if a person presented a threat could he be physically restrained. Tim wasn't there quite yet, but he was close.

Another guard attempted to talk Tim down, but his efforts were wasted. Tim knew the only person that could help was George O'Mara, and he was somewhere behind those double doors. The guard put a hand on the door, a gesture to let Tim know he was a moment away from being physically restrained. Tim calmed for a moment, but only to glance down at the guard's badge that hung from his belt loop. Tim grabbed it, and thrust it to the electronic reader, opening the doors. He shoved the officer back and rushed inside, frightening a couple of nurses and custodial staff who hugged the walls. The guards rushed in after him. Tim was officially a threat now, and they had *carte blanche* to prevent any further action.

Like a team of defensive linemen, they threw themselves over Tim. He thrashed with all of his might, desperate to free himself of their grip.

"Get off of me!"

"Nope, not happening. Cops are on their way. You should've brought your grievances to them first!"

"You don't understand!" Tim shouted.

They put cuffs over his wrists and dragged him into their security office. In ten minutes, an officer radioed that the police were on site.

The doors opened up, and a male and female officer stepped into the office.

"I'm the Chief of Police," the female one said to him. "What's going on? Why are you trying to—"

"That man knows where my fiancée is," Tim said.

"What man?" the male officer asked.

"George O'Mara, the boat owner! My fiancée had scheduled a charter aboard his boat! I can't find her anywhere. I called! I searched the whole island! She's gone! We need to talk to O'Mara and find out what happened!"

"Wait, she was on that boat?" the woman asked.

"Yes!"

The officers looked at each other, each dumbfounded.

Silvia's heart sank for like the hundredth time that day. There was someone else aboard that boat!

"Adam…you sure you didn't see—"

"Nothing," he said. "We ventured out for a few hundred yards, with the boats assisting. We found nothing."

"Nothing? What do you mean?" the suspect asked. He was sweating, his eyes wide. He looked like a man on the verge of a mental breakdown. "What's going on. What happened to my fiancée? What the hell's going on around here?!"

CHAPTER 18

Martha's hair was still damp and stringy. She stared at the ceiling, gradually coming down from the bliss of ecstasy. Lying next to her was her husband, satisfied from the 'lunch break' that he often enjoyed with her.

"I see that smile on your face," she muttered.

"Can you blame me?" he replied.

"Absolutely. Now I'm behind on my work."

"Oh, I'm sure your subconscious was working on it the whole time," he said. He rolled over and kissed her neck.

"Mmm…maybe," she said, smiling at the sensation of his lips.

"Hey, whatever gets you going. Heck, I'll add to your fantasy."

"Oh, Jesus…" Martha had unleashed the goofball.

"Who knows? Those two sharks were probably a couple too. I bet they had their 'couple's time' this morning, went out for breakfast, and were in for a 'shock'!"

Martha shook her head. "That's so bad."

"Hey, for all we know, those eels had to be close together. Maybe it wasn't a pack—maybe they were a couple too! Just on vacation, figured they were tired of the dreary depths and thought they'd see a little sunshine. Then, whoop! They run into some hooligans! The goblin sharks."

Martha rolled her eyes. "I swear, I'm gonna go to my grave asking myself why I married you."

Andy winked, then gave her a peck on the cheek. "I think I gave you a pretty good reason a few minutes ago."

"Maybe."

"Now, back to your eel fantasy…" he continued.

"Alright, you knucklehead!" Martha said, slapping his shoulder.

"Just think of it! You said there might be a swarm of those things, right? Imagine they all got down while swimming in our waters. Maybe in a few months, we'll see a bunch of tadpole-sized electric eels swimming around. Assuming the ones we have are adults."

"Hard to say…" Martha thought about it. Moray eels grew to fifteen feet in some cases. South American electric eels reached eight feet. The specimens were only two, meaning there was room to grow, assuming they were related in any way.

Now, it was on Martha's mind. If there was a school of these creatures, would there possibly be a surge in their population? It was unlikely they'd ever get to return to the Puerto Rico Trench, if that was indeed where they came from.

She got out of bed and threw a robe over herself. Andy watched her leave the room without a word. Had he not known her any better, he'd have worried that he did something to infuriate her.

"I have unleashed the academic," he said to himself. He sighed. *Should've kept my yap shut, or simply went with romantic talk. I was just about warmed up for round two.* "So much for that."

He got up and started getting dressed.

Martha hurried to her office and gathered all of her files on the anatomies of all species of eels, with a focus on the moray and electric. She set up charts as though trying to solve a murder mystery, making sure she had her data on all age ranges. If there was a population of these creatures out there, should they propagate, it may possibly cause problems for other marine species in the area. Trying to get an educated guess on the age of the two specimens would help her determine how long they had before such a thing happened.

Moray eels were usually about a centimeter at birth, referred to as larvae with big teeth. Electric eels were generally four-to-five inches after hatching. If these deep-sea electric eels were anything like the South American species, then they were probably about a year old. Then again, that depended on which species they were more related to. Their basic shape resembled a moray's, except for those freakish teeth, which were larger in proportion.

Martha glanced at the images and notes she had taken of the creature's anatomy. It appeared they had three main electric organs, much like the South American species. There was the main organ on the dorsal side, Hunter's organ, and Sach's organ. Interestingly, the new creature seemed to have several matching characteristics as its two cousins. The reason this was significant in this particular case, was that it allowed her to compare the development stages of the reproductive organs and estimate an age.

She flipped through notes and images of baby eels from both species, all the way to breeding age. Afterwards, she returned to her lab and brought out the carcass of the one she had autopsied.

If she had to venture a guess, it had both male and female parts. Hermaphrodites, like ribbon morays. However, with this creature now on the lab table in front of her, she noticed something that made her heart start beating rapidly. These sexual organs were grossly underdeveloped. Not even to the point that it was a youth; this creature had only recently been born.

She heard Andy come through the door.

"Looking at his junk? I ought to be offended," he joked. She didn't laugh. "You okay?"

"I, uh, yeah!" she muttered. "I just, uh…" She couldn't speak, as her mind was grasping the possibility of what she might've just uncovered.

"Did it shock you again?" Andy asked, half joking. She scoffed.

Not in the way you're thinking.

"I think we might have a baby right here," she said.

"Well, that's not too surprising," Andy replied. "I mean, morays grow up to fifteen feet. It probably has a ways to go before it reaches full maturity."

"No! I mean, I think this thing is a newborn!" she said. "The sexual organs are almost nonexistent. The eggs are microscopic, reminiscent of newborn females from most species. This thing won't be ready to breed for years. Many years."

"You're telling me this thing just hatched?" Andy said. He wanted to smile, thinking she was playing a joke on him. Martha nodded. "A three-foot long newborn, born in a litter?"

"I'm suspecting live birth," she said.

"So, if this thing was an adult—at three feet, let's just say—how big would those eggs be?" Andy said.

"Probably a little bigger than the head of a match," Martha replied.

"That's still pretty small compared to this thing," Andy replied. "If this thing was born from an egg, then its mother would have to be…" He tried to do the math in his head, which quickly proved too much, "…freaking huge! If it was swimming around here, somebody would probably have seen it."

Martha found a chair and sunk into it.

"There was a yacht explosion last night," she said.

"Yeah? So?"

"Say if there was a giant eel like this one here, would it produce a charge power enough to…erupt a full gas tank?"

Andy started to grin, then froze as though paralyzed. For several seconds, he stared at the wall, considering that possibility. If a newborn was capable of producing enough of a charge to nearly kill a shark and knock down a full-grown adult human, a giant one would practically be shooting lightning as though it was Zeus himself. Such discharges would cause dramatic elevations in ocean temperatures, such as the ones picked up by their buoys.

"If there's a big one out there, where the hell is it?"

CHAPTER 19

It was a few minutes after 7:00, and the three crewmen of the *Underwater Kingdom* were beginning to express their desire to call it a night. The day had started off as normal as every other trip. They had made a few passes along the northern banks and found a couple of schools of mackerel. Their numbers were fewer than usual, but it wasn't anything that they hadn't seen before.

Around midday, Captain Brock Giler decided to turn the ship west, thinking the schools had traveled closer to the mainland. Interestingly enough, the waters were nearly vacant over here. Aside from a few small blips on the sonar screen, it was as if all the fish had simply disappeared from the region.

Brock steered the vessel further southwest, where they found some Atlantic cod, then traveled north again as the southern waters were getting cluttered with other fishing trawlers. Usually, by midafternoon, they had enough catch to pay for the whole week. This time, however, he was barely going to cover the overhead. Off days weren't uncommon, much like any other industry, but Brock wasn't going to stand for it. In twenty years, he never came in with less than four-thousand pounds of fish, and today wasn't going to be the day. By 6:00, he was at three thousand.

"They're out here somewhere," he told himself. He liked a good challenge. Unfortunately, it wasn't just the fish that were presenting it. The crew didn't share his ambition. They worked hard and desired a great bounty, but a single off day wasn't going to bruise their egos.

Brock watched the men work as he guided the *Underwater Kingdom* northeast. Just one more pass before calling it quits. There were a few blips over here. Not as many as he liked, but maybe—just maybe, enough to close the gap and make a little profit for the day.

The fish were deeper here for some reason. Brock wasn't the biggest fan of bottom trawling, as it carried more risk to the nets as well as tore up the seabed. But after the long day he'd had, he was ready for anything.

The men readied the nets. There was Carl, slow in mind, but fast with his hands, and so strong, he could wrestle an eight-hundred pound tuna until it suffocated. Standing across from him was Miko, not quite as muscular, but still more than capable of handling any fish that came his way. Plus, he was fast with the wits. Brock's only complaint regarding him was that he was aware of it, and always felt like he needed to make quips regarding every single situation. Or maybe it was because the third crewman, Hamed, had an annoying high-pitched laugh, and he found practically every single joke funny.

But even he wasn't laughing now. Hamed's expression was as tired as the other two as they lifted the nets with the pulleys.

With only a few other blips on the sonar, Brock knew that the numbers were improving. He began to circle the ship back, while grabbing a two-way radio to instruct the men.

"Alright, boys, we're about to make our pass. I'll let you know when to drop the nets." He saw Carl give him a thumbs up. Their lips were moving, their expressions still a bit sour. They weren't too pleased with him at the moment.

Screw it. They had become wealthier than any other crew on Maxwell Island, as well as most that he knew on the Georgia Coast. And it was all because of him and his knowledge of the waters, local and distant. *So, let them complain. Yeah, I see your lips moving, those eyes glancing up my way, Miko. Funny, you just bought yourself a six-burner grill recently. Oh, and there was that jetboat that you paid IN CASH!*

"Wouldn't have gotten that if not for me," he finished the thought out loud. As he hooked to the west, he saw a ship coming in from the north. He recognized the big black pirate flag waving from the bridge deck. The *Red Machete.*

They were out much later than usual as well. Brock wondered if they were having similar luck. On the wall to his left, right beside a Kennedy Summers calendar, was the radio.

"*Underwater Kingdom* to *Toy Boat*...err, excuse me, *Red Machete.* What's going on, Captain Bradley?" He chuckled at the jab in the few moments before the reply.

"*Oh, Toy Boat, is it? Compared to that floating can of Chef Boyardee you're riding on?*"

"Hey! We only use it for bait," Brock retorted. Bradley laughed through the speaker.

"What's going on with you guys? Having similar luck as us?"

"That's what I was gonna ask you," Brock said. "We went about ten miles west before we caught anything substantial. We're gonna make one more pass here before calling it quits."

"Must be an off day for all of us. Had a decent morning, but as the day went on, it seemed like all the fish just vacated. Had to go thirty miles north before we found a good school," Sean Bradley said.

"Thirty miles?! Jesus," Brock said. "Well, at least I know it's not just me. You guys heading in?"

"Yeah. Crew's tired. I'm tired. At least tomorrow should be better. We'll probably head for the same spot tomorrow, rather than jerking around out here."

"Don't be surprised if you see me out there," Brock said. He placed the speaker down then completed the circle. They were now lined up for the pass. The blips were all in the same place, hardly moving at all. He snatched up the two-way radio. "Alright guys, put those nets down. Let's do this."

The nets hit the water, their weights dragging them a hundred feet down to the bottom. It scraped across the seabed, stirring silt into soupy clouds as it captured the creatures below. Brock watched the sonar during the entire pass. To his surprise, hardly any of the dots were making any attempt at escape. It was as though they had accepted their fate and were letting the net sweep them up.

Fine by me.

They passed for fifteen-hundred feet before lifting the nets. Typically, they'd see frantic fish struggling like flies caught in a spider's web, slapping each other with their tails, and trying to wiggle free. But out of this group, there were possibly a few lively ones, but otherwise, the nets looked like a big blue ball of fish heads and tails.

Brock slowed the boat to a stop and stepped out onto the fly deck to get a better look. There were several more fish than he expected, which excited him at first, until he realized at least half of them weren't moving.

The crew brought the starboard net around to the tank and unloaded it, using hoses and pumps to sort them out. The lively ones flopped about, while others lay on their sides, dying or dead.

"What the hell happened here?" Brock said.

"I have no idea, Cap," Carl said. He knelt over to inspect one of the dying ones, then jumped back as soon as his fingers touched it. "Christ alive!" he yelped, shaking his hand.

"You alright?" Miko asked.

"Son of a bitch shocked me," Carl said.

"Shocked you?"

"Yeah, as though he'd been rubbing against carpet and decided to give me a zap," Carl said.

"Gosh, most of them are dead," Hamed said. Brock stared at the catch. Something else wasn't right. There were several more fish than what his sonar indicated.

"We bottom trawled. We scooped these guys right off the bottom. They were dead before we even got here, and the rest were dying," he said.

"Should we report this?" Miko asked.

"I might tomorrow," Brock said. "Right now, I think I'm gonna have to throw in the towel and…"

"Hey, Captain Giler. I have a visitor you might want to meet."

It was Sean Bradley again. Brock stepped back into the wheelhouse again and grabbed the radio speaker.

"A visitor?"

"Use your glasses. About two-hundred feet off my starboard bow. You'll see who I mean."

Brock found his binoculars and looked to the northeast. He spotted the *Red Machete*, then panned right. Nothing. He was ready to grab the speaker mic and accuse Captain Bradley of playing a joke on him, when, finally, he saw the fluke.

"Oh, would you look at that! It's my buddy, Sly," he said. He started turning the wheel to go get a closer look at the sixty-foot sperm whale. Sly often came by, despite his encounter with the drift net which Brock had helped to free him from.

The whale was coming in his direction. It raised its head just over the surface to take a breath through its blowhole, then dipped just a few feet under.

Brock could see the swells generated by its fluke. He wondered if Sly would recognize him. He had spoken with Dr. Martha Cornett, who was also there to rescue Sly from his predicament, and she had stated that sperm whales had spectacular memories. They remembered places they had visited, areas where they encountered threats, possibly even certain lifeforms they had encountered.

Brock wondered if Sly remembered him. If so, he was grateful to be a positive memory. Dr. Cornett had mentioned that studies had shown that these creatures could sometimes hold grudges. If Brock had been the one trying to net it, rather than save it, the sperm whale would remember that detail had it lived, meaning it would probably be a good idea to keep his distance for the rest of his life. Luckily, that's not what played out.

He watched the head rise from the water. The scarring from the net was right there, like a grid covering his left eye. Yep, it was Sly the whale.

"What are we doing, Cap?" Hamed asked.

"Just saying hello to an old buddy," Brock said. "At least one nice thing is coming out of the day."

"Oh, man. Is it Sly?" Miko asked, quickly running to the side. "Hey, there he is!"

"Is that the whale you told me about?" Hamed asked.

"Yep. Right before your time," Miko answered.

They watched the cetacean suddenly whip to its right and go north. There was a sudden urgency to its movements.

"Whoa! What's that about?" Miko muttered. In the wheelhouse, Brock watched the whale increase speed, then dive. His heart started to race. He had read in the past that sperm whales acted this way for three main reason: to feed, to flee, or to fight.

This was not the typical feeding grounds for a mature sperm whale, and Sly was well-known around the island to be fairly docile. Numerous times, he had been spotted near ships, so it was unlikely he was fleeing from the boat. Sly was definitely moving with a purpose, and there was only one other reason Brock could think of.

Brock expanded the sonar range. There was a sizable blip moving to the north; clearly Sly. Roughly a half-mile ahead of him was an incredibly large object gradually approaching. Another whale? *No, too big.* A potential mate? *No, he wouldn't move this aggressively.* Whatever it was, it was moving toward the whale at equal speed.

"The hell?"

****

The enormous mammal moved farther north. Fifty-eight feet long and a hundred-and-thirty-thousand pounds, it was the mightiest in the sea. The length of its head alone was twenty feet, containing the largest brain on the planet. A direct blow at top speed would punch a cavity into an aircraft carrier, or snap the spin of a living creature of equal size to itself.

For years, the whale traveled the waters unchallenged. Even other sperm whales that ventured into the area were smaller than itself. Other than its encounter with the net that marked its face, it had no real struggle. That's why it preferred these waters. The humans generally left it alone. Orca pods tended to stray further west, bypassing the island because of the human activity.

Only recently had its status quo as supreme ruler of the sea been threatened. The whale released a ping, the echolocation marking the location of the challenger. Even at a half mile's distance, it could almost feel the heat radiating off its body, the very heat that caused it to abandon its attack days ago. Since then, it had travelled several miles northeast and circled back around the island, believing the predator may have only been passing through. After all, it did not attack either when it could have.

It could see the giant thing now. The challenger was far larger than itself. Its body was fairly thin and flexible, like one enormous fin. The snout was elongated, the lower jaw yawning open. It was armed with teeth sharper than a great white's, but it was no shark.

The beast was picking up speed.

There was no mistaking its intentions this time; the challenger was not weary, nor was it simply passing through. This was aggressive body language. It was here to fight, to attempt to take the whale's place as lord of the sea. The whale released another ping, hoping that the intense vibrations would deter the strange eel. It did not.

The eel was no stranger to sound. It had lived in deep trenches, where sound traveled fast and wide, bouncing off the walls of the earth. Had the whale's pings been in the enclosed passageways from where it came, they may have done some harm to its senses. But here in the open ocean, they did nothing, except spur the creature on.

They were now within a few hundred feet of each other.

The whale proceeded with caution. The very size of this visitor presented a substantial threat. The whale, being one of the largest animals in the ocean, had never experienced being the hunted. It could not relate to the fear of fish and squid, who from the time of birth were at risk of becoming meals for larger species. Up until now, the whale's existence had been mostly carefree—the life of a hunter with no bounds.

All of that changed in this moment.

Common sense dictated its actions. It was not interested in circling around and sizing each other up as previously done. There was more than the massive size of this visitor that alarmed the whale. The water temperature around it was rising. Minor electrical discharges tickled its flesh. The whale could not make sense of this phenomenon, other than the fact that it spelled danger.

Sly circled wide to point itself in the opposite direction. Its attempt to flee was cut short.

In the blink of an eye, the temperature skyrocketed to a boiling point. A white flash engulfed the water, followed by a bolt of light that burst from the creature's hide. That hot line of light struck the whale's forehead. In that same moment, it felt searing heat. Its body jerked, as though every organ inside was trying to escape. Its vision blurred.

Suddenly, it felt water raining in through its blowhole. The spasm had made it lose control, and as a result, it nearly gasped for breath under the water.

The spasm ended as soon as it began, leaving the whale severely weakened and confused. All it knew was that it needed to expel the water. It raced for the surface and released a plume of water into the air. Its forehead ached. It had never experienced burns before, and had no understanding of electrical shocks. But it did know the piercing pain of teeth entering its flesh.

The whale reared its head high over the water, its jaw wide open as though screaming in misery. Just below the surface, the eel had begun its assault, digging its teeth into its opponent's tail. Those teeth sank deep, drawing blood.

The whale angled its head downwards and tried to dive, but the predator was clinging too tightly to its body, making swimming difficult. Tethered in combat, their combined mass pulled them to the ocean floor.

They crashed down together, the impact shaking the eel's grip loose. Already, it went for another bite, successfully sinking its teeth into the whale's right flipper. More intense pain, far worse than anything a giant squid had to offer. The whale could feel the teeth prodding through its flipper. In a few short moments, it would be torn free.

With all of its might, the whale slammed its bodyweight to the right, bashing the eel against the seabed. It turned its huge head as far as it could, then unleashed a ping that rivaled the vibration of TNT explosives. The soundwave hit the eel and bounced back against the seabed, causing enough discomfort to force it into releasing.

But the carnivore was not done. Despite a ringing head, it was not about to let the whale off easy. It lashed at the fleeing opponent with its jaws, its sickle teeth ripping a chunk of the left fluke. The whale spasmed from the brief, but intense pain. Trailing blood, it circled for another attack, only to realize the eel was closing in. The predator bit at the whale's head and side, slicing deep. Feeling the creature starting to wrap its body like a squid's tentacle around its own, the sperm whale performed another corkscrew motion, then vaulted low. As it 'summersaulted', it spotted the tip of the Eel's tail. It lunged and bit, the cone teeth entering the leathery flesh.

It tasted blood for the briefest of moments. What came next was an intense surge of heat and uncontrollable convulsion. That bright light and its evil force shook the whale's body, singeing the inside of its mouth, and shaking the two titans loose from each other.

Again, the spasm ended as fast as it occurred, the only lasting effect being burning pain, confusion, weakness...and vulnerability. The whale spasmed again, feeling the slicing of teeth along its underbelly. It twisted and went to the surface, slapping the eel's elongated jaw with its fluke.

The eel followed. It attempted to bite, but fell slightly short, its teeth grazing the fluke's right lobe. The whale vaulted over the surface, plunged again, then increased speed in hopes of setting itself up for another ram attempt. But before it could circle, the white flash reappeared, and the bolt of lightning lashed its dorsal fin like a whip comprised of heat.

Now, the whale's big brain was in a frenzy. Its vision was compromised, as was its echolocation. Its enormous heart was fluttering now, its muscles twitching, causing adrenaline to soar. It released a few pings uncontrollably, getting just enough sense of the area to realize something was directly in front of it. It was large, on the surface, and moving toward it.

There was no time for analyzing. The whale was in a crisis. All that mattered was survival. Whatever method was necessary to obtain that goal was inconsequential. Either flee or break through the enemy's skull with its ramming power.

It chose the latter.

Sly flapped its tail with all its might, driving itself toward the surface. It broke the water, landing on its side, then corrected its posture to aim for a collision with the enemy. Its tail splashed water, shooting its mass across the surface like a torpedo.

****

"Oh, shit! Captain, it's coming right at us!" Miko didn't bother using the radio. He was screaming at the top of his lungs, as were the other two crewmates.

So was Brock. He could see the enormous mammal racing toward him. He cut the wheel to starboard and gunned the throttle, but it was too late. Like the famous creature in the Melville novel, Sly struck the portside, plunging his enormous head through the hull. The ship spun, with water rushing into the interior compartments. The whale continued driving itself through the ship, destroying the holding tanks and engine.

The ship teetered to starboard, then back to port, quickly succumbing to the tremendous weight added from the intruding water. Miko and Hamed fell head over heels, hitting the portside, then quickly scrambled for life jackets. Only Carl, the slowest of the bunch, was fast enough to grab the starboard railing and keep himself upright. However, after a few seconds, he was hanging off the bar.

The portside plunged down, the water invading the main deck. Miko and Hamed grabbed for anything they could to stay afloat. Carl, on the other hand, was kicking his legs and screaming.

Brock fell against the bulkhead to his left, then spun around to grab for the lifejackets. He pushed himself to his feet, realizing he was *standing* on the bulkhead. He looked out, seeing the starboard side completely pointed up, the helm protruding from his right as though it was some kind of strange wall design. Water burst through the windows and doorway, knocking him off his feet.

He got back to his hands and knees and crawled to the doorway. Before he could squeeze through, the ship sank deeper, and a huge swell of water swept him back into the pilothouse.

The ship was descending fast. The Captain threw the lifejacket on, then swam for the door again, dragging the other three with him. The water had climbed to Carl's ankles now. Miko and Hamed had been swept thirty feet away, riding huge swells as the whale moved underneath them.

****

Immediately upon impact, the whale realized that this target was not the one it intended. It had sunk the very ship that had saved its life a few years prior. The whale jerked its head to the left and sped northeast. Its vision was clearing up now. It could see the other fishing ship moving closer.

The whale felt an urgency to escape, not out of consequence of its mistake, but a realization it was moments from suffering another attack. It could sense the eel closing in from beneath. There was an intense heat in the water, as well as a series of flashes. The water stung where the strange light had seared its flesh. Whatever this beast was, the whale was no match for it. The challenger's superior size was the least of its problems. Same with its teeth. Whatever this white heat was that illuminated the water, it was more than the whale could handle.

For the first time in its life, the fifty-eight foot sperm whale fled northeast, zooming right past the other human vessel that was approaching.

****

"Holy mother of God!" Captain Sean Bradley shouted, cutting the wheel to starboard as the huge creature came his way. His heart had nearly stopped when he saw the explosive impact against the *Underwater Kingdom*. The boat was now almost entirely submerged, the remains spiraling as though caught in a whirlpool.

He could hear his two crewmen shouting horrifically as Sly the whale raced past them, creating swells so large they rocked the ship.

The Captain fought to keep his balance, while keeping the ship at full throttle. In about a minute, he would be right there to rescue the crew of the sunken ship. As he did, he fumbled to grab the radio speaker mic.

"Hello! Coast Guard? Maxwell Island Police? Anyone! This is a mayday. We have a sinking vessel, one point three miles north-northwest of Maxwell Island. All vessels in the vicinity be aware, there is a violent sperm whale attacking ships! The *Underwater Kingdom* is down, and it nearly attacked us."

He dropped the speaker mic, then kept his eyes on the wreckage. He couldn't quite see the crew yet, as the glare of the setting sun blinded him.

"Keep an eye out, boys! Get the lifebuoys ready! We're almost there!"

****

Miko slapped the water and kicked his legs. With the lean figure he had, it was a fight to stay afloat. He'd seen heavier people drift on their own, hardly in need of a lifejacket. For the first time in his life, he wished to trade bodies with them.

The swells carried him fifty feet from the wreckage. Saltwater constantly splashed his face, making it difficult to get his bearings. Every so often, he'd catch glimpses of the wreckage, but overall, all he could see was water.

Hamed was right beside him at first, but at some point, they got separated. Right before they were swept away, he saw him grab a lifebuoy and throw it under his arms. Now, he couldn't see him, but he could hear him shouting from somewhere to the right.

"Hamed!" Miko yelled out. "Ham—" Water splashed into his mouth, forcing him to gag.

"Miko!"

He heard him! Miko spat the water out, then looked over. The waves fell and began to steady. Between two large swells was Hamed, spinning like a top on the water. He waved to his fellow crewmate, knowing he was moments from losing his strength and sinking to the depths. *I have the buoy! Get over here!*

Miko paddled as though competing for the Olympics. He was forty feet away. Thirty-five.

Suddenly, like a high wind, he felt a current pass underneath him. Whatever it was, it was forcing the water in the opposite direction, like two storms colliding. Miko was caught in another swell, then spun to the left, with his back now facing Hamed.

A horrible scream filled his ears. He turned back, but couldn't see his friend. But he could hear the sounds of struggle. Water splashed, his yells intensifying with each movement.

"Hamed!" Miko fought against the current, then turned. The spiraling waves rose over five feet, and were not stopping. Riding high was Hamed, his back facing Miko. The swells were pushing them together now. At least that made closing the distance easier.

With all of his strength, Miko swam the last few meters. He called Hamed's name, but he wasn't moving. His back was still turned. He was upright, shoulders scrunched from weighing down in the lifebuoy. Miko grabbed him by the shoulder and spun him around.

"Hey! It's me…"

Hamed's jaw was slack, the eyes wide and glazed over at once. His skin was pale, as though all the blood had been sucked out of him. Probably because it had. The water around Miko was red.

"Hamed?" He tried to shake the crewman awake, which only resulted in him flipping over, revealing the bottom of the legless torso. Intestines slapped Miko in the face, then wiggled around like noodles.

Miko didn't scream. He didn't call to God. He was too stunned to do that. He was frozen, his mind lost. At any other time in the same predicament, he would've snapped into focus after ten seconds, then swum for the approaching vessel. But today, he would never get the chance. Only when he saw the immense shape rising below his feet did he realize this wasn't just some horrible nightmare.

It was alive, its huge eyes glaring at him, the snout separating into a set of dagger-lined jaws. They snapped shut over his midsection, shredding his legs and abdomen and crushing the bones. Miko's screams were drowned out by the water as he was pulled deep by the horrible leviathan. It jerked him to the right, then twisted its jaws the other way, severing his lower body. With a snapping motion, it snatched his almost dead remains, sliced them with its teeth, then swallowed.

His killer moved under the water, sensing the vibrations of two other land-dwellers paddling along the surface. Their movements suggested that they were struggling. Weak. As it had learned with the previous two, they were easy to pluck from underneath.

The beast slithered through the water until it reached the sunken body of the floating object. There were only a few fragments that floated along the surface. Splashing between them were its next targets.

It angled its head upward and extended its jaws.

****

Brock rolled with the waves, which bashed him against the various fragments. The ship was completely gone now. He heard Hamed scream, though he was nowhere to be seen. Nor was Miko.

Only Carl was right in front of him. For the first time in his life, his bodybuilder physique was working against him. His muscles were like anchors, wanting to go nowhere but deep down.

Brock paddled toward him, towing the life vests.

"Carl!" The crewman looked around, unsure where the voice was coming from. "To your right. Your right! YOUR *RIGHT!*" Finally, Carl spun the right direction and spotted his Captain. Brock raised one of the life vests high and chucked it toward him. Carl reached for it, but got caught in a swell. He rolled backwards, then flapped his limbs in a panic. He was a few feet underwater, and didn't get a chance to catch a breath before going down.

He felt the blood rush to his head. When he finally opened his eyes, he saw the angle of the light and the darkness 'above' him. He was upside down.

There was movement in that darkness. Something huge was moving toward him. Its skin was grey, its head angular. It was not the whale. It moved like a snake. Its eyes were as round as silver dollars, the pupils big and black. The jaws were open, exposing pointed teeth that each resembled the Grim Reaper's scythe.

The jaws slammed shut, opened again, only to shut once more. Carl's body was mashed up, his insides clouding the water like a broken egg yolk in a bowl.

Brock saw the blood and the shape slithering below it. There was something beneath him. A shark? He didn't know.

The *Red Machete* was only a few hundred feet away. Brock raised his hands and screamed. He could see the crew on the foredeck. One had a lifeline with a donut at the end of it.

"We see you," one of them said.

"Throw me the line!" a panicked Brock screamed. As the boat closed in another hundred feet, the crewman launched the donut with all his might. It splashed down a few yards in front of the Captain, who frantically paddled for it. He slipped through the gap in the center, then waved again. "Pull me up! Pull me—"

Like a bobber in a pond, he was suddenly yanked beneath the surface. The lifeline went taut, pulling the *Red Machete* a few degrees to port.

Brock felt the teeth shred his lungs and stomach. His insides felt as though in a blender. With one last horrific twisting motion, the line snapped, the buoy popping after being impaled. The beast dove and swam off with its prey, chomping once more before swallowing.

The last thing Brock felt was the tip of a tooth in the split second before it entered his skull.

****

Sean Bradley raced out onto the deck and gazed at the thrashing, blood-red waters. From where he stood, the thing below was nothing other than a large shape.

"Jesus, Mary… Sly *ate* them," he said.

Realizing they were next, he rushed back into the wheelhouse and throttled for the nearest harbor.

CHAPTER 20

The snapping of cameras was like nails on a chalkboard.

Silvia Remar did her best to stand straight as she approached the podium. JoEllen Marsh had given her statements to the room full of press, and it was now her turn to give details on the investigation.

Her new thing seemed to be getting ready to leave work for the evening, only to receive an emergency call regarding a vessel in distress. Chopper units from the mainland flew over the area to spot any survivors, but all that was found was the upper body of one of the crewmates. Now, tensions in the island were at an all-time high. Silvia could see the stress in the Mayor's face. Clearly, her sponsors had a long, and not-so-pleasant discussion with her.

And shit rolls downhill.

"Thank you for being here," Silvia said. She didn't mean it. She'd prefer to skip this conference altogether and get right to work correcting the situation. But no, she had to face the heat. She laid out her notes in front of her to keep her wailing mind focused. "I'll start by saying we're getting to work on ensuring safety for the island as we speak. I'm getting in touch with—"

"Chief Remar," Billy Tamos from the *Local Township Times* interrupted. "There have been reports of numerous vessels disappearing. Numerous people missing or confirmed dead. At least ten in the last thirty-six hours. That we know of."

Silvia could feel JoEllen cringe. Just the phrasing was bound to hurt the island economy.

Billy continued. "Do you suspect that this sperm whale is the cause of all four incidents?"

"We have reason to suspect," Silvia answered. "We're getting in touch with the U.S. Coast Guard as I speak. We will work with them to track the whale's movements and decide on a course of action."

"Course of action? Would that entail killing the whale?" Jac Gracey from *NBC* said.

Silvia took a breath. "As I've said, we'll discuss with the Coast Guard Commander and figure out a course of action…"

"You didn't answer the question, Chief."

"Aren't sperm whales on the endangered list? Isn't it illegal to kill them?" another reporter in the back said.

Lightning strike. Silvia twitched and tensed. It was like these reporters were trying to gang up on her and make her job more difficult.

Of course, they are. They're what passes for reporters nowadays.

"If we determine the whale is indeed responsible for all attacks, then it is possible we might have to put it down," she answered. "We will leave that up to the Coast Guard Commander who is en-route as we speak to help evaluate the situation."

"Chief, there are reports that this whale is possibly *eating* humans. The Captain of the vessel *Red Machete* who witnessed the events indicated that they were in the process of rescuing one of the crew of the *Underwater Kingdom*, but that something pulled him down from underneath. Can you comment?"

"It is my understanding that sperm whales are generally docile and I don't believe there's ever been a recorded case of them consuming humans."

"Can you give any comments about the body that was recovered?" Trent Mills from the *Georgia Reporter* asked.

"We're waiting on the coroner's report," Silvia said.

"We've heard reports that it was torn in half right after the vessel went down," Jac Gracey said.

"The body…" Silvia took a breath, "was mutilated. I'm waiting on the coroner's report."

"So, the whale bit the guy in half?" Jac said. It sounded more of a confirmation than a question.

"Large animal that size, with the design of its jaw, hard to determine."

"Wasn't the body accidentally uncovered on North Beach in a similar state?" someone in the crowd asked.

"That's correct."

Someone else raised their hand, but didn't wait to be picked. "And there was wreckage uncovered in that same area. Judging by the remains, that boat was at least twenty-four feet long. By this point, can you confirm that the whale attacked this boat as well?"

"I can't confirm anything until we've completed our investigation. All I know is that the day will be dedicated to developing a swift course of action. In the meantime, we are ordering all vessels not to go out, including fishermen, until we can confirm the threat has been eliminated."

"What about the Belanger Festival?" Billy Tamos asked.

Silvia looked at JoEllen, who watched intently.

"I'll be speaking with Mr. Belanger within the hour and we will provide updates. It is my understanding that the area their vessels will commence their show is shallow, and is unlikely that the whale will even venture near it, as it would risk beaching itself."

Silvia looked to the left and saw Zach Alec from MSNBC.

"Chief, considering there were three confirmed incidents prior to this, why wasn't there a notice to mariners placed in effect sooner?"

And there it was; the question Silvia hoped would come up. She had the chance to do it. Royce and Adam both supported the decision. Then she spoke with JoEllen…

"Chief?"

"Pardon me," Silvia said, snapping into focus. "First, we don't know for a fact that the whale caused those other three incidents…"

"Uh, Chief, hospital staff in Maxwell General have stated that George O'Mara, owner of the speedboat that raced ashore, stated he encountered a large 'monster'. Forgive me, but doesn't it seem like a bit of a coincidence that he'd make such a statement on the same day a near record-sized sperm whale attacks a fishing trawler unprovoked?"

"Though unusual, we didn't have reason to suspect there to be any real danger…"

"No reason to suspect? May I remind you there were three vessels attacked? One which occurred the previous night?"

"That was an explosion, to which we're still determining the cause."

"Many bystanders who witnessed it be towed ashore noted a hull breach…"

"Inconsistent with a whale ramming," Silvia said. "As I've just said, there was an explosion, which originated from within the vessel, possibly because of the use of fireworks…"

"Don't you think the whale attacked, caused a fuel leak, which led to an explosion?" Zach Alec said.

"If the hull was breached inward, the force of the explosion may have bent it back out…" Billy Tamos said.

Silvia felt like she was in the middle of a swarm of wasps, and they were all moving in for repeated stings. These people weren't even waiting for her to answer the questions. Nor were they waiting to be picked.

She waivered left and right, this time noticeably. *God, where the hell is January?*

"Listen, I assure all of you that I'm working swiftly to resolve the matter. The beaches are open. People can go into shallow water. We'll have vessels out on patrol. In the meantime, we will consult with the Coast Guard as to how to handle the situation. Now, if you'll excuse me, I'd like to get started."

Silvia stepped away from the podium and exited through a back door. Being away from the reporters brought an immediate sense of relief, which unfortunately was followed by a new wave of stress. Soon, her face would be all over the television, her name associated with the failure to protect the citizens. It was human nature to seek someone to blame, even for extraordinary circumstances, and Silvia could already feel the storm on the horizon.

The first trickle came from Sergeant Royce Boyer, who stood at the back of the building, arms crossed. He made no attempt to hide the 'I told you so' look.

Yeah-yeah, I know. If you were Chief, Brock Giler and his crew would be alive right now. That instinctive urge to be defensive made her throat tight, and the Sergeant hadn't even spoken a word. And even if he had, it'd be foolish to argue, since he was right.

"Do we have an ETA on the Coast Guard?" he asked.

"The Commander is being flown in separate from Miami," Silvia replied. "I'm told his cutter has already departed from District Seven."

"How'd JoEllen respond to that news?"

"As well as you'd expect," Silvia said. She was quiet for a moment before spilling the truth. "She wanted us to come up with an action plan ourselves. Didn't want the press."

"HA!" Royce said, clapping his hands. "I knew it! I'll get my cuffs, take my boat out, and arrest him right now."

"Knock it off, Sergeant," she said. "I talked her out of it."

"You, or Adam?" Silvia's bewildered expression was enough to expose her guilt. "Yeah, that's what I thought. I know you're eager to protect your job. But I'm not gonna go out and get my ass killed so you can kiss the Mayor's ass."

"Sergeant…" Silvia kept her voice low, "Don't push it. I'll fire your ass right now if you continue."

"Go ahead," Royce replied. "Watch your police force break in two. I guarantee at least ten people will resign in the next forty-eight hours, especially if you plan on sending them out into the water to pursue that whale."

Silvia realized that she'd entered a battle she would not win. As usual, Royce was right. Not only would the force retaliate, but the Fire Chief and other emergency departments would rally against her. It would be a war of internal politics, which would continue through the end of JoEllen's term as Mayor. And they would have major influence on her successor, which would result in a new Chief of Police, and no job for Silvia Remar. She'd be back on the mainland, and as far as she was concerned, most police departments were not on the lookout for cops to perform light duty tasks.

"Take a boat out and patrol the island perimeter. Make sure nobody ventures off the island," she said. "Don't go out too deep. If that whale is causing all of this, then our patrol boats would never stand a chance."

"Yeah, fine. I'll do that," Royce said. "You, on the other hand, go talk to the Coast Guard Commander. Make sure Adam's there so the guy gets a correct assessment of what's going on. Not just what the Mayor wants."

Silvia resisted the urge to respond to that remark, and proceeded to her truck. She slowly and carefully pulled herself into her seat, then started the engine. She glanced at the time. 9:04. The Coast Guard had informed them that Commander Dale Riley was en-route twenty minutes ago by chopper. It was a conversation she could not wait to be finished with.

She watched Royce pull out of the lot first in his Interceptor.

"Can't be less pleasant than talking to you."

CHAPTER 21

"Martha, I would leave it alone if I were you."

She ignored her husband's warnings as she looked at the sky with her binoculars. In the distance, the helicopter looked like a mosquito. Only when it came within a half mile could she make out the orange and white colors. It approached the island from the northwest and was beginning its descent. In black letters below the cockpit were the words United States Coast Guard.

"Martha…" Andy said.

"You saw the broadcast, Andy. They're gonna go after Sly," she said.

"I don't like it, but you know Sean Bradley. He wouldn't lie about this. The whale killed Brock."

"Andrew, you *know* there's more to it than that."

Her husband slapped his hands to his legs, frustrated. Yes, he suspected the same thing she did, but he lacked the certainty that they could talk the authorities out of their plan of action. Who would believe the story of a giant electric eel lurking about in these waters without proof? Martha had the gift of science and compassion, while Andy had empathy. He could put himself in the shoes of others and understand their perspectives. All he knew was that if he was a Police Chief or a Coast Guard Officer, and someone came up to him with the news Martha was about to present, he'd laugh that person off the island.

"I get it. There's something going on, and it involves that thing out there…if it's out there—we haven't proven it yet…"

"We have strong evidence," Martha said.

"Nothing that'll convince those guys!" Andy replied. "If those specimens are, in fact, babies, we still technically have no solid basis on how big the mother is. An undeveloped egg sack doesn't cut it. We have no solid data on their lifecycle, nor their growth rate, or how big they are when they're born."

"I'm not letting them go out and kill my whale," Martha said. She watched the chopper pass to the north until it was out of sight, then started marching to her car. "If I can't convince them, then maybe I'll go to the press. Public opinion might sway them."

"Public opinion is to get these waters opened back up," Andy said. "Knowing Marsh, they want to do it pronto. And people here are afraid. They think he's *Moby Dick*. He followed her, wincing as his mind searched for the right words to say. "Regardless of what happened, Sly has taken human life. He's a confirmed threat. Anything you tell them is not going to hold any water."

Martha opened the door of her SUV and got in.

"I can try. You gonna come along?"

"My inclination is to say no," Andy said. "But I suppose somebody's gotta go along to make sure you don't interfere to the point of getting arrested." He worked his way to the passenger side and buckled himself in. Martha started the engine and gripped the wheel.

"You think they'll actually kill him?" she asked, her voice shallow. Andy looked out the window.

"Probably. I'm no veteran, but I've never heard of an operation to lure one specific whale out of an area before. There have been tricks to lure some away from fishing zones, but those methods are used with bait. I don't think that's gonna work with Sly."

Martha shook her head. It was her duty as a marine biologist to preserve endangered species. She wasn't going to falter now. She pulled out of the lot and drove inland to the airfield.

****

Lieutenant Adam Henry was already there waiting when Silvia arrived at the airfield. He stood, arms crossed, watching the Coast Guard chopper slowly descending onto the landing pad. He glanced over his right shoulder just long enough to see that it was her parking beside his vehicle.

There was a slight coldness in his eye, a hint of judgement, but also empathy. Even with their warnings, there was no way she could've predicted the sperm whale would've randomly attacked a fishing vessel. There was no point in bringing it up. He saw the press conference and how JoEllen threw her to the wolves. Then again, he didn't feel too badly, considering the meeting that morning before the conference. He was still frustrated on how he had to interject himself into the conversation when JoEllen expressed how badly she wanted to avoid having Coast Guard intervention at this time.

Silvia stepped beside him. For the first few moments, she was silent.

"Thanks for your help earlier," she said.

"Mmm-hmm," was his only reply.

"With a little luck, this'll be behind us by the day's end," she said. "I'd kill for my normal problems at this point."

"Good thing you're not headed where I'm going," Adam said. Silvia's attempt at a smile faded. He wasn't joking…and he was also right, which hit hard.

The chopper set down. The fuselage door opened, and a six-foot-four man in a blue Coast Guard jacket and trousers stepped off. His face was stone-hard, almost mechanical. He immediately approached the officers.

"Lieutenant Commander Jim Davidson," he said. Just in the way he spoke, it was clear he was the no-nonsense type that despised wasting time.

"Chief Silvia Remar. This is Lieutenant Adam Henry." They shook hands.

"I understand we have a rather unique situation here," Davidson said.

"Correct," Silvia said. "I can't explain what caused it, but the fact is, we have a near-sixty-foot sperm whale swimming in our waters. It is certainly responsible for the sinking of one boat, and likely three other incidents."

"A yacht, a speedboat, and a Rustler 24, correct?"

"Affirmative," Adam replied.

"Alright. Then that makes my plan of action easy. If it's that dangerous, I'm gonna have no choice but to put it down. I have a cutter coming in from the Gulf, which should arrive at thirteen-hundred."

"Excellent," Silvia said. "If I may ask, what means will you use to put it down?"

"An animal that large and violent, unfortunately, does not provide me with many options. Either we'll use depth charges, or if it surfaces, the Bushmaster."

Somehow, hearing those words made Silvia sink even lower. There was no pleasure to be had in killing a whale, especially one like Sly, who was well known by most of the island population. And now, he was summoned to death.

"Do we know the whale's present location?"

"Not at the moment," Silvia said. "There should be a researcher on the island who might be able to help us. I don't know her well personally, but I believe she has tracked the whale in the past…"

"Would that be her?" Davidson pointed past her at an SUV pulling into the driveway.

Two people stepped out. One was a woman with butterscotch-colored hair, roughly the age of forty, dressed in a white shirt and tan shorts. The other was a man in a button shirt and khaki shorts, about the same age.

"Chief, I don't believe our paths have crossed, despite being on the same island for so long," the woman said. "I'm Doctor Martha Cornett. This is my husband, and assistant, Andy."

"Obviously you know me," Silvia replied.

"Everyone does," Martha said.

"I take it you're here regarding the incident," Adam said.

"That's correct. Officers—Commander," she acknowledged Davidson's presence, "please listen. What I'm about to tell you might seem unbelievable. I think we have a new species swimming off our coast."

"Beg your pardon?" Davidson said.

"I don't think the whale's fully responsible for what occurred last night," Martha said.

Silvia took a moment to think about the information she was just given, watching the creatures in the carpet, before looking back over at Martha.

"Doctor, we have eye-witnesses stating that the whale rammed the *Underwater Kingdom,*" she said.

"I'm not denying he did it," Martha said. "What I am saying is that I don't think he's the real threat."

"He sunk a vessel. In the previous twenty-four hours prior, we've had three other boat incidents," Adam said, being careful not to sound accusatory.

"I understand how it looks, and I even understand something might need to be done about Sly," Martha said. "But there's a piece of the puzzle that I think you should know about."

"You mind filling us in?" Silvia asked.

Martha hesitated, bracing for the possibility that they would not believe her.

"Within the last three months, there's already been increased seismic activity in the Puerto Rico Trench. Then, when the meteor struck, an earthquake measuring eight-point-four on the Richter scale was recorded between the Caribbean and North American Plates, causing tsunamis across the Caribbean, Mexico, and the Gulf. I think that earthquake caused a shift in the landscape deep below the sea."

"An earthquake didn't sink that boat, Professor," Davidson said.

"No, but I think it's awoken something that did," she replied. "Over the past thirty-eight hours, our temperature buoys have been recording temperature spikes all across the island, particularly the east, north, and west sides. But only one at a time. It's almost like they're tracing the movements of a huge heat source."

"A heat source? I don't understand," Silvia said. "What heat source could be moving around out there under the water?"

"A living organism," Martha said.

"Pardon me?" Adam said.

"We believe the earthquake stirred a large organism up from the trench. A *very* large organism, and it's now feeding off this area. Sean Bradley...the Captain who, well, responded to the incident, met with me yesterday. He caught two goblin sharks. They were still alive, but just barely. They died as we took them in. The next part was more incredible: We found evidence that they had swum up from the trench and traveled to this area. Furthermore, in their stomachs were the remains of an undiscovered species of eel. One was still alive, enough so to emit an electric charge."

"Wait, you found an electric eel in a shark's stomach?" Silvia said.

"Something similar," Martha clarified. "Whatever they are, I think they came from the Puerto Rico Trench. I've been keeping up with various reports of strange findings along the Mexican Coast, the Gulf, Florida, as well as the Caribbean. There've been continuous findings over the course of the last couple months."

Silvia looked at the Commander to gauge his response. There was not even a hint of interest in his expression.

"Have you seen this creature, Doctor?"

Martha hesitated. "Well, no, I—"

"Has anyone seen it?"

"Those who have are dead," Andy said, backing his wife. It didn't faze Davidson one bit.

"I'm not going to run an operation based on a hunch," the Lieutenant Commander said.

Martha was shaking. "Sir, you must listen—"

"No, ma'am, *you* must listen. We have a violent animal swimming around out there. I'm sorry, but I have no choice but to put it down."

"Put him down?! He's almost seventy years old. He's endangered as it is. Never has harmed a human being in his life until now. Believe me, I knew Brock Giler. I'm not downplaying his death. I want the thing *actually* responsible to be handled, not a whale that was caught in the crossfire."

"It's not about what you want," Davidson said. "You're telling me there's an electric eel swimming in our waters, blowing up boats, and making the other creatures crazy. It's gonna take more than conjecture to make me spend resources on that, when I have confirmed sightings of the real threat."

"Haven't you heard the reports of dead fish popping up everywhere? Fishermen have stated they've had to travel further out to find anything."

"Just for one day," Silvia said. "Is it really the end of the world?"

"For this island, yeah," Martha said. Davidson was shaking his head now.

"Doctor. Do you have a tracking device on the whale?"

Martha hesitated. Andy was cringing as he read his wife's mind. *Don't do it, babe. They'll get a court order done so fast— The institute will be pissed when they find out. They'll pull our funds for interfering in a military operation. Don't do it.*

It was clear she wouldn't give up the tracking info.

"I got it for you," Andy said. Martha spun on her heel and bored into him with blazing eyes. "Sorry, babe. This was a battle we weren't going to win."

"You're getting Sly killed."

"His fate was already sealed when he hit Brock's boat," he replied in a soft voice.

"He's right," Silvia said. Her throat was tight. She felt responsible for the mental anguish that the scientist was experiencing right now. Even Jim Davidson felt something, though nobody could see through that rough exterior.

"Where can I get that info?" he asked.

"I have a laptop that's linked to it," Andy replied. "I'll give it to you."

"Thank you for your help, sir," Davidson said. He looked back at the officers. "Once the cutter's here, this op shouldn't take long. I'll inform you when it's complete. We'll tow the creature into deeper waters and provide it a decent burial at sea."

"Like you care," Martha snapped.

"I do, ma'am. Believe me, this gives me no pleasure. Not in the slightest. But I have my orders. And I care about the loss of human life. This has to happen. I'm sorry."

He turned around and returned to his chopper.

With a disgusted "Ugh!" Martha returned to her vehicle, not bothering to say another word to Silvia or Adam. Andy took a breath before joining her. Though the drive home was less than ten minutes, it would feel like hours.

Silvia and Adam watched them leave, then exchanged confused stares.

"You think there's any truth to what she was saying?" Adam asked.

"I was about to ask you the same thing," Silvia replied. "Sixty-foot electric eels? What am I to make of that?"

"I don't know." Adam watched the SUV pull away. Through the windows, he caught glimpses of a very irate Martha Cornett at the wheel. "I don't know the words, but I know that music. That woman's gonna do something dumb."

"Royce is on boat patrol. I'll tell him to keep an eye out," Silvia replied. She checked her watch again. "Thirteen-hundred hours. Can't get here fast enough."

CHAPTER 22

Martha was on the deck of her vessel *Infinity*, studying the sounds of whale clicking through her headset, making sure the frequencies were accurate. She didn't speak a word to Andy, who stood on the dock, bitterly watching as she lowered an underwater speakerphone into the water. She tested it once in plain audio.

Perfect. Sly should think it's a pod of females.

"It's not gonna work, hon," Andy said. "It's summer. Fun time for those guys usually takes place in the winter months." Martha turned her back, frustrating him. "Oh, quit acting pissed off at me. You know I didn't have a choice. You know what would've happened if we didn't hand over the data."

Martha didn't reply right away. In her mind, she was hurling insult after insult at him, while envisioning slapping him in the face. Nothing she would dare act out in reality, but when angry, the mind does crazy things. Seeing her husband turn over their tracking computer to the Coast Guard Commander was enraging. He had thrown Sly to the wolves. Now, like the good shepherd she was, she was determined to lure him away and save his life.

"Babe, please," Andy said.

"You would've had a spine," Martha said.

"Martha, you need to stop. If you go out and do this, you're, A, putting yourself at risk. B, you're gonna get arrested, either by the Coast Guard, or the police!"

"I can get out there and lure Sly out of the area. If I can get him into deeper water, maybe he'll dive."

"He's not a submarine, Martha. He'll have to come back up for air. You're not thinking clearly...and that's rare for you!"

Martha tied off the rope from the dock and started for the pilothouse.
"You coming or are you staying here?"

Andy stood on the dock, flabbergasted. "You're really putting me in a pickle, you know that?"

"You contributed to this."

"I was complying with military authority," Andy argued. "I was trying to keep us from getting our asses booted out of here. But now, you're ensuring that'll happen. And worse."

"I'm leaving, whether you like it or not. So, make a choice."

"Martha…" Andy took a breath. Either he went out with her and almost certainly get arrested, or he remained here, and risked the possibility of his wife getting injured while out alone. "You're my wife, I love you…but you can be a real BITCH sometimes."

"Fine. Stay here." She started climbing up to the pilothouse.

Andy listened to the engine come to life. He clenched his fists, closed his eyes, and sneered. *I can't believe this is happening. We're going to end up in jail, or worse.*

Yet, he couldn't let her go out alone.

"Alright! Hold on! I'm coming!" He climbed aboard and raced into the pilothouse. Martha already had her computer activated. The screen loaded, then displayed Sly's position.

"Thanks," she said.

"Babe, I really don't think this'll work. Not only is it not mating season, but he's over sixty years old."

"He's old. Not dead," Martha said. "Yet."

She steered the vessel away from the dock and steered northeast. She looked to the sky as the boat sped away from the island. The chopper was nowhere in sight. There was not a single boat in the water. So far, there was no sign of the Cutter. It was a few minutes past 1:00 p.m.

Any moment now, she would see it on the horizon.

****

Assembled in the Bollinger Shipyards, the *USCGC Richard Denning* was first launched in May of 2012. Like most Sentinel-Class Cutters, it was designed to perform rescue missions, port security, and the interception of potential threats. In its first operational year, it intercepted a boat containing ten Cuban refugees that had veered off course. In its second year, it intercepted a fishing vessel containing Columbian drug smugglers. After the smugglers opened fire on the ship with automatic rifles, the crew was forced to put the M242 Bushmaster to use. The assault resulted in the death of four smugglers and the surrender of the remaining three.

One-hundred-and-fifty-four feet in length, the fast-response vessel was manned with twenty crew and four officers, including Petty Officer First Class Tom Elway. Additional to the Bushmaster, its armament included four Browning M2 machine guns. Equipped with Command, Control, Communications, Computers, Surveillance, and Reconnaissance (C4ISR) system, designed by L-3 Communications, it performed numerous surveillance missions in the Gulf, including storm aftermath and interception of drug smugglers from Mexico and South America. At the rear was a stern launching ramp, which allowed the ship to launch or retrieve auxiliary boats without coming to a full stop.

The *Richard Denning* spent most of its operational history along the Florida Coast, the Bahamas, and the Gulf of Mexico. Only three times did it venture north into the Georgia Coast. The first time was in 2017, assisting in search and rescue operations following Hurricane Matthew. In the aftermath, nearly nine-hundred people were rescued by Coast Guard and private boat crews between Georgia and North Carolina.

The *Richard Denning's* second venture north of Florida was to intercept a reported cruise liner sinking two-hundred nautical miles east of Wassaw Island. With the assistance of two other Cutters and various Air Sea chopper units, over a thousand people were pulled from the failing vessel with few casualties.

The third was to respond to various boat sinkings and disappearances, possibly due to a hyperviolent sperm whale lurking off the coast.

At first, Tom Elway thought the report was a joke. In his thirteen years in the Coast Guard, he had served on four Cutters and had taken part in hundreds of operations across the Atlantic. Several of these operations involved intercepting whaling ships from Europe as well as others that traveled from as far away as Africa.

Five hundred nautical miles south of Bermuda, aboard the *USCGC Raymond Evans*, he assisted in taking down the fishing vessel *Natt Ulv*, which was actively pursuing a forty-five foot sperm whale. The vessel had three motorboats in the water, and one harpoon in the creature's back. The whale could've attacked, but instead, it was intent on fleeing.

However, as they continued to receive reports from the local government on Maxwell Island, it became apparent that the situation was indeed real. Tom Elway, who had assisted in the countless rescues of the fabulous marine creatures, was now finding himself on the dreaded opposite side of the continuum. He was now going to assist in the destruction of one, and not just any whale, but an elder that had been recorded, been featured in documentaries, and was, in its own way, a celebrity in the coast of Georgia. Now, it was going to be remembered for the wrong reasons, and Tom Elway feared that the *USCGC Richard*

Denning's reputation would suffer along with it. It was an unfortunate situation, but what else could be done? Ten people missing or dead, with witnesses confirming the whale as the cause for the sinking of the fishing trawler *Underwater Kingdom,* which just so happened to occur right after three other incidents.

Perhaps it was a brain illness of some kind, or perhaps someone tried to hurt it, and sent it on a rampage. It was all speculation, and in the end, it didn't matter. Even if they somehow diverted the creature, wherever it would travel, it would carry danger with it. Who's to say it wouldn't attack anyone off the coast of South Carolina? Or in the Gulf?

It was early afternoon when his ship arrived at the island. Jim Davidson had already announced via radio that he had completed his aerial reconnaissance and was now arriving at the chopper by boat.

A Maxwell Island Police patrol boat approached from the southwest corner of the island, carrying Davidson to the stern ramp. After completing the transfer, the Commander made his way to the bridge.

"Commander." Tom Elway saluted Davidson, who saluted back. He held a laptop under his arm. "Go shopping at a used electronics store while you were there?"

"Very funny," Davidson replied. "No, this is something that will make our job easier. There's a biologist on the island that has tracking on the whale. It's swimming about three-point-four miles north-northeast of the island."

"So, we're actually going to gun it down?"

"Sadly, yes," Davidson replied. "Not exactly what I had in mind when I was given command of this ship. But we have our orders."

"Were you able to get a visual during your reconnaissance?"

"Negative. It's traveling below the surface. They take a breath every hour; if we wait long enough, we'll be able to catch it when it comes up for air."

None of this sounded right to Tom Elway. Just talking about blowing up this whale was making him sick to his stomach.

"Aye-aye, sir."

Davidson opened the laptop, given to him by Andrew Cornett. The blip in the screen displayed the creature's location.

"Let's get this over with. All ahead, full speed."

CHAPTER 23

"Alright, he's around here," Martha said. She watched the monitor. The map screen displayed Sly's location a few hundred feet behind them. Andy was out on the aft deck with the speakerphone, which was connected to a long cable. Hopefully, Sly had come up for breath recently, because they needed him to be as deep as possible.

Andy's stomach was bothering him. He felt guilty, knowing full well he was interfering with Coast Guard operations. When they were caught—and he was confident they would be—Martha would have a hell of a time explaining it to the institution. On top of that, they'd be lucky not to face jailtime for this.

He spent the entire trip glancing about, scanning the horizon for any ships. So far, they were the only ones out here. That tight feeling in his gut worsened the more he dwelled on their predicament. It was clear that neither he, nor Martha, had thought this plan through. So, what if they got Sly into deeper water? It didn't change the fact that they had a tracker on him. The Coast Guard would continue to follow him...and when Sly would ultimately come up for breath, his days would end.

"Put the line as deep as you can," Martha radioed.

Andy hesitated, resisted the urge to make her turn back to shore, then begrudgingly lowered the line to a hundred feet. All the while, he tried to think of a way to convince his wife to abandon the mission.

"Speaker is activated. Let's see if he'll take the bait," he replied.

Martha slowly steered the vessel northeast. "Please work," she whispered, praying with her eyes closed. She activated the recording.

Soundwaves traveled through the water below. Clicks and pings from numerous sperm whales went far and wide.

She watched the monitor for several minutes. Sly was continuing straight north, not northeast. From the looks of it, he was just traveling in circles.

The plan wasn't working.

Andy couldn't help but feel a little bit relieved. Sensing his opportunity, he raised his radio to his lips.

"Honey. We have to abort. No good will come from this." She didn't reply. "Listen, we can't save him, Martha. They're tracking him. They won't stop just because he'll swim further out if he follows us. It's not going to work."

Martha stepped out onto the fly deck, her face wrinkled with anger and desperation.

"I'm not having this discussion again," she said.

"It's not a discussion. It's a fact," Andy said. "You don't get it! This won't help Sly. It doesn't matter how far we lead him away, even if he was following the frequency. The Coast Guard will follow him across the Atlantic if they have to. They have orders and they have to follow them. No room for personal sentimentality. If that tracker wasn't on, then maybe we'd be able to make some kind of difference. But, unfortunately—" He shrugged his shoulders.

Martha stood up on the fly deck, ready to make a counter-argument. But there was none. He was right. With her emotions running high and adrenaline soaring, she'd overlooked the most basic fact that she would've caught instantly if not under duress.

"He needs the tag taking off," she said. Andy felt his gut was about to rupture. He knew what she was thinking.

"No. NO! Hell to the no!" he said. Martha hurried back into the pilothouse. Andy was ready to scream to the heavens. *I should've called the damn cops on her. Yeah, she would've been pissed, but at least she wouldn't be doing THIS!* He darted for the pilothouse and found his wife already out of her clothes and pulling out her diving gear. "Babe, this is insane!"

"He's calm. He won't hurt me."

"Normally, I'd agree, but he's way too unpredictable now."

Martha fitted her suit over her figure and dug for her mask and air tank. Before exiting the pilothouse, she moved to her computer. The whale calls were still playing. So far, Sly hadn't swum out of the vicinity. Perhaps he was studying the calls? It was hard to say. She increased the frequency, then hurried out onto the main deck, with Andy right behind her.

She grabbed a toolbox and flipped it open. She strapped her air tank over her shoulders and pulled her flippers over her feet. Andy knelt down beside her.

"Let me go down instead," he said.

"No. I need you to monitor his position," she replied. She stopped at the diving ramp then turned around. "Andy, you're right. I can be a real bitch sometimes. But I must do this. If there's any danger, I'll head right up."

"Martha, I beg you—" She interrupted him with a kiss on the lips, then placed her rebreather in her mouth. She tucked the goggles over her eyes, dug into her toolbox for pliers, then launched herself into the water.

Andy hit a fist on the transom. "Damn it!" He watched her under the water until she disappeared. His gaze moved up to the southwest. "Oh, shit."

From a distance, the Coast Guard Cutter looked like a small cloud in the horizon. Very gradually, that cloud was getting larger.

****

Its mouth raised, then closed slowly, then raised again. Water fanned over its gill-slits, satiating its blood with oxygen during its slumber.

The eel dug into the deepest crevice it could find, shielding itself from the torturous sunlight above. Gradually, it was adapting to its new world. The bright shine above it wasn't as strenuous on its senses as it had been during its initial arrival to the shallows. Still, the beast preferred the cover of night. Though the will to feed was strong, the drive for self-preservation was stronger. Sometimes that drive involved the slaughter of other lifeforms, namely dangerous opponents, like the one it had encountered the previous night.

The eel awoke to the familiar echoes of clicks, nearly identical to the whale it recently fought. The difference here was that the soundwaves indicated a large number of these organisms. Several foes were venturing into its new territory. And as it had learned by observing dolphin pods and killer whales, these species often tended to stick together.

Only the Eel's incessant need to feed had allowed the mammal to escape. It proved to be no match for its lightning flash. If one whale would succumb to the bolt, so would an entire pod. It didn't matter how many organisms there were around the Eel. The creature would light up the entire ocean if it needed to. It was a living storm. A swimming hellfire. It would burn anything that threatened it, no matter the size, no matter the number, no matter the odds.

And the beast was threatened.

It raised its head. The clicks were southwest, less than a mile away. With a flutter of its fin-like body, the creature ascended. Initially, it stayed close to the seabed to protect its eyes from the stinging sunlight. Considering the threat in the water, it was forced to observe its surroundings. So, it took the pain. Pain was a part of life; a reminder that it was still alive. Little did the creature know it was adapting its senses. Soon, that blurry vision would clear. Soon, it would dominate both the night and the day.

With only a few hours of sleep needed to recharge its pineapple-sized brain, the electric eel would be unstoppable.

It didn't matter the circumstances surrounding her. Her racing heartbeat, her tense mind, the horrible tightening in her stomach; none of it mattered down here. All of Martha Cornett's problems vanished with the sheer majesty of the ocean depths. The sunlight above, the colors around her, the reef below—even now, it created a calming atmosphere.

Martha descended a hundred feet. She could see the seabed below, possibly another couple hundred feet down. She heard the clicks from the speakerphone behind her...and the clicks of the creature ahead. Sly was near. She wasn't sure if he was responding to the speakerphone or not, but it didn't matter. He was moving slowly, and that was all she needed.

All she had to do was get close, slice that tag off his back, then gradually ascend. Her deed would be done, the whale free to live out the rest of his life in peace, and right away, she would commence the search for the real threat to the ocean.

She stroked her feet, gliding with her arms at her side like a tiny serpent. Finally, she found him. Sly was moving slowly, his fluke slowly waving up and down. He looked like an enormous shadow looming over the seabed. He sensed her presence and turned slightly, revealing his scarred head.

My God.

He was covered in scars. The fluke and right flipper were red from bite marks and showing signs of infection. Something had bitten this whale...something unbelievably huge.

There were more than bite marks. There were lacerations. At first glance, he looked as though he was struck with a whip like in ancient times. Then she saw the charred folds of skin. These were no cuts—they were burns.

Her fist tightened around the tool. She was right. That beast was out here somewhere, and Sly had encountered it. How it led him to crash into the *Underwater Kingdom,* she would probably never find out exactly, but this was enough to know he didn't just attack out of unprovoked rage. Hell, her boat was right above him and he wasn't doing anything.

Martha could not afford to hesitate. She swam closer, while being cautious. An injured animal was the most dangerous. So far, he didn't seem to take an interest in her. She was sixty-feet away now. She could see the tag near his tiny dorsal fin. She raised the pliers over her shoulder. Almost there. She could get close, pry it loose, and return to the boat. If only she had brought a camera! Pictures of Sly would help convince the authorities that there was something lurking in these waters.

"Babe. Hurry up. The Coast Guard's on their way. They're closing in fast. We don't have time," Andy radioed.

She couldn't reply, nor could she curse, which was what she wanted. Adrenaline shook her body. She closed in on Sly, slowed, and reached for his dark leathery skin.

Suddenly, she was rolling over her shoulders, as though caught in a vicious current. Sly had juddered his fluke and took off to the northeast.

No! NO!

Martha wanted to scream. Why did he run? Pain? She was careful not to touch any of his scars. She was so close. Another five or ten seconds, and she could've had the tag removed.

She watched him travel another few hundred feet. He ascended into the brighter, crystal waters above, which made him easy to see with the naked eye. Maybe he was taking a breath?

Then she saw it. From far away, it looked like a squiggly line in the background. As it moved closer, it took on a more definitive form. Martha's mind flashed to the dying eel she had pulled from the goblin shark's stomach. Its mother looked almost identical, except with a more brightly silver-colored skin, and an additional hundred-and-thirty feet of length!

My God. My God Almighty. How on earth has this thing gone unseen all this time?!

The answer was simple. Her husband even said it to the Coast Guard officer.

Because everyone that encountered it is dead.

Its posture was an aggressive one. While its body fin waved, its head was cocked back, like a rattlesnake ready to strike. Then there was blinding light and intense heat.

Martha gasped. She saw the bolt strike the whale. Her body shook. Electrical charges traveled at lightspeed across the surrounding water, sparking a seizure. Her body juddered for a short, but intense moment. At the end, she was nearly unconscious.

"CHRIST!" Andy shouted, jumping back after witnessing the huge flashes under the water. He shouted into his radio. "Martha? Martha?! MARTHA?!" He was on the verge of panicking. "Get back up here. There's something going on!"

The ocean was coming alive with intense waves stirred by ferocious activity underneath.

Something was wrong. Even despite how determined she was, there was no way Martha would put herself in danger under these circumstances. She was in trouble.

Andy yanked off his shirt and shoes, threw a pair of goggles over his eyes, and dove into the water. There was a slight electrical jitter when hitting the water, as if it contained a charge that was fading away. It was nothing he couldn't recover from right away. Already, he felt the intense current sweeping in from over his right shoulder. It was like something was fanning the ocean from the northeast. He looked, and in that moment, even despite the terror of not knowing where Martha was, he was lost in the awe of seeing the two battling titans.

My God, she was right!

There was a blood cloud billowing between him and the creatures. The sperm whale was squirming like an invertebrate, bleeding profusely from where the eel was biting at its midsection.

The whale was trying to whack its enemy away with its fluke, but could not get the angle it needed. The motions were taking both of the creatures toward the surface. Right now, they were a hundred feet or so beneath.

Andy glanced around for Martha. His heart thumped. He had only a minute or so of oxygen left before he had to go back up for air. He turned around, saw nothing but water, then turned south...THERE!

She was alive and moving, though weakly. She was drifting on her back, arms reaching high, almost like someone awakening from a deep sleep. He recalled the flash and the slight electrical shock he felt when diving. That thing actually was electric, which alarmed him further. It could shock again at any moment, and anything in the water around it was doomed to be zapped.

Andy's lungs were starting to burn. There wasn't much time left. He paddled closer to Martha. Another wave struck his body, propelling him toward her...while also pushing her further away.

However, it looked as though her energy was coming back. Martha saw her husband's figure against the bright surface below. The sight of him sparked a new energy within her, especially when she realized he had no rebreather. She fought against her weakened muscles and kicked toward him. They met in the middle, embraced, then traded off the rebreather. Andy took a couple of breaths, felt his insides re-energize, then gave it back, then put his arm around his wife's waist and paddled to the surface... where the two monsters were now fighting.

The scientists stopped and watched in horror. The fight was getting closer to their boat. They rolled over each other, fins slapping the water, the eel constricting its body over the whale, now biting under its left eye. Sly slapped his tail out of desperation, carrying them off blindly. Like a spiraling meteorite, they collided with the boat.

The explosive *crash* echoed throughout the water. The resounding shockwave traveled down to the seabed, carrying the two scientists along with it. They separated, both reaching out for the other.

Andy hit the bottom first. His wife was thirty feet directly ahead of him. He had to get to her now, not just to help her, but for the rebreather. It was three hundred feet to the surface and he had lost some air in the hit. He would never make it to the surface on his own.

Martha turned around and saw him coming. They reunited a second time and traded off the rebreather. They looked up. The bright surface above was clouded with dark obstacles. Their vessel had been broken in two.

The titans spiraled through the wreckage, the deep-dwelling being unrelenting in its grip. Together, they moved as one body.

****

"Bogey's moving. One-thousand yards," the sonar operator announced.

"It's been hit. There's no mistake, sir. Tracking and visual confirmation. The whale struck the civilian vessel," Operations Specialist Bannerman announced to the bridge.

Lt. Commander Jim Davidson stepped out on deck and gazed with his binoculars. The whale's fluke rose over the water, then disappeared. There was debris everywhere. It had struck a vessel as large as itself so hard that it split in half. The bow had turned over. It was slowly descending beneath the frothing waves, while the stern took a little more time.

"Christ! What were they doing out here?!" Davidson lowered the binoculars and turned to face Elway. "Target's moving twenty-degrees north. Target it with the Bushmaster."

"As for the civilians?"

"Wait for it to move another hundred yards out," Davidson replied. "Can't shoot the beast while they're in that debris field. There might be survivors."

The Bushmaster rotated to port, the barrel elevating to accommodate the distance between it and the target. At the moment, they had lost visual of the whale. Judging by the swells, it was still there, moving frantically.

****

Andy gripped his wife by the shoulders to make her face him. He pointed his thumb to the surface. Martha understood. Saving Sly was no longer an option. Her husband was right all along. They should never have come out here. Now, what had she accomplished other than putting their lives at risk?

She let him take another breath, then together, they swam for the surface.

The eel ripped with its jaws, peeling away large flaps of skin from around the whale's eye. Electrical jolts from its body continuously zapped the mammal, fluttering its heartbeats and singeing its flesh.

The whale had another problem: it needed air. It was losing this fight badly and was smart enough to know it had no chance of winning. It just needed to break the Eel's hold on its body so it could make a final retreat. Considering the Eel's hold, there was only one thing that Sly's enormous brain could come up with.

With a jerk of his head, he pointed himself down at the seabed, then fluttered his tail with all of his strength.

Razor teeth prodded against his closed eye. He felt the slicing of the fatty eyelid, and the screaming of nerves as it was torn away, forcing him to watch the pointy teeth close in again. His left eye ruptured, rendering him half-blind.

The pain added to his desperation. The whale reached the seabed and angled up slightly, sideswiping the rocky ground below.

Ping! Ping! Ping!

Intense soundwaves bounced off the seafloor, assaulting the eel's brain. Each ping was like nails on a chalkboard for the creature. Frustrated, it loosened its constriction.

With the grip released, the whale shot for the surface.

The eel coiled, its body letting out small bolts like the severed end of a high voltage cable. It looked up to see its opponent fleeing, trailing thick volumes of blood.

Something else was in the water. Foreign creatures, not of the sea, but of the land. Two biped creatures swimming for the surface. They swam, then stopped, swam again, only to stop once more. It was almost fascinating for the creature to watch. It had no understanding of depressurization, nor did it care. The eel was fascinated, seeing these creatures that clearly weren't meant for the water struggle for the waterless void above. That fascination gave way to hunger. These humans were easy pickings. It would satiate its hunger, then finish its clash with the whale.

Its immense body flickered with intense hot energy. A wave of its tail propelled the beast toward its new target.

They felt the current. Then the sudden temperature increase. Their skin tingled with mild electrical charges. The current intensified, and like an eagle swooping in to snatch a mouse, the leviathan came at the two scientists.

Martha and Andy shared the same thought. They pushed each other backward, each intending to sacrifice themselves in order to give the other a fighting chance to survive. There were no goodbyes, not even a final loving gaze. The eel's advance would not grant the time.

Their palms struck the other in the shoulders, and in a heartbeat, they were ten feet apart. When Andy's heart beat again, he wished it was his last. In one instant, his wife was there, then she wasn't.

The beast passed between them, snatched Martha in its jaws, and kept going.

Andy's enraged scream was drowned out by the ocean. The beast circled far ahead of him, blood bubbles trailing from its mouth. He couldn't see his wife, but saw the way the beast jerked its head back and forth, and the increased intensity of the blood cloud with each movement.

It angled back, its narrow head now pointed at him, ready to swoop in and take him as well.

The sperm whale broke the surface and expelled a thick mist through his blowhole, then sucked the rich oxygen. Bloody water lapped on all directions. Despite filling his lungs, it could feel its energy waning. It had lost half its vision, blinding it to the rapidly advancing ship coming in from the southwest. Because of this, the sudden rapid sound seemed to come from nowhere, as well as the impact of lead projectiles.

The first three flew wide, the fourth grazing his back, the next several punching through his right side. Pain and instinct forced Sly deep. Projectiles continued to pummel the water, striking his tail and back, ripping flesh and organs. It flailed its tail in a final effort to survive, unknowing that his stomach, intestines, and liver had been ruptured.

The eel reared its head back to strike, only to turn to its right to see the whale barreling down on it. Its rattlesnake strike intended for the human was instead directed at the dying beast that it incorrectly assumed was coming in for an attack. Jaws ripped at the weakened flesh.

The last thing Sly would see was the white flash of a high-voltage bolt that would singe his flesh and explode his heart.

The instinct to survive trumped his grief in the moment, and Andy shot for the surface. He would wait to pressurize; he didn't have enough air in his lungs. The surface wasn't too far. It was just ahead of him, getting brighter and brighter. Just a few more strokes.

With the strobing light came electrical shocks. Andy's body jerked, his lungs inadvertently blowing out some of his dwindling oxygen supply. He overpowered the near-overwhelming temptation to succumb to the jolts and sink. With a few powerful strokes, he burst through the surface and grabbed a piece of debris. Nose bleeding, he lay his head over the piece of decking, while taking in several deep breaths. Finally, with his lungs recharged, his mind returned to the horrible change in his life that he was now forced to endure. Martha was gone. Taken before his very eyes.

The memory played back over and over. Each time it ended, he hoped he'd awaken in bed; that it was just some horrible dream. Instead, he was here, drifting in debris between the two sinking halves of his vessel.

Andy pounded a fist on the board, looked to the heavens, and screamed. In his anguish, he never noticed the Coast Guard Cutter approaching from behind.

****

"We've got a survivor in the water!" one of the crew members shouted.

Petty Officer Tom Elway watched from the forecastle as his men hauled the civilian aboard. As they did, other crewmembers pointed to the north. The target's body broke the surface, its face and body almost unrecognizable from the damage they had done.

"Jesus, we even shot its damn eye out," he said. His tone was not that of a delighted man, but a sorrowful one.

"We did our job," Davidson said. He watched the crew bring in the survivor. Immediately, he recognized the man as the one who relinquished the computer. That man's wife was adamant about not killing the whale…and she was nowhere to be seen. "Oh, no. I think we have a body in this water somewhere."

"Want me to send out search parties?" Elway asked. They listened to the survivor's nonstop wails.

"Something tells me it'll do no good," Davidson said. "Let's get in touch with the local PD."

****

The eel rested along the seabed. The new arrival above was far bigger than anything it had ever encountered before. Its drumming vibrations were unlike anything it had ever experienced. It moved toward the carcass like a thieving scavenger, taking a carcass from an exhausted predator. The eel, determined to be the dominant predator of the sea, contemplated a strike. Instead, it chose to wait. Once again, it had spent much energy in combat with the whale, and this new enemy was very unfamiliar. Rather than battle a larger opponent right away, it opted to hunt for easier prey.

Should the intruder remain in the area, the time to strike would be imminent. For now, the eel moved west.

CHAPTER 24

Silvia Remar was in her office when she got the call from Lt. Commander Davidson. The whale had been eliminated, and as far as they were concerned, the waters were declared safe. The news was not all sunshine and rainbows. The report came with devastating news that Martha Cornett's yacht was out on the water at the time, and had been struck by the whale before they could gun it down.

"My God," she muttered. "Thank you, Commander. Let me know if you need anything else." She hung up, then stared at the wall across from her. Her mind was almost numb. Another death. Yeah, the threat was over, but it would still be another blow to the island's image.

She picked up the phone again and dialed JoEllen's extension.

"Mayor Marsh."

"This is Chief Remar. Coast Guard Lieutenant Commander Jim Davidson just notified me that the operation is complete. The whale is confirmed killed."

JoEllen's voice instantly lit up with enthusiasm. *"Excellent. Thank you for letting me know. Let's prepare a press conference within the hour. We need to inform the public that the waters are safe."*

"Yep. I'll be there, Ms. Mayor," Silvia said.

"Everything alright there, Chief? You almost sound bummed."

"Well, I guess there's been another casualty," Silvia said. "A marine biologist went out there against the restrictions. According to Davidson, the whale struck their boat. Only her husband was found."

"Jesus. I wonder what drove that whale so insane," JoEllen said. Silvia didn't offer a response. Since that morning, all she could think about was the frantic explanations that Martha tried to inform her of. Everyone was so quick to blame Sly for all the deaths, despite the fact

that some didn't make much sense. Sean Bradley confirmed witnessing Brock Giler getting pulled under the water. She couldn't imagine Sly could pull that off without his big head busting through the surface.

"It's tragic. Yeah, they disobeyed the law, but it's still very unfortunate," JoEllen said. *"I'll have my secretary include that in the press release. Please arrive at the Town Hall. It'll be a quick event. In and out. I just want us to do it in person so everyone feels safe to go back out on the water."*

Silvia didn't reply. Her eyes were locked on the image of her computer screen. At the top of the article read in black letters ***ANOTHER EARTHQUAKE IN THE PEURTO RICO TRENCH.***

The image below showed some sort of alien-looking fish with large bug eyes that was caught in the Caribbean. After scrolling further, she saw a photo of the largest recorded squid ever on record, washed up dead along the shore.

Silvia scrolled through more articles, stopping at one particular headline which caught her eye.

***SCIENTISTS WORRIED OF RESIDUAL ENVIRONMENTAL DAMAGE FROM GOTA JA' TITAN* METEOR.**

It was the next report that concerned her the most. To the rest of the world, it was unrelated to the reports of deep sea creatures emerging off the eastern North and South American coasts. To Silvia, it was alarming.

Fishing trawler found ablaze fifty miles northeast of San Salvador. Officials unable to determine the cause.

Silvia scoured the article for any mention of any strange burns below the waterline, but nothing was mentioned.

"Chief?"

"Uh, yes! I'll, uh…" She skimmed the article again. Something didn't feel right. Whatever was going on, it felt unbelievable, but true. "JoEllen, maybe we should keep the waters closed."

"Closed?" The Mayor's voice lost any remnant of humility. *"Are you out of your mind?"*

"I'd like to investigate the waters," Silvia said. "Dr. Cornett stated there might be something else out there. Her explanation was, odd, to say the least. But she was adamant that there's another large organism out there. I think it's worth looking into."

"Nonsense. Every day we wait is money lost for the residents of our town," JoEllen said. *"I expect to see you here at 3:00, Chief. Let's get these beaches opened back up."*

"I'm just saying, maybe we should wait, JoEllen. Martha Cornett stated she was getting some odd readings from the water, and I'd like to get some experts to help check it out."

"Odd readings? Like what? Toxins?"

"No. Temperature fluxes."

"Probably just equipment malfunction. She was probably just trying to protect the whale. I don't blame her, Chief, and what happened greatly saddens me. Really, it does. But I'm not gonna keep the island on lockdown because of temperature fluxes that could be explained by anything. If you want to investigate it, you go ahead. But we're opening our beaches today. See you at 3:00."

With that, the line went dead. Silvia glanced at her black screen before it faded to white, then clipped it back to her belt. She looked at the clock. She'd have to get going almost right away. It only took a few minutes to get to the Town Hall, but it was always best in these cases to get there early to go over exactly what to tell the press.

She stood up, turned to shut her computer down, and gasped. The turning of her hips was all it took for her nerves to strike. Silvia yelped, leaned against the desk, and mentally chastised the universe for cursing her with what she referred to as a 'defective spine'.

There was no way around it; she needed her back brace. She didn't care how it looked to anyone else. Just having the pressure there helped her mentally, probably because it provided a sense that she was at least doing *something* to help her back. Meds did nothing, and she was so busy, getting that epidural was impossible.

She pulled her brace from the cabinet, then checked her office door to make sure it was shut. She undid her trousers, then wrapped the brace around her lower back. Before she could connect the Velcro, the brace sprang from her grip, swept over the desk, knocking papers across the floor as well as batting the pencase against the monitor.

The frustration came out of her like a volcano.

"Goddamnit!" she exclaimed.

The door burst open and Royce rushed in.

"Chief? Is everything al—Oh!" He saw Silvia with her trousers undone, then quickly spun around. For the first time in a decade, he felt himself turning red. He was no stranger to seeing a woman undressing…except this was his boss.

As embarrassed as he was, it was nothing compared to what Silvia was feeling. She grabbed her brace, secured it over herself, made sure to tighten the straps properly, then fixed her pants.

What next? Is my truck engine gonna blow up?

"I'm so sorry," Royce said. Silvia initially considered chewing him out for coming in unannounced, but after taking a moment to cool her temper, she backed away from that thought. Yeah, he should've knocked, but in his defense he had just heard crashing sounds. If nothing else, at least he wasn't being an outright dick to her for once.

"Nah, it's alright," she said. Royce turned around. His eyes went down to the brace. Silvia had mentioned back issues before, though she never really elaborated. He assumed it was muscle aches, or at worst, a bulging disc.

"You sure you're alright?" he asked.

"As alright as I'll ever be. Coast Guard's killed the whale. I gotta meet with the Mayor to make a press release," Silvia said.

"I suppose that's good news," Royce said. His eyes went to the windowsill. There was the *U.S. Army* photo on the left. Across from it was a picture of a man in a military uniform. It was the first real time he'd spent more than thirty seconds in her office, as he usually was in and out for quick briefs or debriefs, and never stayed for social talk. Judging by the clarity of the photo, it must've been taken in the nineties.

"Everything alright?" Silvia said.

"Oh, yeah," he said. "Sorry, my bad. Just being nosey. Looking at the military stuff."

Silvia glanced back. "Oh. My dad."

"That was my guess." Royce knelt down to pick up some of the fallen items. He found a few printed reports, immediately sparking a few *administrator chief* comments in his mind. He stacked them, then moved on to the next fallen item: a spiral notebook. He had seen it on her desk before, closed, probably containing more documents for the Mayor. But it was open, with a collage of photos featuring a younger Silvia Remar. There were photos of her running on track, horseback riding, weightlifting, and many other activities from her youth. Many of these photos featured her with a man who, judging by his staunch similarity to the military man on the windowsill, was her father.

He stood up with the book, allowed himself to flip through another page, before handing it off to Silvia. He saw photos of martial arts, tournaments, women's basketball, and her father in a jousting competition.

"Jesus," Royce said. "Were you guys training for the Olympics? Or just a family of athletes?"

"More the latter," Silvia replied. She took the booklet and allowed herself to gaze at the photos. The back-brace seemed to hug tighter as her eyes swept over the still memories of pain free days. "My dad was a real ass kicker. Wanted to compete in everything. That was one of the reasons he joined the service; to pay for all his grand adventures. I guess some of it spilled over to me."

Royce nodded, pretending not to be interested.

"Well, uh, sorry for barging in on you. Heard a yell and a bunch of stuff falling over. Thought maybe you fell or something, but uh...yeah." He wasn't sure what else to say, so he started for the door. He stepped to the hallway then took a right. With one more step, he would've been out of sight. Instead, he stopped. His attempts to ignore that inner calling inside of him were failing miserably.

He looked back. "Hey, uh, if I may ask, what kind of back trouble is it that you have?"

"What *don't* I have at this point?" Silvia said. "Arthritis, bone spurs, herniated disc in the L5 region."

"I see. My advice: get a Purple mattress. It's a memory foam type of material. If you're tossing and turning at night, it's probably making things worse down there. You need a comfortable surface to lay flat on. They're expensive, but they're definitely worth it."

"Okay," Silvia said, surprised to be getting sound advice from the Sergeant. Any other time, she would have ignored it, but at this point, she'd take advice from *Michael Myers* if it meant the slightest chance of easing her pain. "Have you used that kind of mattress?"

"My wife bought one. It's like sleeping on a cloud. The only downside is that it makes it almost impossible to get out of bed. You won't want to get up. And you'll hate your alarm clock all the more." Silvia smiled. "But the main reason I'm recommending it is because I had a buddy that screwed up his back. Make no mistake, it's not a cure, but getting good sleep makes a lot of difference. The body needs to relax. The more it tenses, the more the nerves are compressed."

Silvia nodded. *Damn, I'm getting better info from this guy than any of the doctors I've been visiting.* Her eyes went back to the clock.

"Oh, shit. I need to get going. Thanks for the recommendation, Sergeant. I'll check into that."

Royce stepped aside so she could leave, noticing her deliberate attempt to keep a straight posture while she made her way to the door.

"No problem," he said. Silvia waved 'goodbye' then stepped out into the lot. His fake smile transformed into a frown. For the first time in his life, he felt an emotion toward the Chief he NEVER thought he'd experience: concern. Yeah, she was inept. Yeah, she had less real experience than most of the people she was overseeing. But now, it made sense. The photos, the back brace—all of it illustrated the storm going on in her mind.

An internal force guided Royce's hand to his wallet. He opened it and shuffled through a few cutout photos from his NYPD days. One was actually a cutout from a newspaper of him and two fellow officers sitting on a bench with a kid, after buying him lunch. It wasn't the kid that drew

Royce's attention; rather, the black officer on the right side, his face stuffed with *McDonald's French fries*. It was in the last months that things were normal for Officer Larry Bryan. Royce was there in the gym when he heard his buddy cry out in pain, followed by the sound of weights hitting the floor. One wrong technique was all it took. Two herniated discs.

Months of physical therapy followed, with varying results. The doctors pushed drugs, which did nothing except fill the pockets of the pharmaceutical companies. The doctors declined surgery, stating his age and a bunch of other standard bullshit reasons they didn't want to do it. Risk of infection? Who cares when you can't even stand up straight? His incessant pleas that he needed a fusion were ignored. *"Take the drugs. Try this new treatment."*

Then came helplessness. Larry's temper worsened. Small things such as dropping a pen would send him into an outrage. Going to work every day was a nightmare, especially when dealing with unruly people on the street. And in New York, that was every single day.

Two years later, Royce went to work to see Larry wasn't there. Later that day, the Lieutenant called him in to let him know Larry was found dead in his apartment. He had ended his agony with a bullet in the mouth.

In those two years, Royce learned that pain and helplessness were as bad as any cancer. Had those doctors just done the surgery. *"It only gets worse with age."* He remembered a bunch of people telling Larry that. The effects it must have had on his psyche...

Royce remembered the pain, the feeling of uselessness, the inability to do certain everyday things that Larry loved. After a year, the guy couldn't exercise anymore, and that was his favorite hobby. The guy's whole life was altered.

"Miss ya, buddy," he said aloud, then tucked the photo back into his wallet.

CHAPTER 25

The news report was like a defibrillator to a stopped heart. Maxwell Island, which had been uncharacteristically quiet for the last twenty-four hours, was suddenly bursting with activity again. The word spread like hay fever: the whale was dead, the threat was gone, the water was safe.

Once the word was given, it only took minutes for the mass migration to begin. Within an hour, the beaches were packed. Boats were taking to the water again.

When Lieutenant Adam Henry patrolled along North Beach, he never would've guessed that a body had been found twenty-four hours ago. All the angst the public felt had almost instantly vanished.

Except for his.

He walked on foot, watching the large mass of vacationers splashing in the water. Some swam as far as a couple hundred feet out, where the shark nets barricaded the swimming area from the rest of the sea. He couldn't rid himself of that sick feeling he'd felt since the incidents began.

He was here on North Beach when he saw the AirSea Rescue transport Andy Cornett from the Coast Guard Cutter to Maxwell General. He had received word from Captain Maurice Peterman that the patient had to be sedated, as he was in hysterics regarding the death of his wife.

Another boat destroyed. According to the Chief, the Coast Guard reportedly arrived on the scene right after the whale struck the vessel. The tracking recorder could not be disputed; the whale did in fact strike the vessel. Yet, this news wasn't sitting right in Adam's gut. He was no marine biologist, but he had a hard time buying the fact that Sly, a whale that had been in the area for years, had suddenly become a hyper-violent monster. It didn't make sense from any standpoint. Sperm whales were a docile species, and Sly had been around boats his whole life.

Then there was that visit from Dr. Cornett. In the hours since meeting with Davidson, he had gone over the details regarding the yacht explosion and George O'Mara's speedboat crash. Both reports noted an odd, but similar abnormality. A single burn in the underside of the vessel, reminiscent of damage caused by a lightning strike.

A lightning strike? Underwater?

His mind flashed to Dr. Cornett's warnings of a giant electric eel. It seemed so comical when he first heard it. Then he did his own research, and suddenly, it didn't seem so funny. The plates had shifted, causing all kinds of seismic activity in the Puerto Rico Trench. Considering all the creatures that were coming up to the ocean's surface, only to die from the temperature and pressure changes that they weren't accustomed to, it must've been getting bad in certain areas.

Adam was no scientist. He knew nothing of marine creatures, ocean pressures, the list of organisms living below, nor did he have any knowledge about the hundreds of theories regarding undiscovered organisms. However, he did understand patterns.

These incidents began relatively soon after the earthquakes took place. Considering the two-thousand mile distance between Maxwell Island and the Puerto Rico Trench, the timeframe worked. An organism would easily make that distance inside of a month's time.

Adam walked on foot, actively assuring himself that everything was okay. These people venturing into the water were safe. The threat had been eliminated, verified by the Coast Guard.

Up ahead was Maurice Peterman's Fire Rescue pickup truck. The Captain himself was standing next to it, watching the people swimming. Adam quickened his pace then waved at the Fire Captain.

"Maurice!"

"Hey, Adam," Maurice replied, waving back.

"Out to grab a late lunch?" Adam said, pointing at the café behind him.

"Nah, just keeping an eye on things, just like you," Maurice said. Adam could see the discontentment in his eyes. The Captain looked as though he had seen a ghost.

"Were you in the crew that picked up Andy Cornett?" Adam asked.

Maurice nodded. "He's in bad shape, man."

"Injured?"

"Surprisingly no," Maurice said. "I meant mentally. His mind is lost. I think he saw his wife get taken. It's just so…strange." He watched the water again. "I saw the whale carcass." He paused. Adam knew by the way he brought it up that something wasn't normal, but Maurice couldn't put his finger on it.

"And?"

"Something's going on around here, Adam," Maurice said. "I know electrical burns. Sly was COVERED in them!"

"Electrical burns?"

"That and..." he hesitated, worried that he was going to sound crazy, "bite marks. At least, wounds that looked like bite marks."

"Jesus. You think he ran into a pod of orcas?"

Maurice shook his head. "No. Whatever bit him had to have been much larger. I'm telling you, dude, I got a plain good look at the whale. Had it not been shot by the Coast Guard, it would've died anyway from those injuries."

"Did the Coast Guard Commander say anything about this?"

"No," Maurice answered. "I didn't get a chance to speak with them. Had to get Andy Cornett back here. Besides, their orders were to kill the whale. They're already heading east."

Adam was starting to sweat. It felt like all the pieces were slowly falling into place, and what they were building towards seemed so ghastly and impossible, he was almost afraid to pursue the truth. Electrical burns? Lightning strikes on boats? All at the same time a scientist warns him that an undiscovered species of electric eel is swimming off the coast...

"I don't like that look in your eye," Maurice said. "I know what you're thinking. I'd expect such action from Royce, but not from you."

Adam shook his head. "I don't have a choice. I have to go talk to Andy. I need to know what he saw."

"You think there's something else out there?"

"Nothing around here makes sense, even if you throw in Sly's actions. In fact, *especially* when you consider Sly's actions. And if—" he looked at the crowd, then lowered his voice not to be overheard. "If these people are in the water, and there's a maneater out there, whatever it may be, it's my responsibility to get them out. I need to know if there's a threat."

"The doctors probably won't let you see him."

Adam turned and walked west along the beach toward his vehicle.

"Let them try and stop me."

****

When Adam arrived at the hospital, he figured he'd try a diplomatic approach. He stepped to the check-in desk and asked to speak to the doctor in charge of Andy Cornett, who had been admitted within the last hour. Five minutes later, he was greeted by Dr. Renee Cobb.

"I've been talking to so many police lately, I feel like I'm being investigated," she joked.

Adam smiled. He had met Renee on a number of occasions. Additionally, he read in the Chief's report that she provided information in the George O'Mara investigation.

"Nah, we know you wouldn't harm a fly," Adam said. His smile only lasted a second. "Andy Cornett was checked in. His yacht was sunk and his wife killed. What's his present condition?"

"He's got some lung damage. He must've swum deep and had to come up fast without having enough time to depressurize in the last hundred feet or so."

"Can he talk?" Adam asked. Renee breathed a long sigh.

"It probably wouldn't be a good idea," she said. "I didn't even get started on his mental state."

"Hysterics?"

"Yes. Grief over his wife. Talk about the thing that took her. I presume he means the whale," Renee replied.

"Doctor. It's really...REALLY important that I try and speak with him," Adam said. Renee stared him in the eyes.

"I don't suppose it's something that can afford to wait?"

"It probably isn't."

"Damn it. Alright. But please make it simple and quick," Renee said. "I'd advise not to mention his wife, but if these *urgent* questions are about the recent incident, then I suppose there's no way around it."

"I'll be as delicate as I can."

Adam followed her through a series of hallways until they arrived in Andy's room. He was being given a hyperbaric breathing treatment. He was awake, the black air mask fitted tight to his face.

Adam leaned toward Renee. "Can he talk with that thing on?"

"Yes," she replied. She waited by the door while Adam approached the patient.

"Mr. Cornett. I'm Lieutenant Henry. We actually met earlier today, if you remember."

"I remember." Andy's voice was dry and strained. His eyes were pointed to the ceiling, unblinking. His skin was pale, his hair thinned. It was like the man had aged twenty years in just a matter of hours.

"First off, Mr. Cornett, I wanna offer my condolences for your loss."

"We warned you it was out there..."

"It?" Adam said. He kept an eye on Andy's elevating heart rate.

"You didn't believe us."

"It sounded unbelievable at the time. But something's not right. Mr. Cornett, I need to know if you've seen it."

Andy drew a deep breath. "The water temperatures are rising. It's letting off charges. Killing the surrounding ecosystem. It's feeding on anything it can find."

"Did you see it?"

"It came right between us. It abandoned the whale and went right for us..." Andy's fingers curled. "I felt the charges emitting from its flesh..." His eyes winced and his body shook, as though being electrocuted. "Then it took her. It was no whale! It's an Eel! You didn't believe us, and you let her die!"

Renee and a few nurses rushed into the room.

"Point five ccs of lorazepam," Renee ordered. She glanced back at Adam. There wasn't anger in her face, but confusion and fright. Normally, she'd write off the ramblings of a grieving patient as just that, ramblings. But the fact that Adam Henry, a very respected person in the police force, was concerned about his statements made her nervous. "What's going on? What's he talking about?"

"I'm gonna find out. I'd advise all of you to stay clear of the water." Adam marched out of the room. His fingers found the transmitter to his mic speaker. "Chief. We need to talk."

CHAPTER 26

Tracy Bannister was probably the only person on Maxwell Island that wasn't personally bummed out when the beaches closed. Her stomach felt as though a hurricane was tearing through it. It was misery accompanied by anger—she did not spend three-thousand dollars on a reservation to spend it vomiting.

For the last two nights, she twisted and turned in bed. That damned restaurant! *Wild Bill*, it was called. She would write a scathing review once she felt up to it. 'Fresh swordfish'.

My ass!

Her absence was hardly noticed by her boyfriend, who continued to spend his days at the beach and on the water. Blake wasn't going to let anything like a sick girlfriend ruin his vacation. Nor was his brother Kenneth. For the entirety of the last twenty-four hours, Tracy had to endure his whining about having nothing to do. Blake was the only one complaining. Kenneth, on the other hand, took his opportunity to find a different kind of 'ride'.

Normally, Tracy would've complained about being forced to listen to Kenneth bang his date in the next room. However, as miserable as she felt, it gave her something to laugh about. Blake wasn't amused. On a few occasions, he banged his fist against the wall, muttering "How freaking long are they gonna go at it?!"

To that, Tracy would reply, "What can I say, babe? Some guys can actually pull that off."

That got under his skin, much to her amusement. But then, the threat was cleared and the beaches deemed safe again. For Blake and Kenneth, the timing couldn't be more perfect. They had a jetboat chartered for four o'clock. He had spoken with the owner the previous day, who informed him that if the notice was lifted, he would honor their appointment.

Tracy groaned, still feeling sick and miserable as her boyfriend got suited up in his red swim trunks and open white shirt. He grabbed his goggles, a towel, then was nearly out the door without saying goodbye. His only delay was Kenneth, who was standing outside his hotel room, tongue-fencing with the blonde date he had hooked up with.

"Come on, man," Blake said. Kenneth didn't even look up; he simply held up a middle finger and proceeded with the make-out. Blake stared at the ceiling. "Good God."

"You'll live," Tracy called through the open door. She rested her head on the pillow. She was dehydrated and completely lacking in energy. She refused to look in a mirror. *It would take five pounds of makeup to fix my zombie appearance.*

Blake wandered back inside. His sandy-colored hair was sticking up, unchanged from the moment he woke up that morning. He never bothered showering, in hopes of being able to run out the door the moment he received word that things were back to normal.

"First the whale, and now my brother," he muttered.

"Hey, at least you're going at all," Tracy said. "You could be stuck here with food poisoning."

Blake shrugged, uncaringly. "You're the one who chose *Wild Bill's*. I wanted to try out that barbeque place."

"Barbeque? On an island?" Tracy said.

"Yeah? What's wrong with that?"

She shook her head. "Just doesn't seem to fit the mood."

"It's America, babe. Barbeque fits EVERY mood. Besides, look how well the tropical menu worked for you." He instantly regretted saying that. Just the thought of the swordfish was making her turn green. He froze, hoping somehow he would be able to halt the inevitable upheaval.

Thankfully, she was able to make it to the bathroom. He winced while listening to her gag. So much for sex this week.

At least Kenneth was getting plenty of action. He was still making out with the date he had spent all day banging. Tracy wasn't done gagging when he left into the hall.

"Hope you feel better, babe. We'll be back soon."

"Stick a marlin bill up your ass!" she said in-between vomits.

"Don't blame me. Remember? I wanted barbeque!"

Tracy leaned away from the toilet long enough to throw a bottle of shampoo at him. Blake had already retreated out the door and closed it behind him. The bottle struck hard, exploding white cream all over the door. Tracy saw the mess, moaned, then stumbled back into the bathroom.

It wasn't Blake's fault. If anything, he was right, though she wouldn't admit it out loud. On top of being sick to her stomach, she was angry. Her vacation was ruined. They only had a few days left, and by the looks of it, she'd be spending them here in bed while Blake and Kenneth were out having fun. It wasn't fair. But what could she do about it?

She flushed, stumbled back to the bed, gave one final glance at the mess on the door, then plopped into bed.

He can clean that up when he gets back. She rolled onto her side, looked out at the ocean view, which only served to irritate her further, as that was where she'd rather be. She rolled over, stared at the blank wall, then dozed off.

Blake stood in the hallway and took a breath to recover from his brief sprint. The thud against the door was enough to dislodge Kenneth's lips from his date's.

"Everything alright there, champ?"

"Oh, just dandy. Except I'm gonna have to listen to her complain about this for the rest of the year," Blake said. He glanced at his watch again, then back at his brother. "You done there, stud? Or should I go meet Phillip by myself?"

"Is that who you're seeing?" Kenneth's date said with a laugh.

"Oh, ha-ha," Blake said. *Seriously? This chick doesn't even know me.* Kenneth kissed her once more, then slung his gear over his shoulder.

"Ready to go when you are, bro."

"Finally. Let's get out of here."

"Wait," Kenneth said. He pointed at Blake's hotel room door. "Tracy's not coming?"

Blake stood dumbfounded. He leaned forward, his nose and brow wrinkling.

"Where have you been all week? She's got food poisoning!"

"Yeah, I knew that! But I thought she was getting better."

"Well, I thought so too, until I mentioned the swordfish," Blake said. Kenneth chuckled, then stopped when Blake's annoyed look intensified.

"Wait, we had a reservation for three!" he said, as if he just now realized this.

"I'm sure Phillip will be fine with just two," Blake said.

"No, that's not what I mean," Kenneth said. He hugged his date closer, making sure to get a quick ass-squeeze in the process. "We can take her along in Tracy's place."

"Huh?" Blake said. The blonde lit up with joy.

"Oh, I LOVE waterskiing!"

"Look, uh…" Blake fought to remember her name out of the bunch. Kenneth had been going through women as if he was *Leonardo DiCaprio*. "Uh, Stacie! Yeah, I don't know if—"

"Who?!" she said.

Oh, shit! Wrong one.

Immediately, the date looked at Kenneth, her eyes interrogating him as to how many girls preceded her 'interactions' with him. He panicked briefly, as even he struggled to remember her name.

"No, dumbass," he said to Blake. Directing the attention onto his brother was his method of stalling. "How could you forget, uh…" *Was is Jessica? No. Allison? Michelle? Brittney? SAMANTHA!!!—Sammy!* "…Sammy's name?!"

There was a small grin from Sammy, essentially signaling that Kenneth was off the hook.

"Anyway, *Sammy*," Blake continued, "I don't know if you'll be interested in going with us. We're gonna be out in the sun all day, catching waves, drinking, skiing…it's gonna be busy."

Sammy crossed her arms. "Aren't you idiots from New Jersey?" Blake flushed. He nodded. "Yeah, I *live* here, hotshot. The stuff you're talking about, I do every day. I live it, compared to you doing it every other weekend in the summer. While you're curling up under a blanket in January, I'm out on the water."

Blake raised his hands in surrender.

"Okay, I stand corrected. If Kenneth's good with you coming along, I'm good with it too."

"Damn right I'm good with it," Kenneth said, slapping Sammy on the rear.

"But swim gear…"

"I'm wearing it," Sammy said, pulling down the collar of her shirt to show her green bikini top.

"Fine. Can we go now?!" Blake said, pointing at his watch. "If we're not at the pier in the next twenty minutes, there won't be any boating."

"Hey, you're the one standing and whining," she retorted.

Blake's eyes flared. *Bitch, you're the one who spent the last fifteen minutes making out with my brother!* He took a breath, then looked at Kenneth. *How do you attract these chicks? Must have a thing for bitchy attitudes.*

"Alright, fine. Let's go."

****

Adaption was a painful process sometimes. A lesser being would retreat to its den, or, it if had the technology and intelligence to do so, use an outside substance to weaken the pain.

Neither of these options were viable, for the eel had no dark den to retreat to, nor did it have the capabilities to dull the pains of evolution. The predator did not seek relief, as pain was a reminder of survival, and what critical thinking it had was merely used for determining methods to seek and kill prey. In addition, there was no den or cave to return to. This new environment was its home now, and to survive, it would have to adapt to the alien brightness above.

Nerves surged in its eyes as the pupils evolved to endure the constant intake of light. The eel rested on the seafloor, pumping water through its gills. Blood vessels popped, sending thin clouds of blood trailing its sockets.

The creature rested for hours, until finally, the pain subsided. Its body's natural defenses clogged the small wounds and stopped the bleeding.

It raised its head from its coiled position and gazed at the world around it. It took in every rock around it, every ripple above it, and everything in-between. Its vision was so clear, the creature may as well have lived here all its life.

No longer was the light an antagonistic presence. The eel was free to embrace the night and the day. It swam off the seabed and approached the surface. It was slow and cautious at first, but soon accelerated. Feeling all sorts of vibration from along the surface, the beast prodded its head into the void above. There was no water to filter through its gills up here, but the beast quickly learned that it could go without air for several minutes.

With its head arching over the water like that of a leathery-skinned giraffe, it looked around. There were several of those movable floating objects between it and the landmass. Each one carried one or more of the land-dwellers. Some of them were further out, the vessels making loud droning sounds as they raced eighty-miles per hour.

The agonies of its development had burnt a considerable amount of energy, as did the constant discharges from its electric-producing organs. It needed to feed, and soon.

The eel watched one speeding a thousand feet to its left. Trailing behind it was one of the land-dwellers, towed along at high speed by some kind of line. It had seen these devices before. The eel did not understand the purpose of such actions, nor did it care. It made for accessible prey, as it had learned the previous morning near the island.

During that chase, it learned that it could not outpace the vehicles, but did learn how they moved. To be stopped, they needed to be intercepted rather than chased. After racing in straight lines, they often performed sharp turns and raced back in the opposite direction.

It needed to put itself in the path of its prey.

The eel splashed down, arching its body over the surface like a mythical sea serpent. Tiny bolts of electricity lashed from its hide as it swam toward its new target.

****

Kenneth and Sammy whooped as they watched Blake cruise the water behind them. He hit a wave and bounced, and successfully managed to stick the landing.

"There you go! You're getting the hang of it," Sammy called out to him. He couldn't hear their words, but did understand the tone of voice. Once they got started, Blake noticed that Sammy had warmed up to him since leaving the hotel. She was in her element here. Whatever the case, she wasn't as quick to get angry. In fact, Blake couldn't deny she was actually kind of fun to be around.

The boat driver, Phillip, steered them north. His hair was as long as Sammy's, though his was a dark brown. His shoulders and arms were covered in tattoos, many of which were faded due to constant exposure to the sun.

"Hope your buddy holds on," he said. He turned the wheel to port. Sheets of water jetted high as the hull scraped the ocean.

Kenneth and Sammy watched Blake wobbling hard, then lose his grip and disappear under a huge splash. Both of them exploded with laughter, which transferred over to the boat driver.

"I'm such a dick," he muttered to himself. He slowed the boat and steered it back to pick Blake up. He bobbed along the surface, held up by his lifejacket, muttering a series of f-bombs as he watched the boat come by to pick him up.

"Having a little trouble there, sport?" Kenneth called to him.

"Oh, shut up," Blake replied. "I would've lasted longer if you didn't pull away so fast!" Everyone on the boat, including Phillip, exchanged glances then smirked. "Yeah, that came out wrong. Let me have another go."

"Ah-ah, no sir," Sammy said. "You've already had a couple goes. It's my turn." Without waiting for a reply, she splashed down into the water and shoved Blake toward the boat.

He climbed aboard, muttering, "I pay for this boat trip, and I don't get a say…"

Sammy grabbed the handlebar, propped herself up on her back, using her lifejacket to balance, then gave a thumbs up to Phillip. He throttled, just fast enough at first for her to stand up and get her balance. It only took a few seconds before he was racing across the ocean as if he had committed a crime. Sammy whooped, bouncing over a couple of large swells and landing perfectly.

Blake shrugged. "Eh, so what. I could've done that."

"Uh-huh, sure," Kenneth said.

"You don't have to suck up to her," Blake replied. "She's out there. She can't hear you. Besides, you've already sealed the deal with her anyway."

"Doesn't mean I won't be doing more," Kenneth said with a wink and click of his tongue.

"Great," Blake said.

"What? You jealous?"

"Hell no!"

"You are! I get to bring Sammy to my hotel, while you're stuck with Tracy!" Kenneth laughed. Blake was pissed at his remark, but not due to offence, but because his damn brother was right.

"Why did she have to get food poisoning?" he muttered. He watched Kenneth's date bounce over another swell. She cheered as another one approached. She hit it, went high over the water, performed a forward flip, and landed perfectly. "Damn!"

"She's good. *Really* good," Kenneth said.

"You're referring to the waterskiing, right?" Blake asked. Kenneth grinned and continued watching his date maneuver the waves. His grin gradually faded. He leaned forward. Blake chuckled as he noticed a confused expression take form on his brother's face. "What? Her bikini slipping off?"

Kenneth said nothing. Blake followed his gaze. Then, his own smile faded.

"What the...?"

He questioned his eyes. Could it be a trick of the sunlight? A reflection of some kind?

Bright white lights flickered several yards behind Sammy. The odd view was like watching the edge of a storm approaching over miles of open farmland. Only, this was underwater.

"What the hell is that?" Blake said. He started to stand up for a better look, only to nearly fall overboard when Phillip whipped the boat around.

"Hang on!" the helmsman said.

"Wait! Phil! There's something—"

"Hold that thought," Philip interrupted. He completed the one-eighty turn, glancing back just long enough to make sure Sammy was still trailing behind them. Before turning back to the front, he saw Kenneth and Blake rushing to the front of the vessel. "Whoa! Hey! What's going on—"

Kenneth pointed. "Look! What the hell is that?"

"What the hell is what?" Phillip said. Then he saw the flickering lights. They were five hundred feet away. Within the next few seconds, they closed in over the phenomenon. As they got closer, they saw individual flares, like sparks ripping from the severed end of a high voltage cable.

They passed over it and glanced back at Sammy.

She whooped wildly, having just completed a midair summersault. She landed perfectly and threw a fist in the air. Already, she was lining up for another one.

"Watch this!"

She hit the wave and went airborne. That swell erupted upon impact, as though made out of nitro. Sammy was flung in the air, and not by the water. It was not a cheer that escaped her lungs, but a high-pitched scream. The huge, elongated snout rose from the water like a plesiosaur from the Mesozoic Era, and snatched her out of the air.

The enormous beast quickly turned its head at the fleeing vessel, the bleeding victim clenched tight in its jaws.

Blake was the first to scream. When it escaped, it wasn't out of terror, but of intense pain. Like a special effect in an epic Hollywood film, the ocean lit up in bright white lights. In the instant the electric bolt was visible, it resembled a crack in a large landscape that was about to split in half. The bolt struck the metal hull and traveled up the barefoot bodies of the two men. Blistering heat cooked their skin, which turned from pale to red.

The electric charge concluded in a small explosion along the transom which sent the boat flipping forward. The passengers were launched in the water like badminton birdies, while Phillip was strapped to his seat by the safety belt. The boat bounced over the water like a skipping stone, then settled on its starboard side, half-submerged.

Blake was barely conscious. He couldn't tell if his heart was beating or not. He couldn't feel anything—except pain. His skin was severely burnt and the saltwater did not feel soothing. Rather, it felt like his body was one big open wound.

The thing was closing in, moving like a thundercloud in the distance with lightning reaching from its hide. He couldn't move. Blake was paralyzed, not even able to breathe. He was sinking and forced to watch the monster approach.

It didn't come straight for him. It moved to its left initially, made a jerking movement with its head, then came back into view—with

Kenneth clenched in its jaws. It chomped down, shook its head, then chomped down, breaking Kenneth's body for easy digestion before focusing on the other paralyzed human.

For the second time, Blake wanted to scream, but couldn't. The creature opened its jaws and clamped them over his body. His spine and skull were crushed instantly, sparing him the sensation of being ripped apart.

The eel devoured its prey then turned its attention to the one remaining human.

Phillip clung to the boat, which drifted on its side after somehow finding buoyancy. He looked over his right shoulder and saw that the water had turned red. Behind that red were the electrical lights. They grew brighter. Closer.

Every movement caused the boat to shudder. It threatened to tilt as he leaned into a small storage compartment under the helm. He opened the small metal door and pulled out his flare gun. He loaded a cartridge and aimed for the huge approaching shape.

It neared the surface, its huge eyes appearing brown against its silvery skin.

Phillip squeezed the trigger.

A red fireball plunged into the water and struck the beast on the snout. It whipped violently to the side, the flare fizzling out after a few moments underwater. Phillip wobbled as he reached for another cartridge. If he could just hit it a couple more times, maybe it would go away!

As he fumbled for the cartridge, his eyes went back to the monster. What he saw instead was the retaliatory flash of lightning. That was before his vision blacked out.

The electric current coursed through the boat and up through his body. There was no sense of flexibility; he was as stiff as a metal pole. His insides cooked and his heart ruptured.

When the electric bolt had done its work, Phillip was charred black. His skin was flaking away, his hair and eyes were gone, and the only part of him that retained its original color were his white teeth. The burnt corpse slumped facedown against the drifting side of the speedboat, which proceeded to drift as the evening hours approached.

CHAPTER 27

When Silvia arrived on South Beach, there were already several people gathering in the sand to get their 'front seat' view of the fireworks show. The yachts were getting in place along the water, with several workers prepping the launchers. Nightfall wouldn't be for another few hours, but the workers often entertained the early crowds with simpler stuff like rockets, sparklers, smoke bombs, among other things.

Silvia watched the line of boats. There were at least seven of them, all seventy-foot yachts, each with a dozen or more crew moving about like members on a Navy warship. Each vessel would launch fireworks from the aft deck, middeck, and foredeck. Through radio communications, the crews would launch the fireworks simultaneously. Every year, the whole side of the island would light up in a myriad of colors.

She walked along the beach, her eyes continuously going to the west. Right now, with the exception of the typical boating activity, the water was fairly open. In about four hours, it would be jampacked with yachts coming in from the mainland to view the spectacle. Each vessel would have to wave a blue flag, signifying they had paid their ticket admission to dock offshore. Every year, the police would have to fine a few vessels that tried to sneak in, as well as a few that tried to make counterfeit event flags.

Her back throbbed each time she saw a boat speeding off in the distance. Something didn't feel right. Somehow, she knew that water wasn't safe, but couldn't prove it.

Patrolling the southern side of the island was Boat Two. At its helm was Officer Graft, at the start of another double shift. Leaning over the deck was Zirke. They were a few hundred feet offshore. Even from this distance, she could tell the officers were glassy-eyed. The former had to stand guard at the hotel, as she promised JoEllen they would do. It was a boring, uneventful shift, requiring the officer to stand on foot the entire time. No iPhones, nobody to talk to, nothing to pass the time. Silvia had learned in her life that there were two types of miserable shifts: those that were so busy you couldn't catch a breath, and those with absolutely zero to do, with nothing to occupy the time. It was her opinion that the latter was worse, and she suspected Zirke felt the same way. Now, here he was with Graft, performing favors for another of JoEllen's sponsors. The event hadn't even started yet, but Belanger had requested police presence during the entire setup, as well as during the actual show.

She heard tires scratching pavement behind her. Adam parked his Interceptor then quickly stepped onto the beach where she instructed him to meet her.

He wasted no time addressing his concerns.

"Chief, I think we need to get these people out of the water," he said.

"Lieutenant, I can't close the beaches based on a hunch," Silvia replied.

"I spoke with Andy Cornett. He saw it," he replied. Silvia stood, silent and motionless.

"He said this?"

"In plain English," Adam said. "They went out to lure the whale away. The eel intercepted them. Killed his wife."

"That's not proof. He was under the water. He could've seen anything and mistook it for a giant eel," Silvia said.

Adam exhaled slowly through his nose; it was the best he could do from making a loud, irritated sigh.

"I spoke with Maurice. He says he saw the whale's body afloat when he went to pick up Andy. He told me that whale was covered in burn wounds. Absolutely covered! Nothing in that water can do that kind of damage, including the Cutter." He watched the Chief's silent expression. Indecisiveness. AGAIN! He was one of the more forgiving officers when it came to that, as he understood what she was going through. But enough was enough. "Chief, you're gonna have to do something! I see it in your eyes. You know something's not right."

"I can't close these beaches on a whim," she said. "I tried to delay it, but JoEllen won't hear any of it."

"Close them anyway," he said. "Who cares what she thinks? It won't matter if more people are killed by that thing."

"'Who cares what she thinks?'" Silvia scoffed. "She's the Mayor, in case you didn't notice."

"And you're the Chief of Public Safety, or did you fail to notice *that*?" Adam said. Silvia was startled. She wasn't used to such a harsh tone from the Lieutenant, especially not directed at her. From Royce, maybe, but not him. "Obviously, you like the title and the paycheck, but you don't seem to be willing to fulfill the obligations. You're a cop! Act like one, goddamnit!"

"What the hell, Adam?!"

"Silvia, I like you a lot. You're a nice person, and I hate the pain you go through, but I'm so sick of you cowering down so easily to JoEllen's demands."

"Again, she's the *mayor*, Adam. She outranks me."

"Yes, she can override you. But that's not always what she does," Adam explained. "She's good at manipulation, and that's why she hired you. Because she knew you were vulnerable. Look at how she handled the situation after that body appeared in North Beach. You had a chance to close the beaches and call in all vessels, but she managed to guilt you into letting everyone stay out. That way, *you'd* catch the blame if anything went wrong. I'm sure you're still feeling the sting from this morning."

"Shhh! Keep your voice down," Silvia said, noticing their exchange was drawing attention from a few bystanders on the beach. She walked with Adam back to the parking lot. "You want to get personal? You know why I took this job."

Adam shook his head. He knew what her excuse would be. *"I don't know what else to do. My life didn't go as planned. This is all I have."* He'd heard it all before. He sympathized, sure, but it would be a cold day in hell before he listened to someone describe their disability as a qualification for a position.

"Because it gave you an excuse to be a cop without having to be a cop," he replied. "I get it. Believe me, I do. In fact, I think it's absolutely insane that it's not considered an actual disability. But your injury will continue to control your life, *only* if you let it. Yeah, you'll always be limited regarding the physical stuff, but there's more to police work than that. You need to use your head, Chief. And not just for stupid report writing. You've got to make your own decisions, not always go back on the mayor. Now, I'm gonna ask you a question: Do you think there's a danger out there?"

Silvia hesitated before answering, as her mind was busy taking in everything Adam was saying. The only part he left out was a direct statement as to why he didn't mention her in his resignation letter, though it had become abundantly clear. It took a few moments for her mind to come around to thinking about his question.

"Maybe," she said.

"Maybe?"

"For the love of God, Adam, we're talking about a giant electric eel!" she exclaimed. "Forgive me if I show a little bit of skepticism!"

"The skepticism, I can deal with," Adam said. "The part I can't stand is that you actually do think there is something out there and you're holding back on confronting JoEllen about it. Because you're afraid you'll look like a fool. No offense, Chief, but you've already got that covered."

Jesus! Have these thoughts been pent up the whole time?

"There's no evidence," Silvia replied. "Nothing. There's no footage of this thing. Andy's the only eye-witness, and that can be chalked up to trauma, both physical and psychological. The Coast Guard hasn't reported anything unusual other than the whale itself, which is now dead. And the Island Counsel will not accept burn marks on a sperm whale as evidence of an electric surge in the water."

Andy didn't reply right away. He nearly interrupted her, but then realized that she was voicing frustrations rather than making excuses. She DID believe that creature was out there, but didn't have the know-how to convince everyone else.

He exhaled slowly and let his emotions cool off. He felt the initial waves of regret for being so blunt about his thoughts. Still, it didn't mean they weren't real. In the back of his mind, he wished Royce had gotten the job, as did the entire department. Hell, the entire island. However, JoEllen would never have appointed him. She would've brought someone in from the outside before she hired Royce, and for the very reason she appointed Silvia. If it wasn't her in the role, it would've been someone like her. The reason? Adam glanced at the boats in the water. There, one of JoEllen's sponsors prepped for their Fourth of July show.

Royce isn't the chief. Silvia Remar is. Gotta work with what we've got.

"The only way to prove it is to get footage of it," she said. "We have evidence of burns on two of the boats we recovered. Did Maurice get photographs of the whale?"

"No, but the Coast Guard should have," Adam replied.

"Good enough. We can probably get a request for those. We can get the files from Andy Cornett if he's willing, which'll allow us to display the temperature fluxes that have been happening. However, all this only proves there's an usual problem going on around here. Proving that a unique underwater predator is the cause of those problems will take a little more convincing, however."

Adam felt somewhat uplifted. At least she was attempting to problem-solve, rather than simply bend over backwards for JoEllen. The problem she brought up was a logical one: how the hell do they prove the existence of a large marine animal?

"Where can we get an underwater drone?" she asked.

"I don't know," Adam replied. "You thinking of doing some underwater exploring?"

"I'd rather think of it more as an investigation," Silvia said. "But...yes."

"Damn," Adam muttered. He put a finger to his lips as he thought. He shook his head. "I know our department doesn't have one. Nor does the fire department. The only people I'm pretty sure has one are the Cornetts, but the doctors won't let us talk to Andy unless his condition improves. Which'll take another day at least."

"Ordering one will take even longer," Silvia added. "Damn it."

"There's one other option," Adam said. "In case you've forgotten, I am a certified diver."

"Ah-ah, no," Silvia said, holding a finger to his chest. "If that thing is real, we don't want anyone in the water with it. Going down there would be suicide."

"It might be the only way to get evidence, and soon," Adam said. "Let me get my gear. There're places around here where we can get underwater cameras. I'll charge them on the department's credit card. If we confirm this thing's existence, we can get these people out of the water."

"You accuse me of being a bad leader, and three minutes later you have the audacity to ask me to put you in harm's way?" Silvia snapped. "Besides. Look what happened to Martha Cornett. She was diving, and that didn't work out so well. No, Adam. You're not going in the water."

The Lieutenant bit his lips, holding in a barrage of curse words. Rarely did he ever feel so close to losing his temper, especially on a fellow officer.

"Then what would you suggest?"

"We'll get someone here with a submersible," Silvia replied. "We'll get in touch with the university that Martha worked for. They might have something."

"That'll take as long as getting a drone. We need to find evidence *today*," Adam replied. He pointed a finger to the festival boats. "Every minute we wait puts them in danger. As it does everyone out on that water."

Silvia shook her head. "I'm not putting you in the water, Adam. We're gonna find another way."

He slapped his hand against his leg. Realizing she wouldn't budge on the issue, he stepped back to his vehicle.

"I oughta flash my lights and force these people in right now."

"You'd lose your job," Silvia said. "Not a threat. A promise. JoEllen would have your head in a basket."

"Yeah. With that attitude, that's why you're gonna get people killed." Adam slammed the door and drove off.

Silvia quietly watched until he was out of sight. She wanted to scream and shout. Had nobody else been around, she would have. Already, she had one embarrassing outburst in her office. Last thing she needed was for the public to witness it.

Her phone vibrated. She checked the screen and saw a text from JoEllen.

"Beaches are looking great. Looks like everything is getting back in order again. Well done!" She tucked the phone away without answering, then proceeded to watch the activity in the water.

Are they safe? What is the right call? Do I risk people's safety, or the island economy? What do I do?

Silvia needed info. She needed the knowledge that Martha Cornett would have provided. She needed to look at their computers. But with Andy hospitalized, she wouldn't be able to do that. She needed a judge's order to investigate their home.

"Interference with a police investigation."

She could probably get the courthouse to sign off on that. Silvia pulled her phone out and called the station.

"Hey. Type out a warrant for Andrew and Martha Cornett's residence...Yeah, yeah, I know she's deceased. Yes, I'll be speaking to him once the doctors—Damn it! Will you just do what you're told?! Hurry up, I need it now." She hung up then scrolled down to JoEllen Marsh's personal phone.

"Mayor speaking."

"Hey, it's Silvia. I need a favor from you."

"I beg your pardon?"

"I need you to get in touch with Judge Pendleton. I need a warrant signed within the next hour."

"A warrant? Who for?"

Silvia thought for a moment of how she could tell the truth—without actually telling the truth.

"Andy Cornett willfully interfered with a police and military operation. I need to investigate their residence and seize any data on the whale they had at hand. They might've known it was acting up without warning any of us." She hated throwing them under the bus like that, but admitting concerns about another underwater predator would've made JoEllen hang up.

"Interesting...okay. He should be at the courthouse. I'll give him a call and ask him to wait a little longer before going home. Better get that warrant over to him quick, though."

"Will do. Thanks." Silvia hung up. She got in her truck and hurried to the station.

CHAPTER 28

Even in her dreams, Tracy Bannister could feel the crick in her neck. After cleaning up her mess in the bathroom, she had practically collapsed across the bed. There she remained, unmoving, her head propped up at an odd angle against the pillow. At the time, her stomach felt so miserable, she didn't even care for the odd position she was in. Only when she woke up did she regret not adjusting.

She could hear the popping of fireworks through the window.

Fireworks? She opened her eyes and checked her phone. 7:09. She looked around. Blake was nowhere to be seen. *Are those idiots still out?*

Tracy sat up. To her surprise, her stomach was feeling much better. Perhaps she just needed to get the rest of the bile out and get a few hours of sleep. The difference was so drastic, she even considered putting something in her stomach. Unfortunately, there was almost nothing in the fridge. She got up and checked. Nothing there but a half-eaten sandwich left over from Blake's lunch.

That was at noon. He hadn't eaten since. Perhaps he went out to eat with Kenneth and that chick he was banging? She looked at her phone again. No text or voicemail. Blake could sometimes lack consideration for others, but he was usually pretty good at letting her know if he was running late or out doing something. Probably got caught up in all the fun and just didn't think of it. She took the sandwich out of the fridge and laid back on the bed. She switched on the TV. She flipped through a dozen channels before settling on the local news channel.

Before settling, she sent Blake a quick text.

"Hey!"

"I think I'm feeling better. What r u doin?"

By 7:20, there was no response. Tracy watched TV while eating tiny bits of bread. So far, it was staying down just fine.

"The whale, nicknamed Sly by the local marine biologist, was tracked down by the United States Coast Guard," the news anchor said. The screen switched to an aerial view of the Cutter towing away the whale carcass, then to a Coast Guard Admiral.

"It's very unfortunate that it came to this. Sperm whales are on the brink of being considered endangered. It breaks my heart we had to contribute to that. Unfortunately, with human life at stake, there was no other choice."

The screen returned to the news anchor.

"Scientists are baffled, as there has never been a reported case of sperm whales attacking boats."

She kept glancing to the phone. Now she was getting impatient. She snatched it up.

"Hey! Where r u? Getting late."

Five minutes later.

"I'm getting pissed, Blake!"

With no response, she gave in and called his phone. It went straight to voicemail. She tried calling again, only to get the exact same result. Blake never turned off his phone. She was getting nervous.

She then scrolled through the contacts until she found Kenneth's name. "Where the hell are you idiots?" She made the call. Same thing: no ringing, just straight to voicemail. Like his brother, Kenneth never turned off his phone. It couldn't be a signal issue, since she had called Blake earlier in the week when he was somewhere else on the island.

After waiting a few minutes, she tried again, with the same results.

"What the hell's going on here?" she said. She found their duffle bag and located the pamphlet which had Phillip's phone number in it. She dialed the office number, but nobody picked up. She tried the cell. Straight to voicemail.

They couldn't have gone to the fireworks show. Blake was not the biggest fan of fireworks, and was actually irritated when he discovered there was going to be a big festival taking place on the island. Kenneth, while not as adamantly as his brother, was also not the biggest fan of fireworks. Didn't have anything against them; they just weren't his thing.

Another attempt to call Phillip ended in voicemail. Something was off about this. There was no reason why she couldn't get ahold of them. Her phone was obviously working just fine.

She checked the pamphlet again and saw that there was a secondary number listed. Figuring there was no harm in checking, she dialed it.

"Hello?" It was a female voice. Wife, maybe.

"Hi, uh, sorry to bother you. This number was listed for Phillip's Charters. Is he in?"

"No, he is not." Her voice was trembling.

"He had two clients today. Blake and Kenneth Anese. They were scheduled to go with Phillip at 4:30, I think for an hour and a half, but they haven't been—"

"They haven't called either?" the woman interrupted.

Either? Tracy's heart thumped hard. This person spoke like the concerned wife of a missing person.

"No. No calls. No texts. Nothing. I've tried calling, but I haven't been able to get ahold of anyone. I thought I'd try this number and check." Suddenly, her stomach was starting to cramp again, only this time from anxiety. "Maybe they just got carried away. I can see Blake slipping Phillip a few bucks to stay out longer..."

"I haven't been able to get ahold of Phillip!" Now, her voice was almost panicked. *"I've been getting phone calls from clients scheduled for 6:00 and 7:30. Phillip is always on time."*

Judging by the way she was speaking, Tracy could tell it wasn't the first time she had expressed these concerns today.

"Is it possible they could've..." Her voice trailed off. She didn't know what she was suggesting. She didn't expect to hear such panic from the person on the other end of the line, which was now feeding into her.

"He's ALWAYS on time..." the woman replied. *"ALWAYS. I called the police, but he hasn't been missing long enough—"*

Missing? Police? These words triggered a storm in Tracy's mind. She was worried before, but absolutely did not expect the situation to take a turn like this. Blake had hired Phillip based on reviews and his reputation for being on time. If this local woman said this lack of communication was unusual, Tracy would accept this as fact.

"Oh God. Oh...my God!" She hung up the phone and dialed 9-1-1. "Hello? Yes, I—my name's Tracy Bannister...no I won't calm down, this is an emergency! I need to report a missing person."

****

Adam Henry had checked out from his duties. He should've been working on the upcoming schedules, but he had fallen down the rabbit hole of the internet. Phrases such as *largest deep sea organisms* filled his search history. The information was vast, and he saw creatures that he never thought could possibly exist. Other searches included *theories on large, undiscovered deep sea life.* There were many articles, many of them pertaining to the possibility of megalodons living in the deep trenches in the Pacific Ocean. Some articles were clearly click bait and showed nothing of value. He watched a few videos featuring interviews with people who had made the deep dives, but they mainly spoke about the landscape. No mention of large, predatory lifeforms—and certainly nothing like the creature Andy Cornett warned him about.

Had there not been a knock on his door, he would've spent the next two hours looking into it.

"Come in," he said. The door opened and a dispatcher stepped in. On her face was a look of unease. "Everything alright?"

"I tried to radio the Chief, but I can't seem to reach her," the dispatcher said. "Uh, we just received a 9-1-1 call. Missing person report."

Adam rose from his seat.

"Did they state the last time they saw this person?"

"Today. *After* the ban was lifted."

"Who is it?"

"Phillip Hoskin. A boat charter, with at least two tourists. Maybe a third; the caller wasn't sure. They left at 4:30 and haven't returned since. Caller is a significant other for one of the tourists. The wife tried the non-emergency line. She's reporting the same information."

Adam knew Phillip. He had a specific route he took further out on the northern side of the island...

...not too far from where that whale was killed.

But the Coast Guard did a thorough sweep with their sonar, and detected nothing.

If there was something else in that water, either it can somehow avoid detection on sonar, or it knew to hide.

He checked the time. Almost 8:00. There was nobody to send out. Silvia had their officers stretched thin, with several patrolling around the fireworks show, others at the hotel. If anyone wasn't preoccupied, they were likely checking the beach and town areas, where they were needed. There was simply nobody to send out.

"I'll take a boat out," Adam said.

"You want me to notify the Chief?"

"If you can reach her," Adam said. He grabbed a windbreaker and grabbed a key for a patrol boat. Luckily, he knew where Phillip typically cruised, so he had an idea of where to look.

Before going out there, he would have to take a quick stop at home for his fish finder.

CHAPTER 29

"I just don't see why you need to investigate this house *now*," the locksmith said to Silvia as he worked on getting the Cornetts' front door open. "And don't crime scene investigations usually take a bunch of officers?"

Silvia crossed her arms and rolled her eyes.

"Do I ask you why you use a bolt or a key lock? Or a chrome or bronze handle?" The locksmith looked back at her, then shook his head. "Then stop asking me questions on how I do my job. I have a warrant to search the premises. The suspect is in the hospital. You have all the information you need."

"I suppose I do. Just doesn't add up," the locksmith said. He got the door open and stood out of the way. Silvia stepped inside, found a light switch, and peered into the living room. It was a cozy little area with a carpet made to resemble a coral reef.

They really loved their jobs.

"Will that be all?" the locksmith asked.

"Yes. That'll be all. You know where to send the bill."

Without saying another word, the locksmith returned to his Jeep, leaving Silvia alone to search the premises. She walked across the living room, watching the weaved designs of fish under her feet. Already, her imagination was playing games with her. She envisioned a large mouth opening behind that school of fish, baring razor-sharp fangs. She shook her head, snapped the image from her mind, then continued on.

This first section of the house was as normal as any other residence. Living room; kitchen; dining area; bedrooms; office; bathrooms. Silvia checked the office. It was neatly organized, with some folders displaying typical house documents and bills. Another rack on the righthand side displayed something more to Silvia's interest.

There were handwritten notes, some of which had been duplicated in Microsoft office. *Discovery. Goblin shark.* Dated 7/01/2021. The document went over location of discovery—northside of island. There were body measurements, bite radius, health status during catch, then notes on the internal organs after dissection.

Severe burns in stomach. Possible electrical discharge from prey.

Silvia flipped to the next page.

Stomach contents reveal unknown organism. Animal resembles moray eel in form, but has distinct characteristics that differ. Creature is two feet in length. Distinct dorsal fin running down length of body. Narrow jaw. Capable of producing electric charges. See notes on unknown organism for more details. With said electric charge, the organism likely burned the goblin shark from inside out, stopping its heart. Fish was caught in fishing net before dying.

Silvia's eyes were locked on the words 'electric charge'. Martha had evidence and she didn't share it?! WHY?! Silvia knew the answer. Notes alone weren't evidence. It still would have sounded unbelievable, especially after the eye-witness account of the sperm whale attack. But now, Silvia was waking up to the horrible reality Maxwell Island was facing. Someone like Martha Cornett wouldn't type up notes like these for her own personal amusement.

Her eyes returned to the report; *See notes on unknown organism for more details.* Those notes; where were they? She started digging around. There was nothing printed that she could find. With the computer on sleep-mode, she went for the computer mouse and clicked. Luckily, the computer came on. Even better, there was no password needed. Being in her personal residence, Martha probably never felt any reason to add extra security on her desktop beyond cyber-protection.

There were several files and windows open, most of which contained data that Silvia did not understand. She looked for the word *eel* in every document, but found nothing. Instead, she found several articles on deep sea species that have been rising from the trench. A couple of these articles were the same as what Silvia had been reading in her office. Others were new, such as the article featuring a picture of a strange tentacled creature, but not like a squid, that washed up in the Bahamas.

"What the hell is that?!" she said to herself. The title of the document read *Undiscovered organism washes ashore. Local researchers baffled.* Then there were articles about the earthquakes and theories of possible dormant underwater volcanoes in the trench. She proceeded to read about the tsunamis and coastal damage resulting from the seismic activity, then realized she had fallen down a rabbit hole of reading. She minimized several of the windows, uncovering a map screen. It was a map of the coastal waters around the island. In the water were several black dotes. On the right side of the screen were lists of numbers and dates. Among one of the lists was the symbol for *Fahrenheit*. They were temperature readings. Then it hit Silvia; those black dots were research buoy locations. She proceeded to read the data. Some of the larger numbers were marked with red flags.

Rapid temperature increase—Buoy Three. Rapid temperature increase—Buoy Five.

The current readings for those buoys were normal.

So, something was causing a large enough temperature spike under the water? Silvia was no oceanographer, but she knew that temperature increases like these were not normal, especially in such isolated occurrences.

As she looked back to the map, she realized one of the dots had turned red.

Rapid temperature increase—Buoy Fourteen. 81 degrees Fahrenheit. The buoy was located two miles north of Wesco Peak. Whatever was causing these spikes, it was there right now.

There were no other files on the computer that contained useful information. It would take her hours to scour through the various files. Something as recent as the goblin shark autopsy would contain a recent date.

Autopsy...

Silvia began to think—*If Martha performed an autopsy, then there must be a lab somewhere in here.*

She stood up and followed the hallway to the back of the house. After accidentally ending up in the utility room, she eventually found herself on a path to what initially looked like a garage. Then she opened the door and saw all the high-tech equipment.

There was an OR room for the autopsies, a cleaning room, a chemical storage room, machine storage, a freezer...

She went there first.

The chill hit her like an Arctic wind. The Chief shivered, cupped her arms around her chest, then proceeded inward. There were several large freezer units, coffin-shaped, on the left side of the room. They seemed to contain lids similar to a typical refrigeration unit. She approached the nearest one, hesitated, then lifted the lid open.

Wrapped in an airtight bag were several species of fish, frozen in stasis. Bulging eyes stared back up at her. She recognized some of the species as salmon and tuna. Each one had a white slip tapped on the plastic casing, with a number and colored marking on it.

The next freezer unit was much smaller. When Silvia peered inside, it was obvious why. There were frozen parasites and worms inside each airtight bag. Probably the reason for the autopsies of many of the specimens in the previous container. She could only bear the sight of the purple, red, and pink invertebrates for so long. Silvia slammed the container shut, then proceeded to the next freezer.

She lifted the lid, saw the gaping jaws, then jumped back. After catching her breath, she opened it again, slowly, as though the dead thing in there was about to leap out at her.

Silvia had found the goblin sharks that Martha had written about in her reports. They were laid out side-by-side, taking up the entire length of the freezer. Silvia could see the incision line where Martha had performed the autopsies. Several tissue samples and internal organs had been removed and labeled. She grimaced when she realized she was looking at the shark's removed stomach at the base of the freezer.

"Jesus..."

She remembered the notes; *severely burned.* She leaned in closer. The plastic was crystal clear, allowing her to see the pinkish flesh of the stomach, which had turned a shade of purple due to the freezing process. Even then, the burn marks were visible.

There was another freezer unit on the opposite side of the room. Silvia turned around and approached. This one stood tall like a kitchen refrigerator, with a double door. She pulled them open at once. A cold mist hit her face, which paled to the coldness she felt when gazing at the frozen eels. They hung from a rack like a slab of beef. They were silver in color, with huge bulging eyes, narrow snouts, and needle-like teeth. Silvia leaned in for a closer look. Those teeth were thin, but they looked as sharp as a surgeon's scalpel.

One of the specimens had been dissected, while the other was kept intact. On the white label were the handwritten words: *Unknown Species.*

They looked vastly similar to moray eels. Silvia, while feeling oddly terrified of the dead things, wasn't sure how Martha was confident they were different. She looked at the dissected specimen.

Martha HAD to have copied notes during the procedure. Where the hell are they? The answer was obvious: *Check the damn office, you idiot!*

With the swiftness of reacting to a Drill Sergeant's instruction, Silvia rushed out of the freezer storage and checked the connecting rooms. The office was on the opposite end of the prep-room. It was a smaller desk than Martha's main office, and much more cluttered. Almost all of the notes were handwritten, featuring details on measurements.

On a clipboard was a data sheet with the date *7/1/2021*. Specimen: *Eel species.*

Subject contains physical similarities in bone and jaw structure as moray eel, while its organ structure is closer to that of the South American electric eel. Specimen was still alive during goblin shark autopsy. When removing it from shark's stomach, it emitted an electric shock. I believe this is a defense mechanism against predators, and possibly a weapon used when capturing prey.

Preliminary examination of reproductive organs, when comparing with similar species, reveal that subject is likely a newborn. Whether the creature was born in the waters around Maxwell Island or somewhere else cannot be determined.

However, I must stress the likeliness that a large organism might be lurking in our waters.

Further analysis is pending.

"Oh my God."

Again, the question flashed in her mind: *Martha, why didn't you show us this?* And again, the answer was simple: nobody would have believed her. It would take more than a dead carcass and scientific hearsay to convince the authorities that a one-hundred-and-thirty-foot long electric eel was swimming off their waters. JoEllen Marsh certainly would not pay any attention to the matter.

Silvia had learned enough. Adam was right; they needed to act now.

She grabbed her radio. "Zero-one to two?" She waited. There was no answer. "Zero-one to Zero-two, come in. Lieutenant?" She noticed the blinking red light on her radio. "SHIT!" *How long has my battery been dead?!* She had been working so much, she hardly had a chance to put the radio on its charger.

She pulled her phone and called his number. It went straight to voicemail. Either he had his phone off, which was unlikely, or he was somewhere where there was no signal. She then called dispatch.

"Hey, it's the Chief. My radio's dead. Where's the Lieutenant?" A chill creeped down her spine as she heard the dispatcher's answer. Missing persons?

"He's taken a boat out. He knows where Phillip usually boats. Northern side, I believe."

Silvia's stomach cramped. If he was more than a mile out, that would explain why she couldn't reach his phone.

"I gotta go," she said. She hung up abruptly then took off running. As she tore through the main part of the house, she caught a glimpse of the computer in the main office. That buoy was still marked red. Two miles out, north side.

Silvia ran faster, not even bothering to slam the door shut behind her. She dove into her truck, winced from the back pain, then ignited the flashers. Tires kicked up dust as she sped for the police harbor.

CHAPTER 30

Rockets fly high into the darkening sky like World War Two anti-aircraft artillery. Crew aboard the Belanger Festival vessels lit the fuses to their rockets and watched them ascend hundreds of feet above them, then burst in a vivid display of colors.

They were still firing off basic fireworks to appease the crowd, which was still gathering. Kids with glowsticks ran about. People lined up at the food stands, mixing the smoky air with an aroma of chili and beef. In a half-hour, maybe forty minutes, the real show would begin.

The one thing that Sergeant Royce Boyer appreciated about patrolling the beaches during the festival nights was that there was plenty of activity to keep him awake. He walked the beaches, maneuvering around people sitting on their beach towels and chairs. Every so often, he'd catch another officer patrolling. As the mayor requested, there were seven officers on the beach and two boat units.

He could see one of them further out, patrolling a buoy line between the festival boats and the huge gathering of yachts and sailboats that had anchored offshore to watch the event. There were at least fifty from what Royce could see. Luckily, none were causing any trouble at the moment. In past years, they'd had instances of boats trying to get too close to the buoys, and even attempting to shoot off some fireworks of their own. The memories of dealing with unruly boaters brought a smile to his face. He remembered how it made him feel like a pirate, boarding a large vessel, and confiscating the goods. Unfortunately, they went into an *evidence* cabinet, rather than his personal treasure chest.

"Boat Three, check in," he radioed.

It was Officer Graft who replied. "Boat Three here, Sarge. Nothing to report."

"Boat Four here, Ch—my bad, *Sarge,*" the next officer radioed. Royce smirked. The officer on Boat Four, Jay Noel, had a sense of humor, and like many of the others, was vocal on how Royce was practically the actual Chief.

Speaking of the Chief, where was she?

Royce had been walking about for the last hour, yet saw no sign of Silvia anywhere. Despite his judgements on her leadership skills, even Royce appreciated that she at least put in the hours that she demanded on the rest of her staff. Yet, she was nowhere to be seen. She was ALWAYS here at this festival. In fact, he had heard her check-in a couple hours ago. Her truck was nowhere to be seen. Was her back bothering her so much that she couldn't be here?

"Zero-one?" There was no answer. "Dispatch, is Zero-one in the office?"

"Negative."

"What's her twenty?"

"Unknown."

Royce groaned. He tried calling her number. Straight to voicemail.

"Okay, lady, where the hell are you?"

"Everything okay, Sergeant?"

Royce looked ahead and saw JoEllen approaching. Even in the twilight, it was clear that her hair and makeup had been recently done. Several yards past her was a film crew and reporter, whom she was probably bragging to on how she took swift action to protect the island's interest.

He swallowed his pride, forced a smile—a small one…then answered.

"All's well," he said. He tilted his head toward the boats. "Getting ready to watch the main show. No issues so far. I think everyone's just relieved to have things back to normal."

"You can count me in that crowd," JoEllen said.

Royce forced another smile. *What do you want, lady? You ONLY talk to me when you need something.*

Luckily, he didn't have to wait long for the answer, which came in the form of a question. "Have you seen the Chief? I can't seem to get ahold of her, and I haven't seen her around."

Oh, great.

"Actually, I was just trying to get ahold of her as well. She's not answering her radio or her phone. Last I saw her was right before she did the press conference earlier this afternoon."

"Damn," JoEllen said. She glanced around and watched the event unfold for a few moments. "Alright, Mr. Belanger doesn't seem to have noticed. And so far, everything's going fine."

Yeah, because I'M overseeing it.

"I'll have her get in touch with you if I ever locate her," Royce replied.

"Thank you, Sergeant," JoEllen said. Without saying another word, she walked past him. He waited a few moments, then glanced back at her, just long enough to see that she was going to a different news van. She approached the reporter, shook hands, then engaged in discussion on where to stand while answering questions. Clearly, she was hoping to have Silvia standing with her to affirm that the danger had been eliminated.

"All about the image," he muttered. He looked at his phone again. *Damn you, Silvia, pick up. If the Mayor gets pissed at you, she'll take it out on the whole department.* He dialed again. Straight to voicemail. "Oh, if I had a nickel for every one of your screwups…" he muttered while waiting for the *beep* to leave a message. "Hey. It's Royce. Mayor's looking for you. Call her as soon as you get this. Bye." He hung up, then bit his lip.

For the next few minutes, he tapped his foot on the sand and watched the pre-show carry on. Then finally, through the series of police transmissions, did he hear Silvia's voice.

"Zero-one to Zero-two. I'm heading out your way. Give me your location please."

Royce glanced at his radio, slightly tempted to interject with the question of 'What the hell is going on? Where the hell are you?'

CHAPTER 31

Gentle swells lapped away as Adam steered the police boat north. There was twenty-minutes of sunlight left, and he needed it badly to find the missing boat. The streams of sunlight were almost blinding, forcing him to focus his eyes to the east. Looking west, he saw almost nothing but bright gold and glistening ocean.

"Zero-Two? Do you read?"

Adam didn't answer straight away. His attention was on something in the water dead ahead. Something was floating along the surface and it was large enough to catch the reflection of the sunlight. From his position, all he could really see was its black color.

"Lieutenant?!"

"Zero-Two here."

"I've been updated by Dispatch. What's your location?"

"Close to the Gatto Wreck Site." He looked behind him to see if he could see any police boats. Most of the traffic had shifted to the south, leaving the northside wide open. There was one speck in the water roughly three-quarters of a mile out. "I think I see you. Turn on your flashers." A moment later, he could see the tiny sparkle of red and blue. "Yep, that's you. I'll turn mine on so you can see me."

He did, then turned his eyes toward the thing in the water further ahead. It was too big to be a buoy. Wreckage, perhaps? He proceeded to throttle toward it.

As he got closer, the thing took on more definite form. It wasn't jagged, nor was it round. It was more cone-shaped than anything. The surface was leathery and smooth. Then he saw the dorsal fin.

"Holy—" He realized he was looking at a dead killer whale.

It floated, leaning somewhat on its right side. There was no blood in the water. No sign of struggle. From the angle he saw it, there were no bite marks visible. It was bloated, meaning it had been dead for a few hours.

Adam moved around the snout to get a look at the underside. He was expecting to see a large wound, possibly something caused by a great white. What he saw was completely different. The underside of the orca looked as though someone had hit it with a flamethrower. The flesh was blistered and charred. It was intact, but a shell of its former appearance.

There was no indication that any sea life had been picking at it...another unusual sign. He'd seen dead animals and human bodies before. Hell, the corpse that was discovered at North Beach had signs that it had been fed on by small bottom dwellers. Clearly, this killer whale had been dead for hours, yet, it didn't look as though anything had come near it.

As the sun started to settle, Adam switched on his spotlights. He looked northeast and saw another black thing bobbing in the distance. And another after that. He drove the boat over to investigate, quickly realizing he had discovered the rest of the pod. They were all dead, all burned, all frozen with terrified expressions on their faces.

This time, Adam noticed something different on one of the corpses.

"Hey! Stop pulling away and let me catch up," Silvia radioed. Adam didn't reply. He throttled over to the orca that held his interest. Unlike the first pack member, this one had everything torn away, leaving only a head and left pectoral fin floating with its brethren. Another had been torn in half, its meaty tail stuck to its body by the tiniest of meat threads. The rest were intact, but completely covered in horrible burns.

"My God..."

"My God," Silvia muttered to herself as she passed the first dead orca. The burns on its body made her think of the notes she'd read in Martha's office.

Severe burns in stomach. Possible electrical discharge from prey.

I believe this is a defense mechanism against predators, and possibly a weapon used when capturing prey.

She turned off her flashers and caught up with Adam. As she did, the golden rays of sunlight faded to black. Dusk had officially become night. She switched on the lights in the cockpit and the deck exterior.

Adam's spotlight was fixed on the ravaged corpses of additional dead orcas. Either this was an entire pack, or a large chunk of one. Either way, ALL of them were dead from severe burns.

"Oh no," she said.

"Where the hell were you?" Adam asked, glancing back at her as she steered her boat alongside his.

"My radio went dead. I'm stuck with the boat radio," she replied. "You were right, Adam. We need to get everyone out of the water."

"What are you talking about? I thought you needed evidence?"

"We do, and I think we just found it," she said. "This, and the information I discovered in the Cornett residence. I found their notes. Adam—this thing gave birth around here. She discovered small electric eels in the bellies of goblin sharks. They shocked them from the inside. I read Dr. Cornett's notes. There's something elevating the water temperatures. And here we are, looking at orcas with severe burns. We need to head in now."

"We haven't found the missing boat yet," Adam replied.

"Adam...I don't think there's a boat to find..." Silvia said. The Lieutenant absorbed her words. She was right; Phillip and his clients were gone.

"Then let's tow a few of these guys with us," Adam said. "JoEllen won't simply take our word for it. Get her on the horn while I get a line on one of these things."

"Get a line...wait, you're not seriously thinking of going in the water..."

"We've got a missing person, and evidence that there's another vicious organism out here," Adam said. "She's too focused on pleasing her sponsors to see the truth. So, unless you have a better idea..."

"Adam, it's out here somewhere. The temperature readings I saw on their computer...they have a buoy that had been triggered by a severe elevation."

The Lieutenant didn't listen. He undid his uniform shirt and found a pair of goggles which he had brought along.

He steered his boat near one of the orcas, then brought it as close to the fluke as he could get. After finding a towing rope, he moved over to the diving rack. He tried to reach for the fluke from there, but it had already drifted just out of reach. "Son of a..." Having already anticipated this problem, he removed his boots and duty belt.

"Adam, this is crazy."

"This is police work, Silvia," he replied. He put his goggles over his eyes, then slipped into the water. Silvia aimed her spotlight on him, while keeping one hand propped on her sidearm. The water looked as black as smoke in the night, perfectly obscuring anything lurking below.

She watched Adam swim the short distance to the orca and begin tying his line around its fluke.

"Hurry up, Adam. I don't have a good feeling about this."

"This is the only way. So, let's bring back something to convince the Mayor," he replied. He spat vile tasting saltwater that contained the taste of charred organic fluid. "Jesus!"

He fastened the knot, then gave a thumbs-up to the Chief.

"Put your light on one with a bite mark," he said. Silvia panned her light to the left and found the orca that had been bitten in half. Adam started swimming for it. "Toss me a couple lines. I don't expect this guy to hold together for the trip back."

Fixing the light in place, she grabbed a rope, made sure it was secured to the cleat, then tossed the end out to Adam. He grabbed it, then completed the journey to the dead orca.

The smell was atrocious. This creature had been burned AND mutilated. Some of the insides were practically cooked, having a rigid, plastic appearance.

Adam slapped away a few of its intestines, then reached for the fluke. He looped the rope around the tail, fastened it, then swam for the head.

"Where's that second rope?"

Silvia tossed it out to him. It landed right across the dead orca's face, intentionally so. Adam took the rope, then observed the corpse for a minute to determine the best method of tying the rope. There was no way around it, really; he'd have to loop it around the head and fins like a harness, or else, it would slip out of the loop.

He dove under the creature, dragging the line under its midsection. He reemerged on the other side, then tossed his line over the top of the carcass. He looped it over and around until the rope made an X on both sides.

After securing a tight knot, he swam back for his boat. "See?! Wasn't too hard, was it?!"

Silvia kept the spotlight on him as he swam. Her heart pounded harder and harder. Her intuition wouldn't quit. They needed to leave. *Now.* Her breathing was shaky, as were her hands as they guided the light.

Then, the thought dawned on her: deep sea organisms use light to lure and track prey...

She switched it off, leaving Adam in darkness. He stopped and looked back.

"Something wrong?"

"Just get back to your boat now, Lieutenant." His deck lights were on, giving him enough visibility to see where he was going. Without questioning further, he swam the remaining distance. Finally, he reached the deck and climbed aboard.

Silvia closed her eyes in relief. *Oh, thank God.*

After quickly wringing out his clothes, he went into the wheelhouse and pulled out a camera. He returned aft, snapping numerous photographs of the pod. The flash strobed across the night air with each click.

Tension gripped Silvia again. "Wait...don't do that!"

"We need the pictures," Adam said, holding his hands in a *what the hell?* manner.

"The flasher..." she pointed out. "We could attract that thing." She turned around and started switching off the deck lights, leaving her in perpetual darkness. Realizing she had a point, Adam did the same.

The radio blared.

"Zero-one, I'd like to know what's going on!" It was Royce again. Silvia grabbed the speaker mic.

"Sergeant, this is the Chief."

"Mayor's on my case again, Remar. She wants to know why you're not at this event."

She could barely hear him through the barrage of fireworks in the background.

"Royce, listen. Listen carefully. Get everyone in. Use your sirens, use your—"

Silvia froze when she saw it. Her mind's description of the event, though she wouldn't know it, was like all the victims that came before her. A lightning storm beneath the water.

****

"Say again?" Royce said. Silvia had spoken so fast, it was hard to catch what she was saying, especially with the deafening fireworks popping overhead. Flickering red, green, white, and blue lights strobed across the beaches as the vessels commenced the show.

Audience members cheered and clapped their hands, adding to his struggle.

"Please repeat. Did not receive transmission." He waited a moment. "Remar! What's going on? Did anyone catch that?"

"Negative," Officer Zirke replied.

"Something about using sirens," another officer said. Hell, even Royce could barely hear their transmissions, let alone the Chief's.

"I'm ready for this summer to end."

****

They both saw it. They were huge white flashes, each more blinding than the last. Whatever was causing them, it was moving in. Adam switched off all of his deck lights, then waited quietly. He glanced back at the lines, then cursed himself for attaching six-thousand pound deadweights to their vessels. They had trapped themselves.

No way would they be able to outrun the thing towing these orcas.

"Kill your engine!" Adam hissed, doing so for his vessel. "*Quietly!*"

Silvia almost messed that up by almost tripping over a toolbox that somebody had left on deck. She got into the wheelhouse and switched the engine off. She drew her weapon and quietly stepped back onto the deck.

The flashes were almost a hundred feet away—so close that they could see individual streaks of electricity stretching out from the source.

"Silvia..." Adam's voice was low and intense, "keep your lights off...and DO...NOT...MOVE."

Maybe it'll pass under us. With a little luck, it might think we're one of the dead ones...

...Unless it's here to feed on them.

Silvia tensed. The flashes were almost right under them now. Her heart pounded so hard, she shook with each beat. Her teeth were clenched, her pistol twitching in her grasp.

The flashes were only a few seconds apart. It almost seemed as though the thing produced more electricity than it could contain. Were these discharges intentional, or uncontrollable? Were they warnings? Acts of intimidation? Or were they the prelude to a massive bolt, like cocking the lever to a revolver handle?

The memory of the burning yacht tortured Silvia's mind—and the fact one of the bodies wasn't found. This thing had no reservations on attacking humans. It had tasted the flesh of man, knocking him from his place at the top of the food chain.

The thing was maybe thirty feet down. The flashes revealed a shape. It was serpentine, narrow, flexible...and enormous. She could make out the head; a horrible, narrow shape that made her think of needle-nose pliers...just like the offspring in that lab.

It stopped. As it did, so did the flashes.

She took a shallow breath, then looked to Adam. With the lights off, she almost couldn't see him. There was just an indistinct shape twenty-feet away from her. The Lieutenant was stiff as a bone. Neither of them dared to even wiggle a finger.

Where is it?

The tension had her whole body in a knot. Silvia lifted her finger from the trigger guard, not trusting herself to prevent an accidental discharge with the uncontrollable shaking.

There was a faint noise; steel sliding against plastic. Adam was slowly unholstering his weapon.

The ocean was still as ice. The only sounds that could be heard were the echoes from the fireworks show. They were like thunder from a distant storm, which fit seamlessly with the image of flashing lights…

…which reappeared directly behind Silvia's patrol boat. She whipped to her left, pointing her weapon, then shrieked as the water erupted. The beast snapped its jaws over the severed tail of the dead orca, then dove. The rope went taut and the vessel was yanked backward for several feet. As soon as it began, the line snapped. The boat rocked to-and-fro, its occupant slightly crouched to keep her balance.

Silvia watched the slack coiling of rope behind the transom. Its teeth must've sliced through. However, what if it went for the other half of the corpse? Would the rope break? She saw how tightly Adam fastened it…

Not eager to find out, she went for the cleat to untie the rope. Her fingers barely touched it before the ocean sprayed her again. The eel raised its head like an ancient plesiosaur, bit down on the corpse, then ran again. Once again, the boat was racing backwards, only this time, there was no release.

Silvia fell backward and landed with an audible *thud!*

The creature was going deep. The stern was dipping. Already, the ocean was just inches from the waterline.

"Silvia! Cut the line!" Adam shouted. He couldn't believe it. His pursuit for evidence caused them to be anchored here. He sawed at the rope with his pocketknife until it fell loose away from the boat.

He could hear Silvia's vessel tearing through the water, bumping carcasses along the way. Realizing he had no chance of landing a shot, he holstered his Glock, then grabbed the nearest spotlight. He aimed it at the water and unleashed a white beam.

The creature stopped, and Silvia's boat leveled out. The rope scraped the transom as the creature turned. There was a shaking motion as it tore apart the remains of the orca.

Silvia was on her hands and knees when she reached the cleat. The rope was too tight, forcing her to use a knife to cut it loose. She was near the point of hyperventilating. The blade was barely doing the job. It took several slices just to breach the initial threads. She pressed down on the blade with one hand, then continued the sawing motion.

The creature finished the job for her. It tugged again on the line, snapping it at the cut. The severed end slapped her across the face as it whipped into the water like a serpent.

A moment later, a raw blubbery mass erupted along the surface. In that same moment, something passed through Adam's beam of light under the water.

"Go! Make a run for it!" he shouted. He was detaching the spotlight from its post. He tossed it into the water, its beam swirling in circles as it sank several meters. It disappeared abruptly as the creature attacked it.

They both started their engines, then raced south toward the island. Silvia's boat bumped as it hit a couple of corpses along the way.

Adam's boat was to her left, trailing just a few meters behind her. Behind him were the horrible electric flashes. The beast was pursuing them. Silvia watched it intently. From the looks of it, they were gradually pulling out of reach. Just gradually.

Massive streaks traveled along the surface. The eel breached, its dorsal fin resembling a butcher's knife as it cut along the water.

Silvia engaged the autopilot, keeping the boat pointed south, then drew her sidearm again. She sprinted to the transom, aimed at the beast, then fired several shots. Bullets struck its hide, drawing blood, and causing the beast to dive suddenly. Silvia continued firing at the flashes.

Then, in the span of a heartbeat, the ocean turned completely white. It was like the flash of a nuclear bomb. Instead of a shockwave, that flash condensed into a single bolt of electricity that traveled in a perfect zigzagging line that struck the keel of Adam's patrol boat. It struck with an explosive flash, knocking the Lieutenant against the helm.

The boat stalled. There was smoke rising from the stern. The propellers were either gone, or no longer functional. There was no time to figure out which. The beast was flickering its lights again, gearing for another blast.

Adam sniffed. The boat was leaking gas. The protective rubber layer around the tank must've been breached. He ran across the deck, climbed over the gunwale, and leapt as far as he could.

The eel blasted its lightning bolt, electrifying the steel hull, which in turn ignited the fuel tank. The force of the blast pushed Adam, still in midair, several meters further. He hit the water like a skipping stone, then immediately started to sink. He unclipped his duty belt and let it fall, not before unholstering his sidearm. Relieved of the weight, he paddled to the surface.

"Hold on!" Silvia yelled to him. She swung her vessel around and steered toward him. She beamed her forward spotlight down and located him. Adam still had his pistol in hand. As soon as the white flashes reappeared, he was firing into the water. The creature itself couldn't be seen, forcing him to shoot at the center of the 'lightning storm'. One of those bullets must have landed, because the source dove abruptly.

Adam tossed his empty weapon aside then turned to face the boat. Silvia slowed to a stop, then hurried to the portside. She leaned over the gunwale and extended an arm.

"Come on! Grab my hand!"

Adam reached but fell short. After floundering for a moment, he reached up again. Their hands clasped.

Silvia clutched his wrist with both hands and pulled. Adam kicked the water and clawed at the vessel. The light got brighter underneath him.

"Pull me up," he said.

Silvia bared teeth as she put all of her strength into lifting. She leaned up, hoisting him to the gunwale.

Then she screamed.

It was as though her spine had split in two. Nerves soared through her lower back and left leg. All at once, she fell forward against the gunwale, losing her grip on the Lieutenant. Adam disappeared beneath the waves, only to resurface again.

Silvia was against the gunwale, her eyes wide with intense pain. She groaned with every movement. Despite this, she reached again.

"Ad—AGH!" She couldn't even stand up properly. She could see him swimming up to the boat. His face was alive with fright. He tried reaching but fell short.

Another flash revealed the elongated snout of the creature beneath him.

Screaming in agony, Silvia lunged over the gunwale, her fingertips grazing the water. The creature flashed again.

It was like touching hotwire on a livestock fence. The intense shock knocked Silvia backward, causing her to fall against the console. The rounded knob of the throttle prodded her back, her weight shifting it to maximum speed. The propellers came to life, pushing the boat south.

"No!" Silvia shouted, pushing herself off the console.

The creature's head rose from the water. Behind the sounds of crashing waves were the screams of Lieutenant Adam Henry, followed by the crunching sounds of agony as he was impaled in its teeth.

Silvia's screams turned to cries.

"No! No!" She collapsed on the deck, lost in a heap of mental and physical torture. Meanwhile, the boat continued to race toward Maxwell Island.

The beast swallowed its meal, then changed direction to pursue the other boat. It had already put a few hundred feet of distance between them. The distance didn't matter. The creature had now been wounded.

Its injuries were modest, but enough for it to consider these land-dwellers as the enemy.

It followed the water displacements to the landmass. As it entered shallower waters, it detected new vibrations. They were a couple of miles away, on the other side of the island, but they were distinct. A single land-dweller vessel would not create detectable distortions and vibrations at this distance. No, this was a whole pack of them.

The electric eel altered course and swam along the western coast, gradually making its way to the buffet that awaited.

CHAPTER 32

Silvia crawled on her hands and knees toward the console. She couldn't even stand up at this point. Her back was pounding. Every movement, particularly in her legs, created a nerve spasm. She reached up for the speaker mic on the console. She missed several times before finding the thing.

"Zero—AGH!" She winced, took a breath, then tried again. "Royce! Royce, come in!"

"Chief? You alright?"

"Get everyone out of the water! Get them all out! Now!" She released the transmitter as an uncontrollable whimper escaped her throat. Tears streamed down her face.

"Chief?! What the hell are you talking about?"

"Please, Royce..." she muttered to the night air. She raised the transmitter again, then spoke with authority. "Goddamnit! Get all the boats in! There's something in the water and it's coming your way!"

****

Royce stood dumbfounded for a moment. Was Silvia seriously asking this? At best, she would be reamed by the Mayor. And what was this 'something in the water'? Another sperm whale? What would he tell JoEllen, who was rapidly approaching from the bleachers? One of the patrollers was standing nearby, and she probably overheard the transmission through his radio. In fact, Royce was sure that was the case, as he noticed the flustered facial expressions from the people sitting nearby.

JoEllen marched up to him with the pace and scowl of a woman scorned.

"Sergeant—" A series of fireworks popped overhead, making any dialogue inaudible. Angered further by this, she waved him over to follow her. Royce rolled his eyes as he did so.

"Ms. Mayor, Chief Remar has reported a danger in the water," he said once they stepped a few yards behind the bleachers. "I'm gonna have to oversee the clearing of this area."

"This isn't acceptable," JoEllen said.

"It's a *fireworks* show," Royce retorted. "There'll be others. But I'm not keeping these boats on the water if there's a significant risk."

"Give me your damn radio," JoEllen said. Royce grimaced, then relented. She snatched it out of his hand and raised it to her lips. She was so angered, she didn't care if the entire island overheard the exchange at this point.

"Chief Remar, this is Mayor Marsh. Update me on the situation, please."

"Lieutenant Henry is dead. There's something in the water. We were wrong about the whale!"

"Something in the water?" Royce snatched the radio back. "Sergeant!"

Royce ignored her. "Say again?! Lieutenant Henry's deceased?!?!"

"It killed him, Royce. It's a giant Eel. It can discharge bolts of electricity. That's how the yacht exploded. Royce, it's coming your way."

"You're not seriously believing this, are you?" JoEllen said.

"Shut up," Royce replied, much to her dismay. He didn't have time to take satisfaction in the gasping expression on her face, as he raced back to shore.

"All inland units, converge on South Beach. We are evacuating the water. All patrol boats, initiate your flashers. Get everyone into the shallows. Dispatch, broadcast a radio alert to all vessels."

A series of "ten-four" blasted through his receiver. Royce and several other officers raced to the shoreline. People sitting on the beach watched nervously as the cops ordered people to move away from the water.

The blasting of fireworks abruptly subsided as patrol boats sped alongside them with flashing lights. Officer Graft shouted demands at the crew. Confusion and anger followed.

"What danger?" one of the crewmen shouted back.

Graft pointed to the shoreline. "I don't have time to go over it. The Chief's demanding everyone head in right now."

"You're gonna need to tell me more than that," another crewman shouted.

"Fine. How 'bout I follow it up with dock your boat, or I'll arrest every single one of you?"

An exchange of curse words followed.

Meanwhile, the other patrol unit raced beyond the buoy line, with one officer blasting his voice through a bullhorn.

"Everyone, bring your boats to Kennedi Pier in an orderly manner!"

Confusion followed. Only a handful of the yachts bothered to steer toward shore, a few others to the mainland, while several dozen remained in place.

Royce splashed water with his boots as he hustled along the shoreline.

"Move back. Now!" he shouted to a defiant young couple.

"Hey, we paid good money to be here," the twenty-year old male replied. Royce removed his taser.

"Wanna pay more?"

Message received. The girlfriend took her flabbergasted boyfriend by the hand and led him further up the beach. The Sergeant gazed at the long beachline, seeing fireworks continuing to pop off from the vessels further to the east.

"We need more boat units out here, stat. Any available patroller, head over to the pier and get over to South Beach. We've got more people here than we can handle."

****

Silvia screamed as she pulled herself to her feet. Her knees wanted to give out beneath her. With a groan, she stood up, only to immediately fall against the console.

Looking ahead, she saw the porchlights of beachfront properties and streetlights. She was a few hundred feet from beaching on shore. She turned the wheel to starboard, taking the boat around the west side of the island. After clearing Wesco Peak, she slowed. The motion of looking back made her squeal in agony.

She couldn't see the 'storm' under the water. Perhaps the thing had given up? Maybe it remained further out? She wanted to believe that, but her gut told her that the danger was only just beginning. Either it had ceased its electrical flares, or it was moving around the east side of the island.

She pushed the throttle then radioed the Sergeant.

"Royce, what's the status on the evacuation?"

"Not going well. Lot of people here, not enough cops."

"Copy that. Dispatch, get ahold of Captain Maurice Peterman in the Fire Department. Call him *directly*. Tell him to get his chopper in the sky right now and fly over the east side of the island. Inform him to look for any bright lights in the water." She could imagine the confused expression on the dispatcher's face. "You heard me right. Don't ask questions. Just do it. NOW." She let the speaker mic drop from her hand as she tensed again.

She tried standing up away from the helm, but couldn't. Using the instruments to balance, she continued pushing the vessel south.

****

"Flashing lights?" Maurice said, leaning forward in his office chair as he took in the words from the police dispatcher.

"It's what the Chief instructed," the dispatcher replied.

"She's *not* talking about fireworks?" Maurice said.

"No, sir. Nor is she joking. She's ordering a clearing of the beaches, against the Mayor's instructions."

Maurice stood up. Whatever was going on, it didn't make sense. BUT—if Silvia Remar was going against JoEllen Marsh's instructions, then it was serious.

"Alright. I'm on it." He hung up the phone and went into the lobby. Luckily, the firemen on duty had not gone to sleep yet. "Lieutenant, get a crew over to South Beach on the double. They're getting people in from the water and there are likely to be injuries. I'm taking the chopper."

"Chopper?"

Maurice pointed a finger at his crew. "Apparently I need to spot for something. Anyone want to come with?"" One young man, Allen Lloyd stepped forward. "Alright, come on."

****

Per orders from the Sergeant, Officer Graft abandoned the argument with the fireworks crew in favor of engaging with other vessels anchored further east. Royce would direct the additional maritime units to deal with the disorderly crew now behind him.

He passed the next of the five vessels, slowing long enough for Officer Zirke to shout through the speakerphone at the crew. To their pleasant surprise, the crew on that particular boat replied with a thumbs-up and began steering their vessel around to the harbor.

Zirke lowered the speaker, then waited for Graft to bring them along the next vessel.

"Is this really happening?" he said. "Are we really evacuating the beaches because of some giant electric eel? Has Remar lost it?"

"I—" Graft couldn't even bring himself to state an honest answer. It all seemed so ridiculous and unreal. However, he was focused on the news of Lieutenant Henry being killed in action. *Remar wouldn't make that up.* "I don't know," he finally said.

As they came across the next boat, Royce's voice shot through the radio. *"Boat Three, give them a quick warning with the bullhorn, then keep going. Focus on the first boat furthest on the east side, then work your way back down. The other units will work their way toward the middle from here."*

"Copy," Graft said.

Zirke lifted the bullhorn to the crew of the vessel *Atlantic Robinson*. "This is the Maxwell Island Police Department. By orders of the Chief of Police, you are instructed to dock your vessel immediately. Proceed to Kennedy Pier on the southwest side of the island."

He didn't wait for a response as Graft increased speed again. They passed the fourth vessel, the *Pile Driver*, and repeated the same message. The cursing coming from the deck gave the two officers the impression that this crew would not be particularly cooperative.

Graft brushed his mustache and dreaded the upcoming argument with the fifth vessel, the *Hoelzer-Spahn*. He pulled up alongside the vessel and brought the policeboat to a stop.

Again, Zirke repeated the message, "By orders of the Chief of Police, you are instructed to dock your vessel immediately. Proceed to Kennedy Pier on the southwest side of the island."

One crew member leaned over the side of the yacht with a smug look on his face.

"Yeah, uh, we only take instructions from our boss."

"We're not going to argue," Zirke said. "Get your boat to shore, or you will all be arrested."

"Can't arrest us. We have a permit to be here. Unless *you* plan on paying our bills?" a female voice replied. Zirke glared at the stocky woman hobbling toward the gunwale with a condescending sneer on her face.

"We can and we will," Zirke replied. "There's been a dangerous threat reported in the water. You will take your boat around the southwest corner of the island and dock in Kennedy Pier."

"I'm Belanger's VP. If we go in like this, we're certain to have to refund most of the tickets purchased for this event."

"We're waiting on word from Mr. Belanger," the VP replied.

"My word's good enough," Zirke said.

"Not for me, bozo."

One of the crewmembers stepped forward. "Uh, Ms. Spahn, forgive me for being blunt, but I don't want to get arrested for being out here..."

He cringed as she shot him a burning glare.

"Or…you can do what I pay you for." She looked back at the cops. "Mr. Belanger should be getting in touch with the Mayor any moment now."

Zirke and Graft shared the same annoyed glance. The latter got on the radio.

"Boat Three to any other available unit. We're gonna need assistance here with the *Hoelzer-Spahn.*"

A series of radio traffic flooded the receiver, as the other cops were dealing with similar situations involving the yachts. The sound of loud cracks dulled those transmissions. Graft and Zirke looked back at the other boats, seeing a couple of them resuming the show, as though in direct defiance.

****

The sight of green and red lights fizzling in the sky only added to Silvia's anguish. She arrived at the south end of the island and immediately saw that the situation had turned into chaos. Two additional policeboats arrived ahead of her and were converging on the nearest fireworks boat, which was only now starting to move.

Royce and a few other officers were on the shoreline, forcing people to go back. And then there was JoEllen, with her phone pressed to her ear. No matter how this played out, it was certain that Belanger would never bring his festival to Maxwell Island again. Not only that, but news of this chaos would spread to the mainland within the next few hours.

And Silvia couldn't care less.

She glanced behind her for any sign of the Eel. Nothing.

"All units, watch the water. Look for white flashing lights resembling electrical discharges," she said into the radio. She switched to the Fire Department frequency. "Maurice. This is Chief Remar. You there?"

****

Maurice and Allen had just ascended from the airfield when Silvia's voice burst through the receiver. In the couple minutes prior, they had been listening in on the police transmissions. It wasn't clear what was going on, but it was serious.

"I'm starting to think she's lost her mind, Cap," Allen said. Maurice nodded, then proceeded to steer the chopper to the east. In the span of a minute, they were over East Beach and heading out over the water.

"Maurice?"

"This is Captain Peterman. I'm in the sky. Talk to me, Chief. What's the deal with these 'lightning flashes' your dispatcher told me about?"

"Captain, you'll think this is a joke but it's not," Silvia said. The firefighters noticed a few pauses in her voice, as well as a strain in her tone. *"There's...it's...it's an organism! The burn marks that the Fire Inspector pointed out on the yacht and the speedboat. They weren't accidents! The whale, it went crazy because it encountered this thing. It killed Lieutenant Henry and last I saw it, it was heading toward the island."*

Maurice was about to redirect the chopper back to the airfield, and only stopped when Adam Henry's name came up.

"What? Adam's dead?" He didn't even register Silvia's response, as he recalled seeing the burns on Sly's body when airlifting Andrew Cornett from the Coast Guard Cutter.

"Cap?" Allen said. Maurice remained quiet, his expression a dumbfounded one. "CAP?!" Finally, Maurice looked over. "She said 'lightning storm', right?" He pointed to his right at the southeast coast.

Maurice rotated the chopper to starboard until the cockpit faced south. Then he saw it. White flashes, with individual bolts streaming from their source. Had he been on the west side of the island, he would have speculated it was from electrical discharges in the power cables that connected the island to the mainland. But this was the east, and there was nothing that should have been causing this kind of electrical display.

"Chief? I see it...My God...I see it." He was convincing himself at the same time while relaying the info. He watched the flashes and compared them to specific landmarks on the beaches.

"It's *moving*," Allen muttered.

"It's heading south," Maurice said. He drew a breath. "Chief, it's tracking the vibrations in the water. It's going toward the festival."

****

Silvia switched frequencies back to the police, only to find a barrage of transmission blasting her eardrums. As she waited for a break in the airwaves, she gunned the vessel toward the group of civilian yachts still anchored past the buoy line.

"Listen up," she told her fellow officers, "you'll think I'm mad, but what I'm about to tell you is true. There's a large underwater animal moving in from the east side of the island, and it's coming fast! It is capable of intense electric discharges that can burn through boat hulls and rupture the fuel tank. That's how the *Dream Wrecker* exploded a couple nights ago. Do what you have to do, but get everyone out of the water NOW!" As she finished speaking, she arrived at the group of yachts.

The adrenaline managed to somewhat distract her from the pain, though it still hurt like hell to pick up the bullhorn. Her red and blue flashers glinted off the hulls of over a dozen tightly grouped boats, with countless others spread for a mile down.

"This is the Chief of Police. I'm declaring an emergency. Please vacate the waters immediately. There is an active *violent* threat in the area." The emphasis of the word 'violent' did the trick. She hated implying that it was an active shooter or terrorist scenario, even if she didn't explicitly use those words, but common sense told her that yelling 'sea monster' would not have done the trick.

Most of the yachts turned and retreated west for the mainland, while a few decided to go for Kennedy Pier. Silvia sped east to continue addressing the next group of boats.

She still couldn't stand up straight. Her body shook from the jitters and from fighting the urge to collapse on the deck. Luckily, some of the yachts saw the activity from those she had already addressed and began to vacate of their own will.

"What is that?!" someone screamed. Silvia noticed yachters pointing to the northeast. Silvia found a pair of binoculars and looked to the island. She panned to the southeast coast.

From a distance, the strobing lights resembled artillery flashes in the battleground of a large scale war.

The beast had arrived.

****

"Look at this!" Ms. Spahn threw her arms above her head as she watched the spectators turning around. "You assholes cost us hundreds of thousands! I guarantee you we're gonna get bombarded with requests for refunds, you twit!"

"Unless you want to add a bail charge to that, I suggest you move your damn boat," Zirke replied. He'd never wanted to taser anyone so bad in his life. *Lord, give me the strength to hold back...*

"I want your name and badge number!"

He didn't.

Zirke drew his taser and aimed it up at her. "Alright, I've had enough of your bullshit!"

"Zirke?" Graft said.

"I'll say it one more time! Redirect your vessel to Kennedy Pier..."

"ZIRKE?!"

Zirke shot a glare at his partner. "Knock it off, man! I'm doing this—" He realized Graft wasn't questioning his actions, but drawing his attention to the anomaly dead ahead. "What the—"

The source of the electric flares was moving rapidly—so rapidly that they could see the shape of the creature it originated from. Zirke holstered his taser in favor of his Glock. The muzzle didn't even clear the hip before the ocean turned a blinding white. Like a special effect in a Hollywood blockbuster, an enormous bolt of electricity took form and struck the draft of the *Hoelzer-Spahn.*

Hot currents surged across the length of the vessel, sparking as it pierced the hull. Within the next tick of Zirke's wristwatch, the vessel's hull was as hot as fire. It was as though it had touched the surface of the sun.

And like a star at the end of its life, the yacht erupted into a thunderball of debris, burning fuel, and body parts.

The explosion shined an orange glow on the entire south side of the island. Swells like mountains struck the police vessel and swept it several yards to the north. Both officers fell to the deck as their boat spun along the water. Fragments of hull rained around them like meteors.

There was no point in radioing what happened, as the explosion was seen for over a mile.

"Boat Three! Get out of there, now!" Silvia ordered.

Graft pulled the Remington shotgun from its compartment and shoved it into Zirke's arms before taking the controls. When the USMC veteran stood back up, he saw the yacht's stern pointed skyward, encased in flames. There were no survivors to rescue. Only themselves.

The ocean was still moving as though pushed by a storm. Beneath the burning wreckage were the flashing lights. The creature was searching for any flesh among the sinking debris.

Another bright flash illuminated the world beneath the waves, and the creature turned its head toward its next target. Zirke leveled his shotgun, baring teeth in fright as the ghostly figure gazed up at him and vanished.

He fired several shots into the water.

"What the hell are you waiting for? Get us the hell out of here!" He didn't realize that the engine had stalled and that Graft was trying to get it started again. He glanced at his partner, saw him twisting the key in the ignition, registered the sound of a groaning engine, then aimed back at the beast. He shrieked at the sight of the narrow head zeroing in on the stern. A white supernova engulfed the shape, blinding him.

A bolt of electricity struck beneath his feet. The overcharge blew resulting in its own explosion unassisted by fuel, ripping the entire starboard quarter from the main body. Zirke was thrown into the water, and immediately convulsed from the electric currents that filled it. A dancing figure in a sea of flickering lights, he was ripe for the taking.

The eel raised its head over the swells, closed its jaws on its victim, swallowed, then dove.

Graft did not witness his partner's fate, for he was clinging to the helm for dear life. The boat was half-sunk, the bow at a forty-five degree angle and steadily rising. Graft's feet dangled less than a meter over the waterline. In addition, he noticed that the swells were getting larger, preceding the arrival of the leviathan seeking to snack on him. He looked over his shoulder and saw the white veins of light, illuminating a ribbon of clothing that was once his partner's uniform.

The creature's snout emerged through the waves. There was no point in zapping this victim, for it was helpless and within reach. The eel opened its jaws, baring sickle teeth that dangled blue fabric.

Gunshots popped off, and suddenly the eel jerked. Like a mythical sea serpent, it looped its body and dove, disappearing under mountainous waves. The gunshots continued, the bullets piercing the water along its trail. Next came the sound of a boat engine, and the sight of a Police Chief that Graft never thought he'd ever be happy to see.

Silvia gasped with each recoil. She could barely maintain a steady aim. To her amazement, she had hit the creature. Slouched against the helm, she dropped the empty weapon and sped toward the sinking boat.

She tried reaching out, but realized the effort would be wasted.

"Climb aboard! Hurry!"

Graft let go of the sinking boat and swam over to her. Immediately, his body was struck by the residual electric currents in the water. Silvia cursed in her mind, having forgotten to consider this.

The lights were getting more intense. The creature was turning back. They had moments before the retaliatory bolt. Silvia looked to the deck and saw the lifebuoy at her feet, tied to a lifeline. She screamed in pain as she knelt down to pick it up.

"Grab this!" she said, throwing it to Graft. Despite the jolts from residual voltage in the water, he managed to catch it and slip his upper body through. Silvia slammed her hand against the throttle, gunning the ship toward shore.

The ocean turned white, leading up to a jagged streak. The creature had missed its mark, the bolt literally breaking through the surface a few meters behind them. It traveled indefinitely in midair for the blink of an eye before vanishing completely.

"Royce! Royce, are you there?!"

"My God," he said. The flash had lit up the entire shore, as though a hurricane was making landfall. Now, all boats were racing unanimously to get out of the water. The large festival yachts made wide turns to starboard, the ones further west making their way toward the pier, while the boat furthest east—and closest to the threat at hand, went right toward shore.

He could see the beast raising its head out of the water, its figure illuminated by the blazing yacht.

"Boats Four and Five, use your shotguns and carbines. Put that thing down," he ordered.

"Negative, Sergeant. You can't get near it," Silvia replied.

"Then what do we do?" He paused for a moment, forced his mind to work through the adrenaline, then lifted the speaker mic again. "Escort the yachts to the pier. I need officers on the shoreline here. Dispatch, get in touch with the Coast Guard and tell them to get that damn Cutter back over here. They killed the wrong animal."

Blaring sirens and strobing red lights lit up the driveway behind him. He turned around and saw the large gathering of fire and ambulance personnel arriving on scene.

The Fire Lieutenant sprinted to the waterline and gazed wide-eyed at the huge beast. It had found a body and was munching on it. His gaze then went to the speeding vessel that was nearing shore. He and Royce ran out of the way, then blocked their eyes from the spray of wet sand as the boat ran aground. It skidded for a couple meters before being permanently lodged.

Silvia switched off the engine and remained propped against the helm. On the contrary, Graft leapt over the gunwale the instant the boat made landfall. She groaned, then looked back to the water.

The beast dove again, forcing her to study its signatures for clues to its trajectory.

"Oh, no..."

It was closing in on the next festival yacht, and fast. The vessel was only two or three hundred feet from running aground. Almost there. Almost...

"Come on, get out of the water."

The beast unleashed its fury. The screams of a dozen crew members pierced the air, simultaneous to the appearance of the gargantuan flash. Then, all at once, they stopped suddenly, as the ship split apart in a red hot burst. Burning droplets of gasoline spurted from the cavity, coating the surrounding water and shoreline with fire.

The eel circled the burning wreckage, generating swells that rolled over the beach onto Royce's boots.

"Coast Guard's been alerted," Dispatch announced.

"God only knows how many people this thing will kill before they get here," Royce replied. A look of disgust twisted his face as he watched the beast inspect something in the water. The reflections from the orange-yellow flares betrayed the tiny splashes generated from a surviving crew member. "Oh, Jesus!" There was nothing he could do but watch as the man screamed his last breath, which ended abruptly as the eel clamped its jaws shut on him.

The Lieutenant nearly gagged. He had seen many bodies and injured survivors in various states of mutilation over the years, but seeing someone eaten alive? It was a horror he never thought he'd have the displeasure of witnessing.

Royce noticed the residual bolts streaming off the creature's body as it fed. "Back away from shore. NOW."

The Fire Lieutenant wasted no time following that order. He hustled inland, not stopping until he was another hundred feet back.

Royce started to follow when he realized Silvia wasn't getting off the boat. "Get down from there! For all we know, that thing might be able to come ashore like some snake, or..." He realized by the way Silvia was hunched that she was in tremendous pain. "Oh, shit. Graft! Help me get the Chief down."

The two men rushed to the police boat.

"I'm fine," Silvia said. She tried to lean away from the helm, only to shriek.

"Clearly," Royce replied.

"Don't worry about me. Help everyone else. Don't let that thing go after the yachts."

"It's not going..." He turned to look again. "Oh shit." The situation was about to get worse from here. The whole ocean was still amass with fleeing vessels going west and east. Most of the vessels here to observe the event had turned toward the mainland. Considering their distance, Royce suspected they were simply fleeing from the explosions. From their distance, it was unclear if they were even aware that a giant marine monster was the cause. What was clear was the clumsiness of many of the civilians manning these vessels. Several had failed to raise their anchors, resulting in them snagging on rocks and crevices in the seabed below.

And the combined displacement of water was gathering the creature's attention.

One particular yacht remained in place. The helmsman tried starting the engine, which stalled with each attempt. His frantic cursing could be heard all the way from the beach.

The eel's glistening signatures were gradually closing in on the vulnerable prey.

"Get her out," Royce ordered. Despite the agony it caused her, he and Graft hastily lifted Silvia off the boat and lowered her into the sand. The Sergeant checked the sand where the boat had run aground. "Lieutenant, get one of your trucks over here. We're gonna push this back into the water."

"What the hell are you thinking?" Silvia said, hanging off Graft's shoulder.

"I need to get back on the water. If it catches up to those boats, there's going to be a bloodbath. We gotta lead it away from them. Graft, take her away."

"Hey. *I'M* the Chief of Police, not you." She went to step forward, only for her knees to immediately buckle.

"Remar, you're in no condition to lead," he said. He waved a hand at Graft, who proceeded to lead Silvia away from the beach. Afterwards, he turned his attention to the Fire Lieutenant. "Well?"

"No can do, Sergeant." He pointed at a breach in the hull. "You wouldn't get halfway there before sinking."

"Damn it," he said, kicking the hull. Distant screams drew his eyes back to the ocean. His anger turned to horror as white light turned to orange-yellow flame.

Several first responders and bystanders gathered on the beaches, unable to take their eyes off the carnage taking place.

The eel's high-voltage projectile had claimed the lingering yacht.

The creature's electric projectile punched through the hull of a vessel in the rear of the group. Like molten lava, it burned through the hull and internal compartments, turning the steel red hot and burning the rubber lining surrounding the fuel tank. The result resembled a TNT explosion.

The eel wasted no time scavenging the remains, for there was a whole school of these land-dwellers to slaughter. Numerous machines, helpless before its might, retreated at top speed.

Its bloodlust rampant, the eel initiated pursuit.

"Boats Two, Four, and Five, converge on the threat. Hit it with everything," Royce commanded through the radio. There was no choice now. The creature was on a rampage, and it would not stop unless it was drawn off or put down. "Keep your distance. Don't get too close. Use rifles."

Speaking of rifles...

He got into Boat One's armory, where the M4 Carbine was stored. He checked it, loaded a fresh mag, installed a laser scope, and after packing a couple of spare magazines in his vest, stepped off the boat.

"I need a boat."

The Fire Lieutenant shrugged his shoulders. "Sergeant, I don't know if that's a great idea. You saw what that thing did to your companions. And the Chief said…"

"The Chief's incapacitated," Royce said. Right then, Captain Peterman's voice blasted through the Lieutenant's radio.

"Coast Guard's reported that they're diverting their Cutter. No ETA at this time. I need the Munson boats in the water once this thing is drawn off."

Royce looked up and saw the chopper. He switched to the Fire Department's frequency on his radio.

"Maurice, this is Royce. Land that chopper down on the beach. I have an idea."

Officer Jay Noel, helmsman of Boat Four, was a hundred yards out from the western corner of the beach. He was a man of thirty-three, clean-shaven, with short black hair. An Officer loyal to Sergeant Royce Boyer, he always maintained a gruff *Dirty Harry* style persona.

That persona vanished when the first explosion occurred. After witnessing the second explosion, followed by the devastation of the spectator vessels, his façade had faded completely, replaced by the panicked gaze of a frightened man. His partner, Officer Corey Wiebe, was equally terrified. Only when they saw Boat Five and Six racing past them to meet the threat did Jay finally push the throttle.

He inhaled sharply, suppressing a scream as he witnessed the beast, three hundred yards ahead of him, toppling over another yacht. Screams and clunking engine sounds filled the air, which now smelled of diesel fuel.

Corey Wiebe shouldered the Remington twelve-gauge and stood near the starboard quarter, watching the carnage become more real as they neared it.

Boat Five and Six split up, with the former circling to the left. The Eel's head was out of the water again, the remnants of its last victim raining from its gums. The shotgun-wielding gunman on Five's deck discharged his weapon, getting the creature's attention, while Six circled around to shoot it from behind with his M4 Carbine.

Buckshot and bullets found their marks.

The Eel's mouth opened. There was no sound, but if there was, Jay and Corey suspected it would've been a cry of pain. They couldn't see the wounds inflicted, but it was clear from the sharp movements that the creature was in pain.

Boat Six's gunman adjusted his aim, planting rounds into the creature's neck.

Then there was a splash which engulfed all of Boat Six's deck and cockpit, blinding them, but not their fellow officers, to the huge tail that was swinging in their direction like a bullwhip.

"Sweet holy mother of—" Jay Noel shouted. He throttled back as he witnessed the cockpit explode into shards of glass and metal. Somewhere in that debris was the body of their fellow officer, who thought he was maintaining a safe distance, but didn't realize that while circling around the beast, they were coming up near its tail.

The rifleman fell backward, bombarded by debris and thrashing water. He was trying to get to his feet when the creature turned around. Like a snake, it began to curl around the boat, constricting it...and him. His last breath came out in a squelching squeal before he was crushed against the wooden deck.

The Eel, and its victims, disappeared under the waves. But it wasn't invisible. The flashes continued, giving the gunman aboard Boat Five something to shoot at. He was infuriated now. His screams could be heard, even over the gunshots.

"Want some of this, you bastard?! Come back up! That all you got?!" He fired, pumped, fired, pumped...*click*. He dropped the weapon and drew his pistol and resumed firing at the now blinding light.

The eel retaliated with its bolt, sending a hot charge through the hull. The gunman, who was leaning over the metal gunwale with his bare elbows, convulsed. He spun, his finger suddenly locked against the trigger. Shots zipped from the muzzle, out into the water. Most strayed into the distance, only to be absorbed by the ocean. Others found their way into Jay Noel's cockpit.

Holes burst through the windshield, forcing the Officer to drop for cover. He didn't feel pain, but did notice the red droplets splattering on the deck. He looked at the shredded heap of flesh on his shoulder.

"Holy shit! Jay, you alright, man?" Corey said, rushing to his side. He started to approach, then stopped and covered his eyes as the eel struck Boat Five with another charge. This time, the fuel tank burst.

"Get us out of here, man," Jay said. He grabbed his radio. "Zero-uh..." In the pain and chaos, he struggled to remember Royce's unit number. "Sarge! We can't get close. Boats Five and Six are down."

"Get yourselves to safety. I'll draw it off."

Jay wasn't going to ask how. He let the speaker mic drop, and rested against the gunwale while Corey took the instruments and sped them toward shore. He cringed when he and Corey were hit by blinding lights. He squeezed his eyes shut, certain that the end had come for them, just as it had for their colleagues. Only when he heard rotors and felt the vertical gust of wind did he open them again.

Flashing red blinkers behind a beaming spotlight signaled the presence of the Fire Department's AirSea Rescue Helicopter. The starboard side fuselage door was open. Leaning out of it with an M4 Carbine in hand was Royce.

"Get me lower," Royce ordered.

"I'll get us lower, but not *too* much. I'm not keen on getting blasted out of the sky by that thing, Boyer," Maurice said. The Captain was starting to tense as they passed over an ocean covered in debris and roaring fire. He thought back on his years of experience and training—none of which would have ever prepared him for dealing with a hundred-plus-foot, super-charged sea serpent. Still, he managed to ease the physical tension he felt, which threatened to return when he lowered the chopper to the ocean surface.

Royce yanked back on the cocking lever then put his eye to the scope. The beast had submerged again, but he could see the residuals. He panned over the surrounding area to ensure that no civilians or fellow officers were in the line of fire.

Those who were, were already dead.

The other civilian vessels had circled wide or continued their exodus to the mainland. He would recommend the highest honors be given to the officers who had just given their lives, as there was no telling how many people they saved by diverting the creature's attention. But now wasn't the time for sentimentality—he had to make sure *his* name wasn't going to be added to that special plaque.

The creature still had not surfaced. Judging by the flickers, it was moving westward.

"Another ten feet," he said. Maurice's voice came through the headset.

"Ten, and not an inch more."

The chopper dipped. The lights flickered again, bright enough to inadvertently outline the shape of the beast. Royce fired, the weapon kicking back against his shoulder. Projectiles punched through the water, disappearing under large, stringy splashes that were quickly lost with the unsettling waves and debris.

It was moving now.

"Keep it level. Go southeast. Lead it away," Royce instructed. Wind assaulted his face as the chopper accelerated. Maurice had wasted no time getting out of the creature's way. His judgement was proven to be sound by the lightning bolt that narrowly missed the tail rotors.

"Christ alive! Royce? What the hell is that thing?" Maurice said.

"How the hell should I know?" Royce loaded a fresh magazine. The chopper was ascending again. "Not too high. Not too FAST! We'll lose it." He was starting to raise his voice. Maurice remembered to ease his tension. He had been part of plenty of risky operations, but never was he ever worried about getting shot down until now. He turned the chopper to starboard to allow Royce a few more direct shots at the creature. It was unclear whether they were hitting it or not, but they had gotten its attention.

Gradually, they led it further out. After several minutes, the boats were all behind the creature. The plan was working.

Royce's shoulder kicked with each recoil. He ejected his empty mag and reloaded it.

Everyone better be getting on land because I'm running low on ammo.

"How far should I lead it out?" Maurice asked.

"Just a little further," Royce answered. His eyes kept going to the shoreline, now a quarter-mile away. A half-mile distance would probably be sufficient. They just needed to hold its attention. He sent another bullet into the water. "Come on, *Flash*. Keep following us."

Gradually, the strobes grew weaker. Darker. The creature was diving. A ping of hope rang through Royce's mind. He hoped that maybe he'd landed a lucky shot into its brain, and that the thing was sinking to its death. That hope faded quickly, as did his optimism for successfully luring it out. The creature was turning around and heading back to the island.

"No…" Royce said through bared teeth. "No, you bastard. Get your ass back here."

"What's the plan, Royce?" Maurice asked.

"Get lower," Royce replied. Maurice hesitated, then descended until the landing skids touched the water. Keeping the chopper level, he pushed forward, slicing the skids through the water, generating distortion.

The plan worked. The creature was turning around and ascending. Maurice saw the ocean turn bright white. He screamed and pulled up on the stick. The chopper soared.

Sparks erupted from underneath it. The Captain felt as though his heart had leapt through his chest for a moment. To his surprise and relief, there were no emergency alarms. The rotors were still performing, the fuel pumps going.

"Okay… that was too close," Royce said. Maurice looked back and saw the Police Sergeant looking over the side. The landing skid was still intact, though heavily burned by the bolt.

Gradually, they led it out further, keeping just far enough away so that it would hold an interest. Finally, enough was enough. Royce fired his last bullet, then rested the empty weapon on the passenger seat.

"This'll have to do. Take us up, Captain."

"No argument from me. Where the hell did this thing come from?"

"I don't know." Royce slammed the door shut then sat on the floor, leaning back on one of the seats. He could feel the tremors taking form in his hands. Not since Iraq had he seen so much mayhem and death. The difference here was that it was completely out of left field. Now, six officers were dead, including Adam Henry. It was all hitting him at once.

"You alright back there?" Maurice said.

"Yeah…" Royce replied, staring blankly. His voice was little more than a whisper. His brain was piecing together all of the incidents leading up to this. All the irregularities, all the bodies, the explosions, boat incidents.

We had all the warning signs.

"Well, one thing's for sure," Maurice said.

"What's that?"

"The Coast Guard's gonna be here in full force by morning."

"Not soon enough."

CHAPTER 33

The great beast glided through the waters. The North Atlantic current offered little resistance to its mammoth strength. As it was king of its deep water domain, it was king here on the surface. The only element that caused strain was the shining light from the bright ball high above the water. Whatever this power source was, it was not present at all times. The huge barrier above this new world appeared to alternate between several hours of brightness and darkness, the latter of which the beast chose to hunt.

Like the many others that ascended after the big crash, it was adapting. Already, the light did not cause as much strain as when the beast first arrived. In another week, the massive organism would be a twenty-four-seven hunter. For now, it swam deep during the bright hours, maintaining a mild pace to preserve its energy.

The dark hours had arrived, and the gargantuan fish was on the prowl. Its nose could pick up a single trace of blood for miles, its lateral line capable of detecting vibrations from up to twenty-miles. An adept predator, there was nothing in that radius that was safe. Whether something could share the waters with it was dependent on its hunger and sense of self-preservation. Through trial and error, it had learned that some of the life in the world above were intelligent beings that embarked the waters atop large machine. From below, these machines resembled whales and other members of its own kind.

There was no remorse for the unlucky travelers, for the beast did not comprehend empathy. All it understood was survival, and often the key to such was striking the first blow. Through experience, it learned that these strange machines were not enemies. Most were simply passing through, blissfully unaware of its presence.

Still, the beast kept a watchful eye on the large one traveling parallel to its left. It was several hundred feet out, its size nearly matching its own. It had made no attempt to attack, minus one strange encounter in which it felt a mild penetration in its dorsal fin. Whatever happened, the beast felt no pain, thus it did not consider the action to be an attack. Since then, the machine simply remained in its presence, while keeping a distance of a few body lengths.

With the initial arrival of the large machine came a small school of small, tiny ones. Like young offspring following a mother, they kept close to the beast. They were not fish, yet they moved in a similar pattern. Tailfins did not propel them, rather they used a spinning system at their rear, similar to those utilized by the big floating ones.

After a few days in their presence, the giant did not care. They did not interfere with its feeding. If anything, they just observed.

What did stir its attention was the large organism up ahead. This one was larger than any of the whales. Electrical discharges stimulated its ampullae of Lorenzini, a sensing organ designed for detecting electrical fields at short distances, usually generated by the movement of nearby prey. Often, these targets were hiding, whether in the sand, under rocks, or remaining still in the darkness. To most predators, these sneaky critters were practically invisible. When in range of the ampullae of Lorenzini, they may as well be swimming in broad daylight.

This presence was different. The water distortion caused by its movements indicated it was not hiding, but getting closer. Twice since it arrived at this new world, did it pick up these strange electrical signals. Days of tracking followed, and were now about to reach their conclusion.

Almost a thousand feet out, the mechanical spectator followed.

****

"Sonar contact. It's directly ahead. O'Brien's moving toward it."

Mark Eurupe leaned over his boss' shoulder to watch the image on the monitor. "What is it? The Eel?"

Dr. Trevor Zenner cracked a smile. "I think we've finally located it."

"O'Brien seems pretty interested in it," Mark said. They watched the giant fish on the feeds, transmitted by the numerous surveillance drones in the water, courtesy of their employer in the U.S. Navy.

One-hundred-and-twenty feet in length, the fish was the largest animal on Earth. The impact of the *Gota ja' Titan* meteor had stirred it and many others from hiding. Not only did it reveal the existence of megalodons in present time, but that certain members of their species grew to over a third larger than what was previously theorized. Trevor suspected certain bloodlines were genetically superior. They could live longer, grow larger, maybe contained a degree of intelligence.

The world was not ready to know of the existence of these creatures. At least, that was the answer used to justify the secrecy. Trevor knew the truth of the matter. Such massive creatures could be put to use, and such utilization could be maximized by secrecy. Already, a plan was in progress. Failure could yield disastrous consequences, but the mastermind was confident in his strategy.

Whether the purpose was personal vengeance or a desire to benefit the world, Trevor did not know. All he cared about was credit for the discoveries, and significant payment in his role in the larger picture.

Part of that role was the cover stories.

A printout of an article rested on his desk. *Fishing yacht presumed lost during storm in Mid-Atlantic. Remains have been found by researchers aboard the vessel Anderson Ernest. Still no sign of survivors.*

Progress required sacrifice. Besides, what was he going to do to stop a one-hundred-and-twenty-foot megalodon speeding toward a civilian vessel? The impact reduced the vessel's bow to scrap. The ocean quickly filled the rest and dragged it into the depths.

The incident did produce positive aspects—for him and his employer, at least. First of all, it brought the shark to the surface, giving Trevor the ability to plant a tracker on its dorsal fin. Second, the attack confirmed the raw physical power the creature possessed.

Trevor's job was to research the specimen, figure out a way to direct its aggressive force at specific targets, and just as importantly, locate other deep sea creatures.

Yesterday, they had finally found one—an eel, capable of emitting electrical bursts. Such a creature, if properly manipulated, could become an extraordinary weapon for military purposes. Perhaps the beast could deliver an EMP blast that could disable enemy submarines and aircraft carriers.

He had made not one, but *two* discoveries of a lifetime.

There was only one problem: they were not the only ones tracking the eel.

Mark Eurupe watched the night-vision feed on the monitors. "I don't see it. How far out is it?"

"Maybe seven hundred meters," Trevor said. He switched to infrared scanning. "Ah-ha! There you are!"

On screen, the thing resembled a little red worm zig-zagging over a blank background. Gradually, it grew larger. Once it took up the entire screen, Trevor switched back to the underwater night vision.

There it was, the python of the sea. Rods on the drones picked up increased levels of electrical discharge flowing through the water. Trevor wondered if this was a constant problem, or if it was an intimidation display.

The eel was undoubtedly a ferocious predator. Its teeth looked sharp enough to pierce a couple inches of steel. Not to mention its size, which surpassed all other modern predators in the sea.

Unfortunately for this specimen, it was not *the* largest predator in the sea, for it was only eighty-feet long.

The forty-meter megalodon increased speed, its lips peeling back to expose its angry red gums.

"Shit. SHIT!" Trevor said.

"He's going after it."

Trevor hit the table. "Yes. And there's nothing we can do to stop it."

****

O'Brien closed the distance, quickly securing a bite on the eel's dorsal fin. The opponent convulsed, bending its head and tail over the shark's head to constrict. Being only two-thirds the meg's length, there was no hope for the eel to outmuscle its way out of its predicament.

It snapped its jaws at the right pectoral fin, piercing the skin, but inflicting little pain. Sensing the futility of that attack, it bit at the shark's neck. Still, none of these methods were successful in freeing itself. Up until now, it had never encountered a creature with such durable skin. Moreso, the denticles in the shark's flesh scraped the roof of its mouth.

Matters got worse when O'Brien began to wag his head, thrashing his victim. The front and back of the squirmy eel flung wildly, like ribbons caught in a fan.

Finally, its main defensive mechanism came into use. There was no illuminous display, no mythical bolt, no concentration of energy. Just a heavy charge which ripped through the eel's body, zapping anything that touched it.

The megalodon lurched, its jaws parting. The shock was over as quickly as it came, but it had successfully completed its purpose. The eel swam free, attempting to ascend over the megalodon's head.

O'Brien was not letting up. Not yet ready to commit to a bite, the massive fish utilized his other favorite attack.

Turning his body one-hundred-eighty degrees, the fish swung his half-moon-shaped caudal fin. The upper lobe smacked the eel across the jaw, sending it twirling.

It righted itself, regained its bearings, then attempted another retreat. O'Brien pressed the attack, swimming in a wide arc until he was in front of the eel.

SMACK!

The eel reeled backward, the impact having knocked a few teeth free. They sank to the bottom like stones, raining around the corkscrewed body of their master.

It took a few more seconds for the eel to recover. Not that it mattered. The moment the eel regained its senses, it was struck a third time by a blow more powerful than the last.

With his prey stunned, O'Brien went in for the kill. This time, it was easy to secure a death grip on the serpent's neck. Eleven-inch teeth plunged into its relatively soft flesh. Thrashing the eel side-to-side, the meg utilized its teeth like saw blades. Every penetrating wound was widened, the arteries inside split like bean pods. Within a few seconds, the shark and eel disappeared inside a nebula of blood.

****

Trevor leaned back in his chair, beer in hand. He needed it. It wasn't every day your big discovery got devoured by a hundred-plus foot megalodon.

He watched the shark emerge from the cloud, the severed eel head clutched in his jaws. It swam in a circle, as though purposefully showing off his kill to each of the drones.

"Yeah, yeah, big bastard." Trevor held a middle finger to the screen. "Screw you, O'Brien."

"My God," Mark said. The young assistant was almost trembling at the hideous sight. He could feel the vibrations under the deck. The fight had seemingly stirred up the entire ocean. The area around the boat likely resembled swells during an intense storm. It was a testament to the strength these animals possessed.

They watched as the shark proceeded to feed on the eel. It was a meal which would sustain it for several days at least.

Trevor switched off the monitor. "So much for tagging it." He downed his beer and cracked open another. Yeah, there was still the discovery of the megalodon. Not that it mattered. As things stood, he wasn't going to receive scientific credit for them anyway. After all, if everything went as planned, they would appear abruptly on the shores of an economic and military superpower.

For the plan to work, the creatures would have to be directed. Sound was the best option.

Trevor had a device, but it was still in the experimental stage. After all, it had to produce the right kind of sound at the right frequency to draw the beasts in. It was not as simple as sticking a microphone under the water and blasting noise.

The phone rang.

Mark picked it up. "Yes?... Hold on." He walked over to his boss. "Sir?"

"Whoever it is, tell them to go away."

Mark shuffled his jaw, looking at the screen. "Yeah…no. Not sure you want me telling this man off."

Trevor rotated in his chair and looked at the name on the screen.

Nope. He absolutely did *not* want to ignore calls from this man.

He snatched the phone and brought it to his ear. "This is Dr. Zenner."

"How's progress, Doctor?"

"Well, I can assure you the megalodon is happy. As for the eel I told you about, well… let's just say he was in for a 'shock'."

"I beg your pardon?"

"Nothing I can do about it, sir. It came across O'Brien. They got in a brief tussle, and the bigger fish won."

"So, it's not near Maxwell Island?"

Trevor flinched. "Maxwell Island? Why the hell did you think it would be there… in fact *where* the hell is Maxwell Island?"

"Doctor, there's been an attack. Multiple vessels have reportedly been destroyed, numerous police and civilians deceased, and reports of electrical surges."

Trevor stood up. "What?"

"I've sent chopper crews to the area. After the attack, the creature apparently traveled east. The crews managed to locate it, thanks to its illuminous discharges. They used spotlights to gain a proper visual."

"How big is it?"

"Well over a hundred feet at least. I'd say longer than O'Brien."

"Well, hot damn! And it's producing enough electricity to explode boats?"

"Rumors are spreading about 'flashes of lightning' under the water."

"My God." Trevor needed a minute for this data to sink in. O'Brien was one-hundred-and-twenty feet. An electric eel as big or larger than that would mean the one he discovered was only a juvenile. "The more mature they get, the greater their electrical capacity. This thing could potentially stall out a naval destroyer or an aircraft carrier. Hell, enough voltage could compromise the engines of a nuclear sub."

"Dr. Zenner, we have the opportunity of a lifetime. The first objective is to erase any existing public knowledge of this beast. Luckily, there was

much confusion in the chaos and low visibility. Sounds like it's mainly the first responders we need to handle. I have several teams flying to the island. Meanwhile, there's a unit working on moving the eel away from the island. I've gotten in contact with the Commander of the USCGC Richard Denning, which was sent there on another matter. He's a team player. Better yet, a patriot who wants the same things I do. A contractor unit has delivered whale meat and chum to them, which they'll use to lure the specimen eastward. It's up to you to keep it out in the open sea, away from civilian populations, until the plan is set to go."

"Well, damn, sir. You work fast, don't you?"

"I didn't get to where I'm at by twiddling my thumbs, Doctor. We'll be in touch."

The line went dead.

Trevor placed the phone down and cracked open another beer, raising a toast to the less-than-enthusiastic Mark Eurupe. "To the meteor and the deep ocean."

CHAPTER 34

The air smelled of burnt diesel and metal. Even twelve hours after the incident, the air over Maxwell Island was grey. It took a dozen mainland fireboats to extinguish the yacht flames. Two Coast Guard Cutters patrolled the waters, though the *Richard Denning* was strangely absent.

Even more odd was the news coverage. Every channel, including the local station and newspaper, broadcasted the incident as a 'possible attack' or 'an accident'. Not one mentioned the presence of a large marine predator.

"I don't get it," Silvia said, scrolling through the various news coverage with the remote control. She spoke through clenched teeth while leaning against her office desk. Her spine felt like a cracked toothpick that was only held together by a few wooden threads. It was as though her entire upper body was about to crash through her abdomen. Standing straight was impossible. Holding a thought in her head was equally as difficult. All of this was made worse by the stress.

She could feel Adam Henry's hand in hers. Every time her mind replayed that attempt to hoist him from the water, a jolt of nerve pain struck.

Another jolt shook her when she heard a knock on her door.

"Hey? You in there?" No surprise, it was Royce Boyer. Silvia stayed silent. Talking to people was the last thing she wanted to do right now, let alone even be seen in this state. Royce knocked on the door again. "I can hear the television."

"What is it?"

Royce let himself in. His uniform was still caked in sand, his boots still damp. Despite this, he stood strong. Leaderlike. It took a sharp eye to spot the little hints that, in reality, he was exhausted. He refused to show it. Lack of sleep was nothing compared to what others were going through.

In contrast, Silvia's eyes were glassy, for she had not slept. Not only did they display exhaustion, burnout, and sorrow, but they projected bitterness. She had been up all night attempting to manage her remaining police force. It seemed every order she gave went unheard. They all turned to Royce Boyer for guidance.

"It's out there somewhere."

Royce shrugged. "Somewhere. Nobody's seen it since the attack." He pulled up a chair and sat down. "Has Adam's family been notified?"

Silvia inhaled. Royce knew the answer.

"It's been a long night."

"Seems you spent most of it in here," he said.

"You're the one who had me dragged off the beach," she snapped. Immediately, she cringed. Every muscle threatened to snap. Her mouth opened, though no stream came out. Just a pathetic croak.

Royce got up and hurried to her side of the desk. He grabbed her by the shoulders and gently lowered her into the chair.

"No, no... oh my God! Help me up."

It was evident from her voice that sitting down was even more agonizing than standing. Yet, one could only stand for so long before fatigue set in.

"This was the point I was getting at," Royce said. "You shouldn't be here.   You   should   be   in   the   hospital."
"There's too much to do. People are dead. We have dead cops. There's that thing in the water. And where's the *Richard Denning*?"

"Someone said they saw it head out to sea. Several helicopters were reportedly heading out that way."

Silvia looked up, alarmed. "Did they find it?"

"I don't know. There hadn't even been any transmissions over the radio. The Coast Guard personnel I've spoken to don't seem to even know anything about a large creature."

"What?" Silvia pushed his hands away. "I better get out there."

"You had your chance, Remar. Your place is in a hospital bed."

"There's nothing they can do," she said. "They'll stick me with some cocktail that'll do absolutely nothing except waste my time. The military doesn't know what they're dealing with. The public needs to be made aware of this creature. Look!" She flipped through the channels. "Everyone's talking about the explosions. Everybody's acting like the cause is unknown. There's not one..."

"Wait. Go back a couple clicks," Royce said. Silvia scrolled back, stopping when she saw the text on the bar.

Terrorist Responsible for Maxwell Bombings apprehended by Coast Guard.

"Wait, WHAT?!"

Even Royce could not contain his astonishment. "What the hell's going on? Why are they talking about bombings?"

"I need to speak with JoEllen."

"Remar, wait."

"It's *Chief.*"

Hunched over, she marched for the door, her left leg threatening to give out with each step.

****

Upon arriving at the Mayor's Office, she noticed two black SUVs parked in the driveway. Silvia had been to this office countless times to the point where she recognized every vehicle. These SUVs did not belong to anyone working in this administration.

Their presence also indicated that the ferry service was operational again, after she specifically issued an order for all boats around the island to remain grounded.

Either Royce reversed the order, or JoEllen did.

Silvia opened the door, then used it to pull herself from the seat. There were only two postures her back would allow. One was hunched over like a ninety-year-old person with a stroller, the other was bent back with her chest out, like a proud superhero. Both made her look ridiculous. She went with the latter, which was also the lesser. At least she didn't look like she was two seconds from falling over.

The oddity of her body language was made clear by the look she got from Stephani Vogel.

"Chief? You okay?"

Silvia's attempt to shift nearly caused her to drop. She partially saved-face by catching herself on Stephani's desk. Partially. Not much. The secretary eyed her phone, as though ready to call an ambulance.

"I need to speak to JoEllen."

"She's in a meeting at the moment. Uh…" She reached for the phone. "Forgive me, ma'am, but you look like you need medical help."

"I threw my back out. Page JoEllen. Tell her I'm heading in."

"My fiancé has a bad back, Chief. You don't look like you threw it out. That looks like a full blown herniated disk, at least."

Silvia slammed a fist on the desk. "Mind your own goddamn business, and page the goddamn Mayor, you goddamn busybody!"

Stephani retracted, eyes wide, hands close to her chest.

A door down the hall opened. Footsteps approached the lobby.

"What's the problem, Mayor?" It was a male voice, one Silvia was unfamiliar with.

"Hang on. I'll take care of it." A moment later, JoEllen emerged from the hall. "Chief Remar. Are you okay?"

Silvia's attempt to march to her came off as a pitiful hobble. "JoEllen. We need to set up a press conference immediately. There's a danger to the public, and if we don't act now..."

"Have you not heard? The danger is over, Silvia."

"Over. *What?!*"

"The Coast Guard caught the terrorists responsible for destroying the yachts."

"Terrorists?! What the hell are you talking about? Where is this narrative coming from? It was a large marine animal. An Eel."

One of the strangers stepped forward. He was an expressionless man, who gave off the appearance of an FBI specialist. He wore black slacks and a white button-up shirt.

"Is this the Chief of Police?"

Silvia stepped between JoEllen and this guy. "That's right. And who are you, exactly?"

"Someone who needs to speak with you." He looked at JoEllen. "Bring her to the office." Without a moment's hesitation, he turned around and headed back down the hall.

JoEllen waved Silvia on, then turned to follow.

The Chief hesitated. Whoever this guy was, JoEllen had no problem taking orders from him. And there was no doubt it was an order. Like the appearance, she recognized the voice. This guy had military in his background, yet, lawyer in his attire. From the way JoEllen complied, Silvia knew his influence was great. And she couldn't help but find it curious that his interest in her piqued with her mention of the eel.

The terrorist story was starting to make sense.

Silvia followed the Mayor to her office. There, she met the second visitor. Like the one she saw in the hall, he was dressed pretty formally. His hair was short. Basic training short. His face was grizzled, yet his demeanor was a strange cross between mercenary and attorney.

She had heard rumors that private contractors often used reps and booking agents for non-combative duties.

The second man stood and offered his chair.

"No thanks," Silvia said.

"You sure, ma'am? You look like you really could use it."

"Silvia, you alright?" JoEllen said. "Maybe you should see a doctor."

"Will someone tell me what the hell's going on?! I have seven men dead. I still don't have a civilian count."

"I know. It's a tragedy," the first man said. "But there is good news."

"Oh, right. The 'terrorists'." She made air quotes. "You guys aren't here for the government, aren't you? Yet, you're covering this up. So, what's the deal? Is this some genetic experiment gone rogue? This a secret biological weapon? A government screw-up?"

The second man chuckled. "Not exactly. But there is potential in its use."

"Not if I have anything to say about it," Silvia said. "I saw the creature. I know what it's capable of. And you can bet your ass I'm going to tell the world about it."

She hoped to see the men flinch. To look at each other and silently seek counsel on how to address this potential leak. God only knew who wanted a giant electric eel and why. If it wasn't the government, it at least had to be someone of influence.

But the men did not flinch, and their eyes remained locked on her.

"Efforts are being made to ensure all victims and their families are taken care of," the second one said.

"Great. Won't stop me," Silvia said.

"You might want to be careful with that decision," the first one said.

Silvia's back pulsed. That tone, while gentle, practically screamed threat. She looked at JoEllen, who had sunk into her chair, watching her.

"Did they threaten you too?"

JoEllen shrugged. "I didn't see the so-called eel. I did, however, see the explosions. And I could not be happier knowing the people responsible have been caught."

"There are no terrorists." Silvia could not believe this. She felt as though she was lost in the twilight zone. The image of that news broadcast scrolled in her mind. She dug out her phone. Google, Yahoo, YouTube… each site had articles and video coverage of the apprehension of the terrorists.

Her eyes went to the visitors. This influence went far and wide. Slowly, it sank in how insignificant her word was. A feeling of defeat swept over her.

"You bastards. You're covering this up. You still haven't told me why."

"It's not your concern," the first one said.

"The hell it's not."

"Would you like to hear our offer?" the second one said.

"Whatever it is, you can stick it up your ass."

"You may want to reconsider. Considering your poor work history and…physical set back… you might have a hard time finding a new career. That said, we can solve the issue of money. All we need from you is a brief public statement, and your silence on the matter."

Silvia squared up, her aggressive stance ruined by a pain gasp. "And if I say no?"

Neither man answered.

JoEllen stood up. "Silvia. Take the offer."

"You can go to hell."

"We have access to world renowned doctors," the second man said. "I'm talking physicians who have fixed broken spines. Gave people back their lives." He tilted his head at her hunched back. "I've seen plenty of injuries, Chief. Based on the way you're standing, you're in need of a hell of an operation. Even with insurance, such a thing can cost a hell of a lot."

"I've heard that some people would rather have the back pain than the debt," the other said.

"It's worse than that. Chronic back problems are the worst. I hear they often   lead   to   suicide."
The room went silent.

Again, Silvia looked to JoEllen. The Mayor did not speak, but her eyes conveyed her message. *Take the offer.*

"What did they promise you?" Silvia waited for a response that did not come. She turned to look at the visitors. "There were hundreds of people present. You won't be able to silence everybody."

Both of them smiled, the second one fixing his collar. "It was dark. Most people could not properly see what was happening. Most could only see the explosions."

"The thing attacked people on the surface. Tore them apart with its teeth."

"Oh, you mean the great white that was attracted by the chaos?" the first one said. "It has been caught and killed by the heroes of the Coast Guard."

"A shark..." She did not bother debating the lie. These men knew what they were doing. "You realize you're using a twenty-pound fish to cover for the existence of something almost as big as those Cutters."

"Eh." The first man shrugged, unconcerned. "It was dark. Most eyes were on the explosions. Terrorists armed with high-powered explosives tend to cause chaos. That chaos, and the dark, may have led to exaggerations."

"My police force saw it."

"Those who are still alive," the second one said. "They're being interviewed."

The use of that last word sparked another nerve explosion.

"What did you do?"

"Police officers guilty of spreading misinformation are dangerous to the public, ma'am."

The implication was obvious. Silvia's heart pounded, and her mind spun into a cyclone of stress. Already, she had lost so many people. Now, Jay Noel, Corey Weibe, Terry Graft—three men who witnessed the attack, had encountered a run-in with these people.

All night long, she felt the attack was the worst thing she had ever experienced. Now, it was second to this interaction. Sure, there were no explosions, no bodies being mutilated, no crocodilian jaws or white hot electricity causing mayhem. Despite all of the horror, she could still chalk that up to a monster hunting for food. Yet, the real bloodbath was behind the scenes. These were humans, preying on and manipulating other humans. In Silvia's mind, that was worse.

"You bastards."

Silvia couldn't take it anymore. These men were firm on their story. They, or the person they worked for, had the advantage of money and connections. Even JoEllen had bent to their will. The Coast Guard bought into the narrative. In less than an hour, Silvia was totally alone in the world.

Her knees buckled, her hands shivering. She breathed through her teeth, her mental safeguards succumbing to pain and stress.

All control was lost. Silvia lunged for the nearest man, ready to strangle him. Her pathetic attack did not make it past the first step, for her back delivered a fireball of nerve pain which stripped her legs of any remaining strength. Silvia screamed and fell forward, clunking her head against the visitor chair.

Her vision went hazy, then faded to black. The only thing she could comprehend was JoEllen's voice.

"Stephani! Call an ambulance."

CHAPTER 35

Silvia slowed to a stop, then hurried to the portside. She leaned over the gunwale and extended an arm.

"Come on! Grab my hand!"

Adam reached but fell short. After floundering for a moment, he reached up again. Their hands clasped.

Silvia clutched his wrist with both hands and pulled. Adam kicked the water and clawed at the vessel. The light got brighter underneath him.

"Pull me up," he said.

Silvia bared teeth as she put all of her strength into lifting. She leaned up, hoisting him to the gunwale.

Then she screamed.

"AHH!"

Sitting up in the hospital bed sparked a second scream. Two nurses rushed into the room.

"It's okay. You're alright, Chief."

Silvia rolled to her side and brought her knees to her chest.

A doctor stepped inside. "Hello, Chief Remar. Can you tell me the pain level?"

"Ten! Ten, goddamnit!"

The doctor made no attempt to argue. Often, when a patient gave that number, it was an exaggeration. In this case, he doubted it was fake.

"Alright. Just try to relax. I have your medical history on file. I'm going to prescribe you some pain medications and we'll see if that'll alleviate your discomfort. Then we'll get you a new X-ray and MRI."

****

Those medications were such a waste of time. Of course, it was the usual crap. Gabapentin, carisoprodol, and a high dose of ibuprofen. All equally useless.

It was sometime in the afternoon now. The X-rays and MRI confirmed severe vertebrae degeneration and a disc herniation.

Silvia was on her right side, still clutching her knees. There was something about this position that was less painful than the others... as long as she didn't move. Even her breathing had to be slow.

The door opened.

"Hi, Silvia." It was JoEllen's voice.

The pulsing of her nerves intensified. "What?" Her voice was strained. For now, it was the only tone available, for her entire body was tensed. Not only had her entire world come crashing down, but here she was in a hospital gown, lying in a fetal position. She wondered if God had personally set out to humiliate her today.

JoEllen pulled up a visitor chair. "I'm sorry about all of this. I'm told you have an epidural scheduled. Will it help?"

"So much for doctor-patient confidentiality," Silvia said. She groaned, a display of agony and madness. "It'll help somewhat. But without invasive surgery, I'm in for a long and miserable life."

"Maybe not." JoEllen leaned forward. "That offer is still on the table."

Silvia's brow wrinkled, her fingers clawing against her legs.

"Who do they work for?"

JoEllen looked at the door, then leaned in. She spoke in a whisper. "There's an Admiral in the Navy. Some guy named Heston. Real big deal. Very powerful, very influential. He wants to study the creature and use it for military purposes, but he can't do that if the American public is aware of its existence."

"And you're happy to go along with it?"

"I don't have much choice."

Silvia lifted her head from her pillow. "Did they threaten you?"

JoEllen looked away. "Well..."

Silvia scoffed. "They didn't have to. They offered you something for your silence—something you couldn't pass up." She leaned her head against the pillow and shut her eyes. "So, what was it? Money? Position?" She peeked, spotting a tick of guilt in the Mayor's face. "They're going to rig a senate election in your favor, aren't they?"

JoEllen took a long breath, ultimately deciding to evade the question. A true politician. Her career was sure to be a long one.

"How's your pain?"

"Like you care."

JoEllen put her hand on Silvia' shoulder. "I care more than you think."

The Chief sighed. "A lot. I can't... I can't even think."

"Then let me help you." JoEllen was whispering again. "Take the offer. Let the cover story run its course. Forget about everything that happened."

"How? How can I forget? How can I work here, with a bunch of my department dead, and pretend there's not a big cover-up?"

"You won't have to," JoEllen said. "You'll resign. You'll give a brief statement to the press, thanking the Coast Guard for apprehending the 'terrorists'. Due to personal distress and physical health, you will step down from office. I'll appoint Sergeant Boyer in the position. He's always wanted the job anyway. Should be an easy one from here on. Nobody will come to this island for at least a couple of years. The rest of the summer's dead for sure."

Silvia refrained from commenting on JoEllen's indifference. Normally, she would be up in arms about the rapid decline in tourism. Now that she had an open door to a high-profile political career, it didn't matter what happened on Maxwell Island.

"What happened to the officers that those men interviewed?"

JoEllen leaned back in her seat, hesitant to answer. "All I know is they refused to go along with the story."

"And?"

"I don't know. I wasn't told. But they're no longer with the department."

"What about Royce?"

"He made his own agreement with Heston's reps. He saw the situation for what it was and figured he may as well go along with it."

"There's still Andy Cornett," Silvia said. "He and his wife tried to warn us about the creature."

"Mr. Cornett is in a medically induced coma, due to trauma from the incident involving the whale."

Of course he is. She could not help but chuckle. If she didn't laugh, she would be crying. There was no point in bringing up George O'Mara. Any testimony about a sea monster from a guy suffering from a severe head injury following a boat crash would easily be written off as delusional.

"So, the only thing in the way is me." Silvia stared blankly, then winced when her back continued inflicting its horrible wrath.

She could not take it any longer. Pain had a way of overriding values. Torture a human long enough, and they would happily sell their soul to the devil in exchange for a single minute of levity.

"There's gotta be a dollar value in addition to the medical treatment I need. If we're facing cold hard facts, then we need to know that my career is done. Nobody will hire me. And frankly, I'm fed up with being a cop. I just want to live in some house in some small neighborhood, and wait out the rest of my days. Preferably pain free."

"That's something that can be arranged," JoEllen said. "I'm assuming you'd like to go to the mainland?"

"There's a neighborhood in Florida I used to visit," Silvia said. "Simpler times."

A much needed dopamine hit swept through her. She was ending the fight, and by extension, ending her misery, both physical and mental. Her back would soon be fixed, and she would no longer have to prove herself to anyone.

Just like her position with the Miami PD desk job, the referral to Maxwell Island PD, and her rise to Police Chief, it was through connections instead of merit. The difference this time was that Silvia Remar was willing to accept it.

If she couldn't benefit the world, she may as well benefit herself.

"Arrange a meeting."

CHAPTER 36

Silvia spent the night in the hospital, where she was visited by the two 'associates'. Her meeting with them was easy to cover-up. "They're officials working with us to investigate the attack."

Nobody questioned it. Nor did they question her decision to resign after giving a two-minute statement in a Town Hall meeting later that day. Silvia spent the next forty-eight hours at home, waiting for the epidural to kick in. After three days, there was some relief. Not much, but enough for her to get from A to B.

Every movement had to be taken with caution. Bending a certain way or twisting too fast would trigger a spasm.

It was one in the afternoon. Silvia was wearing her police uniform for the last time. At noon, Royce was sworn in as the new Chief of Police. He faked a smile for the cameras, shook hands, made promises to ensure safety. The act ended once he was back at the station.

Silvia stood in what was now his office. All of her stuff had been moved, courtesy of JoEllen Marsh and the movers she hired. It was an odd feeling, no longer having a badge on her chest. In a way, it was liberating, while simultaneously humiliating. This was no grand retirement after an honorable thirty-five years of service.

She purged her mind of the facts, for they served no purpose except to cause guilt. She had a new job now, and that was silence. Failure to meet the standards for this new occupation would be worse than job termination.

To this day, nobody had seen or heard from Jay Noel, Corey Wiebe, and Terry Graft. All she knew was what was in the typed speech. They had resigned due to distress and relocated. She was not at liberty to disclose where, as that was 'personal info'.

"It's gotten quiet around here," she said.

Royce nodded. "You surprised?"

"Nope. Just feels like September all of a sudden."

"Yeah, I guess so." He sat at the desk for the first time. His first act as Chief was to look out the window. There was no semblance of the man who campaigned for this position, and who resented Silvia for getting it. He looked like a king of a dying nation. He had no soldiers, few workers, and a struggling populace. Already, there were talks of business owners closing their operations for good. Many spoke of moving to the mainland. Maxwell Island had become cursed in the eyes of the public.

Royce looked at Silvia. "I hear you got a new place."

"Yeah. A small neighborhood in Florida called Goldville. I've got a doctor lined up. I just have to survive the next few weeks. Then, of course, there's the recovery process."

She looked to the window, catching a whiff of the salt air coming off the ocean.

"I can't believe..." She stopped herself. ...*that something like that eel can possibly exist.* "I can't believe that today's my last day here. Everything's changing so fast."

Royce knew what she meant to say, and it was right that she refrained from saying it, even in the privacy of this office. There was no point in mentioning the creature. It had not been seen for days, and the public seemed to buy into the cover story, except for a few low-profile conspiracy theorists.

"You on the six o'clock ferry?"

"Yep. Payment went through. House is mine. Completely paid for. By the way, I managed to add one of those Purple mattresses that you told me about. Hopefully it'll help me sleep tonight."

"Good, good." Royce was monotone. Here they stood, having benefitted from a tragedy that claimed numerous lives, including Adam Henry, and many others. Their names were still on the mailboxes, their positions unfilled.

He tapped his fingers on the desk. "I guess this is it, then."

"Yep." Empty silence filled the room. What else was there to say? It wasn't like Silvia and Royce were best of friends all of a sudden. They just shared a mutual secret, one that if exposed, could lead to disastrous consequences.

With that in mind, Silvia dug into her pocket. "Hey, I thought I'd give this to you." She pulled out a piece of paper and handed it to him.

Royce took it and looked it over. His eyes went back to her. "It's a phone number. You planning to keep in touch?"

"I've changed my number. Helps with the press. Constant calls... I can't stand it. Plus, messages from extended families of Jay and the others, asking where they moved to. I can't take it anymore."

Royce tucked it into his wallet. "Why me?"

"Because, despite our differences, I think it's in our best interests to look after each other. There's bound to be people digging into the facts of the 'terrorist attack'. If so, it'll be helpful to give each other a heads-up if we hear anything."

Royce nodded. "Probably the best call I've ever heard you make."

That got a chuckle from Silvia. She gave the place one last look. It was a day of lasts. Last goodbyes, last looks, last smells...

She looked at her mailbox...

...last miseries. At least she hoped so.

Royce extended his hand. "Good luck, Silvia."

It was weird hearing her first name spoken from his lips. She shook his hand.

"Good luck, Royce."

The End

CHECK OUT OTHER GREAT DEEP SEA THRILLERS

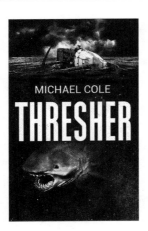

Check out other great
Sea Monster Novels!

Bestselling collection
DEAD BAIT

A husband hell-bent on revenge hunts a Wereshark... A Russian mail order bride with a fishy secret... Crabs with a collective consciousness... A vampire who transforms into a Candiru... Zombie piranha...Bait that will have you crawling out of your skin and more. Drawing on horror, humor with a helping of dark fantasy and a touch of deviance, these 19 contemporary stories pay homage to the monsters that lurk in the murky waters of our imaginations. If you thought it was safe to go back in the water... Think Again!

Tim Waggoner
TEETH OF THE SEA

They glide through dark waters, sleek and silent as death itself. Ancient predators with only two desires – to feed and reproduce. They've traveled to the resort island of Las Dagas to do both, and the guests make tempting meals. The humans are on land, though, out of reach. But the resort's main feature is an intricate canal system . . . . . . and it's starting to rain.

CHECK OUT OTHER GREAT DEEP SEA THRILLERS

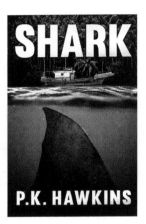

SHARK: INFESTED WATERS
by P.K. Hawkins

For Simon, the trip was supposed to be a once in a lifetime gift: a journey to the Amazon River Basin, the land that he had dreamed about visiting since he was a child. His enthusiasm for the trip may be tempered by the poor conditions of the boat and their captain leading the tour, but most of the tourists think they can look the other way on it. Except things go wrong quickly. After a horrific accident, Simon and the other tourists find themselves trapped on a tiny island in the middle of the river. It's the rainy season, and the river is rising. The island is surrounded by hungry bull sharks that won't let them swim away. And worst of all, the sharks might not be the only blood-thirsty killers among them. It was supposed to be the trip of a lifetime. Instead, they'll be lucky if they make it out with their lives at all.

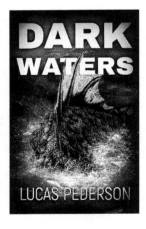

DARK WATERS
by Lucas Pederson

Jörmungandr is an ancient Norse sea monster. Thought to be purely a myth until a battleship is torn a part by one.

With his brother on that ship, former Navy Seal and deep-sea diver, Miles Raine, sets out on a personal vendetta against the creature and hopefully save his brother. Bringing with him his old Seal team, the Dagger Points, they embark on a mission that might very well be their last.

But what happens when the hunters become the hunted and the dark waters reveal more than a monster?

Made in the USA
Las Vegas, NV
06 November 2023